FAITH
farewells

by

JAMES HORNIMAN

First Edition, published in 2020 by J Creative, UK
info@jcreative.co.uk
www.jcreative.co.uk

for Rosemary Ann Horniman

On justice:

'Most jurors don't care about justice let alone Almighty God. They have truncated attention spans, little morality and frankly would rather be at home watching the game or eating their ready meals. Even without these deficiencies, the majority are not smart enough to appreciate the complexities of the law.

Is the jury system not a hindrance to a constitutional and free society?'

An Old Bailey Juror

Introducing Dymtrus Kayakova

Kuznetsovsk, Rivne Oblast, Ukraine
Rivne Nuclear Power Station

A broken heart is inevitable I suppose. Mine didn't break though; it got extracted – unexpectedly and with greater expertise than the work of the most distinguished cardiac surgeon.

I tried to stop it but once again, in my mind, darling Ela was about to die. Rising panic told me the countdown to her final breath had begun; second after second, she fell with tears of pain flooding those exquisite eyes. I tumbled with her, squeezing her hand too hard, crying through her galloping pain. Hurting and helpless, we watched her soul dissolve in front of us.

Despite having been dead for nearly twenty years, when I thought about Ela it was always at this intercept. Thoughts of meeting, marriage and Maria had all faded – only fresh-focussed death repeatedly stood at the vanguard of my memories. Time hadn't distorted my recollection by stonewashing the emotion - it was the way I felt then that I truly remember. I was totally responsible for her death.

Deep in recurring thought, Dymtrus Kayakova climbed the corroded fire escape leading to Rivne Power Station's observation platform control room. The cold late afternoon air caught his face as he stopped halfway up the stairs to catch his breath.

All I had left after she died was the mess; secrets cast in cold stone and a daughter not prepared for the truth.

He had been running flat-out for thirty minutes, so his legs ached when he reached the top step. He ran to be alone with his thoughts, to order his mind. It was worth the pain for a chance to think, to restore equilibrium. Rumination brought with it the risk that his mind would carefully plot its way back to the moments before his wife had died. Then, inevitably, to Maria his only child.

Love without trust is as meaningless as no love at all. You're such a terrible father Dymtrus, you must tell her.

Breathing heavily, he walked over to the platform rail. He paced around thinking about what had been lost and broken, knowing there was only one way to make things right. An instinctive rasping cough interrupted his thoughts and his watery eyes refocused on the view across the frozen plant. The dark thoughts would pass – they always did.

'*Kurva blyat!*'* He had touched the rail with his gloveless hand and immediately pulled it back as the skin tried to stick to the metal. In reflex action to the shock, his hand reached to unzip the pocket of his running trousers to retrieve a lighter and the cigarettes his doctor had long since told him to quit.

For minutes the burning rustle of the tobacco was audible above the constant droning of the plant behind him – it made him think of his grandfather, the one who had convinced him smoking was for real men, working men. Whilst growing up he had idolised his Grandpapa – listening to the stories about the Red Guard, re-enacting the fights with his wooden sword and hanging on his every word. Like all those fortunate children never to witness war themselves, he had always absorbed everything his Grandpapa said, drenched in a childishly positive light.

To the west, the sun was heading towards the horizon, bruising the sky as it fell. It had been another desperately cold day in this, one of the most remote parts of Ukraine where no cloud was brave enough to trouble the frosted skies. The ground had been frozen solid for months; darkness came and went but very little else changed as the ice kept everything held in its sub-zero grip.

*Fuck!

To the northeast of the plant, far in the distance, the adolescent city of Kuznetsovsk looked melancholic as it twinkled in the failing light. It had been built in the 1970's to serve the power station and had not been updated since. This tired city was where he lived. Scanning around from Kuznetsovsk, Dymtrus could see miles of empty fields – the livestock had been taken in long ago. At this time of the year there was very little activity inside or outside the Rivne Complex. Steel and concrete could handle the conditions, flesh and bone required shelter. Dymtrus was starting to feel the cold as he looked up to the escalating plumes of condensation from the plant's four cooling towers which rose high into the windless sky. The massive candy-floss tufts had caught the evening's last light to send all for miles around a warning that it was time to get inside as the night would not take prisoners.

Dymtrus Kayakova, senior engineer at Rivne, had been posted there eighteen years ago and had risen to be second in command. Throughout this time the town had been dreary but he would never tire of the sounds and smells of the Rivne plant – working in the industry was all he ever wanted.

It got dark very quickly at this time of year. It was barely light enough to see as he scanned the uninhabited horizon for the final time that day and drew on the last of his cigarette, inhaling deeply then letting the blue smoke curl from his nose. He took his phone from his running trousers and the emotion flooded back as he stared at the screen-saver.

A life with you was worth losing you forever. Are you proud of me Ela?

His wife had died 18 years ago, leaving him devastated and alone with his daughter Maria. He still spoke to Ela openly and, when it really mattered, she spoke back. Not this time. When he spoke to her they were both still young. It was as if their conversations had frozen in time.

A sudden banging noise from inside the facility gave Dymtrus a fright and made him turn. He saw two indignant crows look up, jump and take flight into the freezing air. They cawed over the crude interruption as the control room door burst open from the second attempt with a strong shoulder, and, in a shower of snow from above the door, two men came stumbling through onto the fire escape carried forward by the momentum from the final push.

Dymtrus dropped his cigarette butt. As he trod down he felt the scrutiny of unfamiliar faces. Both men wore the standard white overalls and hard hats of the mechanical engineering team. Having regained their composure they stared at Dymtrus as they wiped fallen snow from their clothes.

The smells of engine oil and stale alcohol grew stronger as they drew closer, and he started to distinguish more of their features. Although one was much taller than the other both were broad and looked serious, even menacing – shark eyes, piercing with intent. They stopped a few feet in front of him.

'It's going to be another cold one tomorrow by the looks of things boys,' suggested Dymtrus in a low, friendly voice, gesturing to the sky.

Only the drone of the plant could be heard.

'Would you like a cigarette?' Dymtrus gibbered, feeling his right eye begin to twitch

There was still nothing but the background murmur. The men just stood staring with disheartening intensity.

Dymtrus noticed the taller man's tobacco-stained teeth at the centre of his pasty face, as his top lip rose. He looked down – they were both wearing gloves. In the left hand of the shorter man he could see the tip of a knife blade which still managed to catch the dwindling light.

'Is there a problem gentlemen? Do you need me to come back inside?' Dymtrus started to feel a quickening of his heart as they stepped closer, condensing breath rising from their nostrils. His right eye now had a mind of its own.

Finally, the taller one spoke.

'Dymtrus Kayakova?'

'Yes.'

'We've been waiting for you to be on your own.'

'Well now you have me what do you want?' reasoned Dymtrus, his jocularity not hiding his growing nervousness.

'We have a message from friends of your parents,' snapped the smaller man, with a grin on his face and nothing behind the eyes.

One more pace forward. Despite the chill, beads of sweat were appearing on Dymtrus' forehead and his mouth was dry. He darted a look to his left for a possible escape route. He pushed off from his right foot but slipped on the icy balcony as the taller man rushed forward and grabbed him by his baggy running top, pushing him back against the handrail. The shorter man dropped down and grabbed Dymtrus' legs, pulling them up into the air despite the struggling.

'For God's sake, this is ridiculous! What have I done? You have got the wrong man. Please put me down!'

'Some of us still remember,' hissed the taller man as he manoeuvred him to the edge of the handrail.

'What? I don't know what you are talking about, come on put me down and let's talk about this,' Dymtrus shrieked, kicking his legs and struggling to get free. 'What are you doing? It was ages ago; I had nothing to do...'

'SOME OF US STILL REMEMBER!' screamed the taller man, stopping Dymtrus mid-sentence with a punch in the stomach. With a final shove they pushed Dymtrus over the balcony.

The crows had settled once more and looked over with only mild interest as they heard the shriek of a man as he fell thirty feet, then the thud of a body as it hit the frozen ground below the balcony. The men looked over the railing to inspect their work, but all they saw was a buckled, lifeless body with a dark pattern spreading on the snow in the faint glow of the perimeter lighting.

'Die!' both men cried, not caring about the echo around the complex. Both spat over the balcony and, with synchronicity, wiped their tangled beards. Glancing at each other they gave a quick nod, chuckled, and walked back inside, the door shutting behind them with a gentle thud. All that remained, once again, was the soft drone of machinery so consistent it could have been silence.

The sun surrendered to the night. It was to be the coldest one that season.

Central Criminal Court, Old Bailey, London

Sam Waghorne stood at the side entrance of the Central Criminal Court just like he'd been told to. This was where new jurors were supposed to come on the first day of service. Sam was glad to be doing something different today, a break from the constant worries at work. Lately he had been thinking about his Chinese client Xanchu Qin all the time, day and night it had started to consume him. For now he could ignore emails and turn his phone off; he was here to concentrate on something else, fully protected from the stresses of his daily life through distraction.

Despite his exhaustion from a lack of sleep, Sam felt like a new boy at school; he had his forms telling him where to go, what to do when he arrived and even what he was expected to do at lunchtime. As he waited in the queue, he reflected upon the friendly, uncommon breakfast that morning with his wife and children. He normally left for work well before they woke up but today he had learnt more about his family than he had done in the previous two months. Some men must have the chance to enjoy breakfast with their family every day. All Sam could think was he might live longer if he did.

The process of getting through the scanners and security was so thorough it was almost comical. Of particular note were the attitude and general countenance of each guard which made their professional colleagues at Heathrow Airport look like tipsy grandparents at Christmas. Sam wondered if these guys were previous criminals who, having done something really bad, had been sentenced to death-by-boredom in this job. Each officious guard stubbornly ignored the ironic quips of the very British crowd trying to disperse nervous energy in a typical British way. Sam decided to resist the temptation to make a joke and once clear of the scanners and the latent suspicion of being a terrorist, he put his head down and scuttled up the stairs to the main hallway. He briefly took in the high ceilings and the marble that seemed to line every wall but soon caught himself, as he was here to concentrate, not to look around like he was in a museum. Looking down again Sam noticed other recruits shuffling into position to listen to a tall black woman wearing an elegant black suit under a black gown.

'Listen up now! Right that's twenty, so let's get going. Good morning. Welcome to the Central Criminal Court. I am a court usher so will be signing all of you in from my sheet here once we are upstairs. Then I will tell you some important notices about this place. You all have been handed a significant responsibility and I will be here to help you make sure you fulfil it correctly.'

The usher stared purposefully as a wave of obedient silence followed the inevitable childish murmur through the group congregated by the stairs. From members of the public to school children in less than fifteen minutes – Sam chuckled as he thought how quickly the confident attributes of adulthood could be stripped away. Of course, adults had the ability to listen and evaluate but in groups it was always so much more entertaining to pretend they were all eight years old.

Having regained control, the stony-faced usher continued. 'The most important aspect of your jury service is that you do exactly what you are told when you are told to do it. You will notice timing is incredibly important here, the judges might look like crusty old men but they get very cross if a jury is late even by a minute or two. Now hurry up will you. Follow me.'

The usher ascended the marble stairs with her nose pointing towards the vaulted ceiling and her black gown billowing like a vampire. A startled group of peeved women and compliant men followed on immediately.

The Old Bailey - Court Number One

The formidable prosecuting barrister slowly stood, needlessly adjusted his court band and with theatrical timing, turned towards the defendant. His eyes started at the midriff and seemed to gather intensity as they moved up the body in front of him. By the time he reached the eyes of his prey, he looked like a hungry wolf.

'Members of the jury, the victim of this horrendous murder was a loving father and a prosperous businessman. He had many friends and was well respected in the Sri Lankan community around North London.'

'Looking at the defendant before you in the dock, you may well be wondering what on earth such a young, fresh faced woman is doing here!' His final words reached a shattering crescendo.

Like watching a close tennis match the entire courtroom turned as one to look centre stage at the dock, purposefully lit and the size of a boxing ring.

Maria Kayakova sat quivering, her sticky white palms strangulating the rail in front of her. She was alone with her terror, afraid for all she had ever known and felt her grip on liberty starting to slip.

Part I

Keep This Night in Watching

I beseech you, for Jesus Christ's sake, to keep this night in watching and prayer, to the salvation of your own souls while there is yet time and place for mercy...

Chapter I

Kojdanava, Belarus

Maria Kayakova stood in her dressing gown facing a new fire. She felt the pleasant warmth rising up her legs as the blood-orange flames danced in the grate, throwing her crimson shadow around the room. It was well before sunrise and the fire had already made the room snug – a comforting contrast to the unseasonably cold weather of a Belarusian summer morning.

Maria took a framed photograph from the centre of the mantelpiece. The image showed her father hugging her in the snowy garden of their sweet old house in Kuznetsovsk – cold hands but warm hearts meant genuine happiness radiated from both of their faces. It had been taken earlier in the year, but it felt long ago now given the life-changing events of the last six months.

Shaking away her thoughts Maria reached down for the poker; she prodded the fire then threw on another log. The flames licked around it and sparks jumped onto the hearth. Stirring warmth flowed through her as she contemplated the fire which contrasted her life; it was comforting, forever changing; hot and dangerous. She wanted to be as unpredictable as the fire, she wanted the ability to create and destroy if she chose. With her courage building it was time to show the world who she was.

She carefully replaced the photograph and reached for an envelope which balanced behind it. It was from the Belarus State Economic University and was both her new best friend and most valuable asset, not a minute of the day passed not thinking about it. After smelling its importance, she played with the crisp edges as she studied her reflection in the mirror over the fire. This was her golden ticket. Finally, she pulled out the letter to read those beautiful words again, the offer to study International Economics, starting next week. Just four more days in this place and she would leave for Minsk, depart to revel in the freedom that awaited her. Welcome independence, hello opportunity, so-long sadness and farewell frustration! As she read she gripped the letter a little too tightly making it tremble in her hand.

Dear Miss Kayakova, It is with great pleasure…

She read on but the letter couldn't stop her mind from galloping away. She would get a degree, move away from hidebound Kojdanava, and find a job in a faraway country...

'Lunch time Maria, darling.'

Maria didn't hear her grandmother shouting from the kitchen door. She relaxed in the long grass in the garden listening to the cicada symphony once again. As she drew scented air deep into her lungs through her nose, she watched the bees getting to work on the flora with their unwavering diligence. They buzzed to and fro with a single-minded purpose, never getting angry if a flower had been visited by another bee. They carried on regardless as if in fulfilment of a timeless agenda. Back on the ground she noticed a beetle as it fell from a long piece of grass by her foot. She watched as it tried to flip itself, first left and then right. It struggled on with its legs thrashing around but could not turn over. Maria picked up a small stick and used it to help. Once back on its feet the bug scuttled off without turning to thank her. She smiled at the ungratefulness. What are manners to a bug?

Then she turned to the fragile butterflies floating about on the warm air and the birds singing their songs, delighted to be alive on this warm early summer's day. Maria felt content with the world as she watched them swoop and climb. She adored being outside and could spend all day in the garden or in the fields around her grandmother's house. She found comfort in the colours and the fragrance of the flowers but more than that she loved the thought of all the other creatures sharing the garden with her – it was theirs as well as hers.

Maria always remembered her time with her grandmother in Turkey with fondness, it was the happiest time of her life so far and so easy to slip back to when she considered her future – all she knew of happiness related to a foreign place. She often found herself daydreaming, letting her mind wander back to break her routine. Her father once told her this was a sign of laziness and a flaky mind – not helpful or productive. Maria didn't care, it made her glad to rewind the tape to those days where she felt safe and nothing untoward happened. It had been her panacea for many years now; a private remedy which kept her life on course with just a little anaesthetic when required.

There were only ever two people in the house in Turkey; that was how it appeared in her memories. Maria's daydreams were vivid, rich with the colours and sounds of the garden and were always a double act. The memory of the house was hazy to the point of not being able to picture very many rooms. She could recall the small kitchen and dusty dining room which got very little natural light. Once she had remembered her bedroom during a warm evening with the bedclothes thrown back and the window swung wide open to let in the night-time scent of jasmine. Apart from these, the other rooms did not appear at all. In stark contrast her grandmother's face was easy to recall because of how Maria felt when she remembered all those times she looked at it. Her olive skin and those warm moist eyes made Maria feel both safe and loved. When Granny came close and dropped to her knees Maria could see her own reflection in those hazel eyes.

Maria followed the flight of a bird delivering a meal to its young offspring. It fluttered around cautiously before diving into the hole in the tree. Her eyes wandered to a cloud scooting across the sky which seemed to be shaped like a doubled over old man – it was funny to see him travelling so quickly. Her laughter was interrupted when she felt a hand on her shoulder. She jumped and turned around to see her grandmother kneeling down beside her.

'Lunchtime my darling! Did you not hear me?'

'I'm sorry Granny, I was just watching the...'

'Come on my darling, it will get cold. Tarkan will eat it if we don't hurry.'

'He's a sausage dog Granny, he can't reach the table,' insisted Maria with a chuckle.

'Come on! He has learnt to push a chair over with his nose.'

Maria stood, grabbing her grandmother's hand.

'I love you Granny,' she whispered. 'I adore being here with you.'

Maria opened her arms and they hugged tightly, allowing Maria to sink into the velveteen warmth of those familiar smelling clothes. Many moments later they separated and started running to the house, laughing as they went.

By the time they arrived in the kitchen her grandmother had wiped her eyes dry. It would break Maria's heart if she ever asked what made her so sad.

Tarkan lay fast asleep in his basket, lunch and chairs untouched.

A loud thudding on the wall shook Maria from the isolation of her thoughts. Her watch confirmed; six-thirty and late for breakfast. She felt panic rush through her body knowing it should have been ready ten minutes ago. It was time to pack up her fantasies for the day.

'Where are you Maria?' said a voice from another room.

'I'm coming,' said Maria picking up her cherished letter and carefully placing it with the envelope by the photograph, centre-stage on the mantelpiece.

'Hurry up Maria, I am starving and it is time for me to get up! Is there any particular reason you are so slow? What's the matter with you?'

'I'm sorry,' said Maria as she rushed into the kitchen, banging her hip on the door handle as she went past it. She didn't notice the letter wafting off the mantelpiece from her wake. She stifled a yell and rubbed herself vigorously to lessen the pain before putting a pot of water on to boil for coffee. Another bang on the wall made her turn and hurry towards the source of the hammering. She pulled down the handle and leant on the door.

'What time do you call this Maria?' spat her father lying awkwardly in his bed. His face was contorted as he had tried to pull himself up on his own.

'I'm sorry, I had problems lighting the fire.' Maria flashed back, surprising herself at the smoothness of her lie.

She approached the bed and placed her hands under his clammy armpits. As she lifted him she noticed yet again he felt lighter. He was still eating well enough she thought as the subtle yet unmistakable odour of stale vodka drifted under her nose.

19

He made several groans - some real, others melodramatic thought Maria, but once he was sitting up properly, she gave him his book and went over to the chest in the corner of the room to retrieve the cloth and bowl.

After filling the bowl with lukewarm water, she left it next to the bed with the cloth so he could wash himself. Recently he had become less interested in his own hygiene, self-neglect which if challenged would result in defensiveness. He was oblivious to the fetid consequences and often claimed he was too busy doing other things. This time he was immediately engrossed in his book so she left to finish the breakfast and to get dressed.

In the privacy of her locked room, she took off her bedclothes and slippers to study her naked body in the mirror, turning occasionally to appreciate every angle. Something changed when she looked at herself like this; she was seeking something – putting the pieces together to build to full potential. There was an inner confidence she found when evaluating her figure in the mirror – no one had ever seen what she was now observing but one day they would and one day they would like it. The touch of her slender body in its milky skin together with her long blonde hair made her feel self-assured and helped establish the relationship with herself. Moments like this fuelled her inner desire to get out of the house – to find her own life.

With another bang on the wall, Maria instinctively covered herself up with her hands as a wave of self-consciousness flooded back. It was time to get him up, so she rushed to put on her clothes. All covered up, the feelings she had had just seconds ago evaporated as she realised that her father's hunger and therefore anger would not be held back in deference to the delicate sensitivities of his only daughter. The building of her confidence suit-of-armour would have to wait.

Back in work mode, the omnipresent home help was, once again, present and ready to help. Letting out a slow breath she passed a quick, ironic smile to herself in the mirror before heading for his bedroom. Although the smile was artificial, it provided her daily make-up - face paint to ensure she got through another day with her dear father.

'Come on Papa - let's get you into your chair. Breakfast is ready.'

Dymtrus and Maria Kayakova had been living in their two-bedroom house in Kojdanava for almost six months. The house sat on the outskirts of the town in beautiful countryside but still close enough to provide for all of Dymtrus' needs. After the accident which had almost cost him his life, Dymtrus wanted to get away from Kuznetsovsk, away from the Ukraine and to come home - back to Belarus.

His recollection of that fateful February day was acute. He knew what had happened and why, although it was easier for him to pretend otherwise and claim that he could not remember, relying on the doctor's report to piece things back together. It made uncomfortable reading; a broken back had left him unable to walk or feel his legs; he had a broken left arm with a shattered radius and ulna. The bones had mended to a degree, but the damaged nerves had left him unable to write. The most serious damage sat unrecognised inside his head. This is where the real danger was concealed.

Dymtrus had been lucky, he had been found just after the fall by a security guard on an early evening patrol. Life-saving first-aid given by the paramedics preceded a rush to intensive care in the town. He was critically ill for two weeks with initial estimates of only a slim chance of recovery. When Maria heard she was sure he was going to die, he was so damaged a revival didn't seem possible. She recalled sitting next to his bed with those wires and tubes, his face bruised and body distorted. She had felt frightened and alone next to him; realising this was the first episode in her short life when she was genuinely worried; how control can be taken out of your hands, just how fragile precious objects are.

The truth around the events that left Dymtrus dying in the snow had never been revealed. The story went that he remembered smoking on the icy fire escape – the handrail was perilously low so it was within the realm of possibility that he had slipped and fallen. The doctors had found severe bruising to the abdomen consistent with a sudden impact. They concluded it was Dymtrus landing on his arm, so badly had it shattered.

Once Dymtrus had been declared non-critical and it became apparent he would survive, his employer decided he could never work again. The company also concluded the accident was not its fault and made it clear that any compensation claim would be pointless. However, as a gesture of generosity to reflect Dymtrus' contribution over many years, the company was willing to provide a reasonable top-up to his pension and promised to help fund a suitable house for Dymtrus to live in. He agreed that it had just been a terrible accident and promised to retire with as much dignity as he could muster.

Shortly after leaving hospital Dymtrus and Maria had moved up from Rivne to Kojdanava in early April and settled into the new routine. Maria, just eighteen, had been allowed to study and take her exams at home, so she could be there to care for her father.

After breakfast, Dymtrus Kayakova contemplated the day ahead from the security of his chair by the fire. This is where he was forced to spend most of his day – the reading or just thinking had made him deeply reflective to the same obsessive extent as he used to be physically active. There was no doubt this was starting to define the second part of his life – after mobility comes stillness. The predominant recurring thought which haunted him was the matter of Maria. She would be leaving soon and he was torn inside. Go for her, stay for him. He had been a proud, hardworking man all his life and was delighted his daughter would one day attend university and then settle down with a family of her own. Today something else burned in his head; a rage borne from selfishness and the thought of her not being around. Apart from Oksana, his useless, transitory girlfriend who worked miles away in Lithuania and a couple of friendly neighbours who popped in from time to time to cook and proudly deliver carefully reared wonky vegetables, he had nobody in his life. This frightened him; Maria's presence gave him the courage to suffer. When she went away he was lonely and afraid. Most days started with the best intentions but more recently his irritation at not being able to look after himself and the thought of being alone had left him agitated and depressed. Today he felt angry knowing full well it was the cumulative effect of the prison he sat in. It encased an array of guilt, shame and vulnerability.

'So, you are off next week are you Maria?' said Dymtrus tentatively, knowing full well she was planning to leave on the first day of September.

'Yes Papa. I am so happy. It is all I ever dreamed of,' said Maria with care. 'Are you going to be alright without...'

'I'll cope you silly girl, I have Oksana and next door to help me. It's not like you're moving away or anything, you will be back home every day won't you?' said Dymtrus, the inflection in his question providing a glimpse of his fragility.

'Yes Papa, I will. I still want to be able to help you. I will do all I can,' said Maria trying her best to prevent an argument. She and

Oksana did not see eye to eye. She went out whenever her father's sponging, boring lady-friend ever came around, and this only happened when she could be bothered to drive over and typically wanted something.

'But if you get a job, how can you work to earn money for us and still get back here? You can't do both you ridiculous girl,' Dymtrus stared at his daughter. 'Your priority is here.'

'I will try my best, Papa. We need the money and a change of scene will do me good. Let's talk about this later shall we, I need to get some things from the shop.'

Maria had delayed if not defused the situation.

That evening, when Maria returned from the tired and frugal village shop, she found her father still in the warm sitting room but now he was sitting in his wheelchair reading a book. She suspected a neighbour would have helped him shift across from his chair so he could quietly wheel himself around the house and possibly on better days, the garden. As she drew closer she realised something wasn't right. He wasn't looking at the book, but somewhere above it, his eyes filled with tears. As she drew closer, the book made a small but noticeable shift and his moist eyes tried desperately to focus on the pages once more.

'Were you thinking about Mummy, Papa?'

Maria put her bags on the floor and knelt beside the chair. She noticed the smell of alcohol as she drew closer. She knew he drank heavily when she was away and found it extraordinary how he childishly denied it every time.

'No, Maria,' he said wiping his face and shifting up in his chair.

'I'm fine, just thinking about some old friends.'

They both knew he was lying.

'I miss her too you know,' whispered Maria. 'At least you had a chance to know her, to love her.'

'You have no idea what you're talking about child; you know nothing about grief, of helplessness, of being lonely. Your mother died giving birth to you, never ever forget that.'

Maria had asked many times about her mother, but never got anything from her father except a feeling that she was to blame for her death.

'I cannot believe you are going to leave me Maria,' Dymtrus hissed, throwing down his book and grabbing her arm. He squeezed so hard Maria gave a short intake of breath. As she looked at him his bloodshot eyes revealed just how long he had been drinking.

'Please let go Papa, you're hurting me.'

'Arrgghh!' cried Dymtrus, releasing and pushing at the same time. Maria fell back into her shopping which sent it spilling all over the cold floor. As she landed her head smashed against the table leg.

Dutifully and very slowly Maria picked herself up and refilled her shopping bags as quickly as she could with tear-filled eyes. Without looking back she walked calmly into the kitchen, the respect for her father having taken another leg down. If she treated him like he treated her he would want her to leave.

Meanwhile, Dymtrus sat staring out of the window breathing heavily. His right hand ran down the inside of the wheelchair looking for the hidden vodka bottle and the small glass.

He still used a glass.

Chapter II

The offices of Wolfenberg Bank, City of London

Sam Waghorne sat at his desk acquainting himself with the consideration of another tedious day. The UK stock market was about to open and his clients would soon be on the phone. They had started to annoy Sam in a way they never used to. Of course he valued their fees which helped pay his hefty salary but recently they were being needy and had been getting in the way; proving to be a distraction to climbing the greasy pole of senior management. Sam's junior staff could look after the tiresome clients as far as he was concerned. He had his team of fifteen to run and managing it was what he enjoyed. He felt this was a real strength in his armoury. Management and fiddling around with his personal investments of course – that was what Sam liked to do.

As he sat waiting for his computer to warm up, he wondered what he was going to do all day. As the screens flickered to life he looked at his electronic diary. It was the first working day of the year and there was a sales meeting planned that morning. Wolfenberg Bank was obsessed with growth and attracting new clients to come to the bank. Most fund management companies in the UK grew predominantly from client referrals but that was not the German way – Wolfenberg expected its staff to go out there and find new business, whether bashing down doors or calling people you didn't know. Sell your granny if needs be - it just didn't matter as long as the money kept rolling in. The company had built a reputation in London as a very aggressive institution with highly motivated and intelligent staff. The truth was most of them were selfish, quick-witted street fighters, lacking any of the characteristics which people outside the industry would recognise as intelligence. Sam was once told there was only one thing better than success in this culture and that was seeing a fellow director, in another team, fail - you could pick up their clients with no effort. It was binary - employees were rewarded handsomely for providing new money and they were fired if they didn't make the cut. The meeting Sam sat staring at in his diary would be the New Year's first call to arms. A tingle ran down Sam's back as he read the invitation. Today the boss was here from Frankfurt – Hail Caesar! Those who are about to die salute you…

'Bollocks!' Sam cried as he read through a trading statement from one of his personal investments. It read like a tragedy. Another financial disaster to hide from his wife…

Feeling he'd had enough of investment research for one day he went back to the safer waters of his diary. Apart from the tedious sales meeting, all Sam had to look forward to was a lunchtime party in the local wine bar. One thing Wolfenberg staff were able to do well was drink. Good teamwork and high pressure fuelled the requirement for serious drinking in the evenings – sometimes at lunchtimes but mostly in the evenings. Upon closer inspection all of Sam's closest colleagues were functional alcoholics in fact. None of them would admit to it but the need was greater than the want in all cases. Any excuse would see the usual suspects head to a local pub or bar looking to throw off the stress of a hard day's work. Sam looked forward to these sessions, a chance to get his team together and hold court for a while.

Sam Waghorne had been a private client fund manager for

twenty years. He was still only forty-two, but he had a great deal of experience in "making rich people richer" as he described his job title when laymen asked at parties. The companies he had worked for had been kind to him over the past two decades and he was able to keep his wife moderately happy. He was married to Lucy and had two sons, both at a criminally expensive preparatory school in Chelsea, where he lived. He loved his family dearly and it troubled him he didn't see them enough. More family time was always one of his New Year resolutions – those promises he kept for a few hours or so at the start of each new year.

Sam blew on his black coffee as his phone rang. The market had opened and it would be either a bored, early-rising client with a tedious question or it would be a try-hard stockbroker trying to get Sam to buy some shares with a weak story or an offer of a boozy lunch. Sam's mood lifted as he realised it was Alec, one of Sam's better brokers and one of his best friends.

'Morning Al,' blurted Sam, recognising the number on the telephone display. 'What's cooking?'

'First day of the test match, that's what's cooking. Have you had a bet?'

Alec's first job was to help Sam position himself on the sports betting websites to maximise profits using the combined experience of two keen cricketing fans. Putting it another way, they needed to investigate alternative ways they could lose material amounts of money betting on a sport they knew the square root of nothing about.

'So, what do we do then? Alec said, starting the ball rolling. 'Australia look pretty shaky in the top order, but they did well in Melbourne.

'I think it will be close but, on balance, I think England will win. I have decided to short Australia and go long England,' said Sam with a degree of conviction.

'Good luck,' said Alec, bursting out laughing.

'The Australians are batting like shit at the moment so they're a straight sell. England look OK. They will like the bouncy Brisbane wicket and the fact it has been raining there for days – it will be like playing in Yorkshire in May. Either way I cannot afford to do too much as I lost my shirt in Melbourne.'

'You were terribly unlucky. Who was to know the entire English middle order would get the squirts mid test match after a team curry with their wives. Oh no, it's all over madras!' said Alec, again laughing at Sam's expense.

'Speaking of chilli receptions, Lucy saw my bank statement and the shit really hit the fan back here too,' said Sam. 'She has been trying to save money by cooking pasta for supper twice a week and she didn't take kindly to seeing a twelve-hundred-pound loss on my account. She's only been buying the *Daily Mail* on Thursdays and Saturdays to economise.'

'Ooops,' said Alec with no compassion. 'Never mind old boy, sounds like pasta four days a week now and the fewer copies of the *Daily Mail* in the house the better in my view.'

'I know, I know – but she loves it, anyway what are you guys doing in the market?' said Sam changing the subject. 'We are desperate for a few New Year tips. Get the clients thinking we care, you know the sort of thing.'

'Looking at buying Simco Group for a potential takeover and

reducing Faxo Medical after the good run it has had,' said Alec, clearly looking through his notes. His voice always dropped when he attempted to be serious. It didn't work.

'Brilliant. Once again another groundbreaking piece of research from "Goldfish Asset Management",' said Sam. 'You told me about both of those before Christmas.

'Did I?'

'Oh for fuck's sake. I thought you guys were paid a percentage of the business you do?' said Sam.

'Yup. Best decision ever to join this lot.'

'Is that the best you can do for a New Year's call? Where are the forecasts, the predictions for the year ahead?'

'I predict you finally get fired for doing no work, being selfish and only looking at your personal investments.'

'Not funny actually, my boss was looking at me in a very funny way at the Christmas party.'

'He must be a bender. Did he recognise you with your trousers on?'

'Ha ha!'

'Touched a nerve have I?' said Alec.

'Listen, I have clients to impress and the *Le Grand Fromage* from Frankfurt is in town today. Do you have anything of any interest to say this morning?'

31

'Buy Simco, sell Faxo. Should that be *Der Grosse Kase?*'

'I repeat, do you get paid for the ideas you have?'

'Yup'.

'Well if you are paid for your ideas how come you are not really poor and thin?' said Sam with his acid tongue firmly in his cheek.

'You're wrong actually, this place is great. Work a bit, muck around a bit, you know. It's like being paid to be back at school. Pa would be pleased to see all those fees didn't go to waste.'

'Do you mean it's a bit like being back in remedial maths with Biffy, Whiffy and Stiffy? A little bit of work followed by a daisy chain in the....'

'Ha ha ha, jealousy will get you nowhere. Actually, for the record, Stiffy was at the other place.'

'I've got to go to a meeting now, any more pearls of wisdom?'

'Nope, oh important one. What's the meeting? Advanced delegation lessons?'

'Sales, old boy. I'll send you a picture so you can see what one looks like. I hope you lose all your money on the cricket.'

After a silent pause Sam spoke again, this time with a serious voice.

'I want to talk to you about something actually. Can I buy you lunch in the next week or so? This lot are demanding more and more from us and I need a few ideas,'

'You mean you need some of my contacts don't you?' said Alec laughing.

'Well perhaps, you could be of some help. This week any good?'

'I'll let you know Sam. An order would be nice…'

Sam put the telephone down. He knew full well Alec would be back on the line several more times that morning, he always was.

The presentation suite was on the fourth floor of Wolfenberg's magnificent offices – 15,000 square feet of money-making real estate full to the brim with young, hungry, fund managers and their support teams, eager to succeed. The room was supercharged with New Year enthusiasm. Sam took his usual seat close to the front of the room so as to be recognised by his bosses but, then again, near enough to the side to make it look like he didn't think about where he sat when he came in. He placed himself next to a crusty-faced director who, remarkably, had survived the merciless regime over the past few years and had seen it all before.

'Here we go again,' he declared as he turned to Sam, 'the same over-optimistic rallying cry from managers who have never spoken to a client in their lives. Are you ready to leverage the upside all over again Sammy?'

'If anyone uses the phrases "holistic approach" or "let's think outside the box", I am going to shout "Vanker" in my best German accent,' suggested Sam with a chuckle.

'I don't think you're taking these meetings seriously Sam Vaghorne, they offer superior added walue and help you with your adwisory clients.'

As Sam finished laughing, a tall and skinny man came storming in. The room fell silent. His blue suit was a touch too tight and he wore his trademark tailored shirt with no tie. This was forty-six year old Jurgen Schneider, the European Head of Wealth Management at Wolfenberg AG. He was over in London to press the flesh and bang the drum at the start of the year. This golden boy of German corporate elitism was universally feared, had a reputation for being beautifully eloquent and was utterly ruthless. People crapped themselves in his presence and he knew it. He wore the tight suit on purpose – nobody would dare tell him it looked like somebody else's…

Sam looked around the room. It was full to bursting with staff eager to hear their boss. Schneider adjusted his glasses, held his hands up like a Caesar and as the room once again fell silent he began.

'Velcome to you all and a Wery Happy New Year!'

Sam nudged the director causing both to stifle a schoolboy giggle, placing their hands over their mouths. Laughing when Schneider spoke would be tantamount to suicide.

'I want to share vith you my wision for year ahead.'

As the room settled into Jurgen's plans for the year ahead, Sam's mind wandered. He carefully took his mobile out of his jacket pocket and opened the cricket page on the Sporting Punt website. England had started badly…

Back at his desk Sam opened his email and looked through the messages he had received whilst listening to Schneider. He forwarded the client related ones to his assistant Richard 'Bomber' Maloney, who was loyal and hard-working and who Sam mercilessly abused by passing almost all client correspondence to him. Nobody knew why Bomber had picked up his nickname and he was reluctant to say. All that was known was that it had been established on a drunken night out during the years which led to him obtaining his first-class degree from university. Bomber was bright but unfortunately he was under the impression that this kind of assistance from his boss would result in a bigger bonus and promotion prospects. He was right of course, but for Sam and not for him.

Sam read an email from Sue Smyth, office lush and Personal Assistant to Peter Heathcliff, Sam's immediate boss. Sue and Peter were very close in the office and, although they thought the office was unaware, most of the team knew they had a fairly passionate relationship outside work too. Sue was Peter's PA alright – Penile Attendant.

Sue had been wondering whether Sam and his team were going to the January Club lunch. This aberration was a tradition at Wolfenberg. Given the propensity of some in the City to regard January as a month of abstinence, staff at Wolfenberg liked to go out on the first working day of the year and buck the trend. They did things differently at Wolfenberg. Jim's Bar was the chosen venue for this year's party; a small subterranean wine bar with all the hallmarks of a successful City watering hole. There were dark alcoves for conspiratorial conversations, hidden recesses for customers with a thirst for adulterous activities and private rooms for plotting. It was staffed by a few of society's odd balls; hard-working, tarty girls with short skirts, a cheeky word and a strong slap for over-eager patrons. Naturally there was an irritating manager – a young toff straight out of school wanting to make his way in the catering industry. Jim's was dark and expensive despite the poor quality food but still Wolfenberg staff were always there. They were able to look beyond minor frailties and enjoy what was important; to outsiders it looked bizarre that this dingy place was visited so often but most people didn't understand. Jim's felt like home to the regulars. Jim's had soul.

Sam furnished Sue with a typically saucy response. Subtle emails were his speciality but his alacrity barely disguised his keenness.

Of course he would be there. Moth to a flame. He wouldn't miss it for the world.

At twelve-thirty precisely, Sam descended the stairs that led down into Jim's. The whiff of stale alcohol served as an arcane welcome to the regulars and helped to keep curious visitors away. There was always a sense of anticipation as he walked down these stairs. Not quite a tremble but close to it. He was not sure if it was the culmination of all the previous times he had been, a reflection of the riotous parties gone by, or just a re-ignition of a warm friendship which had grown through careful cultivation over the past five years. It was an agreeable sensation that only lasted for a few seconds. It was brought to a sudden end as he pushed through the double doors at the bottom of the stairs.

Sam was struck by how busy it was already. He realised quickly that almost all of the people in the bar were from Wolfenberg which was not really surprising given the date. Dotted around were a couple of classic examples of the die-hards, or die-earlies as Sam called them, propping up the bar. Plump, ruddy and already heartily commencing their second bottle of respectable claret. These gentlemen were probably in property or something similar, certainly an industry which allowed them to work for a few hours in the morning and then drink themselves into oblivion through the afternoon. Next to them were two badly made-up middle-aged women. Pork dressed as pork, drinking Chardonnay in their business suits which were at least one size too small for them. Their continuous chat was only punctuated with the occasional nasal laugh as they glugged merrily, completely unaware they were independent witnesses to the first Wolfenberg party of the year.

'Hi Sam, what'll it be? Red or white?' said Sue holding a bottle of each colour in her hands.

'Oh, white. Thank you.'

Sue poured and Sam took the glass. He took a half-glass swig to catch up as he looked around at who had arrived.

'Cheers Sammy?' shouted Sue standing there, now gripping a huge gin and tonic and smiling. He bent down and kissed her on her cheek.

'Careful Sue, you might break the glass,' Sam whispered with a smile, gesturing to her hand.

'Had a skin-full last night Sammy, don't remember getting home. I was shaking like a virgin on prom night this morning. I've only just stopped,' said Sue, confessing all.

'Well cheers and Happy New Year!' said Sam chinking their glasses together and draining his.

As Sam refilled his glass he was already fully aware that today his demand for wine would be insatiable. He regretted not having had any breakfast as he felt a touch lightheaded already. Smiling at what lay ahead, he turned towards a plethora of chattering secretaries.

A couple of hours later the early-season party was in full swing. The bar was stifling and the air was rich with the unmistakable odour of festivity. The merriment recipe was simple – take a generous quantity of alcoholic fumes and remove half the breathable oxygen. There had to be over a hundred Wolfenberg employees in Jim's. Sometimes parties just get going and don't seem to want to stop, and this was one of those. Sam was drunk but, then again, so was everybody else.

Chelsea SW3, London

Although he would not remember it in the morning, it was almost eleven-thirty when Sam got home. He had not spoken to Lucy, his wife, all day. Supper had come and gone. Lucy was a mild mannered, understanding wife and realised there was a certain amount of entertaining and drinking associated with Sam's job. What she hated was not knowing where he was. She trusted he was not up to no good but she worried when the phone didn't ring.

It had taken Sam at least two minutes to get from the cab to the front door of their house in Chelsea – breaking his own drunken personal best. Sam fumbled for his keys and eventually found the one he thought went into the lock. After a few seconds of rattling and tapping, Sam stopped and leant on the door to contemplate the truth - he was shitfaced and this was going to take a little longer.

Without any warning the front door opened and Sam stumbled into the hallway. Lucy stood in silence. She had seen him drunk before but this time something was different, it was like she didn't quite recognise his face. There was a red wine stain all down his shirt and he stank of cigarettes.

'Where the fuck have you been?' said Lucy slamming the front door shut.

'What? Fuck you back! I have been busy talking with Peter about the business,' loud-mumbled Sam, slurring each word of his prepared line. He gave an inane grin, exposing red wine stained teeth. Lucy realised it was his eyes that made him look so strange – the pupils were smaller than normal and they had a fixed glare quality that was very unnerving.

'Why don't you ever call me when you go out? What is wrong with you?' Lucy said, raising her voice. 'Have you been smoking?'

Sam just stared back, his silence driven by alcohol. Finally, he took a giddy step towards Lucy.

'My priority is at work! You have no idea how difficult things are at the moment.' Sam shouted as he raised his hand as if to strike Lucy.

Lucy took a slight step aside but never took her burning eyes off him.

'If you carry on like this Sam, I will take Charlie and George and leave you. Do you understand? Looking after them is hard enough without there being a third child to look after.'

'I'm off to bed.' Sam garbled. With that Sam pushed against the wall as a first attempt to gain enough momentum to mount the stairs. He fell forwards, hitting his head on the fourth step. He picked himself up and stumbled up the rest of the stairs holding on to the banister. He turned back to see Lucy at the bottom of the stairs standing with her arms crossed.

'You don't understand, we had so much to talk about, it's going to be a very difficult year,' he remonstrated, the slurring removing all weight from the obviously inaccurate extenuating circumstances.

'You're telling me!' Lucy shouted up the stairs. 'If you carry on like this you won't see us again.'

Sam progressed to the spare room shouting randomly that he would be fine on his own. Like an inebriated crab he grasped at any handhold he could. He collapsed onto the bed and fell asleep in his suit.

Lucy let a smile broaden on her face as she went back to the sitting room sofa and her film. Part of her was jealous that she no longer had the opportunity to go out like Sam did, to be able to let go and forget your responsibilities.

Chapter III

*The Belorusskaja Železnaja Doroga train service
from Kojdanava to Minsk*

Maria sat with her forehead pressed against the steamed-up window of the train to Minsk. Given the time of year and the heavy rain it was still pitch dark outside. The compartment was packed with commuters, crammed in like animals. The only difference in conditions between this and a cattle truck was that these animals made no noise as they sped towards their destination. There was an occasional cough or a sudden sneeze but generally there was nothing but the mundane rattle and whirring of the carriage as it carried two hundred unsociable people towards the capital city on this cold, damp morning.

As an exception to the rule, next to Maria sat a plump man with a big nose and round glasses. He was wrapped in a thick overcoat. He broke the silence by starting a discussion with the man opposite him.

'Travel in to town every day, do you?' said the man to a skinny, well-dressed gentleman directly opposite. 'I'm not sure if I have seen you before.'

As he leant forward he pressed into Maria to such an extent she was squashed even closer to the window. At least his coat kept her warm in the unheated carriage. Maria was surprised just how quickly the two strangers got to know one another and found it very hard not to listen to their conversation. The man opposite, contrary to normal commuter rules, seemed willing to engage every question with vigour. Soon they had established where they both worked, the location of both their houses and the exact breakdown of wives, children and pets. Maria was amazed people in the right frame of mind could divulge so much in such a short time. It cheered her to hear them talk – most people ignored each other for the entire length of the journey. Maria smirked as she studied the annoyed faces of other passengers. Surely an unwritten rule had been broken, conversations in the mornings, especially the mornings, were not to be encouraged.

Much to the relief of those around them, the conversation fizzled out as quickly as it had begun. Maria rested her head back on the cold glass, and reflected on the past few months. She had been at her new university for twelve weeks now. This was her first day back after the Christmas break and she was full of anticipation for term two and hearing from her new friends. She thought back to the kaleidoscope of her first week. She had been frightened and in the beginning the best friend she had made was with the city of Minsk itself. She toured all over it and quickly fell in love with the place. It was so much bigger than she had imagined, feeling like home from the first moment she arrived. The architecture, the sense of history, the window shopping, the restaurants and bars she had peered into, were more thrilling than anything she had dreamt of and immediately overloaded her senses.

The day was breaking and Maria could see objects appearing in the gloom. A solitary worker's cottage through a copse turned her mind back to her father. She had kept her promise to him, returning home to help get him through the evenings. Despite this generosity, Maria found it remarkable that he often gave the impression he did not love her and that she was an irritant to him. When she had first started leaving, Maria had accepted this on account of his desperate loneliness and the sudden change. His behaviour would demonstrate child-like mood swings - pretending to be upbeat during the daily university updates during which he could barely disguise his envy, to the vodka-fuelled aggression about her absence – lamenting the present in honour of the past. Maria found it staggering at what a grown man was capable of when he couldn't get his own way. Sulks interspersed with violence, each episode pushing them slightly further apart. It was hard for Maria not to blame herself for being away from him and she tried to justify this by linking the aggression with his frustration at not being able to work or get around the house without his wheelchair. It was not his fault his health had deteriorated during the gruelling winter and added to this his sight had weakened further which made him even more vulnerable when alone. Maria was witnessing the relationship with her father dying, poisoned by the gulf between his growing needs and hers. Their hearts no longer lived in the same house.

Fortunately, a helpful neighbour had agreed to come in to support him when Maria was in Minsk but she still felt guilty about spending so much time away, such was her sense of loyalty to him. In a stubborn attempt to prove he was still good at something, he continued to drink heavily during the day, hiding the evidence in a declining series of cunning locations. He could get outside once he was in his wheelchair and Maria had, on several occasions, discovered several empty vodka bottles smashed and broken at the bottom of the garden. Alcohol had gathered him up and enveloped him in its warm embrace. He cared little for the mess he caused whether it was glass or hearts which were being broken.

Maria could use a room at the university, whenever she stayed late either to study or socialise, at very little expense. She had gone out of her way to get to know the university staff well and this had paid dividends already with her tutors' total understanding of her domestic situation. Through a combination of curiosity and the need for funds Maria found work in a lively bar, The Vanishing Eye, near the centre of the city, run by the charismatic Boris Kushner, a shifty but savvy character who knew all the right people in Minsk. Boris' restaurant bar was a favourite haunt for a diverse selection of customers. The warmth of the open fires drew in the cold and the delicious, rustic cooking gathered up the hungry. Most nights were heaving, and the atmosphere was intoxicating. From the minute they met Boris was happy to take Maria on three nights a week and every other Saturday during the day. For Maria it was perfect; the first earnings of her life, a lively crowd and no more than five minutes' walk from Minsk's Passazhirsky station.

Boris acted as the foreman for his regulars and the feedback was that Maria needed to wear his signature uniform of a tight white T-shirt and black jeans. She had been shy at first but as time passed it started to make her comprehend the notion of being noticed – worth looking at. Like the attentions of an admirer, working at 'The Eye' made her feel special in a way she never had before. There was a nice team there too, one of the other girls had lent Maria some make-up and they had spent one early evening rapidly applying this after a half-joking comment from Boris. He liked his girls to look their best for their benefit as well as his.

Maria opened her eyes and looked out of the train window onto an expanse of water, one of the big lakes the train goes past on the way from Kojdanava to Minsk. She focussed on the gentle wavelets breaking on the shore in the milky morning light.

She ran and ran along the beach, her toes barely sinking into the warm rusty-white sand. The sea sparkled with many blues as the sun threw flickers and flashes across it, darting like a thousand golden dragonflies. Maria was chasing a seagull along the shore. As it flew away shrieking, Maria raised her hands and jumped up with gleeful joy. She fell into the surf and rolled over in the warm, crystal clear water. As she sat up she looked over to the rocky escarpment where her grandmother sat, her head completely covered with a floppy hat to keep the sun off her skin. Maria could see her looking over her dark glasses staring right at Maria, beaming a smile. Maria waved but got no reply. She stood up and ran back over to her grandmother. She settled down on a rug and wrapped herself in a soft towel.

'I want to do more reading with you Granny,' said Maria

Her grandmother put her book on her lap and took off her dark glasses.

'Yes of course, my darling,' said she in a calm voice. 'What would you like to read?'

'You choose,' said Maria, wriggling with anticipation.

Her grandmother pulled a random book from the beach bag and Maria settled down next to her feet. Maria's eyes looked like they might burst out of their sockets as she waited impatiently for the first word.

As the story unfolded Maria relaxed in the warmth of the sun and allowed solace to take over from scenery.

Later, long after supper, Maria was blissfully tucked up in bed. It was pitch dark in the room but she was wide-awake having been stirred by a noise. The bedroom door creaked a little as it opened, throwing just a touch of light across the floor. Her grandmother came creeping across the room. Maria closed her eyes and pretended to be asleep.

As her grandmother approached the bed Maria could hear gentle sobs. She felt the warmth of her as she knelt down beside the bed and put her face close.

'God how I am going to miss you.'

Maria lay still.

'Your father will be very proud of you my darling.' Maria felt a hand caress her hair. Gentle and warm, it felt so natural to her.

'Goodnight, my sweet, sweet child.' Her grandmother kissed Maria's cheek then sniffed slowly as she stood up.

As the door clicked shut Maria rolled back towards the wall. She was safe and happy, completely unaware that her time in the warmth and love of her Grandmother's orbit was running out.

'Come on love, time to get off!' said a loud voice. 'We're going back again in a few minutes!'

Maria's thoughts came flooding back to the train as she felt something prodding her shoulder. She looked around and realised she was the only one left on-board and the guard was keen to get her off. They had arrived at their destination and it was time to get to her first lecture of the day. Maria stood grabbing her bag, left the train and ran all the way to the university campus.

Dymtrus Kayakova sat in his wheelchair. He had managed to wheel himself outside into the frosty garden. This had been a serious effort and had taken the best part of twenty minutes. The house near Kojdanava sat on the southern side of the vale created by the Nyoman River. He sat looking down the valley, which extended away from the house and as far as he could see. This was his favourite outlook where he came when he wanted to be alone, at one with his thoughts.

He felt for his bottle, finding it resting in its usual place down the side of the chair. A flood of comfort washed over him as he lifted it from its home. He removed the stopper and took a long slug. A plunging moment was followed by a huge wave of euphoria which cut his sadness in two like an axe. It had been three months since Maria had left for university and he missed her more than he ever thought possible. She still came home to help out and to be with him, but things were no longer the same. He had lost her full attention and she had lost her innocence, her naive charm. This was what he hated most; he knew it was the beginning of her life and the start of the end of his.

'What we look for in others is the very opposite of what they look for in us. You want freedom and I need help when it should be the other way around,' he said out loud with a slow melancholic voice. Talking to himself had become standard behaviour in recent months. He took another hefty hit from the bottle.

Maria had her new life, but rarely talked about the new experiences and friends she had made. He wanted to know all about it but she tried to keep things as they had been. It was the bits he was sure he didn't know which upset him the most. The aspects he couldn't control.

Through his new glasses Dymtrus caught sight of an eagle soaring high above a ridge in the distance. He followed its path as it glided effortlessly across the sky. Close to the horizon Dymtrus picked up the path of the river. A thought always disturbed him when he looked at the dark blue water; something his beloved Grandpapa told him many years ago.

He remembered sitting on his grandfather's lap, ensconced in a large comfortable armchair in the corner of a small, smoky sitting room. There were other people there of course but Dymtrus didn't remember who – only two razor sharp images of himself with his grandfather moving within a blurred extraneous theatre.

All Dymtrus could recollect of his eleventh birthday was the conversation with his grandpapa and the present he had bought him. Twenty Red Army soldiers lying in a wooden box. Crudely moulded from toxic lead but neatly ordered and, to him, perfect. He adored them. Dymtrus sat on the floor as Vladyslav Kayakova told stories of the Russian Revolution – The Battle of Tannenburg, of his friend Felix. Dymtrus moved the soldiers around in formations and mock battles as the story unfolded. Anger, hunger, saving Felix from drowning – they were all played out with childish make-believe.

Dymtrus jumped. He turned his head with feral nervousness towards a voice coming from behind him. Someone was shouting his name from inside the house; it was his neighbour who had come to help him prepare his lunch. He was grateful of course but it was not the same as having Maria with him. Dymtrus took a long draw from the small bottle, put the cork stopper back in and quickly forced the bottle back to its home, down the side of his wheelchair between the canvas and his leg.

Dymtrus used his left hand to turn the chair around to face his neighbour as he approached, smiling in the January sunshine. A short, good-natured man in his thirties, he was kind but simple. He was invaluable around the house when Maria was away but when it came to conversations, they were often ephemeral and always superficial.

'Lunchtime,' came a monotone announcement.

'Thank you Oleg,' said Dymtrus. 'I'll be right in.'

In his right hand Dymtrus still grasped a little lead soldier. The little chap still looked smart in his baggy peaked cap and knee-high boots. He had been bashed and chewed through the years but had survived whilst his other comrades had been lost in action. His red flag snapped off years ago but he had made it this far with no serious injuries. Dymtrus needed him now and would make sure this little soldier did not meet the same fate as his fallen companions.

Dymtrus kissed the soldier, then gently placed him down next to the bottle of vodka and wheeled himself up the path with nothing to look forward to but tepid food and thirty minutes with the clueless Oleg.

Chapter IV

.

The offices of Wolfenberg Bank, City of London

Sam had started to hate days like these. Another colossal hangover shrouded him to the point where he wanted to cry.

He sat at his desk and squinted towards his electronic diary hoping not to see any client meetings. He had come to dread any serious human interaction when he felt like this. Fortunately, there were no meetings but he still felt depressed about the number of things he had to do.

It was a crucial day in an investment banker's life – bonus day. This meant not only would he be called in to a meeting room with his boss to find out the extent of his bonus but also he would call in each of his direct reports and tell them their fate. Results and market performance had been excellent so everyone expected bonuses to be high. The City had come to expect bonuses as an intrinsic part of a banker's pay – long gone were the days when the word bonus had any relation to the dictionary definition. If you did not pay them, people would leave to work with competitors - as long as there was competition, there would be bonuses. Deep down Sam believed the culture of the bonus had got carried away. Given what he and his team did for a living they were all overpaid charlatans. When he spoke at parties to friends of friends who were doctors or writers or barristers, they all seemed impressed with what Sam did but Sam thought otherwise - they all did proper jobs, steeped in morality and supporting society. All Sam did was try to make rich people richer – pathetic really and certainly nowhere on society's helpful people list. Some days he felt he was wasting his life and others, that he would have been more fulfilled if he had trained to be something else. He was well paid, so there was a degree of freedom his job allowed, but it was not the same. Sam's mid-life crisis had started far too early and gross overpayment was inadequate compensation.

Sam reached into his drawer and picked up the conveniently placed Ibuprofen tablets that rested next to the Vitamin C pills. Taking these had become a morning ritual. He took three with a swig of black coffee. He got to his feet and announced across the three panels of desks that it was time for the weekly team meeting. Oh joy of joys he thought to himself - his merry gaggle of team members followed him.

As the last person filed into the room, Sam fired up into life.

'Morning all.'

'Morning,' came a dreary response.

'Ok, ok. Try not to be too enthusiastic. We are into February and we have not shown the bosses any new clients. I wanted to talk to you all about what the fuck you are all doing about it. I mean, last year was reasonable but you know what these Germans are like – they want more growth this year. Last year doesn't matter.'

'When are you giving out our bonuses, Sam?' said Darren, one of Sam's young pretenders, sporting classic hair-gelled mid-twenties look - good with the ladies and full of confidence.

'I did it yesterday,' said Sam.

Darren's face fell for a nanosecond but it was enough for Sam to latch onto.

'I'm only joking, you greedy bastard. I am going to speak to each of you later.'

'Anyway, what are you going to do to grow your client base?'

A few of the secretaries looked at each other, desperate to get back to their celebrity magazines and emails.

'Do you guys have any idea how competitive this place is becoming? If we cannot demonstrate growth then they will take us all on a jolly in the back of a big van and we will not be coming back.'

Finally William Fairfax spoke.

'Sam, do you realise just how shit most people in this country think Wolfenberg is? I heard someone say most clients think we couldn't run a bath let alone a portfolio. How does our illustrious senior management think we should try and grow the client book with that kind of reputation?'

Will was a successful guy and did not normally react like this in public. He was in his thirties, privately rich and had the physique of a man who enjoyed good food and even better wine. It took quite a lot to wind him up.

'You are paid to come up with the ideas guys, I know things have been difficult but other teams are coping and some have seen growth this year.' Sam had effectively agreed with Will's comments by presenting such an obviously weak answer to such a pertinent question. Sam announced the team target that sent a groan around the room. He decided the meeting was over.

Lunch with Alec proved a success, providing sage advice and Dutch courage for the afternoon ahead.

Sam retrieved his bonus announcement letters from his drawer. The alcohol at lunchtime had fuelled him for the task ahead; he was ready for aggression, melancholy, pity and sadness. He was primed to be ruthless yet sympathetic, ready to listen to why people's bonuses were either too low or fantastic. Either way, he didn't really care.

Fake smiles, fake concern.

It was Sam's turn. Old Peter Heathcliff heralded from a different era, from a time when ex-army officers controlled the City with a stylishness developed serving Queen and country. His lonely-hearts profile would have been - tall, handsome and rich. With double-breasted tailored suits, with ramrod straight backs and highly polished brogues, you could recognise his type anywhere in their City regalia. Some people were sad that they had become a rare breed, lamenting the decline of that type of natural leadership too often missing in the new world of too much political correctness. There were too many laws and not enough examples - and now a frown came rather than a nod at the offer of a pint at lunchtime. Sam respected his boss but he knew he had become a cliché in the modern business world. Sam's career had started when his boss was in his prime; now all the people he respected were overlooked for promotion.

'Come in Waghorne, and do take your hands out of your pockets,' said Peter. 'Any net new money this year?'

Sam laughed at the direct question.

'Hurry up man, I need to get to Epsom to watch my son play polo.'

'Mixed response from my lot I'm afraid,' said Sam with a curious look on his face, deliberately changing the subject.

'Not surprised given the shower you have put together. Most of them don't deserve a bonus at all. Now sit down man, I'm busy.'

'They expect to be paid something because it has become part of the deal.'

'I know, shame. When I first started, my Christmas bonus was a five pound note and a ten pound turkey.'

'But that was during the War Peter.'

'Sod off Sam. Anyway, I've got good and bad news for you.'

'Well?'

'You should be pleased, you got a £250,000 bonus, and I'm bumping up your salary by 10%, so your overall pay is 20% higher than last year. If you thought you were overpaid then, you are now.'

'Thanks Peter. Lucy can buy a new hat.'

'The bad news is we are expecting at least £100 million of new client money this year from you. You are going to have to pull your finger out.'

'Any good ideas Peter?' said Sam with a little too much desperate edge for it to be a throwaway line.

'Well funny you should say that actually,' said Peter leaning over and handing Sam his envelope with a casual air. 'I want you to call this chap.' Peter took a single sheet of paper out of a file and passed it to Sam.

'What is this?'

'The next big thing Sammy, and don't start shouting about it because your colleagues would bite your arm off to have that piece of paper.'

'What do you mean the next best thing?'

'China, dear boy, China.'

'China?'

'Yes, China. The growth rates out there are incredible and the Chinese are desperate to come to this country to spend their newfound wealth. I want you to give that man a call.' Peter pointed vigorously towards the piece of paper he had handed Sam.

'My connections in Government are very handy from time to time.'

'Sounds interesting….'

'Yes, it is. This guy runs a very successful property company in China and he is keen to come to the UK to grow their operations.'

'So the company want to buy some trophy assets in London then do they?'

'Precisely.'

'What do you want me to do?'

'They want to start an account with us and use it to leverage loans so they can buy properties across the West End. I want you to be their account director Sam. You know, short-term assets with low risk. Should be a real doddle.'

Sam felt elated as he looked down at the piece of paper that bore one name and one telephone number. Martin Zhao. What a curious mix of East and West. Sam looked up and realised the meeting was over and it was time to get calling.

'Don't fuck this one up Sam,' Peter whispered as Sam got up to leave.

Sam stopped for a couple of seconds. He swivelled round with a smile to match the one he expected on Peter's face. A stony expression was all he saw staring back at him.

He turned and headed back to his desk.

Anxious not to make a pig's ear of his task, Sam set to work immediately. A few minutes later Sam leaned back in his chair - the call to Zhao was very brief and extremely productive. Sam had turned on the English charm and it had been agreed that Zhao, and the other members of his board in London, would come and see Sam in a couple of weeks. Meanwhile Zhao would send through a letter explaining just what his company wanted from a banking relationship in London.

As Sam reached for his coat he reflected on an extremely busy day at Wolfenberg. Bonus day created a unique atmosphere in the office - happy, furious, sad, joyous and grumpy - all sat together with other emotions; like some of the seven dwarfs of banking.

There was only one thing for it, off to Jim's Bar for the post bonus day analysis and debrief, some with champagne and others with the cheapest white. He had already told Lucy he would be home late. She had barely made a murmur when he told her. Just another normal evening in London – Sam drinking to excess with his colleagues while George and Charlie got a bedtime story from their effectively single mother.

Once upon a time there was a happy family who had the love and support of a good father...

A tall story indeed.

Chapter V

The Vanishing Eye Bar, Minsk, Belarus

Maria raced across the city so keen was she to get to work well before Boris expected her. She looked forward to working as it provided everything that being with her father back in Kojdanava did not. She made friends and earned money, which in turn provided secure independence but most of all it made her happy. It was something purposeful to look forward to in addition to the hard work of university life.

As she pushed on the front door of the bar, a waft of warm wood-smoked air greeted her face. There was something very comforting about it, acting as an expectorant for her happier emotions.

'Hi guys!' she said with authentic enthusiasm as she walked in.

Boris was sweeping behind the bar, chattering with one of the male chefs.

'You are early Maria, I sometimes think you have nowhere better to go,' barked Boris with a hearty chuckle.

'I love working here,' said Maria as she headed for the kitchen to locate her 'Boris' T-shirt.

By eight that night the bar was packed. Friends, colleagues and lovers were having dinner in Boris' restaurant and a noisy, good-humoured bunch crowded the bar. There was laughter, cheering and chatter. The tantalising smell of sausages drifted around, encouraging customers to drink too much and, like many times before, the mood became self-fuelling. Energy created from the flywheel of fun…

Maria balanced a tray full of beer glasses – another six large Brovars, the locally brewed beer for the party of boys from The Military Academy of the Republic of Belarus. They were youngsters at the moment but Minsk's famous academy would turn the 'MARBs' into soldiers before too long. They worked them very hard, so the recruits were allowed to sing and drink beer on their one night off a week. For many years Boris' had been one of their favourite places.

A collective cheer went up as Maria arrived at the table with the beer.

'Come and sit here, darling,' shouted one soldier.

'No, over here please,' insisted another as he laughed and banged his leg.

Maria felt no concern at this behaviour. It was all meant in good fun.

'How is your course going, Maria?' said Yamin Shakirov, the self-chosen leader of this trainee group. He told the funniest jokes and drank the most beer. With his physical dominance and quicker wit he was an obvious front-runner and none of the others would disagree. Yamin had dark hair and even darker eyes, which sparkled with intelligence and mischief. He was universally liked by his peers and sat very comfortably at the top of the pile.

'Oh, you know. Hard work, quite dull,' said Maria.

'You enjoying Minsk, darling?'

'Very much so, should have come years ago.'

Maria gave Yamin a quick look that nobody else saw. It lasted for only a second but both knew what it meant. Maria had met Yamin on several occasions after she started at the bar and since the first time there had been a growing interest between them. For Maria it was all about his air of confidence, the way he controlled the others so effortlessly.

As Maria went back to the bar one of the boys patted her bottom and the table gave a big cheer. Yamin watched the soldier as he touched her, showing no emotion on his face at all.

Later that night the mood of the bar had decayed, emphasising the true beauty of the previous hours. People had come and gone, leaving a few hardy souls sitting at the bar with their heads slumped down in alcoholic prayer. There was no discussion needed between the guys at the bar. They were all too involved with their melancholic thoughts or too drunk to talk.

Yamin and Maria stood together at the end of the bar. Their bodies were not touching but were close enough to feel each other's warmth. The pretence of earlier had evaporated; now affection was on full display, not that anybody watched or cared.

Yamin touched Maria's long, blonde hair, letting his finger hook around it and draw towards the floor. His deep brown eyes were fixed on hers.

'I cannot leave you alone. Can you stay a while?' whispered Yamin.

Maria gave a half smile and looked at the floor with a gentle touch of innocence and a degree of calculation.

'I need to get home Yamin, I have to see my father,' said Maria with genuine regret.

'But we are going on manoeuvres and I am not back for at least a week, Maria. This is our opportunity to be together.'

Yamin placed his hand on Maria's wrist and held it tightly.

'I want you to stay with me. We can use one of the rooms upstairs. Boris only has a couple of guests staying at the moment. Nobody would know.'

Maria looked into Yamin's eyes. She wanted to stay with him and she knew if she waited much longer then it would be impossible to say no.

'I must go,' she said with conviction. 'Boris would not approve if we stayed here.'

'Come back to the academy then,' Yamin said with a degree of hope. 'It is easy to get people through the gate if you give the guard some cash.'

In frustration Yamin squeezed harder on her wrists and Maria instinctively recoiled. His eyes narrowed slightly in a way that suggested he was used to getting his own way.

After a few seconds he let go of her arm. The sudden release caused her to stagger backwards. One of the drunks sitting at the bar looked up but clearly couldn't focus.

Maria grabbed her bag in silence and headed for the door. Yamin picked up his vodka shot and knocked it back aggressively. He sat on the stool next to him and let his head slump into his arms.

It would be well after midnight by the time Maria got home. Her father would be furious, of course. Once outside, she looked through the steamy window into the pale orange and brown fuzzy glow of the late night bar. Yamin had his back to her and was negotiating another after-hours shot from one of the other waitresses. Maria felt a pang of jealousy as she saw them talk. She stopped and thought about going back. Torn between her past and present she looked at her watch; she had five minutes before the last train.

She started to run as thoughts of Yamin were superseded by the well-known anxiety brought on by thinking just how cross her father would be.

It was pitch dark inside the house when Maria came through the front door. She pushed it shut and was relieved to hear the gentle click of the lock. This time she welcomed the benefits from her father's drinking as she turned with deliberate caution and crept across the room. She could smell fresh tobacco smoke, so he must have struggled himself into bed not long ago. When required the old goat could manage to roll out of his chair, only occasionally was he to be found in the morning in a contorted mess, asleep on the floor.

With a sudden smack something crashed into the wall just inches from Maria's face. The loud noise startled her to such an extent that she automatically pressed herself against the wall.

Silence reigned once again. Maria peered into the darkness, her heart beating violently.

'Who's there?' she said stepping forward with trepidation.

A soft glow rose up, its orangey redness hovered for a time before growing much brighter, illuminating the face of her father sitting in his chair in the corner of the room. His hair was a mess and his face distorted in a way only possible after an entire day of alcohol abuse. Maria could make out his heavy eyes staring into the room with no particular focus. The glow of the cigarette faded and the room fell into darkness again.

Maria stood in silence and waited.

'Where on God's earth have you been?' Dymtrus boomed at the very top of his voice. 'Have you been shleeping around you dirty whore?'

Nervous shock raced through Maria's body.

'Come over here!' he screamed.

As she grew closer another hysterical pull on the cigarette revealed tear-soaked eyes and an unshaven face. She could not remember the last time her father had not shaved. The gaze had intensified into an out of focus glare directed at Maria. He blew the smoke over Maria as she recoiled.

Maria dropped to her knees to put her face on a level with her father. She thought it conciliatory and hoped it may defuse her father's rage. Instead, Dymtrus hit out with his right arm and connected with her left cheek. She fell to the ground with an agonised cry. She got up slowly, holding her face with a mixture of shock and pain.

'I said where have you been Maria?' Dymtrus screamed. 'Come on girl; tell me before I hit you again. I have never been so angry with you!'

'I have been working father; I have been at Boris' bar and I came straight home I promise you.'

'Ever since you have been going to university you have become unreliable. Are they teaching you how to sleep with men and how to lie to your father? Do you expect me to believe you have been working all this time? You are such a disappointment to me.'

Maria reached into her pocket and pulled out her wages from that night. Notes and coins fell to the floor as she raised a fist full of money.

'Look! See if you can focus upon it, just how much I have earned this evening,' she said waving her hand at her father's midriff.

He hit her hand and the rest of the money went flying across the room making sharp clanging noises that seemed amplified in the dark.

'I wonder where you got that money from you whore! You earned that lot on your back you dirty bitch.'

Maria felt her blood boil. She had been meek up to this point but the thought of her father thinking she had earned her money as a prostitute angered her beyond belief.

Maria stood and stepped toward the light switch on the wall next to them. She felt for a second and then flicked it on. She spun around staring at her father with rage in her eyes, moved forwards and slapped him squarely across the face.

'If you must know I do have a boyfriend actually!' she screamed. 'He is young and handsome; he is kind to me. Do you know what that word means you drunken bastard?'

'He must be doing well looking at all the money he gave you,' Dymtrus said looking away from Maria with his hand on his jaw.

Maria lurched forward. She gave her father another huge slap around the face – this time more of a punch. The sound echoed around the room as Dymtrus recoiled, almost toppling backwards out of his wheelchair. He held his head as he stared in alcoholic disbelief. He looked shocked his daughter could have hit him so hard.

Maria's blow dislodged a tear from Dymtrus' red and lost eyes. They remained riveted to her face as the tear rolled down through a developing bruise before dropping down to his lap.

'I always knew you were evil,' he whispered slowly

'What did you say?'

'You heard me. I have tried to keep the truth from you about your mother but what's the point? I've had enough so it's time you knew. She died giving birth to you. You killed her.'

'What are you talking about Papa?' Maria said with a hint of fear.

'I knew from the day you killed my wife you would be of no good to me. After all I have done to look after you,' Dymtrus sneered at his daughter as he spoke. His voice was slow but the bubbling spit may as well have been venom foaming from his mouth.

'What do you mean?'

'She died giving birth to you, one good soul lost to bring a wicked one into the world. Hardly seems fair does it?'

'I... I can't believe you are saying this.' Maria said, dumbfounded.

'I should have told you years ago, but I thought you were going to grow up a kind and helpful child not the selfish slapper you have become. You deserve to know the truth after tonight.'

'She died to save you. She died so you could live. She died, she died...' Dymtrus stopped as his crying gathered pace, diluting the venom and causing his head to sink into his chest. The vodka had won again. He cried uncontrollably.

Maria just stood staring at her father, a kaleidoscope turning in her mind.

A small argument about her job had turned into a torrent of emotions rushing over the ramparts of her normally steady persona. She sank to her knees and held her head in her hands.

Sometime later Maria awoke with a start. She was still in a foetal position hugging her knees and was extremely cold. She got to her feet very slowly and, rubbing her eyes, she looked at her father. Her fears subsided as she realised he was sound asleep in his wheelchair.

'Goodnight Papa,' she whispered as she reached down and kissed him on his cheek. It was noticeably warm against her own and she lingered there for a couple of seconds. He shifted slightly in his chair before the snoring returned.

Maria left him in his chair that night. Her head said not to wake him but the stronger emotion came from her heart which wanted him to wake up freezing cold in the same place he had so badly hurt her so she took herself off to her bedroom.

How could someone blame a child for the death of their wife? Maria thought as she held her head and fell onto her bed. Why would he hurt her like that? Sometime later she pulled the thin duvet over her and tried to sleep – not helped by the light cast that night from a cloudless sky bearing a heartless moon.

Dymtrus' eyes flickered as he awoke with a start. The room span as he tried to focus on something.

There was a huge crashing sound and all went dark. The air rushed around him and there was pain; pulsating pain through his head. The colours were bright, mostly reds and blues swirling around in a concentric pattern that seemed to generate its own warmth through his skull. He must get up, come on, time to get up now.

The snow had been cold. Deathly cold. Deceptively soft to touch but the deadly chill sapped the heat from anything that touched it. He was unbearably cold yet limp like a discarded woollen glove after a snowball fight.

Finally voices; people rushing around him. He longed to be seen, to get comfort from the kind of hug which could only be dispensed by a stranger.

'Help!' he cried in his mind but they couldn't hear him. Chattering around him but nobody could hear.

Checked for life. Lifted up. The smells of industry sweat, oil and tobacco hitting his nose. He laughs at the prospect of being rescued. So cold now, so cold.

Another explosion. Was that in his head or outside? The helpers start to run. There is panic. Something is wrong. Floating above it all now looking down on himself. This wasn't the accident at Rivne. This was something long before Rivne, this was a different place, a younger memory, something terrible, something huge…

A feeling of falling woke Dymtrus. Breathing heavily he opened his eyes and realised the lights were still on. He was motionless in his chair but he could feel his heart galloping in his chest as cold sweat dripped down from his forehead. His shirt was clammy against his skin which prompted a look down at his trousers, they were wet through with urine. He looked at his watch. 4.30 a.m. Why was he still in his chair? Where was Maria?

Then he remembered.

He looked towards the window by the front door. The sun had started to rise, already the valley was revealing detail through a ghostly flat blue. The pure beauty made his heart jump, prompting him to become self-aware. He instinctively reached for his vodka bottle down by the side of his chair. When the first finger touched the cold bottle he felt a sense of relief. He lifted the bottle, it shook as the stopper was removed. Taking it to his lips he drew a long, hard slug.

As the bottle lowered into his lap he replaced the stopper with shaking fingers. He took the neck of the bottle and, with a scream as from the devil himself, threw the bottle hard against the adjacent wall.

He wheeled himself to his room and struggled into bed. The bed sheets were soon as wet as his trousers.

Chapter VI

The offices of Wolfenberg Bank, City of London

Something transformed in Sam when he saw clients. It was a joyful time which brought a relevance to the sterile task of managing investments. There was artistic licence to take advantage of as he took trusting clients by the hand and used his unswerving bullshit to lead them through the unpredictable minefield of markets. Most clients sat gazing like children as Sam weaved his yarns, relishing the opportunity to carve out new meaning from the research the bank produced.

With a bustling waddle Sam followed Peter into the room as the assembled group stood and bowed their heads respectfully. The home team established themselves on one side of the table, smiled awkwardly and sat down. The Chinese clients bowed again then did the same on the opposite side.

'Welcome to Wolfenberg, gentlemen. It is a pleasure to see you all on such a beautiful spring day. I would like to introduce Sam Waghorne and his investment assistant Joanna Hansen. We are very happy to offer our investment management services to you.'

'Thank you Peter,' said a short, stocky man rising to his feet. Sam realised this was Martin Zhao.

'We are very grateful to you all for welcoming us to your splendid bank.'

Peter and Sam gave grateful nods. Sam liked this guy – charm dripped out of him like fresh honey from a frame.

'Mr Heathcliff. As you know we are representing our parent company Qin Property China and we are here today to discuss our plans in regard to expansion into London. We have grown over recent years and Mr Qin and his team are very keen to develop a property portfolio in your capital city. To facilitate this we need an associate bank which can manage our cash flows and operate as our strategic partner.'

Sam turned to Peter and they gave each other an almost imperceptible wink. A furtive liaison which suggested things were looking good.

'Gentlemen, and lady,' said Zhao, making his last word last for twice as long as the first. He looked at Sam's assistant Joanna with a glint in his eye, giving a slight bow. 'We have been speaking at board level and we all agree Wolfenberg seems capable of delivering what we require. We would like to make sure the people who work for us are suitable.'

'Well, we have put together a top team for you Mr Zhao. Sam and Joanna are amongst our best performers. Perhaps Sam could expand on his career so far and give some detail as to how he would manage your portfolio.'

'Thanks Peter,' said Sam as Martin Zhao sat down.

'I am delighted to be able to meet you and your colleagues today and have the opportunity to run through our investment offering.'

Sam said, trying to match the schmooze of Zhao.

'Joanna and I have been with Wolfenberg for five years and have worked together before we joined. We offer our clients a team to deliver consistency and strong performance. We will look after you through good and bad times and will always have your best interests at heart.'

The assembled group settled into a thirty-minute melted chocolate pitch from Sam and Joanna with Peter throwing in the occasional comforting anecdote. It was Wolfenberg at its very silky best. When Sam had finished, the Chinese clients asked for the Wolfenberg representatives to leave the room whilst they discussed the next stage.

'We'll just be next door,' said Peter as he got up and walked out with Sam and Joanna.

'Good work Waggers,' said Peter with vigour. 'I reckon they will give us a chance. My mates in the Government told me they would be happy to come to us.'

'So you rate our chances do you Peter?' said Sam.

'I think so. My people said they were very impressed with our chairman's recent trip to China. He spent three weeks sucking up to all the top bods there so we should get something in return.'

Fifteen minutes later Martin Zhao appeared at the door. He smiled and this was all it took for the three of them to file back into the room behind him.

'Mr Heathcliff,' he said. 'We have had a brief discussion about using your institution. We feel reassured you have the staff and the resources to look after us. Given this we would like Mr Waghorne and his team to manage a portfolio for us. We can clear up the details later but we would like to start with fifty million pounds.'

Sam felt a sudden rush through his body. He was overwhelmed with the size of the initial investment. This represented half his yearly target and would give the team a tremendous boost.

'Thank you Mr Zhao, excellent news. I speak for everybody at Wolfenberg when I say we are delighted to be representing you and your esteemed company,' said Peter standing up to reach across the table to shake Martin Zhao's hand. The other Chinese guests started clapping. Sam and Joanna looked at each other and decided to join in the fun.

'I think we should celebrate with some lunch,' said Martin Zhao with a beaming smile across his face. 'We would be delighted if you could join us?'

'That would be splendid,' said Peter turning his head to Sam and winking. Peter was back on home territory; he loved a good lunch.

A night of celebrating at Jim's with Joanna meant Sam eventually got home at midnight. The kitchen light was on but Lucy had gone to bed long ago. They had not even spoken that day; Sam had not told her his good news. He felt guilty as he crept from the front door and headed for the kitchen and a glass of water. As he walked into the room he noticed a card and a bunch of flowers on the kitchen table. He picked up the card and read the note.

Sam
Looking forward to working with you.
With best wishes
Martin and the team.

Sam stood and stared at the flowers. How did they know where he lived? Was the fact they had chosen white roses, Lucy's favourite, a total coincidence?

Sam headed up the stairs to the spare room with plenty running through his mind.

Chapter VII

The Vanishing Eye Bar, Minsk, Belarus

Yamin and a collection of his friends sat on stools at the bar in the Vanishing Eye. They were having a quiet drink rather than a full session; those were only occasional because of a lack of time and money. Yamin was holding court as usual which included Maria, staring at him from the other side of the bar. She was leaning forward with her head in her hands listening to her boyfriend tell another story. He was talking about details of a gruelling training session and all present were taking mental notes of what he had to say.

'We had to run for twelve miles up and down a massive hill in the Tian Shan mountains, then the bastard instructors made us do it all over again cos one guy gave them lip.'

'Yep, I was sick on the way back but you can't stop otherwise Shorty comes to find you to beat you up,' said one of Yamin's colleagues.

'I fucking hate that guy, he's pure evil.'

'We should gang-up on him one day and kick the shit out of him.'

'You could do but then he would hunt you down and kill you. He might be short but he is lethal.'

'So we kill him first!'

A cheer went up followed by hearty laughter.

Maria stood and picked up a freshly washed glass and cloth. She dried and polished the glass as she looked at Yamin. She smiled as he laughed. She had fallen in love with him over the past few months but had kept this very much to herself. This kind of relationship was new territory for her. She had so much going on with her new university course and the care she still gave her father. She knew it was likely Yamin would soon want to take the relationship to a new level. This frightened her at the same time as making her feel excited – an independent take it or leave it kind of excitement. This was her choice; finally something which was her choice.

'Can I buy you a drink darling?' said one of Yamin's colleagues to Maria.

Maria looked embarrassed to be asked with Yamin in the group. She blushed as she looked down, a polite way of saying no.

'Not here darling!' said the man leaning forward over the bar and grabbing her arm. 'What about someplace else which is quiet and romantic!'

The group roared with laughter but Yamin did not seem to enjoy the joke. He stood and announced to the gathering he was off to get some air and have a smoke outside. He beckoned to his colleague who had spoken to Maria. As they left Maria felt embarrassed as to what had just happened, a few months ago she would have laughed at that kind of thing but now she could sense Yamin's thoughts, she had grown antenna. She decided to do a dirty glass run knowing she would soon lose interest in the remaining soldiers now Yamin had gone for a smoke.

Outside the bar Yamin and his colleague stood smoking and chatting. They were standing to the right of the front entrance, just into a side road where Boris left his van.

'Our course is almost finished,' said Yamin to his friend.

'I know. It has flown past and certainly doesn't feel like two years since we all met,' said his colleague Sergey.

'What are your plans?'

'No idea. My father wanted me to come and get the best training I could. I suppose I will go back to Russia and get a job there. What about you Yamin?'

'Me? I am off to London to work for the Russian Embassy. They want me to start in August. One of the staff at the academy has sorted it all out for me,' said Yamin with no emotion.

'Lucky sod. So your father has pulled a few strings has he? You always did have it easy.'

'You make your own luck in this world and anyway, you are too lazy to get a proper job.'

'You do too much hello darling daddy and brown-nosing senior officers for my liking.'

Yamin fixed a stare at his friend. He dropped his cigarette by his side and let it roll towards the parked van. With alarming speed he lunged forward and punched Sergey squarely in the face. He fell to the ground with no resistance at all. Yamin looked both ways to see if he had been spotted then jumped down on top of him.

'If you ever try and chat up my girl again I will kill you,' he said through gritted teeth but with a calm voice.

Sergey could only stare back, having been immobilised by the blow. Blood was running from his left nostril as he tried to nod.

Yamin stood, looked down at Sergey and spat in his face. He wiped his mouth and kicked Sergey squarely between his legs.

'Never again,' he said quietly as he turned away.

Maria was watching from the window. She had moved over to the other side of the bar during her glass sweep. She could not quite believe what she was seeing. As Yamin walked up to the window Maria turned and hurried back to the bar not knowing what to think. She was doing the late shift and had told her father she would be using one of Boris' spare rooms. She had plenty of time to ask Yamin what was going on.

Moments later Yamin came back into the bar.

'Where's Sergey?' said one of the group.

'He had to go home,' said Yamin with disinterest. 'He has drunk too much.'

Nobody gave this a second thought.

Later that night Maria and Yamin sat together at one of the tables in the bar. All of the lamps had been switched off and a single candle on the table provided a gentle orange glow. It flickered and threw gentle shadows on the walls around the table as it blended with the silence. All Maria would have to do is lock-up and go up to the room on the top floor used for when staff did the late shift.

Maria leant forward and touched Yamin's hand in the candlelight. She sat staring into his eyes, trying to read them.

'You seem tense,' she said chancing this was the best way to start a conversation about the argument she had witnessed.

'Oh, it's nothing. We are coming to the end of the course here and they are really pushing us. I'm just tired.'

'So what do you guys do next? Is there more training after Minsk?'

'I want to talk to you about that, but first I want to do this,' said Yamin with authority as he raised himself up and reached across to kiss Maria.

She was a little reluctant at first and her natural reaction was to pull back from his approaching face. But his eyes never left hers and like a shark homing in on its prey she felt her instincts change as his mouth came closer. Yamin stopped his face an inch in front of Maria's. She could feel the warmth coming from his body; she could hear his breathing, the smell of his tobacco-infused breath. Maria tilted her head to one side like a curious dog. This was Yamin's signal and he went in with pace and passionate force, kissing Maria squarely on the lips.

Maria melted into the kiss and was intoxicated by it. She closed her eyes and pushed back against Yamin with her own force. Her mouth parted with his and they both entered into a fabulous world of stimulating sensation and closeness. Yamin put his hand on Maria's head and pulled at her hair with force. Maria pulled away from him and gasped for breath with a laugh.

'Slow down!' she said, wiping her mouth. 'There is no rush!'

Yamin fell back into his chair and crossed his arms in an indignant fashion. The mood had fallen flat as quickly as it had risen.

'What?' he said grumpily.

'I really like you and the past few weeks have been amazing but don't rush me please.'

After a few seconds Yamin looked up from the table.

'Ok, ok. I'm sorry. Let's have another drink; there is something I want to talk to you about.'

With both wine glasses refilled, Maria sat back in her chair with her glass held in both hands almost as a security blanket in front of her chest. The atmosphere had settled back down and took on an intriguing slant as Maria looked up to listen.

'Sergey and I had an argument outside,' Yamin said after a brief pause. Maria stared but he looked away as he spoke.

'We are all under a lot of pressure and he told me a few things I didn't want to hear.'

'Like what Yamin?'

'He thinks I have had a privileged upbringing and my father will find me a job when I leave the course.'

'Well has he?'

'Oh for fuck's sake! Not you as well!' Yamin shouted, slamming his fist down on the table. Maria jumped back in her chair and felt her pelvic floor muscle twitch several times.

'No, no Yamin please. I was just asking what you are going to do next.'

'Please Maria, you at least can be on my side.'

Maria gave a half smile. She was an intelligent girl and pondered Yamin's last comment whilst looking into his tight, opal shaped eyes. He seemed to be strong and weak at the same time. How peculiar that he was able to sound so aggressive one minute and behave like a sulking schoolboy the next. With her experience of dreaming she was able to speculate; perhaps there was a dark secret in him, some event in his history that created this polemic psyche. It made her want to find out more.

'So go on then, tell me. What is it? What are you going to do?' she said after a heavy, moody silence.

Yamin lifted his head and refocused on Maria. Here he comes she thought, conventional Yamin had re-entered the building.

He narrowed his eyes before he spoke. Maria detected menace.

'I have been offered a job in the United Kingdom.'

'My goodness,' said Maria with genuine surprise. 'Doing what exactly?'

'I have told you before we are being trained to be security

experts. I cannot tell you everything about our training but there are a lot of companies and organisations out there that would want the type of service we can provide. Security, you know, that kind of thing.'

'So what are you going to do?' said Maria after a long slurp of wine. She was starting to get drunk but she did not care given the gravity of the conversation they were having. It felt like the right thing to do.

'This is what I wanted to talk about,' Yamin said with slow pronunciation and lower than normal volume.

Maria leaned forward, anxiously waiting for him to continue.

'Your English is as good as mine and you would love it so I want you to come with me.'

Maria stared in silence.

'I want you to come with me and see London. I'm going to be a trainee security guard for the Russian diplomatic service.'

Maria burst out laughing but this dried up when she saw the seriousness in his eyes. This was preposterous. She would have to leave her course. She would have to leave her father. She had never done anything like this before.

'But, but...'

'This is what you need Maria. This will get you away from your father, your course is not important to you anyway, you know that. We don't need you to get a job; they will pay me well enough to support us both if you don't mind doing some casual work to stop you from getting bored.'

'You patronising shit! Are you being serious?'

'Absolutely. Sorry but this is a big opportunity for me and I would like you to come too.'

'I need to think about it, I need to explain to my father, not that he cares very much about me anymore.'

'Why do you say that?'

Maria explained the fight and how their relationship had deteriorated since she started university. She hated herself for telling Yamin, it sounded like betrayal as she spoke. She mentioned her father's drinking and how she felt when she went home. Having spent all her life with this man it made her sad to think so much had changed.

'Sounds like a perfect time to go, Maria,' said Yamin with a simplicity that cut straight to the heart of the matter. Maria stared back in deep thought; she had had too much to drink to think clearly.

'Let's not worry too much about it tonight shall we,' said Yamin sensing Maria's weakened state. 'Let's have another drink.'

'Because I speak English and would like it or because you need me there?'

Maria gave a mischievous smile and settled back into her chair giving the signal to Yamin to open another bottle of wine. She knew it was naughty and she would have to explain to Boris some other time. The takings had been good that evening so perhaps she could get away with just the one bottle.

It was approaching two in the morning and both Yamin and Maria were talking freely about what they would do when they arrived in London. The sights they would see together, the friends they would make. Both were very drunk so the openness of their conversation went beyond the normal boundaries of a new relationship. It is incredible how much people get to know each other when the inhibitions drop away, safe in the confidence-building kingdom of the bottle.

Yamin stood to help Maria to her feet – she was in a worse condition than him. He put his hand under her arm as she turned from the table and attempted to walk towards the bar.

There were two spare rooms at the top of the Vanishing Eye, which Boris kept for the occasional traveller in need of a bed. Most of the time one of these rooms was used by a member of staff doing a late shift or the chef if he had to be back at his restaurant early in the morning to prepare for a special event. Maria had used them before and had told her father she was on the late shift and would be using one tonight. He got upset she did not come home but the vodka soon took the pain away. Maria wondered whether he would remember in the morning.

Maria turned to Yamin. She was giggling as she tried to walk towards the bar. He caught her when she started to lose balance.

'Come on, I'll take you upstairs.'

'I'm fine, honestly. We need to lock the doors.'

Maria stumbled again so Yamin stooped down and picked her up in his arms. Maria's head fell against his chest. He walked to the door leading to the stairwell and carefully opened it with a spare hand. At the top of the stairs he turned into one of the spare rooms and put Maria down on the bed. She flopped down and her head sank into the pillow.

Maria's head drifted as the room span. She heard Yamin come back up the stairs after, she suspected, a cursory attempt to tidy up and lock the front door. He came into the room again. She felt him take her shoes off, hearing them hit the floor. Then he slowly took her black jeans off, struggling to get them over her knees. She was too tired to resist. He pushed her across to the other side of the single bed and got in next to her. He had taken his clothes off. He hugged Maria's back as she faced the wall. She drifted further and fell into a deep, turbulent and drunken sleep.

A narrow strip of light through the curtains woke Maria. She looked at her watch through half closed, puffy eyes. It was 6.00am. She was coming round slowly as she turned over and jumped a little as she saw Yamin next to her. The memory of the previous night came back to her and she rushed to pull all her thoughts together. Yamin was sleeping soundly with his mouth wide open. She smiled at the peaceful expression on his face as she slithered down the bed trying desperately not to wake him.

In the bathroom many thoughts were whirling through her mind. She still had her T-shirt, bra and pants on so she didn't think Yamin had taken advantage of her. She checked herself as she sat on the loo but all seemed normal.

After a long drink of water she went back to the bedroom. Yamin was still fast asleep, lying there with his boxers on. His body seemed to be made from marble in the half-light of morning and Maria felt turned on as she took her T-shirt and bra off and climbed back into bed as quietly as she could. This is what it is like; finally this was her chance. She lifted Yamin's arm and curled herself into his body. As she settled, she placed Yamin's floppy arm across her chest and pressed it to her with gentle assurance. Yamin shifted in his sleep but soon resumed his deep and lengthy breathing. She felt safe and warm. Slowly she sank back into a dreamy, comfortable sleep.

Two hours later a small droplet of sweat fell from Yamin's nose as they lay together in each other's arms. Their breathing was heavy but in harmony and both were happy, intoxicated this time by a different drug – the scent of each other. Maria felt Yamin was a part of her, like she had known him for a lifetime. What had happened was in a different world to any other of the brief encounters she had had in her life. At times he had been like an animal, rough and mechanical but Maria had let this happen and the resulting pleasure had been magnificent. She slowly stroked Yamin's muscle at the top of his arm, it was smooth and as coolly strong as stone.

Like a grumpy Labrador disturbed from his sleep, Yamin rolled over, drew himself up and shuffled to the bathroom. Maria lay staring at the ceiling thinking of London and the freedom it would bring her. She knew in her heart that the decision to leave had already been made but what would her father think? She would have to introduce Yamin to make her father see the sense in going. She looked at her watch. 8.50 a.m.

'Fucking hell,' she said panicking, realising the time. She desperately tried to get dressed as quickly as she could, falling over as she tried to get her underwear on. Lectures were due to start at nine and she was going to be late. She flew past Yamin in the bathroom barely stopping to talk.

'Can you get out tonight?' she said starting down the stairs.

'Guess so, why?' said Yamin from the bathroom through a mouthful of the communal toothpaste.

'Let's go and tell my father this evening.'

'Tell him what?'

'London!' shouted Maria as she jumped the final three stairs and ran past the bar to get the front door key and her bag. A shower and breakfast would have to wait.

'Boris will be here at nine!' Maria shouted as loud as she could as she opened the front door.

'Tell him you got pissed and I let you sleep upstairs!'

'See you at the station at six. OK? Don't be late!'

Maria slammed the door and starting running up the road. She laughed when she realised she was still in her work clothes and didn't care one bit.

After a day of listening and learning nothing Maria met Yamin at six precisely. There was a train at twelve minutes past so they did not have to wait long before they were on-board and flying through the Belarus countryside on the way to Kojdanava to see Maria's father. Both sat in comfortable silence as the train glided along – not pensive, just the type of healthy silence familiarity brings. Contented and tired with a little piquancy delivered through the thought of the night before running through their minds.

Eventually it was Maria who spoke.

'Last night was amazing, perfect,' she said with a low, almost apologetic tone.

'I hope you didn't mind me waking you like that.'

'There's a first time for everything I suppose,' said Maria. 'I arrived twenty minutes late because of it.'

'All part of your educat...'

'Stop it!' Maria blurted, feeling herself redden as she smacked his arm.

Maria had no idea how her father would react when she introduced Yamin. Many thoughts were going through her mind. Would he be angry? Would he get violent? Would Yamin hurt him? She turned and stared out of the window at the passing scenery. The summers in Belarus were pleasantly warm but far too short. Maria saw green trees, grass and the odd cow merge into one high-speed country setting. She had been in the countryside most of her life but the city had made her cynical. Was she still travelling home or just visiting her father? Once allowed out of the bag, youth and development would never see eye to eye with the slow-paced constants of peace and tranquillity.

'Just be yourself, OK?' Maria said after a few minutes of mildly bumpy train silence.

'Oh, I thought I might do some impressions.'

'Come on, be serious, he can get pretty scary when he has been drinking. Just relax and I will tell him about London.'

'Fine,' said Yamin as he shut his eyes and tried to catch up on some sleep.

Maria turned back to the green fields, pressing her forehead against the glass. She was tired as well so sleep was not too far away...

'I think this is our stop.' Yamin said some time later.

The station signs for Kojdanava started to pass by the window.

Maria jumped up and grabbed her bag realising she must have been asleep for half an hour or more.

'Sorry I was miles away.'

'I know. Are you OK?'

'Yes fine,' Maria looked at Yamin and smiled. 'I'm fine'.

Most times a city train came in there would be a bus waiting and luckily they were not disappointed. They ran to the bus and sat pressed together near the back. Nervously Maria turned to Yamin when the bus doors closed. She was about to say something when he stopped her by placing his index finger to her lips.

'Shooosh,' Yamin said quietly. 'There is plenty to get right today so let's not get all soppy.'

Maria was embarrassed and turned away from him. He tried to placate this by reaching for her hand but she pulled away. The rest of the seven-minute journey was spent in super-charged juvenile silence.

The bus stopped just up the road from Maria's father's house.

'Two minutes,' said Maria.

'Ready. I have been trained for this.' said Yamin.

'Perhaps. Did I ever tell you he doesn't like Mongolians?'

'What do you mean, I am Russian,' said Yamin with modest indignation.

'I'm only joking. Some of your mates from the academy swear you look more like a Chinaman than a Russian. They say your mother must have slept with a Mongol.'

'Who said that? I will kill them.'

'All of them.'

'Here we are,' said Maria with a chuckle as they approached a cottage just off the lane they had been walking along.

Yamin straightened his back and became the soldier he had trained to be. He looked over to Maria as they walked towards the front door. Smoke billowed from the chimney despite it being a summer's evening. It still got cold, especially for those who did not move around much and had thin blood.

Maria grabbed Yamin's hand and gave it a squeeze. She let go of it and knocked on the door and waited. It felt stupid given she was entering her own house – she put it down to nerves.

As she pushed the door she heard the familiar rolling squeak of her father's wheelchair coming from his bedroom and approaching the sitting room. She looked over to Yamin and they both entered with fear. An elongated shadow approached the room, cast by light from a bedroom. Frozen to the spot, they waited to see what mood they had caught him in.

Chapter VIII

Kojdanava, Belarus

'Is that you my darling?' said Dymtrus Kayakova, briskly wheeling himself into the room. He was clean shaven and wearing a fresh shirt. Maria could see a beaming smile across a warm, welcoming face. The very opposite of what she had expected. He looked very respectable.

'Good evening Papa, I want you to meet a friend of mine. This is Yamin Shakirov. He is studying at the Military Academy in Minsk. He comes to the bar I work at.'

Yamin stepped forward and lowered his six-foot frame by bending at the waist. He offered his hand to Dymtrus who accepted it without saying anything. Dymtrus stared into Yamin's eyes and gave his hand a good firm grip.

'You are training to be a soldier, yes?' Dymtrus said after a lengthy pause.

'Sort of sir, I am doing a course in military techniques and defence. I hope to work in the Security Service one day,' said Yamin. Maria was impressed he could keep his emotion under control knowing he was there to discuss a certain 'one day'.

'Good. I like soldiers. You are very welcome in my house. Please take a seat. Maria please can you get two glasses and a bottle of vodka from the cellar stairs, I think we have run out up here. Yamin and I need a drink. Have a think about what you should cook for supper too,' said Dymtrus wheeling himself to the chairs by the fire. 'You get yourself a glass if you want anything,' Dymtrus said as an afterthought.

Maria was overjoyed with the cordial introduction, so she scuttled off to the kitchen where she could still overhear the men speak. From initial impressions it sounded like her father was delighted with Yamin. He was never normally this nice to her let alone anybody else. It might be a reaction to the only male company he normally got – Oleg his neighbour who was kind but so painfully simple. Maria felt a warm glow enter her, a relief that her father seemed willing to receive Yamin into his house. She had a feeling his mood might have something to do with running out of vodka the previous night, forced sobriety from an inability to descend the cellar stairs. Whether or not this genuine hospitality would survive their news, for the first time in ages she was glad to come back into the sitting room with the drinks and a smile.

'Ah! There you are. Come on Maria, the man is thirsty after his long journey,' Dymtrus said with an animated keenness only alcoholic dependency can bring. Yamin sat with a smile on his face but no emotion in his eyes. He was very much on guard.

Maria poured three glasses having decided to get one for herself to help her courage. She handed a glass each to the men. Yamin waited for Dymtrus' move.

'Shlang!' Dymtrus said.

All three of them raised their glasses and downed the vodka.

Maria was the only one who gave a noticeable cringe as the strong liquid slipped down her throat.

'The same again girl!' Dymtrus said with force. Maria was happy to oblige but gave Yamin a mocking smile only he could see.

After a couple more rounds Dymtrus, Yamin and Maria all settled down around the fire. Maria would be expected to prepare supper at some point so she thought it important to get some of the groundwork covered. More importantly it would help if they could set out their plans before Dymtrus had too much to drink.

'So when do you leave the Academy, Yamin?'

'This is my last term – I have nearly completed the course.'

'So what are you doing next? Have you got a job?'

Yamin flicked a quick glance at Maria sitting opposite him. She noticed he was on edge and shifted ever so slightly on his seat. He gave a nervous cough that would have sounded innocent enough to a stranger but she knew this was crunch time.

'I have been offered a job in London. I will be working with the Russian Embassy helping them on the security side,' said Yamin in a proud voice.

'My goodness, how exciting. Congratulations,' said Dymtrus leaning forward to offer a mildly trembling hand to Yamin who shook it politely.

Maria looked at her father. She knew he had guessed the purpose of their visit together. He was an intelligent man and his brain was first class when the drink and depression from his physical condition were not allowed to put their barriers up.

'When do you leave for London?' Dymtrus added.

'I start in September. I want to go across to find accommodation so I will probably go mid-August,' Yamin said apologetically.

Dymtrus stared back with interest. Maria could sense the calculations going on inside his head.

'Sounds great; you must be very excited.'

'Now what are you going to cook for supper Maria? You both must be starving after your journey,' Dymtrus said, changing the tempo and direction of the conversation. Maria took this as a signal her father wanted to talk with Yamin alone, so she nodded, stood up and headed for the kitchen.

'Oleg put a chicken in the fridge,' Dymtrus yelled.

Maria didn't mind being asked to prepare the food and she was able to pick up most of what the men were saying in the sitting room. Supplies were low but she thought she had just enough to make a reasonable stew. Good honest fare for her men. She set about chopping the vegetables with one ear on the conversation next door.

A few hours later they had finished a simple supper and were chewing on bread with some local cheese. Maria had opened a second bottle of local wine which was saved for special occasions. She was quite surprised it had survived for so long. They were all merry and the conversation flowed easily. Against all of Maria's expectations the evening was going well. She had to jump in with both feet.

'I'm going to go with him,' Maria said after a lull in the conversation.

Another silence followed, only interrupted by Dymtrus putting down his cheese knife. He looked at Maria as he finished his mouthful.

'I see. So despite all I have taught you about education and loyalty, you want to run away from your course and leave me here to die?'

Here it comes again Maria thought, it had taken some time but Nasty Papa had returned. Yamin looked serious and was keeping his head down avoiding everybody's eyes.

'It's not like that, Papa.'

'Well what is it like? Have you got any feelings for my welfare? I need your help damn you!'

Yamin lifted his head to Maria with an instinctive defensive action.

'Your neighbours and friends can help you. They have been whilst I have been away.'

'What would your mother think?' Dymtrus said taking the argument to a higher level.

'Father if you are going to talk like that then I will leave tonight. I am nearly twenty years old and I deserve to make my own way in life. I love you but you must let me have some space, some freedom of my own.'

Dymtrus pushed his wheelchair back and headed for the front door. He opened it with some difficulty and pushed himself into the dark, moonlit garden to his favourite spot, looking into the valley. Maria sat still during her father's struggle. She knew about this place – he went there to think and to be alone so it would be futile to follow him. As she started to clear the table Yamin announced he must be getting back to the barracks. If he left now, he could make it back before midnight.

Maria kissed Yamin and said she would see him tomorrow. She wanted to talk more about their plans and what she would need to arrange for their move. Yamin walked to Dymtrus who was sitting under an old renovated street lamp that was placed near his favourite spot to make nocturnal visits possible. Maria watched as Dymtrus shook Yamin's hand in the moonlight. It was polite but the friendliness had gone. Like the sun going down on a brief encounter - there was little warmth left at the end of the day. Maria wept as she watched him leave. Surely there would be further trouble now she was alone. Her bedroom was the safest place she could think of.

Maria woke with a start. She looked at her watch on the bedside table – it was six in the morning. She had expected a visit from her father after she had gone to bed but there had been no such call. He must have put himself to bed. It would have taken him time, but he was resourceful when he needed to be. The other odd thing was he normally woke up early at this time of the year, so it surprised her there had not been a customary banging on the wall with the cry for assistance.

Maria got up and headed for the kitchen. En route Maria was alarmed to see her father's wheelchair sitting exactly where it had been the night before, facing away from the house down the valley framed by the blue light of morning. Despite being summer the nights got cold in Kojdanava. She opened the front door and ran towards him.

'Papa! Are you alright?' she said as she approached the chair. She dropped to his level in front of him and found he was fast asleep in the morning sunshine, looking like a baby. There was an empty vodka bottle upturned in his right hand down by his side.

Maria turned the wheelchair and took her father back to the house. As they went in, he woke from his sleep.

'What? Where are you taking me? Wait!' Dymtrus said, still delirious.

'Papa it is only me, Maria. You fell asleep outside. I am bringing you in for breakfast!' Maria said with a laugh.

Dymtrus was silent. The sleep had interrupted his anger and this took a couple of minutes to rebuild inside him. Eventually the full memory of the night before had manifested in his head.

'You leave me alone you selfish cow. If I want any help from anybody I will ask Oleg or his mother to come and help me.' Dymtrus spat venom at Maria.

'But Papa, can we not discuss this sensibly? This is my big chance to see the world. Why would you want to deny me this opportunity? Why did you have to mention Mama like you did last night?' Maria said with a tear growing in her eye.

'You never met your mother, don't you dare tell me when I can and cannot mention her name. She died bringing you into this God forsaken world.'

Maria just stared back at her father. He was not going to listen to anything she said and was certainly not going to act rationally.

'I think I'd better go,' she said with a calm voice.

'Fine.'

'I will pack my things.'

'Fine. Don't come running back here in a hurry. You will not be welcome,' Dymtrus snapped back.

'Papa don't be like that, you should be proud of me.'

'Please get out now. Do you not see how disappointing it is to see a child who I raised singlehandedly stab me through the heart?' he said wheeling himself to his bedroom.

Maria ran to her room and packed her bag as quickly as she could.

Ten minutes later she carried her bag into her father's room to offer her final goodbye. He had turned his wheelchair away from the door and sat facing the wall. She turned and ran from the house. Tears ran from her face as she left, knowing the only thing in the world she had left was the support and newly found love of Yamin Shakirov.

Dymtrus could not see straight because of the water in his bloodshot eyes. What was he going to do? How was he to cope? He loved his daughter more than he could possibly tell her. Where did he start with the true story of his life? Letting her go was the easy option, the path of least pain. She was better off not knowing the truth about the past – she had too much on her mind and far too much to look forward to. He would tell her one day, when she had found a husband and could rely on a family to support her through the pain of what he knew. One day she would understand.

He wheeled himself into the garden stopping by the lamp, looking down the valley. He cursed the empty vodka bottle by his side. At least Maria had brought some more up from the cellar stairs during her brief visit. He would go and get another later on.

The thought of drinking and the gentle breeze through the conifers calmed his soul. Sometimes, when he thought of the past, the memories came back in a flood, haunting him for days. Other times they were ephemeral, encased in a vivid nightmare. The duration was totally unpredictable, the effect was always frightening.

Dymtrus was twenty-five again. He was sitting with his parents in a cafe in Kiev on a beautiful summer's day. People all around them were laughing and chatting as they ate and drank. The bustle of this popular cafe in full flow was as exciting as the quality of the food.

Dymtrus turned to his parents. Both were handsome and dressed well. Given his father's profession this was not a surprise. Accountants were well paid even back in those days. Dymtrus was proud and content, happy to be able to join his parents for lunch on his mother's birthday.

'How is your job going Dymtrus?' asked his father.

'I love it Papa, the best thing I have ever done. The people at the Station are so helpful, really teaching me to do my job properly. Some say it is dangerous but as long as it is done correctly, there is nothing to worry about.'

'I am glad, I know my father would be proud of you if he could see you today.'

'I know Papa. I think about him; especially when I am told I am doing well.'

'We are both proud of you too son,' said Dymtrus' father grabbing the hand of his beaming wife as he spoke.

Dymtrus smiled back as he stood to go and use the bathroom. Walking away from the table he floated, safe in the knowledge his parents were able to give him so much love.

As he stood by the urinal there was a massive explosion. It threw him against the opposing wall and knocked him off his feet. For several seconds he was still, dazed and unsure as to what had happened, what to do next. Tentatively he got up, opened the door and was hit by a cloud of dust and screaming from every direction. He started to panic wondering what on earth was going on. Ducking his head down he tried his best to remember his way back to the restaurant without using his sight, the dust was so thick he could barely see in front of his face.

He turned the corner back into what used to be the main room of the restaurant. The air cleared slightly as he walked to where their table had been. He dropped to his knees. There were bits of people scattered like an impossible human jigsaw, blood all over the floor and all up the last remaining wall. Broken glass, shredded linen, twisted plastic and smashed china was strewn everywhere in one chaotic mess only the devil could have requested.

'Papa?''Mama?'

Chapter IX

West Hampstead, London

Maria flew for the first time with a mixture of fear and excitement. She tried to squeeze as many clothes as she could into her bag as she had read the United Kingdom was colder than Belarus. Equipped with all her thermals, jumpers and coats she knew the weather could not defeat her.

Yamin had travelled before her to secure a place to live and to meet some of his new colleagues. He had warned Maria that the Russian Embassy was obsessed about secrecy so he would not be able to tell her much about his activities or movements. So much so, he would be told very little about the place as well – the less you knew, the less trouble you could get yourself into. He neglected to tell her that she had been followed by workers for two weeks before she left.

After an enjoyable flight which was more liberating than frightening, Maria travelled from the airport to North London on public transport that was surprisingly easy to understand. She arrived at her new home in high spirits and earnestly spent time tidying the small flat on Lyndale Avenue, a few minutes' walk from the main streets in West Hampstead.

The previous tenants had clearly not been as fastidious as Maria, having left the place in a total mess. Yamin had had no time to clean up as he had barely been in the flat since he had arrived. The mess was one of the two reasons it was cheap. A reminder of another reason came every five minutes or so when a commuter train rattled past the window, shaking the fragile flat until it had passed. When quiet was restored the flat was still not much to look at but it had functional simplicity so Maria was happy.

Once the flat was clean Maria felt an overwhelming desire to explore her new environment. She had promised Yamin that she would acquire a mobile phone so they could stay in touch in a country with reliable network coverage. Having safely purchased on the high street, she went to have a look around.

After a few minutes Maria noticed an advert for a job in the window of a bar just off the Finchley Road. This was a place Yamin had told her about – he had mentioned the name of the bar after walking past some days earlier. He was keen to increase their income and he was concerned she might get bored all alone.

Part-time waitress required. Restaurant service and bar work. Apply within.

Maria walked towards the edge of the pavement to see the name of the bar and get a feel for the place. As she looked up she held her hand to her eyes, shielding them from the early morning sun. She squinted as she read.

The Running Leopard
Fine Sri Lankan Cuisine

She looked around at the street and the other shops nearby. It was clear that West Hampstead had a strong community of residents with Sri Lankan heritage. There were specialist food shops, cafes and restaurants dedicated to the cultural requirements of the Sri

Lankan way of life. The Running Leopard seemed to be just this sort of place; big heavy red curtains and plenty of gold ornaments – mostly celebrating the elephant. Maria walked to the glass window and held her hand up so she could see inside. A repeat of what she could see from the curb – green plants, red chairs and a well-stocked bar at the back. Maria liked it and wondered whether a place like this would be happy to employ a girl from Belarus. She pushed on the front door. It was open.

Despite it being well before lunchtime, Maria was hit by an exotic mix of spices and stale alcohol as she walked into the restaurant. The door chimed a couple of gold elephant ornaments as they gently brushed into each other.

'Hello. Is there anybody there?'

She looked at all the different colours and shapes of the various bottles behind the bar. Not quite sure what the boys back home would think of this she thought, it looks more like a pharmacy than a bar. Just then she realised she was not alone. A short Sri Lankan man in chef's uniform was standing by the door into what she presumed was the kitchen.

'Can I help you madam?' said the man with a heavy Sri Lankan accent.

'Hello, yes good morning,' said Maria in a mild fluster. 'I saw your sign in the window. Are you still looking for help?'

The short chef looked Maria up and down whilst holding his chin. Maria felt self-conscious and could feel herself turning red.

'Best come back when the owner is here. Mr Darsha normally gets here at midday. I'll let him know someone came in. Who shall

I say called?' said the chef with indifference. It sounded like he wanted to get to the market or chop something up.

'Maria. Maria Kayakova,' said Maria, offering her hand to the chef. He had already turned back to the kitchen.

'I'll tell him you came in,' he shouted pushing on the door and disappearing into the kitchen.

Maria looked back at the bar and wondered whether she could be bothered to come back. Chefs made very bad advertisers – they were rude when they were busy so she decided she could discount that. Looking around she liked the place; it might be fun and they could certainly do with the extra money.

At midday she took the pleasant stroll up to the restaurant. She timed the six minutes it took her door to door, all along well-lit streets. Perfect if they wanted someone to work late into the evening. She pushed through the door and heard that pleasant chiming sound merge with the spicy aroma. In front of her sat a thin man in an open shirt at one of the tables nearest the bar. He looked like a man who could own a place like this.

'Mr Darsha?' she said in a pleasant tone as she approached the table.

'Yes, you must be Maria? He replied in a soft low tone that didn't match his physique and was quite unexpected to Maria. The clipped well-educated voice gave her a jolt of encouragement.

'I was interested to know whether you are still looking for someone to help you. I have just moved to London and have some experience in bar work.'

'Yes we are. We are very busy and I am desperate to get someone to help out. Tell me a bit more about yourself. Please do sit down.'

Maria gave Mr Darsha a summary of why they had come to London. She ran through her duties at The Vanishing Eye and the kind of hours she worked. After about five minutes Mr Darsha put his hand up.

'Stop, stop! When can you start?' he said with a pleasant smile. 'I think you will fit in perfectly.'

'Well, I suppose straight away! But I need to talk to my boyfriend. Perhaps tomorrow?' Maria said in a rush.

'I really need help in the evenings and we open the bar at six. Why don't you come down tomorrow at say half past five and we can introduce you to a few people and show you the ropes. We need to work out the days that suit you and what nights you can stay late. Some of the Sri Lankan locals go on a bit you know. We also need to discuss what to pay you.'

'Thank you Mr Darsha. I will see you tomorrow,' Maria said writing down her new mobile number then getting to her feet. 'I won't let you down.' She reached out her hand and he took it.

'Good. See you tomorrow, oh, and please, call me Kumara.'

'See you tomorrow, Kumara,' said Maria walking to the door with a spring in her step.

Maria thought it would be enjoyable to make Yamin a special dinner to celebrate her new job and the extra income that would come in. She bought some lamb and some fresh vegetables to make a stew – one of his favourites. There was even some crusty bread to mop up the sauce. Yamin had been coming home in variable moods, surely like any job where elements either met, exceeded or disappointed relative to expectations. There didn't seem to be much middle ground with Yamin – things were either great or terrible. It had just passed seven in the evening as she waited for him on their lumpy sofa, everything just about ready.

By eight she was starting to worry. The oven had been turned down low and the candles blown out. He did not know about her new phone yet so there was no way for him to call her. She noticed the cheap clock on the mantelpiece and the quiet ticking started to irritate her.

Eight thirty. Maria's phone beeped telling her she had an SMS. She rushed over to where the phone sat. She looked at the message.

Looking forward to working with you. Best, Kumara

Another fifteen minutes passed, still nothing. She turned the cooker off and sat back down on the sofa with her glass of wine. She had opened it at seven and now most of the bottle had gone. The clock ran at a watcher's half speed - where the hell was he?

Finally, at nine a key entered the door and Yamin came through the doorway into the flat. Maria sat on the sofa with a tear in her eye. She had drunk a bottle of wine and her emotions were running high.

'I cooked supper,' said Maria.

Yamin stood staring at her, almost like he didn't recognise her at first. Maria noticed he had a swollen left eye and looked like he had been in a fight.

'Is everything alright Yamin?' she said, getting up and coming over to his side.

Yamin clearly did not want Maria to see him so started towards the bathroom. Maria grabbed his arm but he shrugged her off with a force that sent her falling back.

'I'm fine, we had some trouble at the embassy. I'm sorry I'm late. I won't be a minute.'

Yamin went into the bathroom and slammed the door shut. Maria stared at the closed door. What on earth had been going on? She went to the bathroom door and banged on it.

'Yamin, what has happened to you? What have you been doing?'

There was no answer. Maria thought about using her shoulder but eventually went into the bedroom and lay down on the bed. Perhaps coming to London was a mistake. She wondered how her father was coping without her and what was he doing - drinking too much and moaning about Oleg whilst still relying on his help.

There was a click of the bathroom lock. Yamin came out naked apart from a towel around his waist. He came into the bedroom turning his face away from Maria so she could not see the extent of the swelling to his left eye. He sat down facing the wall.

'What have you been up to Yamin, why has somebody hurt you?' Maria said turning towards him. 'If this is what moving to another country means then I want to go home.'

'Never ask me about my work,' Yamin said slowly and deliberately. 'The Russian Embassy asks me to do various things I am not able to talk about – not even with you.'

'But you are hurt. You don't get paid enough to be hurt like that.'

Maria moved to where Yamin sat and very gently lifted his hair to look at his swollen eye. There was a cut above it and already the yellowish purple of a big black eye. She had a small intake of breath as she saw the full extent of his injury. She leant over and kissed the intricate tattoo on his neck like a target and whispered she had made Yamin's favourite lamb stew. The kiss on the neck was like finding Yamin's on-switch and he smiled for the first time that evening.

'I bought two bottles of wine so let's have the other one,' Maria said with a cheeky grin.

'You've finished one already?' Yamin said with surprise.

'You were late!' Maria giggled again and ran to the kitchen to resuscitate supper and to open more wine.

Over supper Maria told Yamin about her new job at The Running Leopard. By the time they sat back on the sofa after eating, everything had returned to normal. Maria was still worried about what Yamin had been up to but she also knew he was a trained soldier and some things were better left.

Maria had developed a love-making scale of how rough Yamin was and how that correlated with his mood. A happy and playful mood usually ended up with a nine or a ten out of ten in terms of duration, comfort and satisfaction for her. When he was fractious and preoccupied she was treated badly and the force he used increased – like she was being used to release his frustrations. A quick, angry and uncomfortable session only scored a one or a two.

She had hoped his mixed mood could have brought home a six. She got a three.

Later, as Yamin lay sleeping, Maria reached for his mobile to add her new contact details. Curiosity grabbed her and she looked back at him before looking at his messages. He didn't move. Scrolling up she found the latest one from a random number with no name:

ALL, 2D PRACTICE

A message from his work no doubt – it made no sense at all.

Maria arrived at The Running Leopard at five-thirty on the dot. She liked to be punctual, to set the right impression from the start. She walked in to see Kumara Darsha sitting in the same chair as the day before, going through some papers with an official looking man in a suit. As the elephant chimes announced her arrival Kumara turned to her whilst encouraging the little man to head to the kitchen. He quickly took the papers they were looking at and scuttled off.

'Maria! Do come in. Take a seat,' Kumara said as he extended an arm to the chair the little chap had just vacated.

Maria and Kumara ran through her responsibilities which included working behind the bar - she would have to learn the names of all those funny coloured liquids in the potion bottles - and serving food to guests in the restaurant. Kumara told her what her hourly wage and weekly schedule would be and Maria felt pleased. That would help them make ends meet and might help Yamin improve his mood.

As the regular staff arrived, they gave Maria several shifty looks before they were invited over to meet her. All the others were of Sri Lankan descent and Maria felt a little out of place. Kumara could see this and made a point of stating that his paying customers came from all walks of life and he was pleased Maria could bring a different cultural background to his humble restaurant. This cheered her up no end as she didn't feel much warmth from the other waiters she had met. If you added the chef, they made a miserable bunch. Perhaps they were a close team and behaved like this when they met people for the first time but Maria liked Kumara and he was in charge; that was the important thing.

'You'd better start learning the menu and the drinks Maria. There are quite a few bottles there!' said Kumara standing up and pointing to the kaleidoscopic bar.

She could see the little man in the suit was hovering by the kitchen door.

'I will see you later. These guys will look after you,' Kumara said, heading for the exit. The little man in the suit scuttled across the restaurant like a crab, a whole stack of papers under his arm. Kumara opened the door and they both left together.

Maria looked up to see all the other staff had disappeared into the kitchen, no doubt off for a good gossip. She took the menu from the holder on the table. She opened it and started to familiarise herself with the myriad of dishes the chef liked to serve.

Chapter X

The offices of Qin Property Company, Portman Place,
Regents Park, London

Sam and Joanna sat in the reception hall of the Qin Property Company's London headquarters. They had a meeting at midday to update the client on progress with their portfolio. Sam looked around him at all the reception had to offer. They were used to a degree of opulence at Wolfenberg but nothing could have prepared them for this. There were Carrera marble pillars rising up from a chess-board stonework floor, the smell of the burgundy leather and the solidity of bronze statues. Sam thought it was all a bit over the top but he didn't say anything to Joanna because she looked like she was enjoying it.

'Is this like your flat Jo?' said Sam trying to kill a few seconds.

'Stop it Sam, I like this. It's much better than going to see boring corporate clients in boring battleship-grey coloured banks,' Joanna said trying her best to remain professional.

'Suppose so, but they don't get taste do they, just pile in as much art and grandeur as possible. Too much money this lot.'

'Come on Sam, try to take this seriously, this is now our biggest client.'

'It's amazing how they can make it smell Chinese.'

'Sam! Stop it,' said Joanna with a serious look, she was gesturing to her left.

There was a soft tapping on the marble and a diminutive Chinese lady in an elegant knee length suit came walking towards them. She gave a modest bow and said Mr Zhao and his colleagues were ready for them.

Sam's feet sank into thick carpet as they climbed two flights of stairs and were led through a large wooden door into a huge office. All the board of Qin stood around a vast oak table.

'Come in please Mr Waghorne, Miss Hansen,' said Martin Zhao. He was smartly dressed in a tailored suit and highly polished shoes.

'Coffee for you both?'

'No thank you,' said Sam. There was too much talking to be done and it would only make him hyperactive.

'Water would be great, thanks,' said Joanna.

'We would like to discuss how the relationship is going in your eyes, Mr Waghorne. It has been a few months since we came to Wolfenberg and the directors would like an update on the money we gave you to manage. Mr Qin and the board back in China are willing to commit much more to this country; he sees the London Property market as an excellent opportunity. If we are satisfied, then more funds will be coming your way.'

Sam looked at Joanna. This was incredible news. At this rate the client was going to provide most of his net new money target for next year as well as this. He shifted nervously in his seat trying not to look too keen to impress.

'Over to you Mr Waghorne, what's been going on?'

Joanna sent a review document around the table, one for each of the directors. When they were all settled with a copy Sam started.

'Good morning gentlemen, Joanna and I would like to update you on the progress on the Qin Property Company portfolio this afternoon and give you our thoughts on where we are in world markets and what is likely to happen in economies for the next few months.'

All the directors sat watching Sam weave his magic. This is where the true art of the fund manager came out - melding fact with fiction, welding events in history with likely or unlikely events in the future all brought together in a smooth monologue.

At Wolfenberg they charged a whole percentage of the fund every year for the privilege of being a client. This was big money for the bank and only really perpetuated on the trust the client put in their manager. That is why Sam and Joanna were paid so well, they were the gatekeepers to the client's money.

'As we all know markets have been strong in the past three months and I am delighted to tell the directors the portfolio had grown by five point six per cent in the quarter since you came to Wolfenberg.'

A murmur of pleasure went around the table and Sam paused to soak it in. This was nectar for a fund manager and, like any actor, Sam absorbed the credit. Sam openly thanked Joanna for her contribution. All the men around the table seemed to welcome

Sam's English chivalry.

'So we have outperformed the benchmark you set for us. Our performance is quoted after fees as well gentlemen, so I hope you will agree with me that our contribution has been meaningful,' Sam added, looking for an encore.

Sam and Joanna spent the next sixty minutes running through the stocks and bonds they had bought and sold during the quarter. It was clear to Sam that Martin Zhao and his colleagues had lost interest shortly after hearing the portfolio had done well. That was all most clients cared about. The detail was for the experts – that is why clients used professionals and didn't do it themselves. Sam had made them money and that was that.

At the end of the presentation Martin Zhao stood and started clapping. This was a first for Sam and Joanna went bright red.

'Thank you, Mr Waghorne, for such a comprehensive presentation; I speak for all of us when I thank you both and Wolfenberg for such an impressive start.'

Sam nodded appreciatively and smiled as he clocked the face of each of the directors as they applauded. Plenty of meetings had been terrible through his career and experience told him to enjoy the praise whilst it lasted.

'Oh, one more thing,' said Martin Zhao, looking at his colleagues.

'Can you please provide us with details of how we take funds out of the account? We have identified some property assets here in London – quite a few are coming up for purchase you know, so we would like to be able to get money quickly if necessary.'

'No problem, I will get Joanna to email them over to you later today,' said Sam.

'Thank you. You are joining us for lunch?' Martin Zhao said rhetorically.

'Fantastic,' said Sam, standing up and smiling at Joanna. She had a face like thunder. Sam thought it was because, despite her protestations, he still treated her like a secretary and not an assistant fund manager.

'Well done today, Jo. Excellent. All go OK do you think?' Sam said as the taxi pulled away after lunch.

'I'm not comfortable Sam. They have only just signed up with us and they talk about taking money away. We get taught to be suspicious of these things you know. People do try and launder money you know.'

'But they run a property company. Surely it is reasonable for them to have their own money back when they identify something to buy?' Sam said with a noticeably defensive tone. He was relieved Joanna had not picked up on his reliance on her administrative skills at the end of the meeting.

'Zhao saw your long face as well Jo. I hope he doesn't think badly of us. Surely asking for some of his money back from time to time is not unreasonable?'

'I'm sorry Sam but something is not right there. It's all too good to be true.'

'Stop worrying and think of this year's bonus for goodness sake. These guys are handing us our annual target on a plate. Why would you worry about anything? Compliance has done the checks and anyway this one came in from one of Peter's contacts in Whitehall. We are covered and just doing our jobs,' Sam said more forcefully.

As they headed back Sam watched the busy London streets on the hot summer's afternoon.

'Ugly race the British,' he said watching sun-burned skin flop around the streets.

'Oh, and if you treat me like your secretary in front of clients again, I will kick you in the bollocks.'

The rest of the cab journey was silent.

Sam got home at a reasonable time that evening and was able to spend a few hours with his wife and sons. He knew Lucy had always understood his job was going to keep him away from home for some of the time but it was the boys he felt guilty about. Charlie and George were still at preparatory day school in London and they missed their daddy.

It was just before seven when Sam had come through the front door so he missed the watery riot which was bath time. All he heard was screaming and shouting from the bedroom the boys shared. He ran up the stairs two at a time and almost went straight back down headfirst as he tripped on a discarded towel. He headed for the noise and found Lucy changing the boys into their pyjamas.

'You're back nice and early,' said Lucy with a degree of edge suggesting it was the first time in quite a while.

'Hello My People,' Sam said opening his arms and letting the boys run to him. George, younger of the two at just five, tripped on his half pulled up pyjama bottoms and fell to the floor with a thump. Sam scooped him up and he hugged both of them with each arm.

'Bundle!' shouted Sam and rolled on his back. The boys took this as their queue and started jumping on his chest laughing and returning the chant.

'Come on, stop that will you,' Lucy said interrupting the fun. 'Not just before bedtime please. They won't sleep if you rev them up too much. Perhaps you could read them a bedtime story instead?'

'Yeah!' said the boys in unison.

'Sure, no problem. Let me get changed and I will be right there.'

Sam loved reading to the boys when he got the chance. He could use his imagination; take them off to faraway places that didn't exist. So much better than the real world he thought as he hung his suit up and put on some shorts.

After a little light television whilst Charlie played with a toy robot and George had a glass of milk, Lucy announced it was bedtime. The boys, both keen to get the best spot on Daddy's lap, raced upstairs whilst telling their mother they loved her.

Sam was already in the boy's bedroom sitting down by the radiator, his special place for bedtime stories. He had a book on his knee, taken from the many dozen in the bookshelf but all three of them knew he was not going to read from it. Daddy made his stories up. Sam wondered when the boys would realise that's what he did for a living.

'Can we have the story about the kittens and the spider?' Charlie said pulling at his father's shorts. 'I love that one.'

'Which is that one? I haven't heard of it before. Is it in a book?'

'No, we made it up,' added George, laughing and cueing his brother to stand.

> *Five little kittens, sitting in a web.*
> *Along came the spider and now they're dead.*
> *Five little kittens, sitting in a web.*
> *Along came the spider and now they're dead!*

George and Charlie paced around their father chanting the lines again. Sam sat in wonder with no idea what they were doing. He decided to intervene.

'Right, let's stop that and I will read one I know about.'

Sam pushed past his dancing boys and took an old favourite from the bookshelf. Soon the boys had settled down to listen to their father's odd sounds, vivid descriptions of pirates, dinosaurs and aliens. Sam loved to embellish each story he read.

After twenty minutes and a mild skirmish in the bathroom to brush teeth, Sam tucked his sleepy soldiers into bed. He turned off the light and pulled the door to leave a couple of light giving inches.

'Goodnight Charlie Farlie! Goodnight Georgie Porgie!' said Sam in his best fatherly voice.

'Goodnight, Mr Daddy,' said the boys in unison.

Sam smiled as he went down the stairs thinking he really should try and do that more often.

Over supper Sam told Lucy all about his new Chinese clients. They had not had a proper catch-up for a while and Lucy made the most of it. Occasionally Sam would get annoyed by her insightful questions which cut through the descriptions of problems at work like a hot knife through butter.

As they were eating, Lucy suddenly jumped.

'Oh, there was some post for you today darling.'

 She stood and went over to the fruit bowl by the cooker. From underneath it she pulled out a couple of letters.

'This also came for you,' she said. There was a wrapped box in the shape of something alcoholic.

'Who is that from?' said Sam undoing one of the envelopes. This particular letter had drawn his attention because of how formal it looked. It was too formal even for a bill. He tore the envelope open.

'Oh for fuck's sake!' he said with sharp disappointment.

'What is it?' said Lucy sitting back down, staring at her husband. The wrapped present suddenly took a backseat.

'It is a fucking jury summons, that's what it is,' said Sam with annoyance.

'When do these people think I am going to have time for this?'

'I've always rather wanted to do it actually. I think it would be very interesting, you know, doing your civic duty and all that,' Lucy said, trying to be pragmatic.

'That's because all you do is drive the boys to school and go shopping.'

Lucy didn't want an argument tonight.

'When do they want you to do it, and where? Anywhere good?'

Sam was reading the green letter with care.

'Seems they want me to do it in November at the Central Criminal Court. That's the Old Bailey isn't it?'

'Yes, just by St Paul's Cathedral. That would be a great place to do it surely – I think they do the juicy stuff there, you may even get a murder!'

'Sod that, I want something small so I can be in and out in a few days.'

'I think you get asked for two weeks don't you. One of the mums from school was telling me the other day. She got a trial which went on for a month.'

'Thanks. That's all I need. Hang on, it says here I can ask for it to be deferred. I wonder by how much?'

'Call them in the morning and ask. Now, open the package. A nice man dropped it round this afternoon. He played with the boys. There's a card taped to the side.'

Sam looked at Lucy and then took the card from the side of the wrapped box. He looked at Lucy again before opening it.

'Did you see who it was from?'

'Yes, of course. A car pulled up and a tall man in a suit got out. The driver stayed in the car. I saw him approach the house from the bedroom window, carrying the parcel.

'Where were the boys?'

'Charlie and George were back from school so came out from the sitting room to see what was going on.'

'Did you chat to him?'

'Yes, for a few minutes. He was nice. Seemed to know about you and Wolfenberg so I assumed he worked there.'

Sam opened the card.

Thank you for all your hard work.
Xanchu Qin.

'Who is that?' said Lucy.

'My new Chinese client. They are becoming very friendly. I have never met this guy Qin, just his lieutenant Martin Zhao.'

Sam unwrapped the box with increasing alarm. He did not want his family to be involved with any of his work affairs. It was not good for them.

Sam was shocked. It was a bottle of ten-year-old *Talisker* – his favourite whisky.

'But, but,' he looked at Lucy. 'How did they know this was my favourite?'

Lucy looked perplexed and just shrugged her shoulders.

'It's not like it's an unpopular whisky is it? Lucky guess?'

Sam knew these guys did not guess. Something made Sam very nervous.

Later that evening Sam fought the urge to have a dram from the new bottle. He decided on an early night with his wife.

Two hours later, as Lucy slept with blissful contentment, questions kept streaming through Sam's head making sleep impossible.

Chapter XI

The offices of Wolfenberg Bank, City of London

Sam sat at his desk watching his computer screens like a child would cling to a security blanket. It was late in the afternoon and nothing was going on. He was checking the prices of his own privately-owned shares. Some fund managers could legitimately claim they made money through this activity; others, about ninety-five per cent, would claim progress despite losing quite considerable sums over time.

The phone rang. Sam grabbed it immediately; it was his compliance officer, Aaron Snee. Snee was a forty something 'lifer' in the Compliance department. He was dull, boring, keen on chess, single and perfect for the job. He knew Sam well and they got on primarily because Aaron was the man responsible for signing off all of Sam's personal trades. Some of them were quite speculative and occurred at a frequency which had drawn the attention of senior management.

'Hi Aaron,' said Sam as he put the phone to his ear.

'Hi Sam, all well?' said Aaron out of Wolfenberg instilled politeness rather than any interest in Sam's well-being.

'Sure Aaron, how can I help?' said Sam looking at Will Fairfax opposite with a 'what does this loser want' look.

'Sam, I think we have a problem. Your Chinese client seems to be paying money into their account normally but we have noticed money is starting to go out as well. We've had a few requests for smaller sums to be sent back to the client's Chinese bank. Do you know anything about this?'

'I haven't seen any requests. When did they come in?' said Sam with a degree of indignation.

'We have asked your team to send requests to us if a new client pays money away. We got a couple in this morning.'

'What do you want me to do? I know they said they wanted to send more money and they did that last week. They also said they were looking at several properties. Perhaps they want to buy something?'

'Could you call the client and ask what it is for?'

'Sure, I will let you know what they are doing. Are you concerned Aaron?'

'No just doing my job Sam,' said Aaron as he put down the phone.

He put the phone down gently and turned to Joanna next to him. She was looking back having heard the discussion.

'I sent the payments to Aaron this morning; just following procedure.'

'I know, I know. Thank you. I'll call Martin Zhao now.'

Sam was worried. What had he got involved with? This client was starting to dominate his life; he was concerned about what they were up to and hated his family had been involved. Sam pulled up his contacts and tapped Martin Zhao's mobile number into his phone. Martin answered on the second ring.

'Hello?'

'Martin, it's Sam, Sam Waghorne.'

'Hi there Sam, what's up? Markets look good today, are you making us plenty of money?'

'Sure Martin, but there is something we need to talk about as well.'

'Ok Sam, what is it?' said Martin with a bit more seriousness.

'It's your payments. Compliance here have picked up that money has been coming in and out of the account. The people down in Compliance go crazy when there is something interesting for them to do.' said Sam, trying to inject a bit of humour to numb the pain.

'What do you mean?' said Martin after a pause. 'I told you we would be looking at some properties. We have identified two we want to purchase.'

'They need to see proof, Martin. These guys need to know you guys are telling the truth.'

'What! Sam, are you being serious?' said Martin, his voice rising in tone and volume.

'I'm sorry, we need to prove to the Regulator you are not laundering the money!' said Sam, immediately regretting his jocularity.

'This is crazy, we chose you guys because we thought this kind of thing could not happen. This is outrageous; surely what we do with our own money is no business of anybody's but ours!'

'Just send in details of the properties and we will be able to make the payments.'

'Sam, I need to talk to Mr Qin and the Board about this. Let me tell you, I am not happy!'

With that Martin Zhao cut off.

Sam replaced the phone and sat back in his chair, blowing his cheeks out. He looked over to Joanna but she had gone. Will Fairfax did not make eye contact with Sam as he stood and walked from his chair. Sam knew he had told Martin too much about why a bank would be nervous of client money flows but this client was too important to him and, frankly, too important for the bank.

Sam sent a quick email to Joanna asking her to tell Aaron and his team that Zhao would be sending in details of the properties they had been looking to buy. Sam knew this was unlikely before he had a chance to speak with Martin again. He needed to make the call outside the office, from a non-recorded line. The email would buy him some time and by now he needed a drink – he would surely find an assembled quorum in Jim's, there always was.

Three hours later, after a good session in Jim's, Sam walked from the tube at South Kensington. It would be a nice surprise for Lucy and the boys; Daddy home early again. Sam had consumed quite a number of glasses of wine but nothing a bit of fresh air and a mint or two could not cover up.

It was a warm afternoon and Sam had his suit jacket over one shoulder as he walked. His mobile phone rang. He scrabbled around in the jacket and pulled the phone out.

'Hello?' Sam said with a degree of trepidation. Would it be Peter asking Sam to stop drinking so much and do a bit more work in the afternoons?

'Mr Waghorne?'

'Yes.'

It wasn't Peter.

'Good afternoon, Mr Waghorne. This is Xanchu Qin speaking from the Qin Property Group.'

Sam froze.

'Um, yes, err, yes hello Mr Qin. How nice to hear from y...'

'I thought this an appropriate time for me to give you a call,' interrupted Qin with a smooth deep voice.

'How can I help?'

'Well, Sam, can I call you Sam?' Qin did not stop to let Sam answer.' I hear we have had some people from your noble institution questioning our integrity? I really just wanted to remind you that this is a very serious and important venture from our side and I would hate anything to get in the way of our success.'

Sam felt like he needed to sit down, his heart increasing its beat all the time.

'Well, what um, what did you want me to do?' said Sam with nervousness running through his voice.

'We just need to make sure you know how important this is to us. We are looking for many, many properties in your capital and we need Wolfenberg to be there to support us.'

'I'm not sure what Mr Zhao has told you Mr Qin but please, our compliance checks are just routine.'

'Just make sure things go smoothly Sam, that's all I ask,' said Qin with a quieter voice but one which contained much more malice.

'But there is no...'

'Juust .....bbe ccccertain. Certain. For Lucy and the boys, please bbe certain. You must nnot betray us.' spat Qin this time with a pronounced stutter. Sam instinctively withdrew the mobile from his ear, from the volume. Qin was furious.

'Mr Qin. I will make sure...'

The line went dead. Sam, who had not moved during the conversation, looked up and found the nearest wall to lean against. He put his head into his hands. What on earth was going on? What the hell had he got himself involved with?

Next morning Sam was in the office early for two reasons – because he had been unable to sleep and to try and get his head around Qin. He had to make Qin realise Wolfenberg had been the right choice. He had meant to call Martin Zhao the night before but the call from Qin had rather dispensed with the need.

As Sam sat down, with his first and most necessary cup of black coffee, his phone rang. It was Peter Heathcliff from his office.

'Morning Waggers, have you got a couple of minutes?' said Peter with jovial charm.

'Sure, I'll be...'

Sam stopped as he realised Peter had already put the phone down. Rude bastard he thought as he picked up his coffee and walked the forty odd paces to Peter Heathcliff's corner office.

'Morning Sam, come in!' said Peter as he saw Sam coming towards him. 'Please shut the door.'

Sam realised this constituted more than just a pep talk; the door request was only issued if Peter had a problem.

'I won't beat around the bush, Sam,' said Peter when the glass door had closed against its magnets. 'Compliance tells me your Chinese clients are playing silly buggers. Money going in and out of the portfolio just like a Hokey Cokey. What the fuck is going on? I thought they were respectable clients Sam?'

Sam stood there looking at Peter in his big leather chair behind his desk of solid oak. Peter was a great fan of Sam; he had been one of Peter's better hires. But Sam could see all was not well. Suddenly Peter looked distant and unfriendly, his double chin looked ugly and not fatherly, his tanned hands sinister not guiding.

'All I know is Aaron and his freak colleagues are crapping themselves that this lot are money launderers. I have explained

Qin wants to buy and sell property in the UK so there will be payments in and out but he is insistent they tell us precisely what they want to buy. I spoke to Zhao and he broadly told me to fuck off and that he had not assumed a bank like Wolfenberg would not and could not trust its clients.'

Eventually Peter spoke.

'You do realise how important this account is to the bank don't you?'

'I get the idea Peter, Government links etc. Yes.'

'So you must smooth it all over. I had Zhao on the phone to me yesterday evening and he was pissed Sam, really pissed.'

'Ok, Peter. I will try my best.'

Sam stood to leave but remembered one thing.

'Sorry, Peter do you have another minute or so.'

'Yes of course' said Peter purposefully looking at his watch with frustration. 'What is it?'

'I had a court summons.'

'What the fuck? Why, what have you been up to?' said Peter dropping his pen.

'No, sorry,' said Sam laughing. 'I have been sent a jury summons to appear at the Central Criminal Court in November. I want you to write them a letter to delay it,' Sam said, explaining the situation.

'Christ, not you as well! You are the fourth person in the company this year. Sure, we can't have you buggering off for two weeks in November, it is one of the busiest times of the year. Can you defer it?' Peter said with anger.

'Yes, I can request a delay for up to six months but that still means I will have to go before April next year,' Sam said.

'Ok, that's fine. You will probably enjoy it. All those crooks and men in wigs,' Peter said with a hearty chuckle.

'Oh, Sam,' Peter said as Sam opened the door.

'Make sure this Chinese issue is sorted.' Peter had his right index finger pointing at Sam.

Sam's head was full of conflicting issues. They knew about his two children and his wife's favourite flowers. Why didn't people trust each other anymore? They were legitimate, of course they were. It was time to get Martin Zhao back onside, Sam did not want another call from Xanchu Qin.

Chapter XII

The Running Leopard Bar, West Hampstead, London.

Maria had been working for a few weeks in her new position at the 'Leopard' as it was called by workers and patrons alike. She had thoroughly enjoyed it since she started and she thought she had won favour with Kumara Darsha, the flamboyant but modestly shifty proprietor of the bustling bar and restaurant.

As the last remaining customers paid their bills and contently floated to the door, Maria settled into a seat by the bar and asked the barman for a glass of wine. Staff were allowed to have a drink when things had been tidied up and the place was almost empty.

'I love this place you know; you have all made me feel so at home,' Maria said, as the friendly barman poured her a well-deserved glass.

'You're welcome – you have been a tremendous help. Where is real home?'

'Oh, I was born in Ukraine but I lived with my father in Belarus, in a little village west of Minsk.'

'So, what brings you to London?'

'I had to get away from something. I miss the bar I used to work in, it was a bit like this but there are things back home that made me miserable.'

'Like what if you don't mind me asking?'

'My father mainly. He is such a proud man and when he was hurt at his job and couldn't work again, he got so frustrated that he often took it out on me.'

'Does he hurt your mother?'

'She died when I was born and my father blames me for it.'

'Christ! You are such a sweet girl and your father sounds like a prick,' the barman said in summary as he spotted Kumara Darsha approaching the bar. He winked at Maria and turned away as Kumara sat down.

'Mind if I join you?' he said, turning to Maria. Kumara was looking dapper in his customary dark blue suit, no tie and a borderline effeminate silk handkerchief in his top pocket. This was his evening uniform and the guests loved the effort he made.

Before Maria had a chance to reply, Kumara said something very quickly to the barman and the latter instantly reached for a brown bottle on a high shelf. It was amongst the other colourful bottles and Maria watched intently as the barman poured a good quadruple measure into a glass. Kumara noticed her gaze.

'Sri Lankan rum, Maria. That's my bottle. Nobody else likes the taste!'

'I'm not surprised,' replied Maria. 'I can smell it from here. I'll stick to my wine if that's alright.'

The barman looked at Maria for a second too long as he said that he had to get home. He took his bar apron off, threw it on the bar and went into the kitchen to get his things. Maria looked around the bar and realised that all the staff had gone home or were in the kitchen having an inner-sanctum chat and post-service drink with the chef. She turned back to Kumara and caught his eyes leaving her breasts and then trying to find something to focus on. He shifted on his stool when he realised he had been caught staring.

'Cheers!' said Kumara lifting his glass of neat rum. Maria raised her glass and they chinked glasses.

'I am very glad I found you Maria, you have proved to be an excellent catch,' said Kumara after he had drained half his glass.

'I am very happy to work here, it reminds me of home.'

'Tell me more about you,' Kumara said as he stood away from the stool and went around the bar. He reached up on tiptoe for his own bottle of rum and poured himself another quadruple on top of the double he had not drunk.

'I was born in Ukraine but lived with my father in Belarus until recently. It was mostly cold and boring, and I wanted to see more of the world, so I came to London.'

'Why London?'

'Back at home they say it is the finest city in the world.'

'Do you agree?'

'Perhaps. It's too early to say I suppose but the people are not as friendly although the sense of history is incredible. It's everywhere you look. There is so much to see and learn about, I suppose that is the main difference.'

'Why were you unhappy at home?'

Maria lifted her glass in a suggestive manner and Kumara got the hint. If there were to be any personal disclosures, they would have to be marinated with more wine. Kumara filled her glass up to just below the rim. Maria looked at him in a quizzical way.

'Steady on Kumara, you will get me drunk,' said Maria as she carefully lifted the brim-full glass and took a long slug.

'My father is a proud man. I loved him with all my heart,' said Maria as she looked at the floor. She could not bring herself to look at Kumara as she spoke.

'He had a terrible accident at work which left him unable to walk and confined to a wheelchair, so he needed looking after. His body may have been broken but his pride was the biggest casualty, he was a hard-working man and not being able to work left him frustrated.'

'Did he take it out on you?'

'Sometimes. I went to university to continue my studies. He got used to me looking after him and when I was not around all the time, he got angry with me. I was stuck between him wanting me to do the best with my life and him getting cross when I was not around to cook him supper or to get him another bottle of vodka.'

'So you came to London?'

'Yes. Anyway that's enough about me. Tell me about this place. How long have you been a restaurant owner?'

Kumara looked at her for a few seconds and a smile gathered up on his face. He had keenness in his eyes as he stared at her. His face was as dark as ebony but those eyes sparkled with a mixture of fire and ice.

'I bought this place about ten years ago from an old Sri Lankan man who had had enough of cooking for customers. He started to lose money like any restaurateur who doesn't keep the place fresh and takes his eye off the ball.'

Maria had nearly finished her glass so Kumara carried on talking as he went around the bar again to recharge their glasses. Maria noticed this time he had to hold onto the bar to steady himself.

'Business is good because the Sri Lankan community really look after each other here. I have been lucky I suppose because some of the big hitters in the area have chosen my restaurant as a central meeting place.'

Maria found this very hard to believe. She did not think there was much left to luck in Kumara Darsha's life. He was far too smart for that. If something was successful it would be because he had organised it.

'Do you do anything else Kumara?'

'What do you mean?'

'Oh, any other businesses? You seem to go out of the restaurant a lot and all those men in suits who come in...'

'I have a couple of other business interests, all above board I assure you.'

Maria gave a false chuckle. What an odd thing to say. She was starting to feel a little lightheaded. She looked at her watch and saw it was ten minutes after midnight. Yamin would be back at home and he would be wondering where she was. She normally got home at about this time if she had been working on the late shift. She had a sudden desire to call him.

As she walked to the washroom she took out her mobile and called Yamin. The line rang and rang and finally went to voicemail. She pressed the red button before the tone to leave a message. How odd he was not answering. Perhaps he had gone to bed early.

When Maria returned she saw Kumara had refilled both their glasses. He must have had close to a third of his bottle. Kumara rose slightly as she sat. Maria liked her boss; he was a gentleman. She was surprised by how drunk he was; he must have been drinking during the day.

Maria noticed Kumara had started to lean on the bar top and his eyes had become watery and red.

'Where do you live, Kumara?'

It took a couple of seconds for Kumara to respond. He turned his head slowly and had trouble focussing on Maria.

'Where do you have to get back to?'

Kumara gave an inane grin, looking slightly over Maria's left shoulder. Maria was amazed how quickly he had gone from being able to laugh and joke to being unable to focus or communicate.

'Derring Park Rod' he said with slur.

'What?'

'My flat, one one two Derringha Pork Rud.'

Maria hesitated slightly.

'Do you want me to get you home? I am happy to help you.'

He smiled and put his hand on Maria's knee. She let him keep it there for a few seconds before gently picking up his hand and placing it back on the bar. Kumara leant forward and tried to kiss her. She withdrew from her stool as he came in, so he fell forward onto the floor. His arms did not prevent him smashing his head on the carpet. Maria gave a gasp and bent down to help him.

Maria, crouching next to him, asked him where the keys to the restaurant were. He pointed to an overcoat hanging on a hook by the bar. Rummaging around she found a large set of keys in his coat pocket, many more than the restaurant would need. Maria wondered what on earth all these keys were for.

Maria went into the kitchen. There had not been anybody here for at least twenty minutes. She located the backdoor key with some difficulty and locked it with the fifth key she tried.

By the time she came back into the restaurant Kumara had struggled to put his coat on and was slumped against the bar. He was making a desperate attempt to pull himself together. Maria thought it was a last effort to sleep with her – this had clearly been his intention but he had got too drunk.

'We can get a taxi outside,' Maria said as she held her arm up and gestured towards the front door of the restaurant.

Kumara lifted himself up from the bar and took a step towards the door. Maria had to catch him on the second step as he stumbled and fell. He was a slight man so Maria had no problem supporting him. Despite the efforts he was making to salvage the evening of romance he had planned, he was too seriously drunk. With one arm around Kumara's waist they walked towards the front door.

Maria managed to support him the other side of the door as she locked the restaurant and put the keys into her pocket. The first step of the exercise had been completed, now to find a taxi home. The restaurant was on a busy road so plenty of taxis came past even this late into the evening. Within minutes a welcoming yellow light came cruising along the road, so Maria hailed it and it drew up next to her.

'Where to love?' said the driver.

'Do you know Derring Park Road?'

'Derringham Park Road? Sure it's just around the corner; given what your boyfriend looks like you had better jump in. Make sure he is not sick on my seats.'

Maria opened the door and with some difficulty pushed Kumara through into the taxi. He fell onto the floor of the cab but with determined effort,managed to pull himself into the seat.

Maria settled back down on her side of the cab and felt the mobile phone in her pocket; it was far too late to call Yamin, so she sent an SMS saying she was on her way home. Once sent, she looked up to see the taxi driver staring at her through his mirror. He looked away when she noticed him.

The cab sped away from the address on Derringham Park Road. It was a smart street with well-kept, small houses on each side of the road. They seemed to be divided into maisonettes with upstairs or downstairs accommodation. Maria took the keys and managed to open the front door easily, in the cab she had established that it was the only Chubb key on the key ring. She flicked on the light switch just inside the door and a light came on upstairs. One one two was an upstairs flat and there were stairs going up to a long landing almost as soon as the front door was open. There was some post on the floor and Maria collected this as she followed Kumara up the steps. He was hanging onto the banister as he rose slowly. At the top of the stairs he pirouetted on his right foot and headed towards a poorly decorated sitting room with very little furniture. He flopped down onto the sofa in the corner. Maria went straight on down the landing and entered a kitchen. It was just large enough to accommodate a round wooden table with four cheap chairs. She put his keys down on the table and had a look around.

It was a small flat and not very clean. There were dirty dishes in the sink and a curious smell, probably from a takeaway curry consumed at lunch time. A single light bulb hung from the centre of the ceiling throwing a weak, milky light around the room. It didn't seem anybody spent much time in this flat, it didn't feel lived in - just like a place used for sleep. Totally the opposite of what she had imagined for the well-groomed dandy.

Maria span round in surprise when she heard Kumara come into the kitchen. He had obviously had a second wind because he seemed to walk without the help of the wall. His eyes were much brighter.

'Time for a small drink Maria?' He said with a half-smile on his face. His voice was clearer.

Maria was astonished. Five minutes before he had been almost unconscious in the back of a taxi, now he wanted a nightcap. He must be a regular drinker if he could recover like this. He rubbed his nose. This made Maria think he may have taken something to perk himself up.

'I don't know what's wrong with me; I am normally able to drink much more than this. I must be stressed or something. If you want a drink there is a bottle of whisky under the sink. Pour me one would you?' Kumara said as he sat down on one of the kitchen chairs.

There was a thumping knock at the door. It was so loud Maria jumped as she came back with two glasses of whisky.

'Who could that be?' Maria asked.

'Did you pay the taxi driver?' Kumara said, taking his drink.

'Of course.'

There was another bang on the door. This time much louder. Maria hurriedly put her glass down and ran down the stairs.

Maria opened the door and Yamin burst in pushing her out of the way. He mounted the stairs two at a time. Maria had been thrown to the floor by the force of the door. She picked herself up and shouted up the stairs.

'Yamin. What on earth is going on? Yamin!' screamed Maria up the stairs.

There was no response.

Maria ran back up the steps and into the kitchen to find Kumara on the floor and Yamin standing next to him. Kumara was doubled up, holding his rib cage with both hands.

'Yamin, what is going on? Yamin!' Maria screamed again but there was no answer. Yamin had fury in his eyes and Maria wasn't even sure he had heard.

Yamin slammed his right foot into Kumara and Maria heard a crack followed by an agonising groan. He dropped his knees down on Kumara's chest and this prompted another cry. Yamin then grabbed his neck and began squeezing. Maria could not just stand there and watch. She had no idea what was going on but instinctively ran to Yamin and grabbed his shoulder.

'Darling, what are you doing? Stop please I beg of you, stop!'

Yamin turned, his eyes red and furious. He stood and looked directly at Maria but she felt he was looking straight through her. Yamin pushed her away, quite harmlessly at first. The second time though he pushed her back with greater force and she stumbled. As she lay on the floor, Yamin picked Kumara up like a father lifting a child. He drew Kumara's face close to his, then with a quick flick of his wrist threw him across the room. His fall was broken by one of the kitchen chairs which disintegrated as he landed. Another horrific scream tore through the air after the sound of smashing wood.

Maria wanted to go to Yamin again to try and stop him. Something told her a third time might put her in danger, so she lay down watching Yamin continue to beat Kumara up.

'Stop! I'm only here to help him, nothing has happened!' Maria yelled as terror grew in her.

Yamin was like a wild animal; his eyes had a fixed stare as he turned to Maria. He came running at her and picked her up with one arm, carrying her out of the room with his momentum. Maria screamed as she was carried along. They got to the top of the stairs and Yamin let Maria go. She tumbled down the first few stairs trying desperately to grab onto something. Not managing to stop herself, she rolled over, banging her head on the wall on the way down and slid to the bottom of the stairs, coming to rest by the front door. Dazed she looked back up the stairs. Yamin had gone back into the kitchen. Maria tried to get up but the mixture of wine and the fall made it impossible. Her head flopped onto the soiled carpet amongst some stale shoes and soon her eyes were closed.

Maria woke with the smell of Yamin next to her. Her immediate reaction was one of contentment, she felt safe when he was lying next to her. She reached across and instinctively put her arm over his shoulder. Her slumber had yet to welcome the memories of the night before. The dawn kept Maria in blissful semi-consciousness.

The arm moving across his shoulder woke Yamin. He turned to Maria and she could feel his intentions as he came into contact with her stomach. He pulled her towards him and without talking buried his head into her shoulder. With a flood of anxiety, the events of the previous night came flooding back to her. She froze, not at all sure what to do or say. She was frightened.

'Let me go to the loo,' she said to buy some time against Yamin's obvious intentions.

Maria took longer than usual in the bathroom. For minutes she sat glued to the loo. Shaking feebly with cold sweat across her forehead and caught between confusion and the fear of getting hurt.

When Maria had plucked up the strength, she walked to the bedroom with purpose. Stopping in her tracks, she let out a muffled sigh of relief when she realised Yamin had gone back to sleep.

Never had she slipped back under the sheets so cautiously.

With light streaming in through a gap in the curtain, Maria was eventually stirred by a noise from outside. She reached over with her arm and was alarmed when all she could feel was cold sheet. She turned over and saw the bed empty beside her.

'Yamin,' said Maria, thinking he could be in the bathroom. No answer.

Maria got out of bed and went to the kitchen. He would be there getting a glass of water. She could hear a noise as she approached.

'What are you doing?' Maria said as she came into the kitchen. The radio was on but there was no sign of Yamin. Maria grew nervous as more of last night's memory crept back into her mind. She went to every room looking and calling out his name.

Maria resigned herself to thinking he must have gone out to buy something for breakfast. She looked at her watch. Eleven thirty. She had a second flood from the previous night's activities. She fell onto the bed and looked around the room. Then it hit her. Yamin's things were gone – his clock that sat next to his side of the bed and his shoes that normally rested neatly by the wardrobe. Maria jumped up in an immediate panic and opened the wardrobe. All his clothes had gone. Everything. His bag, which should have been on top of the wardrobe, was not there either. Maria started throwing things around trying to find any evidence of Yamin's presence. What was going on? Where was he?

Maria couldn't find her own mobile no matter where she looked. She collapsed onto the sofa not knowing what was going on. The full memory of the night before engulfed her senses.

'Where are you Yamin darling? Where are you?' A panic spread through her like she had never known as thoughts of Yamin's text came racing back to her.

ALL, 2D PRACTICE
11 2D PR

112 Derringham Park Road

Chapter XIII

The offices of Wolfenberg Bank, City of London

Sam gazed out of a dirty office window across to St Paul's Cathedral. The huge dome still dominated the skyline despite being almost three hundred years old. Just as impressive, next to the cathedral, was the golden statue of Justice standing proudly on top of the dome of the Old Bailey – sword in her right hand, scales in the other. She was the guardian of English Justice and Sam would be going there in a few months to see it all for real. Although he appeared to Peter and his colleagues to be dreading the jury service, he was actually looking forward to it. Just something different for him to think about, far away from the pressures of trying to grow his client base, away from Martin Zhao.

Sam glanced down to see an opened letter on his desk; it was from Qin Properties. He leant further forward as he read; his mouth wide open. He couldn't quite believe what he was reading. It was a payment instruction from Martin Zhao to transfer ten million pounds to a bank account in Uzbekistan.

Sam read the letter again. He still could not believe it. Martin had made it quite clear they would want to transfer money for UK property purchases, so why would they want to send money to Uzbekistan? Where the fuck was Uzbekistan in the first place?

Sam would struggle to put the pin in the atlas in anything like the right place. He picked up the phone and called Martin's mobile.

Please leave a message after the tone...

Sam didn't know what to do. He was sure the signatures were correct, so there was no doubt Zhao wanted the money sent and therefore he would have to send it. Just then Sam's phone rang. Sam could see it was Aaron from Compliance.

'Hi Aaron. I have a feeling I know what you are calling about.

'Sam,' said Aaron cutting through any attempt at light-heartedness, 'I put that letter on your desk after Tony dropped it off with us.'

'Have you tried telephoning the client, because I am not happy paying into a bank account in Uzbekistan without any reason or prior knowledge?' Aaron said, again not letting Sam speak.

'I have just tried the client and there was no answer.'

'OK Sam but I do not feel happy about this. I am going to do some digging,' Aaron said and put the phone down without any goodbye.

Sam replaced the receiver slowly and turned to Joanna.

'Could you make the payment? I am going home.'

With that Sam switched off his computer, locked his desk and went home for the day. It was a quarter to three.

Chapter XIV

Kojdanava, Belarus

Dymtrus sat alone in front of the fire. The flickering flames threw shapes of orange-gold around the poorly lit room. It was dark outside but a pale blue light fell through the window from the moonglow reflecting off the winter snow.

Dymtrus was in his wheelchair with a blanket securely wrapped around his legs. Oleg had given him supper and would be back later to put him into bed. Dymtrus had a large glass of neat vodka in his hand. He sipped it slowly and listened to *Der Fliegende Hollander* playing on a cassette player in the corner of the room. The music flooded the house as Wagner's magnificent violins sang to him. He looked at the flames and thought about Maria.

It had been over five months since she had left and he had yearned for her every day. She was his only family and he missed her company, her laughter and her voice telling him about university. He had a long drink as the music came to a crescendo, sending a tingle down his once strong back. What a fool he had been to force her away.

Dymtrus turned to the window. He could just see the snow that had built up against the side of his lamp in the garden. It was probably ten below out there now. He noticed his breathing had increased and he could feel his heart in his chest beat faster. He looked back at the fire. Dancing flames licking over the oak logs, changed as they burned, consuming everything...

Dymtrus felt somebody roll his sleeve up and inject something into his arm. Then he was being lifted from the frosted ground. He could not feel his legs but he could definitely feel his back and rib cage which both hurt beyond description. He was placed on a stretcher and he gained some relief. He was so cold he had stopped shivering. He tried to turn his head to see who was helping him but there was no way he could lift it, too much agony. He started to relax and realised a wave of drug-induced calm was starting to pass through him. From agony to contentment, a blissful peace arrived.

He awoke in hospital. The pain in his back had returned and still he was unable to feel his legs. There were tubes and machines everywhere. He could smell the sanitary conditions and there was a faint but unmistakable aroma of hospital food. He saw a red button dangling down from the side of the bed. He moved his arm and pressed the button. A starchy nurse came bustling into the room after only twenty seconds.

'Is everything OK, Mr Kayakova?'

'Where am I?'

'You are in hospital in Kuznetsovsk. You had a terrible accident at the power station three days ago. You are very lucky to be alive.'

'What happened?'

'I have no idea my darling. All I know is two men were captured on a CCTV camera leaving the Complex. Don't worry about it now please; the police are looking into it. All I care about is what happened to your body and how we are going to make you better. Now you get some rest.'

With that the nurse took the alarm out of Dymtrus' hand and efficiently tucked in his sheet the way only nurses can. Dymtrus took his glass of water and settled his head back on the pillow. He started to wonder how on earth he had ended up in hospital.

'We have a message from some friends of your parents.'

'For God's sake, this is ridiculous! What have I done? You have got the wrong man. Please put me down!'

'Some of us still remember.'

'What? I don't know what you are talking about, come on put me down and let's talk about this.'

'SOME OF US STILL REMEMBER!'

Dymtrus jumped and spilt his vodka down his legs. He knew who these people were and why they had tried to kill him. The same reason his parents had been killed all those years ago in Kiev. The flames from the fire had died down and the room was dark. He was panicking. He didn't know what to do. He tried to take deep breaths. In out, in out. He felt his heart was going to beat out of his chest.

Dymtrus drained the remains of his vodka and immediately felt better. Wagner had moved on to the third act, *Senta* had just arrived when the telephone rang on the dresser next to the kitchen on the other side of the room. Every time the phone rang in his house Dymtrus thought it would be Maria and his spirits lifted. He put his empty glass down and wheeled himself to the phone. He steadied himself and got ready to talk to his darling daughter.

'Hello?' he said as he put the receiver to his ear.

Silence. International line he thought, it would take a second or two to be connected.

'Hello, Maria darling?' Dymtrus said again.

'SOME OF US STILL REMEMBER,' a low, cold voice said.

Dymtrus froze. There was no point thinking how these guys could have got his home telephone number, they could get their hands on anything they wanted.

'Let it go,' said Dymtrus with a fragile voice.

'NEXT TIME WE WILL KILL YOU.'

With that the phone went dead. Dymtrus carefully replaced the receiver and wheeled himself back to the fire. He felt warm again but only on the outside. Inside he was scrambled. He had let secret build upon secret and now the burden was killing him.

'Grandpapa!' Dymtrus shouted.

'What were you thinking?'

There was a sound outside. Dymtrus turned and heard someone approaching the front door. The muffle of boot on snow grew louder. There was a hand on the front door. The handle dropped and there was a creaking as the door opened. Dymtrus could not move. His eyes were fixed on the door as it moved. The music once again came to a mighty roaring crescendo.

Snow blew in through the open door and Oleg fell through the gap. He looked at Dymtrus with the countenance of a simpleton.

'Bed time Dymtrus,' He said with a chuckle.

Dymtrus managed a half smile as his shaking hand retrieved his glass and took it to his mouth in a reflex action, only to realise it was now, like all those times before, depressingly empty.

Chapter XV

The Barr Al Jissah Resort & Spa, Muscat, Sultanate of Oman

Sam sat reading on a sun lounger next to Lucy in the searing heat. It was the off season for Oman but it had still managed to creep up past thirty-five degrees. The unrelenting sun came up in the morning and stayed bright in the sky until about four in the afternoon. Most people had given up sunbathing by then anyway. Only the true sun-worshippers carried on whilst the fair skinned amateurs went off to dig the Aloe Vera out of the minibar.

Sam let his book drop down to his waist. It came to rest against a modest pool of sweat which had collected in his belly button. He looked across to his wife who was fast asleep with her face pointed towards the sun. If Sam was keen on the sun, Lucy was the President of the Suntan Club of Great Britain. She loved it. The D in Vitamin D for her stood for Devotion. Up early to catch some sun before breakfast – certain nationalities liked to place towels on loungers on the way to breakfast to ensure a good spot but that was just child's play compared to those who liked to worship the rising sun on the room's balcony, without sunscreen, whilst most people were still in bed.

Charlie and George were off at children's crèche. From nine in the morning to one in the afternoon they were looked after by the hotel staff. It meant Sam and Lucy could spend the mornings together and then the family could have a fun packed afternoon by the pool.

Sam took a sip from his beer that rested on the cool box by his lounger. Despite the cost, the only downside of any holiday at such a luxurious hotel was that he would get materially fatter from all the food and drink. Although he had vowed to do at least one bit of exercise every day, he could feel himself getting larger. To hell with it; he was on holiday.

'She is so thin!' said Lucy turning her magazine around to Sam. She had woken up and now had her nose back into celebrity gossip.

'It doesn't look like she has eaten for a month,' Sam replied, the irony of his last thoughts not going unnoticed.

'I am surprised her husband still fancies her, looking like that.'

'You'll be OK,' said Sam laughing.

'Sod off Sammy,' said Lucy with a smile and a laugh, 'Do you think I am fat?'

'Only joking. You look lovely.'

This was much more like it. This was the kind of banter they were used to and what had been missing in recent months; just spending some time together.

'Do you want lunch darling?' Lucy said.

'Perhaps later. I am off to have a snorkel. I'm getting far too hot.'

Sam bounced off his lounger and headed to the beach. This was the happiest he had been in a long time. He looked back at Lucy. She waved when she realised he was looking. He did fancy her and seeing her in that bikini still turned him on. He thought about an early night as he marched off with a spring in his step. It was amazing what a few days away from work could do for the soul.

Later in the afternoon the family were all playing in the hotel pool. Sam and Lucy were contented and fooled around with Charlie and George with carefree happiness. George had found a plastic football, so Sam marshalled an impromptu game of water polo between the Waghorne family and a random family also staying at the hotel. Sam took his turn defending the Waghorne goal, which consisted of the steps on the far side of the pool. He relaxed as the ball was with Charlie at the other end of the pool. Charlie was just about to score by throwing the ball into the opposition goal - the plants in an oasis at the other end. Sam looked up to see all the suites around the hotel pool. This was an amazing complex with five-star family accommodation. Each suite had its own balcony and all of these faced the pool. There must have been a hundred of them.

'Daddy!'

Sam looked back at the pool to see the ball flying straight towards his face. He fell forward and punched it as hard as he could in the general direction of his wife. He returned to look at the balconies. There were a few people sitting on them having a quiet afternoon or spending a few minutes out of the sun. His eyes continued to scan and then suddenly he stopped. On a balcony at the end of the building right at the top stood a man looking down at the pool and at Sam in particular. He was dressed in black trousers with a black polo shirt. He looked completely out of place in the heat surrounding him.

Sam squinted and held his hand to his eyes. There was something familiar about this man. His dark hair and his pale skin.

'Oh my God!' said Sam as the penny dropped. This guy was one of Martin Zhao's colleagues from Qin. He had met him when he and Joanna went to see Qin Properties in Portman Place. No doubt about it. Sam's mind started to race. What was he doing here?

'Come on Dad!' said George as the ball whistled past Sam's ear and flew into the goal. The opposition family gave a whoop of delight as Sam retrieved the ball from under an unamused old lady's lounger.

'Sorry,' said Sam getting back into the pool.

Once he had disposed of the ball, Sam looked up at the apartment with the man from Qin. The balcony was empty and the curtains of the suite had been pulled.

Part II

St Sepulchre's Bell

You prisoners that are within, who for wickedness and sin, after many mercies shown you, are now appointed to die tomorrow in the forenoon, give ear and understand that in the morning the greatest bell of St Sepulchre's shall toll for you in form and manner of a passing bell...

Chapter XVI

The Central Criminal Court, Old Bailey, London

Up on the fifth floor of the Old Bailey, the twenty new jurors were issued with instructions from the usher and were led through a security-coded door into the jury waiting area. Sam had been expecting what he had seen of the notorious courthouse so far but the illusion that jury service was an exclusive club for a couple of dozen people was shattered as he came into the room. It was like the business class lounge at Heathrow Airport. There must have been two hundred people sitting in the room, on a variety of tatty 1980's cloth-upholstered chairs. Looking around, there were so many people that all the seats had been taken. In the corner of the room was an empty restaurant with plastic chairs around a number of tables. The food, even from twenty yards, looked greasy, soggy and disgusting.

Sam felt like a new boy at school as he walked towards the jury service manager's office. It had a sliding glass window and a table full of different coloured forms. There was another queue to get your lunch money vouchers and to get your name on the system. Sam had another look around, this time at the people sitting in the room. Most were watching morning television on the three large screens placed around the waiting area. Sam saw the faces of the people watching a show about who might well be an ugly baby's father. He chuckled to himself as he then scanned the gormless faces of those being mildly titillated by observing other people's misfortune; he would hate to be the defendant who had to be overseen by this lot.

'Jury for court number eight to your court waiting area please, that's jury for court number eight to the court waiting area,' announced the man through a microphone in the office.

Sam queued and took his lunch card with the standard three pounds fifty per day electronically added and announced to the Old Bailey Jury Manager that he was available for service. The manager gave him an 'I'm busy' look, so Sam turned, spotted a spare chair in the corner and went for it. The room had cleared significantly as serving jurors from on-going trials were called into court.

'Jury for court number five to your court waiting area please, that's jury for court number five to the court waiting area.'

Sam had come prepared. He had a couple of books and a fresh copy of the *Telegraph*. Although everybody wanted to get out of the traps quickly, Sam had read that the truth of it was, there could be a significant wait until you are called into action.

A woman in a black gown walked into the room. This was it. The first new trial of the day needed a jury. She walked around the perimeter of the room with a slow purposeful gait. All the new jurors watched her as she went. She knocked on the Jury Manager's door and went inside. The jurors watching collectively felt a disappointment when she vanished into the office and the sound from the television was, once again, the only distraction.

Two minutes later she came out of the office holding a microphone. The televisions were switched off and the expectant crowd fell silent again. The waiting area had turned into a theatre. The orchestra had stopped and the first act was about to start.

'When I call out your name could you please answer with a clear 'Yes',' said the usher in black with a thick London accent.

'Stephen Scott?'

Yes.

'Miranda Westwood?'

A pause then a hearty 'Yes!'

'Rashidi Yobo?'

This time a quiet yes came from one corner of the room which was hardly audible.

'Sorry was that a yes?' said the usher with a strict voice. She looked like a lady not to be crossed.

'Yes.'

'Good. Thank you'

'Sunil Bhutia?' the usher went on.

This carried on until she had read out twenty names. Sam knew twelve were selected for any one jury so why did they start with twenty people? Then he put two and two together. Some trials take more than the allotted two weeks that each juror was expected to stay. If there were multiple defendants surely some trials could last for months. More than twelve were chosen to make sure they all could sustain a long trial; Sam realised he could tell how long a trial was likely to be by counting the number of people they chose. A sudden chill ran through Sam. What if he was chosen for a really long trial? What would he say to get out of a three monther?

'Could those people I have called out please follow me,' said the usher who put the microphone down on the table by the Jury Manager's office and went sweeping back from whence she came. Various people from around the room stood, collected up coats and bags and followed her.

During the morning, several ushers repeated the exercise of calling out a series of names for trials starting that morning. Sam was not chosen for any of them and just sat in his chair with his paper. After a couple of hours wait, he decided it was time for a coffee and went into the brightly lit, highly disinfected kitchen area. There was a drinks machine in the far corner, so Sam walked past the service area where a few tired looking sandwiches had been laid out in the hope of attracting the attention of a starving man or anybody else insane enough to buy one. Egg and onion was one of the combinations.

Sam pressed the button for a black coffee and a grey brown liquid reluctantly slopped into a skinny polystyrene cup. He picked it up and was relieved to find it possessed one characteristic of coffee – it was scalding hot. He carefully took it to the woman sitting in a semi-redundant position at the till.

'Two fifty,' she said with a total lack of interest in human interaction.

'Shit! I could get a Starbuck's for the same price,' Sam replied with a mocking smile.

'Well go on then. I don't care.'

'Your heart's not in this job is it?'

'What's that dear?'

'Never mind,' said Sam deciding to drop the subtle irony for fear she would take it the wrong way. He had to get back to his crossword.

Sam sat in reflective silence for the rest of the morning, watching jury servants come and go as their trials ebbed and flowed. He picked up his joining instructions and reread them for a third time.

Jury members must not discuss their trial with other jury members or anybody else at any time.

Sam chuckled as he saw a huddle of fellow jurors sitting together in the canteen of the jury waiting area. It seemed obvious their trial was all they wanted to talk about. The furtive looks and hands to the mouth gave the game away. Coming from the fund management industry, he was well used to recognising the signs of clandestine conversations and bubbling gossip. The strange thing was, this open and deliberate breach seemed to be ignored by the Jury Service Manager. The rules were one thing, human nature quite another.

Sam looked up at the television which was still spewing the same mid-morning dross.

'This is absolute rubbish isn't it?' said a voice sitting opposite Sam.

A small middle-aged woman with glasses smiled back at him as he looked up. She had put her book on her lap, clearly disturbed by the sound of the television.

'It's dreadful isn't it? I'm not sure what is worse, knowing people actually watch this or the people on the program actually exist,' Sam said with a chuckle.

'Quite,' said the women with a subtle French accent. She looked at Sam with a warm and welcoming face. 'I am trying to read but I keep on getting interrupted by people I do not wish to know about,' she added bluntly.

Sam looked down at her book. It was old and very tatty in a plain red cover.

'What are you reading?' Sam said without really thinking.

'Oh,' said the woman looking slightly embarrassed,' it is an old novel I have been asked to adapt for the stage.'

'Goodness me, that sounds interesting. Is that your job?'

'Well sort of, I lecture in Creative Writing and specialise in scriptwriting.'

'You're a playwright? Fantastic. So, what are you doing at the moment?'

'We are taking this book and turning it into a stage production,' she said lifting the old novel in the air. 'I am going through the first edition to see whether I have missed any of the author's original thoughts, you know, picking up on the emotion of the man.'

Sam's interest went to another level. He had often wondered what it would have been like to do some creative writing of his own; it would be so much more interesting than his job at Wolfenberg.

'Sorry, I am being very rude. I'm Sam, Sam Waghorne,' Sam stretched out his hand towards his new friend. She took it heartily.

'I'm Martha Quinault,' she said with beaming smile and letting her French accent roll all over and through her surname.

'Have you been picked yet?' said Sam

'No not yet. I am a very unlucky person so I suspect I will be the last to get chosen. I reconcile this with the hope I will get a good old murder when I do get selected. I can use the material for my next play.'

'I'm not sure I can take much more of this television. Are we allowed out yet?'

'I think the Jury Service Manager needs to release us for lunch but we could get called at any time.'

'I'll go and ask.'

Sam stood and went over to the office in the corner of the room; the nerve centre of the jury service at the Old Bailey. He tapped on the little sliding glass window and heads from all inside the office turned to look. Each face had a degree of indignation and Sam felt embarrassed having disturbed them. Name tag sitting proudly on his lapel, Tony the manager came to the door and opened it.

'Can I help you sir?' he said with forced cheerfulness.

'Yes,' said Sam.' I was wondering whether we are allowed out for lunch yet. I have not been called to a trial and I am not sure I am brave enough to try the food here.' Sam smiled, immediately realising he had been too rude. He noticed the faces in the office turn as he finished his sentence.

'I will be able to release you when we get the word no more trials will be started until after lunch. We are really in the hands of the judges you know. I'm sure it won't be too long now.'

Sam looked at the name tag on his lapel.

'Tony, could you let me know when I am likely to be asked to be on a jury? It is getting terribly boring just sitting around trying to read my newspaper whilst being subjected to pond-life television on full volume,' Sam said in a light-hearted way.

'I'm sorry sir,' said Tony with a chuckle. 'We choose our juries at random so you never know when you may get selected. I do know there are a couple of cases starting this afternoon, so I'll keep my fingers crossed for you sir. I know there are some naughty boys up for trial so you may get a really juicy one,' said Tony over emphasising 'juicy' and lightly touching Sam's arm. With a slight kick of his left leg Tony turned back into the sanctuary of the Jury Manager's office. The door closed with modest bang; no more silly questions please.

Sam headed back to Martha. He plonked himself down and sighed.

'He told me to wait.'

'Oh, for fuck's sake!' said Martha

Sam turned and stared at his new friend. Where did that come from? He was finding her more and more intriguing.

Thirty minutes later the remaining potential jury members were put out of their misery and told they would not be required until ten minutes past two. Sam and Martha agreed to have lunch in a sandwich shop around the corner and had hurried out of the Old Bailey to maximise the time they had.

When they had found a suitable place, Sam kicked off the conversation with a mouth full of sandwich.

'So, tell me about being a writer. How did you get into it? I have always thought about doing it but never...'

'I wouldn't recommend it,' Martha said, cutting Sam off and allowing him to finish his mouthful. He was like a child sometimes, asking too many questions in quick succession.

'You have to be totally committed from day one if you are going to make any sort of career out of it. It is so competitive as the number of scripts or drafts chosen to be published is so small. You will find most things have been thought about and written down before. A new idea is incredibly rare,' said Martha with a flat tone.

Sam was surprised. He had expected Martha to be upbeat, to be excited about his interest.

'The thing people forget about writing is it is a job first and enjoyment second. If you are serious about writing anything you have to commit to it.'

'How did you get into it then; it sounds like you have learned the hard way if you have become bitter about it.'

'You could say that. I have been doing it for about thirty years, since I left university and I am cynical because I have only just started making any money. I am sorry, I don't mean to be negative, but I meet so many budding writers who are not willing to commit enough effort and think their work will have a magic touch. Life is just not like that – any success is the product of a great deal of hard work.'

Sam sat and thought for a while. He found Martha fascinating. She was intelligent and thoughtful but at the same time her attitude was off-putting.

'It can be the most rewarding pastime in the world if you find a subject you are passionate about so the idea starts to fly. Like nothing else, it starts to develop a life of its own and you are only helping it get down onto paper; the ideas just keep on flowing.'

'Do any of your students ever get published?'

'Sure, quite a few but very often it is the ones who do not want or expect it. They are the ones I like the most. Humility is a wonderful quality in a writer – the best ones never forget where they have come from.'

Sam let this sink in. He always had an ambition to write something, he had never known quite what. Martha was putting him off.

'If you write anything, I would be happy to read it of course. I am sorry I am such a negative old bag.'

'Thanks but I was called to be a banker. I have no writing talent and certainly no good ideas.'

Martha gave Sam a look that reminded him of elements of his

mother and his school matron. He knew the conversation was over. He was not knowledgeable enough to engage Martha in a conversation about her work and she had become bored. A change of direction seemed appropriate.

'So tell me, what kind of trial do you think you'll get? A murder? I am looking for attempted murder. So much more interesting,' Sam said going back to default Jury Service member conversation.

'Why is attempted better than actual? No great trials have been concerned with attempted murder.'

'Because the victim is in court and they can tell you what happened. Murder is assessed on the past – attempted murder can be studied in the present,' Sam said looking at his watch. He jumped as he realised it was time to get back – five to two and the judges would be finishing their glasses of port and walking back to court.

'Come on, we need to get back; Dr Crippen awaits…' Sam said clearing up his lunch wrappers.

'Yup, let's go.' Martha stood and marched to the door.

Sam had to run a couple of steps to catch up with her. Martha turned to Sam as they hurried back.

'You know Sam, it is easy to see you work in finance. Every now and again there is a beautiful diamond to be found amongst the general crap you speak…'

Sam resigned himself to another few hours of afternoon television studded with the occasional daydream. It was his first day and the lack of activity had already become unbearable. To be offered an opportunity to sit on a jury and then make you wait so close to the courts was exasperating. Back to the crossword he thought as he saw Martha come back from the loo and sit in a different area of the room.

Sam must have drifted off because he wasn't sure if he was dreaming when a crow-like woman entered the waiting area. Just like before she glided up to the Jury Manager's office and prepared herself by pinning a ruffling radio microphone to her lapel. Sam sat up and grew excited as the television muted and the room, once again, fell into theatrical silence.

'I am going to call out some names now; will you please answer 'yes' when you hear your name,' said the court usher as the microphone crackled against her gown.

'Nicholas Mumbly?'

A resounding 'Yes!' rang through the room. It was heavily pregnant with the emotion of finally being chosen. Sam would make his louder.

'Sandra Goldstein?'

A soft, nasally 'Yes'.

'Martha Quin err Quin halt?'

'Martha Quinault, yes.'

This made Sam burst out laughing as Martha unsympathetically corrected the usher before replying. Sam was pleased she had been chosen.

'Varinder Singh?'

'Yes'

'Bernie Grantham?'

There was silence as people started looking around for Bernie. The usher waited for a few seconds before trying again, this time much louder.

'BERNIE GRANTHAM?'

'Oh, sorry. Yes miss, sorry.' Clearly Bernie had been asleep. A communal tut swept around the waiting area.

'Sam Waghorne?'

Sam was so shocked he lifted out of his chair as he shouted 'Yes!' A couple of people turned to him with looks suggesting there was something wrong with him. The usher gave him a haughty glance and then carried on calling out names.

Sam was so excited. He tried to catch Martha's eye but she didn't see him as the usher reeled off a list of twenty-five people.

'If those people I have called out could follow me to the lifts I will give more instructions there.'

Sam picked up his newspaper and tucked it into his coat pocket – this was it; the time had arrived. He stood and made his way to the lifts via the loo.

Sam and the other twenty-four candidates stood listening to the usher explain what happened next. She explained that twenty-five people had been chosen because it was likely to be a four month trial. There was a collective intake of breath from the group as calculations and plots started, some would love to spend four months helping - others had work, holiday or family commitments and started to think of excuses. Sam was confused. Part of him wanted to see the system and get involved; the other part told him four months was far too long to be away from work. His mind raced back to the Qin clients. What would they all think if Sam took this sort of time off? He would have to think of a good excuse quickly.

'Right if you could all follow me please,' said the usher, floating off down the circular stairs with her gown billowing like Dracula's school mistress.

Sam caught Martha's eye. She seemed totally unhappy about the length of trial, perhaps four months away from her work would scupper her new show. Sam smiled back, happy to have met her. She would think of something, of course she would.

Sam was the last person into court. Number eight was one of the modern courts located within the new part of the building. Sam had it in his mind's eye there would be plenty of polished oak and green leather straight from a period courtroom drama but what met his eye had very much a new world feel, yes green leather but modern wood and plastic positioned for purpose with no elegance.

Sam was struck by just how many people were present in the court. There were at least twenty barristers in their wigs and gowns, the judge on his bench clad in black, Sam had expected bright scarlet, and about another dozen people dotted about the court. Quite a circus thought Sam as he turned towards the dock. Then the penny dropped. Sitting there with a security guard chained to each were six young men; two white and four black. That's why the trial required so much legal support and could take at least four months.

They all looked so young. One of them caught Sam's eye so Sam quickly averted his gaze. A huge wave of reality hit, taking Sam from the cosy institution of the Old Bailey straight out into the streets of East London, or wherever these frightening defendants came from. What Sam was looking at was real. Something really bad had happened. This wasn't a game; a silly financial challenge where the only threat was the loss of somebody else's money. This was a different kind of reality, the like of which Sam was neither used to nor prepared for. What had happened had and would change people's lives forever. Sam had not felt this kind of fear ever before.

'Ladies and gentlemen,' said the judge in a soft, authoritative voice.

Sam looked up and saw a man in his sixties wearing half-moon glasses peering down at the twenty-five candidates. He looked terrifying.

'This is a murder trial and as you can see there are six defendants; as I am sure you have been told, because of the complexities of this trial and the number of defendants, it is likely to take at least four months.'

Sam looked at the barristers and they all seemed to be pleased this was the case. Think of the fees. None of them were smiling but they were all quietly smug – Sam could tell, he had been getting away with charging outrageous fees for many years doing his job.

'For this reason, I will be asking each of you chosen for the jury in this trial whether you have any objections to serving for that length of time. I would like to remind all of you that doing jury service is a civic duty and therefore I will only accept representations which have genuine merit.'

Sam started to feel uneasy. He had not had time to concoct a reasonable excuse – what if he was chosen first? Christ, he better start thinking.

The clerk of the court stood. She was a plump, officious looking woman in black robes with a wig. She held up a piece of paper and cleared her throat.

'I will now call out some names. When you hear your name please proceed to the jury box if you have no objection to sitting on this trial. If you are certain you cannot commit and have a valid reason, please make your way up to My Lord's bench and he will speak to you directly.'

There was palpable tension amongst the twenty-five people waiting to be selected. Sam was desperately trying to think of a reasonable excuse not to have to sit and stare at the six terrifying defendants for four months. He was not sure the excuse of work commitments would be good enough given the judge's comments about civic duty. The judge might well laugh and tell him to go and sit down.

The usher read the first name and a well-dressed woman walked straight into the jury box. Great, thought Sam, one down eleven to go.

The next called walked in the same direction as the first but instead turned sharply right as he went past the bench. He wanted to talk to the judge. He climbed the three steps up to where the judge was sitting in the middle of the bench. The judge bent down like an owl to listen to the reason. The man stepped back from the bench after a minute chatting to the judge.

'Mr Peppiatt, I am releasing this man from the jury due to holiday commitments. He has paid for his flights and is happy to prove this to the court if necessary,' said the judge, addressing the prosecuting barrister. Mr Peppiatt was standing at the front of one side of the court where all the barristers sat. He gave a brief nod as the excused jury member shuffled off past the waiting jurors and out of the court.

Holiday commitments thought Sam, what on earth did that mean? Everybody had holiday commitments of some sort. He felt better about having legitimate work commitments.

Another two names were called and both walked straight into the jury box. Three down.

A young woman was next but she headed straight for the judge. They spent less than thirty seconds talking before she headed out of the court.

'Mr Peppiatt I am releasing this lady due to childcare issues.'

Very interesting thought Sam; he could mention his children as well. George needed to learn to ride his new bicycle and Sam had promised Lucy they would all go off and practice during half term.

Three more went straight into the jury box; that made six. Halfway and still seventeen names to choose from. Sam felt the odds were getting better.

'Martha Quinault,' said the clerk.

Sam's heart rate picked up. He saw Martha walk purposefully straight up to the bench. She had a good two-minute chat with the judge and Sam wondered if he was enjoying finding out about her interesting career. There was the odd shake of the head and some smiles as the judge listened in. Eventually Martha walked back from the bench with a fixed smile, rebuke or embarrassed pleasure wondered Sam. She arrived at the T-junction, left for freedom from four months with the six meatheads and right to enter the crucible. She turned left and as she walked past Sam she turned and looked him in the eye, giving a subtle wink. She had flirted with the judge and he had let her off.

'Mr Peppiatt, this young lady has pressing work commitments, so I have decided to release her,' said the judge with a great deal more feeling in his voice.

Mr Peppiatt nodded as Sam looked quizzically at the judge. Martha was in her mid-fifties and it was probably ten years since anybody had called her a young lady; these judges may look old and past it but their flirting seemed to be razor sharp.

Two more went straight past the judge and sat happily in the jury box so that made eight. The box was starting to fill up and Sam felt a tingle of relief, two thirds of the way there.

'Sam Waghorne.'

Sam went into autopilot and as he walked, he felt his legs a little lighter under him. Sam noticed his palms were sweating as he approached the T-junction. He turned right towards the judge, climbed the two stairs and approached the bench.

'Good afternoon Mr Waghorne, perhaps you would tell me why you are not able to serve on my jury?' said the judge looking at Sam with piercing eyes. The voice was friendly however the glare could have melted ice.

'Yes, good afternoon My Lord,' Sam thought some manners might score him some cheap early points. 'I am not at all sure I can commit to such a long trial. I have a client facing job and also a holiday booked with my family.' Sam continued feeling uneasy about the latter part of his excuse because he was technically lying in court.

'What is the nature of your work Mr Waghorne?'

'I am a fund manager at Wolfenberg Bank, I look after private clients.'

'Yes, yes. I am aware of the company. I am also aware of how big the group is. I am comfortable it will survive without you.'

'But I have hundreds of clients who speak to me all the...'

'Yes, I do understand Mr Waghorne but you also have a civic responsibility. Now then you mentioned a holiday. Have you paid for the trip?'

'Well I am not going away as such. I intend to spend a week at home. I need to teach my youngest son to ride his bicycle.'

The judge stared at Sam for a few seconds. Sam didn't know whether the judge was cross or perplexed with the honesty of Sam's answer.

'Well if you haven't booked it then I am confident it can be rearranged,' said the judge with a hint of frustration.

'I do understand the importance of my civic responsibility My Lord, but why should someone who has spent twenty pounds on a discount airline flight be permitted to leave your court when a man planning to spend time with his children is asked to stay. Why should a small financial sum be the swing factor?' Sam said realising he was pushing his luck.

'Mr Waghorne I suggest you go and sit in the jury box. I will be having final representations tomorrow so why don't you have a think about your situation and if you still feel strongly that you cannot serve then perhaps you could obtain a letter from Wolfenberg to confirm this?' said the judge with noticeable frustration.

'Thank you My Lord.'

Sam turned and proceeded toward the T-junction. He would be the only person so far to turn right instead of left. What a loser – his excuse was not good enough.

Sam looked around the court as the final few names were chosen. He really did not want to sit here for four months. The defendants scared the hell out of him. The thought of a situation like this would put anybody off crime – they should film this and show it on morning television instead of that pointless rubbish he had been subjected to earlier.

Some of the remaining candidates had an issue for the judge but it took only ten minutes more to have fifteen people sitting in the jury box. The judge cleared his throat.

'I will be releasing you soon as we will need to do some more work before the trial can start tomorrow. I have asked for fifteen of you to be chosen because I will be conducting final representations before we start. If any of you wish to speak with your employers, this is an ideal time to do so,' said the judge. Sam felt himself blush, everyone must have realised the judge was addressing him.

176

'I would like to make a start at ten tomorrow morning,' said the judge with finality.

With that the clerk of the court stood and indicated to the usher that the jury should leave. Sam and the other lucky winners all stood and filed out of court eight in silence. Some people looked pleased, however Sam could not hide his disappointment. He would get Peter to draft a fabulous letter which told half truths about how important Sam was. Sam would insist that the number of clients he looked after should at least double overnight. He would make it impossible for the judge to say no.

Out in the fresh air Sam felt his mobile phone vibrate in his trouser pocket. He looked at the screen and saw Martin Zhao's name. He had sent a text message.

Call me. It's urgent. Martin.

The next morning Sam walked to the tube station with a spring in his step. He had gone back to work after being released by the judge and had spent a good hour telling all who would listen about life inside the Old Bailey. He had been particularly pleased with the letter Peter had written in an attempt to get Sam out of a long trial. It was always nice to receive written evidence that someone appreciates you. Peter had embellished the truth and set the letter up in such a way as to make Sam sound pivotal to the bank's day-to-day functioning. It was a work of art.

Thoughts of Mr Qin and his colleagues entered Sam's head and popped his happy bubble. What if Sam couldn't get out of the trial? Zhao and the others would be furious with him. Given how close they had got to Lucy and the boys, what would they think of next to make Sam understand how important this relationship was to them? Then he realised he had forgotten about Zhao's message from yesterday. Sam felt a chill run through him, Martin would be furious.

Sam stood on the platform composing a text in response to Martin. He already knew he would be very unhappy that Sam had not got back to him the day before. The relationship with Qin and Martin had soured in the last few weeks and this would not help. He thought he had better call Joanna in the office.

'Morning Jo. What's up?' said Sam with as much cheerfulness as he could muster.

'Oh, Hi Sam. We have a problem with Qin. They want to take out another big slug of money and send it abroad.'

'Where to this time?' said Sam fearing the worst.

'Same as before, Uzbekistan. But this time a new bank and new account details. Compliance is crapping itself.'

'OK, I will try and come in later. I have enough to worry about here. If I get put on this trial Martin is going to kill me.'

'Yup, he sounded very pissed off with you yesterday. I would leave your phone on vibrate if I were you.'

The same usher came floating into the waiting area and asked for the jurors to make their way to the jury waiting area outside court. Fifteen plus the usher entered in silence.

It was like time had stood still. Everybody was in precisely the same position as the day before. All the barristers and court officials wore the same outfits and each of the defendants was in the identical place in the dock. Dozens of pairs of eyes fixed on the jurors as they entered. Sam stood at the back of the bunch as it settled by the side of the barristers waiting for the clerk to stand.

'Would each member of the jury make their way to the jury box? If you wish to have further discussions with the judge, please turn right at the bench and speak to him.'

Sam realised his error. His should be first not last. If he was first, he could get his claim in early. He decided to promote his position and as the assembled jurors shuffled about getting ready to move forward, Sam deftly shifted up through to be placed about fifth or sixth.

Sam watched like a hawk the movements of the first few jurors. First one straight into the jury box, second in, third stopped at the bench. Chat to judge. Dismissed. One down. Fourth juror in, fifth chat with judge. Judge seems to disagree with juror and sends him to the jury box. Sam's pulse quickened, it was a very real prospect for the judge to overrule. Sixth straight in and then it was Sam's turn.

With legs feeling heavy Sam walked to the now notorious T-junction and stopped. He turned and headed to the judge who, when Sam looked up, was watching the performance. There was a 'please hurry up look' on the judge's face, so Sam jumped up the two steps.

'Good morning Mr Waghorne. Have you contemplated why you cannot sit on my jury?'

'Good morning My Lord. I have been given this letter from my boss at work. I believe he sets out why he feels that, much as he appreciates how I relish the opportunity to sit on your jury, the tenure of four months is just too long for me to be away from Wolfenberg.'

Sam put his hand into his jacket pocket and pulled out the letter. He handed it to the judge and noticed his hand was trembling as he did so. The judge took the envelope and took what Sam thought was an age to open it and read it. He looked back at Sam a couple of times as he went through what Peter had written about Sam. It was clear to Sam that the judge didn't believe a word of it. He must have seen this a thousand times before. Finally, the judge broke the silence.

'Surely Wolfenberg is able to cope without you? Well actually, thinking about it, after the recent performance from banks, perhaps not,' said the judge with a hearty chuckle.

'Mr Waghorne you are released from this court.'

The judge forcefully handed the letter back to Sam. Sam took it and turned back to the court. He noticed everybody was glaring at him with the same annoyance the judge had shown. He must have been there for several minutes and these people were getting frustrated. Sam took this to be his cue to get out. As he scuttled to the T junction and turned left, a billowing voice behind him echoed around the court.

'Mr Peppiatt, I am releasing his gentlemen due to extremely pressing work commitments.'

The judge may as well have said he was releasing Sam to go and buy some pornography for all the good the word 'extremely' did in his sentence. He had made it clear to his court this man exiting stage left was a lightweight with no feeling of civic responsibility.

If Sam had had a tail, it would have been between his legs as he walked out. With his head down he hurried out of the court door. He pressed the lift button and soon was back in the relative sanctuary of the jury waiting area. It was eleven fifteen and morning TV was in full flow. Sam buried his head in his hands.

Half an hour later Sam and a few remaining jurors not serving on a jury were sent home. There were no more trials due to start that day. Sam collected up his things and left; so much for this being exciting. It was actually turning out to be a real pain in the backside.

Chapter XVII

The Central Criminal Court, Old Bailey, London

It was eleven in the morning when Sam turned up to the jury waiting area. The manager had told them to come in late due to a lack of trials starting. Sam had packed additional material with him in anticipation of another boring day. He had ensconced himself in a corner of the room as far away as possible from day-time television. He had a copy of the *Financial Times*, his usual *Telegraph* and a new paperback he had purchased on the way to the Old Bailey. He was fully prepared for a day of reading.

Sam didn't see the usher sweep into the room. He was engrossed in the market review section of his paper, unaware of what was happening around him. He didn't even look up when the television was turned off. Markets were starting to perform badly, driven primarily by a collapse in confidence in the banking sector. This could be serious thought Sam as he scanned the pages.

Sam heard his name the second time it was called out. The usher had increased her volume and this caused Sam to jump up, his paper falling to the floor with a crisp rustle.

'Yes.' Sam said loudly. The usher looked over to acknowledge the response. She looked at Sam like she had just trodden in something nasty.

He followed the usher with the others out of the waiting area. They all congregated by the lifts and fidgeted with childlike anticipation. This time there were only fifteen people asked to join the usher by the lifts which Sam hoped indicated a much shorter trial.

'Ladies and gentlemen, could I please have your attention. My name is Chantelle and I am your usher for this trial.'

Sam recognised her immediately having not really looked properly before now. It was the same usher who had welcomed the new arrivals on his first day. She was black with jet coloured hair which was tied back away from her attractive face. She was tall and had a particular presence in front of this crowd.

'When I have finished, I would like you to make your way down to the doors outside Court Number One. You lucky people are going to serve on a jury in the most famous court in the world. If any of you have done any research into the Old Bailey, you will know this court has seen some of this country's most notorious criminals.'

'Is it a murder? We all want a decent murder,' said a small man at the front of the group. He sounded like a child going off to the cinema.

'Calm down now. The judge will explain when you get inside the court. Anyway, there are fifteen of you because the trial may well last two weeks.'

There was a sigh from a group of people who had not been party to Sam's previous experiences. Sam was relieved and felt a degree of his original excitement flood back to him.

'If you could all follow me please.'

Chantelle turned, letting her gown fly up to the left. Sam watched her as she walked. Despite being at least five ten, she wore heels which made her well over six feet tall. The shoes pushed everything forward which reminded him of a gazelle walking whilst grazing. He wondered what she would look like if she started to run.

Congregating by the doors to Court One, Sam was struck by the sheer beauty of the older part of the Old Bailey. Court Eight was in the new section and frankly was a bit of a let-down. Court One in contrast was in the middle of the old section, which was adorned with marble, archaic inscription, busts and statues. Barristers scuttled from court to the stairs whilst other court staff busied themselves carrying boxes or documents. This was more like it.

'Please could you remain silent and sit in the benches at the back. The Clerk will call you up one-by-one and you can go to speak to the judge if you have any objection to serving for more than two weeks.'

Sam was looking at the inscriptions on the walls. Chantelle coughed and Sam looked back. She was staring at him with a 'there's always one' look on her face.

'Come on, try and pay attention please,' she said as she reached for the brass handle and opened the double doors which led into the most notorious court on earth.

The first thing to strike Sam was the sheer scale of the court. At the front sat the judge with white wig and black robes. He sat staring straight at his new flock. His eyes pierced through to them despite being about fifteen metres away. He was watching every move the jury made as they each sat carefully on the benches at the back of the court provided for the press or other non-public representatives in any trial.

Sam looked around him as the musty old-world smell drifted into his nose. The light was as real as it could be for a room with no outside windows. There was a huge light unit in the middle of the ceiling that gave everything a November morning kind of look, like a widow's house in the country, trying to save money.

The wooden benches were all covered in green leather reminding Sam of the television images from Parliament. Sitting perpendicular to the Clerk were four barristers. They were busily looking through notes in front of them; it looked like they were rehearsing their speeches and remembering the order of each section of the trial. Sam was quite surprised there were only four of them. There had been many more in court eight with the six defendants.

The dock sat in the middle of the court. It was surrounded by a continuous wall of glass above a wood panelled frame. The glass was about three feet high and made the dock look like you could play squash in it. It was big enough to take twenty would be criminals and their guards if necessary. This time there were three figures quietly sitting in the middle of the huge space. Sam could only see their backs but it was immediately obvious that all three were women.

Up to the right was a public gallery. There were a couple of people sitting there leaning on the rail staring down at proceedings. It made him feel awkward at first, people coming in off the street and looking directly at the jury. They were not allowed to take anything like mobile phones or cameras into the viewing areas but still Sam and the others had to leave the building every night and you never knew who might recognise you as you left – the brother of the defendant wanting to cause trouble, the sister of the victim wanting to flatter you? Sam would consider a few mild disguises when he got home – perhaps a hat or a high collared coat?

The judge interrupted Sam's visual tour.

'Ladies and gentlemen welcome to court number one,' he said.

'You will all have noticed there are fifteen of you sitting in the press benches of this court. This is a trial for murder so I would anticipate the trial lasting for two weeks, that is I expect we should be able to get through it in ten working days,'

'Now the length of the trial may well be dependent upon any unexpected events which arise during the case and of course how long the jury needs to deliberate. Therefore, for this reason, I have asked for fifteen of you to be chosen so we end up with a selection who can commit to such a length of time.'

Sam looked at his fellow jurors, they had no idea. Two weeks was a walk in the park.

'If any of you who are called up have any objection to serving for that length of time please come up to my bench and I will listen to your representations.'

'Please,' concluded the judge as the Clerk took her cue and stood up to read out the names.

'When I call your name please come and sit in the jury box or head to the bench if you want to converse with My Lord,' said the Clerk as she held out a single sheet of paper.

The potential jury members shifted nervously in their seats. This was it.

'Barbara Smallbridge'

A lady scuttled into the jury box.

'Kevin Ward'

Again, no complaints from a small man in jeans; Sam thought he must be a decorator, he was convinced he could see flecks of paint on his trousers.

'Sam Waghorne.'

Sam jumped out of his seat. He could not quite believe his luck. This was going to be perfect; a good murder case in a fantastic court for a reasonable duration. He had no intention of missing out on this one, so he gladly walked straight into the third vacant position in the jury box. As he sat down he got a whole new perspective of the court. He was sitting directly in front of the barristers who were staring back intently, already trying to assimilate what kind of jury they were going to have to deal with.

'Well ladies and gentlemen; that is all twelve of you in place,' the judge said after a few more minutes. He looked over to the female barrister sitting closest to the defendant.

'Any concerns?' said the judge and immediately the barrister jumped to her feet and turned to what Sam thought must be her client in the dock.

'No, My Lord,' said the female barrister with a voice as smooth as melted chocolate.

'Good, good then let's get you lot sworn in shall we?'

Chantelle had taken her seat by a desk in front of the jury during the selection process and she now stood, picking up several cards and a book. She went to each jury member in turn, asking them which religious card they would like to read from. When it came to Sam's turn he grabbed the bible and, typically, made a garbled hash of the printed words on the card. Chantelle gave a coquettish smile as he eventually finished.

When everybody was sworn in, Chantelle sat down again and the judge cleared his throat.

'Thank you, ladies and gentlemen. We are now ready to begin.' His voice was more serious than before. 'As I have mentioned, this is a murder trial which should last for about two weeks. The first thing I would like to do is remind all of you of your duties as a juror. Now some of you may well come from walks of life where you work for ten hours a day in an office or out in the open. We tend to do things differently here. Our sessions are broken down into two per day and these tend to last no more than three hours at a time. This may seem short to some of you but it is of paramount importance that you apply full concentration during each of these sessions. There will be a lot to take in and if I see any member of the jury flagging, then I will adjourn the trial. I will not tolerate anybody sleeping in my court, so if any of you feel tired, please pass a note to me via the usher. It is important you all concentrate.'

The judge took another sip of water.

'I would also like to remind you that it is your civic duty not to talk to anybody about this trial as it progresses. It is vital you listen, consider the evidence presented and make your own minds up on the balance of this evidence. Talking with other people may well lead you to come to conclusions that prejudice the defendant so please resist the temptation to discuss this case with anybody, even between yourselves.'

'The other warning I would give is to firmly ask you not to try and find out any more information about this case on the Internet.'

Sam looked around to see his fellow jury members look at each other with indignation as if they had had a civil liberty removed.

'I am fully aware of the temptation to find out what happened but again, it is crucial you base your opinion on what you find out during this trial. Adding the opinions of journalists will only serve to confuse you.'

'Right, that is quite enough of that. Given the time I suggest we call it a day here and start at ten sharp tomorrow.'

The judge looked down at Chantelle who stood and indicated with her eyes that it was time for the jury to vacate the court. They all stood as one and shuffled out, the first couple of jurors on the back row passing by the witness box and heading past the barristers. Sam looked at his watch as he walked. It was five to four. Should he go back to work and undoubtedly end up in Jim's talking about the trial or should he go home and spend a few hours with Lucy and the boys?

Sam wanted a clear head for the trial so, after much consideration, he chose the latter.

Chapter XVIII

R. v. Maria Kayakova

Day One

A loud bang on the cell door made me jump. I turned to the sound. The door opened and in came my barrister with a female security guard.

'Miss Eleanor Sechford-Jones,' I said slowly as an elegant woman walked into the cell with her head held high and a broad smile on her face. What a magnificent lady she was. She had a serious but attractive face under neatly positioned but ultimately very long blonde hair. She carried her wig under her arm and wore a smartly tailored suit. Most of it was hidden by the folds of her black gown.

The security guard was a different story. She was not so friendly and was a right sight; she had a face like a bag of spanners with broad shoulders like an ox and a very unfeminine knitted jumper with official pips on the shoulders. Her black boots completed the ensemble making her four inches taller than she actually was.

'Good morning, I hope you had a good journey in. Shit it's cold in here,' said my brief, with an attempt at good humour, as she rubbed her hands together.

I had come from prison in the back of a security van and the journey had been anything but pleasant. They treated you like a convict all through the day, talking about you in front of your face like an animal at the zoo. A couple of guards had a bet on the length of my trial yesterday. I almost laughed before the truth sank in.

'Morning,' I said. 'What happens today?'

'We start the trial for real today. The judge has called for all of us to go to court. You know the way, up the stairs to the left.'

The dank cells were collected in an intricate maze beneath the courts in a setting that looked like nothing had changed for two hundred years. It seemed each court could house defendants in separate cells, so I had the place to myself. Earlier there had been several throaty screams from the other cells on the floor. A stark reminder of where I was and what kind of people were entertained here.

'You remember all I told you yesterday don't you?' Eleanor said after a few seconds of silence.

'Yes. I need to look meek, polite and above all, innocent.'

'Good, right-o, let's go then,' Eleanor said with haughty optimism. I stood and submissively let the guard handcuff me on one arm. She caught some skin as she pushed the cuffs closed. I recoiled slightly but the guard did not seem to notice and she certainly didn't care.

It took only a few seconds to climb the damp, grey stone steps to a door marked with a solitary number '1'. It creaked open and all of us entered the court. Eleanor led us to the three chairs placed in the middle of the enormous dock. I looked up to see the prosecuting barrister staring at me like an eagle just about to attack a lamb. He had his wig on his head for the first time and his eyes were like lasers burning into my head. He made me feel awkward just by looking at me. I suppose that was his job.

I sat down and the brutish security guard kindly unlocked my wrist. I suspect I was now deemed safe inside the dock. I turned to Eleanor for a final briefing. She talked for a while but I didn't really listen, I was scanning the court to check what else had changed since yesterday. There was no judge. He must be finishing his breakfast. A woman sitting in front of the judge's bench was engrossed in deep administrative conversation. She wasn't there yesterday.

Up to the right in the public gallery sat two people, I had no idea who they were. One was looking around like it was her first time in court – perhaps she was a legal student coming to witness the law in action. The other guy looked like a disinterested journalist, told to come by his boss, sitting there in a dirty suit which looked like it belonged to a larger man.

'Good luck,' said Eleanor with sudden formality. Things were about to get going.

She stood and went out of the side half door of the dock placing her wig on with urgency. The security guard allowed my interpreter into the dock then closed the door behind her. She sat back down next to me with such a thud I thought for a while the chair would collapse under her. The journalist in the gallery leant forward in anticipation.

'All rise!' said the gowned lady in front of the bench who had risen to her feet.

Like children at school we all stood and looked to see from where any activity may come. There was a buzz in the air. I suspect not dissimilar to the buzz a Roman crowd gave off before the Gladiators appeared. Whoever was coming next was good – they made us wait.

Eventually the door to the side of the bench opened and in he came. His Honour Judge Oliver Barniston QC. I had met him at the pre-trial and again yesterday but it still took an effort to remember his full name in the right order. This time he came sweeping into the court like a massive fruit-bat, his black gown billowing out behind him as he walked with purpose and sat down in the tallest chair in the middle of his bench. He ordered his papers as the court settled down. The two barristers had taken their positions to my right with their seconds behind them. The two public gallery members sat with expectant looks on their faces. After a few more moments the judge broke the shuffling silence.

'Are we all ready?' he said looking down at the two barristers.

Silence from the counsel indicated we were ready to go.

'Clerk, please call them in.'

The clerk picked up a telephone to relay the message. Everybody apart from me seemed completely at ease with proceedings – the machine was starting.

A couple of minutes later, from the back of the court, I heard a door opening. The sound of feet heralded the arrival of twelve jury members. They shuffled past me to sit in the jury box. I wonder how many of them had looked at my trial on the Internet despite the judge forbidding it. I bet they all had. One man looked at me, but the others looked too scared to do anything other than walk in a straight line.

The judge cleared his throat and the ambient sounds ceased.

'Ladies and Gentlemen of the jury,' he said with a low steady voice.

'As I mentioned yesterday this is a trial for murder. You will first hear from the prosecution. Mr McOmish will present the case for the Crown over the next few days. When he has finished you will then hear from Miss Sechford-Jones, who is representing the defendant. I will sum up and you will then have the opportunity to gather together to deliberate what you have heard. I urge you again to only consider the evidence you hear in this court and you are not to be tempted by external influence.'

The judge took a sip of water.

'You will be introduced to witnesses through the trial and, again, I urge you to pay particular attention to what each of them says. Their evidence is crucial in this case.'

The judge stared straight at me over the top of his glasses. He gave the impression I was guilty already. Perhaps he was always like that. He looked over to his left.

'Mr McOmish.'

With this cue the prosecuting barrister jumped to his feet. He settled over a curious cardboard box staring straight down at the floor. Clearing his throat, he lifted his eyes to the jury. It was like the start of a play and I had a front row seat.

'Members of the jury; let me take you through some introductory points which will set out the background to this case. It is the prosecution's assertion that this defendant was involved in the murder of a certain Mr Kumara Darsha, a businessman and restaurant owner from north-west London.'

McOmish looked down to locate a large bundle of paper in front of him. He shifted from one leg to the other.

'As My Lord has pointed out, I will be calling witnesses as I set out our case. Each of these will be relevant to a particular piece of the trial as it develops, so you each have been provided with an empty file to order your notes.'

The junior barrister behind McOmish was shuffling and ordering papers. I thought it was quite off-putting but McOmish ploughed on regardless. This must be part of the job.

'Members of the jury, allow me if you will to take you back to last year. October last year. This is when Kumara Darsha was found dead in his flat in West Hampstead.'

I settled back in my chair. This was going to take some time.

'Mr Darsha was a man in his forties. He had two children, a son and a daughter, from a marriage which was dissolved two years ago. His children spent about half the time living with their father, the rest with their mother. I want you to picture this man. He was a loving father, a successful restaurateur and a businessman of some repute in his particular area of London.'

'Why was this man found dead in his flat on the morning of 17th October? Over the next few hours let me tell you what we have managed to find out about this terrible crime and what we consider to be the involvement of the young lady you see sitting before you in the dock.'

'Mr Darsha was found approximately thirty four hours after the pathologist suggests he died. He had multiple injuries. We will of course come on to the extent of these and how, in the prosecution's view, they were inflicted.'

'The flat he was found in on Derringham Park Road is in a quiet, peaceful part of West Hampstead. He had lived there for five years and it was no more than a ten-minute walk from the main road. It was also very close to his restaurant. The day after he was murdered his two children came to the flat to see him.' McOmish said. He paused and looked up at the jury for a few seconds.

'At nine in the morning of the 17th October his two children had decided to go around to see their father. When they knocked on the door there was no answer. After many attempts to reach him on his mobile phone they contacted the police who finally knocked the door down later that morning, finding him dead in the kitchen of the property. The police said that from immediately obvious observations, he had been beaten to death in the early hours of the 16th October.'

I looked around the court. Everybody was looking at this man standing with his arms out in front of him. They were all hanging on every word. He was eloquent and kept a beautifully moderated tone. Even my barristers sat with mouths slightly open as they listened to his introduction.

'Ladies and gentlemen of the jury, you have in front of you two very important documents.'

I gazed over to the jury box to see each member looking down in front of them. Each had pencil and paper for notes and a small tumbler of water. It was just like being back at school.

'Each of you has an admissions pack which contains sections which will be relevant to certain parts of this trial. We have compiled this to make your job easier, it is where most of the information is kept,' said Mr McOmish holding up a thick white file and waving it around as he spoke.

'The other document is printed on larger paper,' he said waving a white but very much bigger document above his head. 'This contains a long list of information relating to various mobile phone communications in the days preceding and the days after the alleged murder of Mr Darsha.'

I took a long look at the document from my position. I was not allowed to see any of this but even from ten feet away I could see it was quite thick. Where did they get all that from? What was in that pack?

'I will be using this information when we run through events in detail. I do realise it looks very complicated but you must bear with me if we are to get to the truth.'

Mr McOmish turned to look directly at me.

'This is Miss Maria Kayakova. She is twenty and was born in Ukraine. She was well educated there after which she came to the United Kingdom to broaden her experience of the world. She speaks many languages and managed to find work in London when she arrived last year. She did not come to London alone,' Mr McOmish paused to lick his thumb and use it to turn a page divider over in the big folder.

'If you could all turn to section six in your main pack please, My Lord the photograph in question is located at page fifty-eight of My Lord's bundle,' said McOmish submissively, pausing for a sip of water as the jury shuffled papers to locate the photo.

'This is Yamin Shakirov. I apologise for the quality of the image however this was taken from a CCTV camera at West Hampstead tube station.'

I could not see the photograph so instead looked at the jury. Their faces studied the image as the barrister spoke.

'This is the man we believe committed this crime together with the woman you see before you in the dock. Maria Kayakova and Yamin Shakirov were a couple, they came to the UK to be together.'

It is interesting when you hear things about yourself spoken by another. It is almost irresistible to nod your head when you hear something you agree with. No doubt there would be plenty to refute later in the trial.

'The details on Yamin Shakirov are patchy. He decided to flee the country after, in our opinion, he had committed this crime. The Police are actively searching for him with the help of their international colleagues. As you can see from the photo, he is a rather…menacing looking character.'

My barrister rose to her feet. What was she doing?

'My Lord. I must object. I think my learned friend should be careful not to give the jury too much of a character reference just from a photograph.'

'Thank you Miss Sechford-Jones. Yes, Mr McOmish, he may look menacing to you, but there is no evidence to suggest he was. Please be careful. Continue.'

'I apologise My Lord. Members of the jury, you will need to come to your own conclusions as to Yamin's character. I will refer back to this photograph when we run through the pathology.'

Mr McOmish spent the next thirty minutes running through the background to the trial. I drifted in and out of what he was saying. There were CCTV images of me and Yamin in the local high street. There was an image of me with Kumara outside his restaurant. All of these had times and dates, so the prosecution were able to put a time line together putting me and Kumara in his flat at one in the morning on the day he died.

Pictures of the dead body were analysed with the jury seeming to swing between repulsion and gory fascination as they ran through the images. I had no way of knowing what they were looking at. My memory of that night had been terminated when I ended up at the bottom of the stairs. It may have been the drink or the bang to the head but the first memory after that was in bed the next morning.

The jury looked at one of Kumara's shoes, which had been found half way up the stairs. There was also a pair of glasses, which had been smashed and left in the flat. This was all evidence of a struggle between Kumara and Yamin.

After a while I found myself drifting having lost interest in proceedings. It is hard to concentrate on things you cannot influence or get involved with, after a while it starts to wash over you. I was roused by the judge instructing the jury they had probably had enough for one day. He discharged them and they shuffled past me one-by-one. What a sorry bunch they looked. Not one of them looked like they were enjoying themselves and most looked thoroughly bored. When they had all gone the judge said a few things to the barristers and then spoke quietly to the clerk.

'All rise,' said the clerk with an authoritative tone.

I stood because everybody else did. The judge stood up and went flying out of the court with his gown billowing. Batman had another emergency to deal with...

I didn't know what to do so I sat down again. Moments later I was being ushered down the cold stone steps, back to the cells with another night in prison to look forward to.

R. v. Maria Kayakova

Day Two

Shower and teeth: socks, pants and jeans on. Always the same. I walked to the corner of the cell where I had left my bra and put it on again. It was slightly damp and filthy.

There had been a bang on the door to wake me, but it had also woken my cellmate. Tough. The poor girl had got involved with crime after her husband left and her children had been taken away; a victim of the drugs cycle. Take them, run out of money, steal to pay for them and then repeat. The routine continues until you get caught. It's amazing how quickly things can deteriorate. We got on despite the cramped conditions; I was lucky as apparently not all the inmates at *HM Holloway* prison were that friendly.

After a pleasantly smooth drive through north London handcuffed to a guard with no windows to admire the view, I felt a degree of déjà vu ascending the same old steps to my chair in the dock. All the usual crowd were there. Oliver, the judge staring at me like

I had, once again, run over his dog in my car. All four barristers with their noses down calculating and plotting – at least though the judge had the decency to look at me when I arrived.

The judge looked down at the clerk and said something I could not hear. I was much more alert than the afternoon before and was looking forward to the day's proceedings. The chat must have been a jury alert because a few minutes later in they came, all eager after a good night's sleep. Once they settled, the judge barely lifted his hand and Robert jumped to his feet.

'My Lord, with your permission, I would like to call the prosecution's first witness.'

The judge shifted in his seat having been reminded there were special conditions around this first witness. I noticed as he looked at his notes that several television screens had been placed around the courtroom.

'Members of the jury, the first witness is the daughter of the victim. You will remember that Kumara Darsha had two children, his son Bahir, who is currently nine years old and Meniki, who is seven. I need to explain to you what the procedure will be as we ask the first witness, Meniki, some questions,' said the judge in a matter of fact way.

'We are able to ask children to be witnesses here in court but we have certain procedures which differ from a normal witness. Meniki is here at the Old Bailey but she is in a secure room away from this court. There is a closed-circuit television link and I will be asking Mr McOmish and Miss Sechford-Jones to ask her questions via the link.'

'From our experience children tend to lose interest quickly and their attention span can be very short, especially if they are feeling pressure. The interviews will not last for more than ten minutes and I will stop proceedings if I see any sign Meniki is uncomfortable.'

'Mr McOmish,' said the judge with his arm extended towards the prosecution.

'Thank you, My Lord' said Robert McOmish as he stood. I thought I would call him 'Bob' principally to fulfil a silent protest but also because you could never imagine anybody calling him Bob. He was a Robert if ever there was one.

'Just before we start could I ask each of you to remove your wigs,' Bob said as he looked at the judge, Eleanor and the seconds behind them. Each took their wigs off revealing their hair. The judge had greyish white hair that looked like a thinner version of the wig. Eleanor had lots of beautiful blonde hair tied neatly at the back. Bob had very little hair on top of his head. What he did have left had congregated around his ears and slipped down towards his neck.

The televisions flickered into life. The one nearest me showed a little girl sitting in a big chair. It looked like her mother had made sure she was in her best clothes for court. There was another frame within the main one. We could see Ollie the judge in the top left-hand corner. He looked strange without his wig, almost normal, but this is what the little girl could see.

I had never met her before. My dealings with Kumara Darsha had only been in his restaurant. This little girl looked so vulnerable in such serious surroundings. I suppose that was the point of this first witness, to give the jury a real impact on what a murder actually did to society – it took people away from their loved ones; it made little girls and boys vulnerable. This was an obvious early goal for the prosecution. 1-0 to them.

'Good morning Meniki, can you hear me?' Bob said in his best Daddy voice.

'Er, yup. No problem. Thanks,'

The illusion of innocence was tainted by a confident and almost cocky response. I scanned the jury and they seemed to be surprised by the sureness from a seven-year-old girl who audibly came from North London.

'Meniki, this is Robert, I am going to ask you some questions if that is ok?' said Bob, again with a friendly voice.

'Hi Robert, that's cool. What do you want to know?' said Meniki.

I couldn't work out whether she was trying to sound self-assured or this was her natural character. Either way, it was strange to see the image saying one thing and the sounds something else.

'Perhaps I could ask you to tell me a little bit about your life. You and your brother saw your father quite a bit, didn't you?' said Bob with deliberate caution.

'Yes. Dad and Mummy didn't live in the same house, so we used to go and see him about twice a week. We would like err go round his flat in the mornings and spend the day with him when he was there. He would take us out or we would play in his garden. He loved to see us.'

'Was your father kind to you Meniki?'

'Yeh, all the time, right. He would buy us treats and stuff, look after us well. He was well busy, so we didn't see him as much as we wanted. After school sometimes but you know, mostly we saw him at weekends sort of thing.'

'How did you get to your father's flat Meniki?'

'Err, we took the bus or walked. Mummy lives with Ronnie up by the station at Brondesbury Park so it takes about ten minutes on the bus I suppose.'

'So, you visited your father often?'

'Yes, as I said, like at least once or twice a week. We used to play with him in the garden and he took us for pizza and that.'

'Thank you, Meniki, I know this must be difficult for you. Are you ok?'

'I'm sweet.'

'Was your father a good man? Did he look after you?' said Bob escalating the emotion.

'When he was around he was a well-good father, it was kind of terrible when he split up with Mummy but these things happen though. Nothing lasts forever.'

I noticed the jury fluster at hearing such a deep, adult style answer. Bob had taken things too far and he knew it. He concluded his questions there and sat down.

It was Eleanor's turn. This was her opportunity to neutralise the witness.

'Miss Sechford-Jones, would you like to question the witness?' said the judge, still looking silly without his wig. It was like a dress rehearsal for a play.

It was clear Eleanor was uncomfortable with the prospect of questioning such a young witness. I sat further forward on my chair.

'Yes, just one question My Lord.'

Eleanor turned to the camera which connected the court to the room Meniki was in.

'Meniki, this is Eleanor. I am here to make sure those who were responsible for your father's death are punished correctly.'

You could see the prosecution look towards the judge, this was clearly close to the bone.

'Yes, I know. I love your hair, it's well cool,' said Meniki with a touch of innocence which prompted a ripple of mirth from the jury.

'Thank you. I have just one question for you Meniki. When you arrived at your father's flat that day, you knocked on the door several times. You rang his mobile phone but there was no answer.'

There was a pushiness in Eleanor's voice which was inconsistent with the surroundings. What was she getting at?

'We have had the chance to review the statements you gave at the time. You mentioned in this document you saw a large man at the window of the flat. Is that right Meniki, did you see a big man at the window when you arrived?'

'Yes, I think he was at the window. He was looking out of the window. Definitely but I did not recognise him mind. He was very big. Big muscles, you know, fit, very strong. We ran. Went straight back to Mummy's.'

The judge noticed Meniki was now out of her depth. He asked the clerk to end the interview and Eleanor reluctantly sat down. I could tell the jury had not been impressed with her style.

The television screens went blank. I looked around for a second or two trying to work out what would happen next. A quick whisper from the judge saw the jury ushered out for a mid-morning break. We had not been in court for more than thirty minutes – he must want to talk to the barristers.

The barristers shuffled and the judge scribbled during the jury break. I was completely ignored throughout. This is when you feel like a small cog in a slow but steady machine. My life was irrelevant here – what mattered was the process. I could have been a naughty monkey for all the front of stage people cared. I was the reason they were all here yet none of them cared about who or what I was. Animal, vegetable or mineral - all that mattered was the crime, the associated process and, of course, the pay.

When the jury arrived back from their break Bob announced he was calling his second witness. This was Amal Darsha, Kumara's younger brother. The usher held out a book and a card. Amal Darsha was sworn in and everybody settled back to listen to the questions Bob McOmish had for him.

I looked at Amal and recalled our previous encounters. I had seen him several times in the restaurant working there for his brother from time to time. He was taller and much thicker set than his brother, in fact his physical size gave him greater presence than

Kumara ever had - Amal was menacing and he knew it. He used it to his advantage with me, there were a couple of evenings I remember him coming on to me; trying to ask me out for a drink. There was charm there but also something else, a feeling he gave you that you weren't quite safe.

He had darker skin than I remember and this set his immaculate linen suit off beautifully. He gave a broad smile which brought his over-white teeth out against the contrast of his face. He looked good and knew it.

'Good morning. Are you Amal Darsha, brother of the victim Kumara Darsha?' Bob said in a matter of fact way.

'That's right,' said Amal in that familiar deep, rich tone. He had a great voice.

'Well good morning Mr Darsha. I wonder whether you would be kind enough, for the jury's benefit, to run through what you do for a living?' Bob said.

'I suppose you could call me an independent trader. I buy things, sell them on, you know. I also helped Kumara in his restaurant. Not all the time, just when things were busy,' Amal said with confidence.

'Would you say your brother was an honourable man?'

'Yes, of course. It was a shame he separated from his wife but he has two beautiful children who he adored. I used to help him look after them when he was busy.'

'So you knew him well and saw a lot of him?'

'Yes, that's right. We were close both personally and in business.'

Amal looked around the court with a cocky impatience that clearly questioned where Bob McOmish was going with this.

'Your statement mentions you are of good character Mr Darsha. You have no criminal convictions do you?'

'That's right. Kumara and I were brought up to be honest and fair. Our business activities always reflected my father's views,' Amal said with pride.

'Did Kumara have any enemies Amal? Were there people who did not like him?'

Amal stared at the high ceiling in the court. It looked like he was trying to remember his witness statement. Suddenly the pressure of the court was getting to him.

'I am not aware of any. He had no bank debts and owed nothing to others. He was loved by his client base at the restaurant. Sure, he had an eye for a bargain and did not suffer fools gladly but not so much as to get killed.'

'So there was nobody you know of who would have wanted to commit this crime on him?'

'No, not at all. He was popular. No.'

'Thank you Mr Darsha, no more questions My Lord,' Bob sat down with a reverent bow towards the judge.

'Miss Sechford-Jones?' Ollie raised his hand, giving Eleanor the chance to question the witness. She rose slowly.

'Mr Darsha, perhaps I could ask you for a little more clarity about your business activities. You mentioned you did some trading with the support of your brother. What kind of trading are you referring to?'

'We sold a few properties in the area'

'West Hampstead?'

'That's right, local buildings, shops mainly. We sold some office space; the odd flat.'

'What else?'

'We would buy and sell second hand cars. There were always a couple of deals to be had in our community. Once people trust you, they want to carry on trading with you.'

'Quite the entrepreneur then?'

Bob looked over to Eleanor as her tone shifted to be more confrontational. I was starting to get excited. Eleanor had a plan here.

'We made a living; trading and Kumara's restaurant kept us out of trouble.'

Eleanor stared at Amal.

'What is your full name Mr Darsha?'

'I'm sorry?'

'It's a simple question sir, what is your full name?'

Both the judge and the prosecution looked at Eleanor. Surely this was a stupid question.

'Amal Darsha.'

'So that is not an abbreviation?'

Amal shifted from one leg to the other.

'It is but nobody has called me by my birth name for about twenty years, certainly since I have been in the UK.'

'So how old are you now then?'

'I am forty-one. I arrived here with my family when I was just over twenty. I have been known as Amal Darsha all that time.'

'So what is your full birth name please?'

'Ravinda Javed Darsha Sangakara.'

'Thank you.'

Eleanor looked down at her notes, composing herself.

'You stated on your witness statement you were a legitimate and honourable businessman,' Eleanor said in a raised tone, reading from a single piece of paper in her hand.

'Yes.'

'Well you wouldn't be surprised to hear we have done some digging around what you call your legitimate business interests. Members of the jury, the man you see in the witness box seems to have led somewhat of a double life. We asked the police as to whether Amal Darsha had ever come to their attention and the answer was no. We then asked as to whether Ravinda Sangakara had been of interest to them. We had much better luck this time. They had this name on file. They would like to question this man in relation to drugs charges and a string of transactions involving stolen cars and computer property in the north London area. All they had to go on was other people arrested mentioning Ravinda Sangakara's name in a trade-off for leniency.'

Amal continued to fidget in the witness box. He was looking around him for support but there was none to be taken.

Eleanor resumed after her big right hook.

'You mention you have not used your full name since you have been resident in the United Kingdom. That's not true is it, Mr Darsha. You have used it often in an attempt to preserve an image of honour whilst having a dark secret.'

'Yes, but....'

'Was your brother involved in any of these deals, Mr Darsha?'

'No! Absolutely not. He was an honest man with a good restaurant and a loving family. Well, all that before he was murdered,' Amal said with real passion. He looked over to me as he finished.

'I'm sorry, Mr Darsha. I find it very hard to believe what you say. You have lied in this court claiming to be legitimate when in fact the police wish to question you on a number of offences which occurred very close to where you live. You claim you helped your brother in a number of ventures. Are we really supposed to think he was not aware of what you were up to?'

Bob McOmish stood but the judge was too quick. Eleanor sat immediately upon hearing the judge.

'Miss Sechford-Jones, please try to keep within the scope of the trial. Supposition is for novelists not advocates.'

There were smirks from the jury, especially the men. There was a thinly-veiled misogynistic tone to his reprimand.

'I'm sorry My Lord,' Eleanor said rising to her feet.

'Members of the jury, it is the opinion of the defence Mr Darsha is not to be trusted. You have discovered a conflicting truth between his witness statement and reality. I suspect the police will want to question him further on that issue.' Eleanor had reduced the volume since the warning.

'I suggest you think long and hard about the credibility of this witness. He has told you in this court he was very close to his brother. You must consider whether this crime which has been committed could well be linked to this shadowy underworld we have uncovered.'

'But, can I just say...'

'No further questions My Lord,' Eleanor cut Amal off mid-sentence.

Bob McOmish shook his head, he had no follow-up questions. He looked flustered as Amal left the witness box looking half the man he had on the way in. It was amazing what five minutes at the Old Bailey could do to you.

After a few seconds Bob stood and looked directly at the jury. He had been rocked by the last witness and Eleanor's questions which called his integrity into question.

'Ladies and gentlemen, I thought this would be an appropriate time to recap,' Bob said reaching for a red file in front of him.

'We have a dead man. He was of good character with no previous associations with the police,' Bob said in an ironic tone, offering a quick glance at Eleanor.

'We know Kumara Darsha was found dead on the morning of the 17th October; he had been left for dead by his attackers. The woman you see before you has admitted she was in the flat when Yamin Shakirov brutally killed Kumara Darsha. It is the opinion of the Crown this woman was involved with the murder. We will go on to set out why we think she was and exactly how her involvement led to this man's death. First, I want to get a couple of points clear in your minds,' Bob said with directness, getting to the heart of the trial.

'We have seen Kumara Darsha ran a successful restaurant, we have heard he was a loving father and supportive brother. There seems to be no reason why anyone would want to kill this man. So why was he murdered?'

'My Lord, with your permission I would like to call the next prosecution witness.'

The judge nodded his head which commenced activity at the back of the court. A young woman came past me. She was dressed in her best work clothes and looked like she was a stranger to court. She looked nervous as the usher swore her in.

'Are you Miss Helen Smallwood?'

'Yes.' The woman said with a feeble voice.

'Perhaps you could start by telling us your address?'

'I live at 114 Derringham Park Road in West Hampstead.'

'So you live in the house next door to where Mr Darsha was found?'

'That's right; I live in the flat on the ground floor of the converted house. Mr Darsha's flat was next door and upstairs from mine.'

'Thank you Miss Smallwood. I wonder whether you could explain to the court exactly what you heard in the early hours of 16th October.'

'I had a friend staying and we ate at about eight-thirty. We then watched a film in the sitting room and went to bed.'

'So what time would that have been?'

'Oh, I think about midnight. My friend slept in the bedroom at the front of the house and I was in my room which is towards the back.'

'Go on.'

'I was woken by loud screaming followed by several terrible crashes. I looked at my clock and it was one-fifteen in the morning. I went to see my friend at the other end of the flat but she was fast asleep. When I returned to my room I heard voices, people shouting. It was quite muffled.'

'Could you tell what sex the voices were?'

'Definitely two male and I think one female. Some of the screams were definitely female...'

'So, you think there were two men and one woman?'

'Yes.'

'Good. Thank you. What happened next? Did the screaming continue?'

'I was not able to sleep; the sounds were still very loud. The crashing continued and there was a dragging sound. Like something heavy being moved.'

'How long did the sounds last, Miss Smallwood?'

'Oh, I should think for about an hour. Then things went quiet. I was going to call the police but these things do happen in our area whether on the streets or in people's houses. I thought they wouldn't be interested.'

'The female screams continued through this time?'

'Yes, I think so. I was tired. I put a pillow over my head.'

My mind wandered as Bob asked more questions. I noticed there were six men and six women on the jury. A lucky split perhaps. If juries were random how did they make sure the split of the sexes was equal? It got me thinking because in life when things look unplanned it is often the case that they actually have been.

I was helped back on track by Bob interrupting the witness.

'You heard three people in the flat and the sounds came from all of them during the disturbance?'

'Yes, there were moans and lots of thuds but the screaming continued, yes.'

'Thank you Miss Smallwood. One further question, did you at any point hear anybody leave the flat next door?'

'No. I just heard the screaming and then it went quiet. I must have fallen asleep once it had quietened down I guess. I'd had a busy day.'

'Thank you, no further questions My Lord,' Bob said and sat down with his gown puffing out.

Eleanor sat still. I noticed the jury looking at her. They were getting the hang of the procedure. Eventually she stood up. She looked like she was on a roll after the success of Darsha's brother.

'Yes, Miss Smallwood. You say you live on the ground floor and Mr Darsha's flat is upstairs.'

'Yes, that's correct,' the witness said with increasing confidence.

'Do you normally hear noises from the next-door flats?'

'Not usually, the flat next door is normally quiet.'

'The walls between the flats are quite thick wouldn't you say?'

'I don't know. I suppose so.'

'How could you be certain there were three people and specifically two men and one woman if the walls were thick and they were upstairs and you were down?' Eleanor increased the sternness in her voice.

'That's what it sounded like. Three people. I suppose it could have been two or four but it sounded like three; definitely one woman through.'

'And how can you be sure of that?'

'I think we would all recognise a women's scream, don't you? It was unmistakable each time I heard it. It sounded terrible.'

'And you didn't want to call the police? It sounds like you should have?'

'I didn't think I suppose, I regret it now of course. I watched as the body left the flat. It's terrible I could have heard him being killed.'

'I bet you do. I put it to you that there is no way on earth you could have known who was in this flat that morning. Thank you Miss Smallwood,' said Eleanor as she sat down.

Well that wasn't much bloody good was it I thought, as the judge thanked the witness who left with a scamper. Not much questioning on my behalf. I stared as the witness went past.

'A good time for lunch I think,' the judge said as everyone stood. He went flying out via his side door. I felt a grip on my arm; back to my cell for lunch. I wonder what it would be; steak or poached salmon perhaps? I gave an ironic chuckle as I was escorted down the stairs.

The afternoon was taken up by a cross examination of the policeman who arrested me down in Exeter. He looked young and nervous. I hadn't been concentrating so I missed his name. He was asked questions about my arrest a few months after the murder. I had been picked up at the house I was staying at whilst I worked in a local coffee shop – the only work I could find in the area. They took me to the local police station and interviewed me about Kumara and where I thought Yamin had gone. I don't know how they traced me because Yamin took my mobile phone. Either way I was taken to London.

This was the first part of the trial which was personal to me. The policeman was asked to go through the statement I had made and what kind of suspect I was. Did I cooperate? Did I resist? I had made claims of being mistreated during the first two days of arrest. They had been rough with me and I had put this in my account.

I had told the truth in my statement. Kumara had been too drunk to get home that night. I was trying to be helpful that was all. Bob made references to the obvious. He insisted I went back to Kumara's flat for sexual reasons, to gain favour with my boss. My defence was based around being helpful, but the prosecution were looking for something else.

I can still see Yamin's burning eyes. I have recounted this over and over again; was he jealous of Kumara having found out I was there? I suspect I will be asked this when it is my turn to stand in that wooden box. I suspect the fact that I couldn't remember anything after being pushed down the stairs would go down rather badly.

As the policeman went on I thought about Papa in Belarus. I still worried about him. How I longed to be with him again, away from here. The clerk stood and said the 'all rise' thing. The court soon emptied. I was left with my guard, having let the afternoon wash through me. When it is you they are talking about the court is a very different place. You feel like an animal in the zoo - people stare, ridicule your ways and would poke a stick at you if they could. They stay with you for a while but the conclusion was always the same, after a while people tire of you and seek out the next curiosity in another cage.

I went back to prison in my private van. I was tired and knew the difficult part of the trial had not yet started.

R. v. Maria Kayakova

Day Three

When everything settled, Bob McOmish waited for several seconds then stood slowly.

'My Lord, I would like to turn to the nature of Mr Darsha's injuries. We have all heard accounts of what happened that night but I think it is time we took a look at some facts, the details of the injuries inflicted on the victim during this prolonged and vicious attack.'

'I would like to call Dr Battersby-Sykes. He was the pathologist engaged to assist with this case.'

There was a sound from the back and a short man wandered to the witness box. He wore what looked like somebody else's grey woollen suit and his nose supported little round glasses. He couldn't have carried off the learned doctor look any better; looking like he was going to a medically themed fancy-dress party as a chaotic but hugely experienced medic.

Once sworn in and credentials read out, the court understood he was a pathologist and not a party-going charlatan. Bob McOmish stood again.

'Good morning, Dr Battersby-Skyes.'

'Please, just Dr Skyes, that is the name I use most of the time,' the witness had a low, authoritative voice.

'Of course; for the court perhaps you could explain your involvement in this case.'

'I was asked to perform the autopsy on Mr Darsha,' he said with a hint of derision.

'Very good,' Bob said in a condescending manner.

'Dr Sykes, I want to focus on the injuries inflicted on the victim. Perhaps we could start with a description of what caused his death.'

Bob turned slightly to face the jury.

'Members of the jury I would ask you to turn to section four of your jury packs where you will find photographs and computer images relating to this issue.'

Once again I sat there not being able to look at the images and join in. I could not remember much about that night and would have been interested to see just what Yamin had done.

Dr Sykes had his own notes and ordered them with a rustle as the jury sorted out their paperwork. Bob lifted his arm when Dr Sykes was ready.

'Mr Darsha died between the hours of 2 a.m. and 4 a.m. on the morning of 16th October last year. This is as precise as I can be, given the length of time from discovery to autopsy. He died from multiple injuries sustained to the upper half of his body, most notably severe and numerous head injuries undoubtedly received from a heavy, blunt instrument.'

Dr Sykes spoke like he was reading from a shopping list. He did this every day. I looked at the jury and the reaction to the description was somewhat different. They all looked uncomfortable, some looked horrified.

'After examination, was it clear the victim had been subjected to a significant amount of physical abuse in the period that led up to his death?'

'Yes, in my experience any one of approximately twelve blows to the head would have rendered the victim unconscious. When you add them together it is not surprising he died. Then of course there was the chest.'

'Please go on, Dr Sykes.'

'Further examination of the torso provided quite an unusual finding. When I say unusual, that is in the context of my industry, not in normal society of course. In society this is extremely rare.' Dr Sykes said and chuckled to himself. It was remarkable how light-hearted he was whilst discussing something that could hardly have been any more serious.

'I observed what we call a flail chest. Every single one of his ribs had been broken in at least two places. Some of the larger ribs had been broken three times. His rib cage had become detached from the chest wall.'

There was a collective gasp from both the jury and some other members of the court.

'I think this would be a good point to look at some of the images in our packs. Jury please could you turn to page two in section four in your files,' Bob said, jumping on the emotion of the moment to really drive home this point.

I could see the horror on the faces of the jury as Bob led Dr Sykes through each of the images in front of them. Dr Sykes described bruises and cuts, broken bones and blood loss in his low but jolly voice.

'The thing about a flail chest is that it renders the victim unable to breathe normally. This incapacity is a matter of the chest not being able to operate in a normal way. The ambient pressure in comparison to the pressure inside the lungs causes what we call a paradoxical motion. There is a huge increase in effort to breathe and it is incredibly painful.'

Dr Sykes put his hands together, linking his fingers.

'A flail chest is invariably accompanied by pulmonary contusion, bruising to the lungs and loss of oxygenation. In this case one of the broken ribs punctured the pleural sac which caused pneumothorax. Put very simply, it is very hard to inflate a popped balloon.'

The jury seemed shocked by this analogy. Dr Sykes had used a great deal of clinical information to describe the condition but the truth was that Kumara was beaten so badly his lungs stopped working. Bob let the gravity of the situation sink in before continuing.

'Thank you, Dr Sykes. In your opinion how did these injuries come about? What kind of force would you need to do this?'

'The most obvious cause was deliberate blunt trauma. I see a number of cases with extensive thoracic trauma but very few have a flail chest. A significant force needs to be applied over a large area of the chest. My conclusion was that the victim suffered significant trauma once he was unconscious.'

'What brought you to that conclusion?'

'Well it is my opinion that he received the injuries to his arms and head, all of which are consistent with being punched or hit. The bruises to the upper arms are particularly interesting; like they were made by a pipe or stick of some kind. The chest injuries are likely to come from stamping or heavy objects being dropped on the victim. In my professional opinion stamping once unconscious is the most likely explanation.

The judge must have thought the jury were green enough when he called for a break. Bob thanked Dr Sykes and suggested he came back after the break to discuss more of the autopsy. I was asked to remain in the dock.

Suitably refreshed and with queasiness decanted, the jury came back in. I caught a whiff of cigarette smoke as one member walked by. He was the little chap who looked like a builder. I wonder whether his business would survive the trial, I hoped so; he looked so sweet and out of his depth.

'Mr McOmish?'

'Thank you, My Lord. I would like to turn to some other findings from the autopsy of Mr Kumara Darsha. Dr Sykes, perhaps you could continue?'

'I would like to turn to the analysis we conducted of the victim's blood, other fluids and other pathological checks we do on the internal anatomy.'

'I have described the lungs and tissue in the chest but it is also worth noting that he suffered internal bruising to his liver, kidneys and stomach. One conclusion I am capable of coming to is that, due to the sheer number of injuries inflicted, this assault must have happened over a reasonably long period of time.'

'Or by more than one person?' Bob said jumping in. Eleanor shot a quick glance at Bob and then at the judge but remained silent.

'Yes indeed. That is certainly possible,' Dr Sykes said in a matter of fact way before continuing.

'The other point about this bruising and bleeding internally is that it allows us to estimate the length of time of the attack before death.'

'So that is?'

'I would say between one and one-and-a-half hours.'

The jury members looked at each other in surprise. Were Yamin and I in the flat for that long?

Bob let the jury murmur die down before continuing.

'Just to be clear, the victim died between two and three in the morning and was *tortured* for around one and a half hours?' said Bob, dwelling on the new verb with care.

'In my opinion yes, that's right.'

'We know Yamin arrived at the flat at around one a.m. so if the attack commenced soon after he arrived that would tally wouldn't it?'

'Yes it would.'

'Very good Dr Sykes, please continue.'

'I would like to turn to the analysis of the victim's blood. This is normal procedure during an autopsy where we check for levels of any stimulants which may have been in the system when the victim died. I would like to comment on the volume of alcohol I found in the blood. His Blood Alcohol Content was 0.24. This represents, in modern parlance, over three times the legal amount for driving a car.'

There was a whisper through the jury – I had no idea what this meant in the UK – the rules in Belarus were a little less specific.

'The alcohol levels alone would have slowed down the responses of the victim but it is hard to say just how much because it also depends how used to drinking he was. I did examine his liver and this showed no signs of cirrhosis.'

'The defendant has pointed out in her statements that both she and the victim had been drinking heavily that night so there is no contention there I feel.' Bob said looking at Eleanor. She didn't meet his eyes.

'I conducted further analysis of the blood and found something very interesting, very interesting indeed.'

The judge stopped writing and looked up at the witness.

'Dr Sykes, I would appreciate if you could concentrate on delivering your autopsy findings without too much artistic licence or delay, we do have a great deal to get through.'

'Yes, of course My Lord. Well you see the blood sample contained a significant amount of Jatamansi.'

Everybody looked blank. What did he say?

'Sorry. *Nardostachys Jatamansi* in Latin, common name Musk Root or Indian Spikenard. This is a herb which originates in the foothills of the Himalayas and is used for many applications including promotion of appetite and digestion, treating epilepsy but most notably as a strong sedative. In small doses it can be used as a reproductive stimulant.

The judge flicked another glance at the witness.

'Sorry. It is most unusual. I have only seen it a couple of times in twenty years.'

'Can you tell how this drug was administered Dr Sykes?'

'Well it is produced as oil from the root and leaves of the herb. It can then be concentrated to a degree. The amount I found was high, so I suspect it was taken orally within six or so hours of death. Perhaps longer if the concentration was higher.'

'So Kumara Darsha was drugged the night he died?'

'Well I cannot tell you who administered the drug but I see it as very unlikely that he would have taken this amount of it by himself. The quantity was only ever going to slow him down. Given the amount of alcohol he had taken as well, it is a wonder how he got up his stairs to be honest.'

'Dr Sykes could you talk a little more about this drug; where did you say it came from?'

'It originated in the Himalayas but we have seen reports that it can be grown more locally – it needs altitude to flourish however. It is not very easy to get hold of you know.'

'Does it taste of anything? You said the likely ingestion was oral; with a strong drink perhaps?'

'I recall the taste as bitter and I believe it is hard to emulsify with water, much better in alcohol.'

'Thank you, Dr Sykes, I think I will leave it there.' Bob looked over to Eleanor to see whether she wanted to examine the witness. She stood.

'Thank you, My Lord. Dr Sykes perhaps I could ask you one question.

'Of course.'

'You mentioned this drug can be used as a sexual stimulant and it is quite possible Kumara Darsha could have indigested it himself.'

Dr Sykes looked at Eleanor for a few seconds.

'Yes, I think that is correct. That is possible yes.'

'So, Maria Kayakova quite possibly had nothing to do with any of this given his intention to sleep with my client? Given his weakened state he could have got the dose wrong?'

'Yes, I suppose so.'

'Thank you, Dr Sykes.'

Eleanor was pleased with herself and had a half smile as she turned to me.

'I think that would be a good place to pause for lunch. I would like to talk to counsel,' the judge said. His mind was clearly on food. 'I know it's a little early but you have had a great deal of technical information to absorb.'

The usher got the jury to leave the court. It had been an interesting morning all in all. All that medical chat had left me hungry.

After lunch a young woman turned up in the witness box; Mrs Becky Haversham. She was in her twenties and as thin as a pole. Her bottom was tightly packed into a smart dark blue skirt which looked borderline inappropriate for court. I saw all the jury members look down at her lower half as she walked past – a difference of opinion clearly split the jury. Tart? - the men thought. Tart! - thought the women.

Once the skirt had been lowered to an acceptable resting position, the court was ready to begin. Who was this woman? What could she have to do with this trial? She couldn't have been more than twenty-five. After she was sworn in, Bob stood to help us with the conundrum.

'Good afternoon, Mrs Haversham. Perhaps you could help the court by explaining who you are and what role you had in this investigation,'

'Yes, good afternoon. My name is Rebecca Haversham and I work for the Metropolitan Police as a Blood Pattern Analyst,' she said in a confident voice which matched her tight skirt.

'Would you please explain what that role involves?'

'Certainly. We operate within a specialist branch of Forensics and we are capable of determining actions and timings as a result of bloodshed. For example, we are able to show where any bloodshed occurred, the nature of the instruments used to cause bloodshed and the movements of individuals during it. We also examine bloodstain patterns and the way in which blood is transferred onto objects like walls and carpets.'

'Very good, thank you. Members of the jury please turn to section seven of your packs. This shows various images of the flat where the victim died. Mrs Haversham will be able to help us to explain what we are looking at.'

'Mrs Haversham, perhaps you could run through your analysis of this case.'

'Well, yes. The first few photographs show the flat stairs and the hallway which runs to the kitchen at the back of the flat. I conducted forensic tests on the carpets and walls in these areas on 17th October. I found what we call passive bloodstains on the carpets on the stairs and in the hallway; towards the kitchen door side of the hall I found drip patterns and a pool pattern– indicating the victim would have dripped blood there and had rested there for some time.'

'On the walls of the hall, I think here in image four.'

Becky was pointing at her copy of the photo pack.

'Yes, this is our first glimpse of what we call MVIS, Medium Velocity Impact Spatter.'

'Mrs Haversham, could you explain that in simple terms?'

'Sorry, yes,' she gave a nervous giggle. 'This tries to assess the type of force that would have caused the blood to spatter in this particular way. Medium refers to the likely force of the blow the victim received. From my analysis, I suspect this is where the incident started.'

The jury looked engrossed with this witness. I for one did not realise this kind of analysis actually existed. Imagine doing that for a living. I expect it went some way to explaining the shortness of her skirt, she spent all day bagged up in a white forensic suit after all…

'Do go on, Mrs Haversham.' Bob looked amazed as well.

'I also found some evidence of expiratory blood on the carpet in the hall by the bedroom doorway. This is blood that is blown out through the nose or mouth from a victim. It is probable he hit the floor here I would conclude.'

'There is a high degree of possibility the victim was dragged into the bedroom from here as there was a quantity of flow pattern on the floor into the first bedroom. The mattress in this bedroom was covered in deep blood stains so I suspect this is where the majority of the attack took place. There was evidence of HVIS, high velocity spatters on the walls by the mattress and also significant pool patterns on the mattress itself. The direction of travel analysis on the walls would indicate the victim was lying on the mattress when the high velocity blows were inflicted.'

'So, to be clear, you determined the attack was conducted in the hall and the first bedroom. For the jury's benefit this is the room off the hall to the right of the stairs,' Bob said trying to clarify the situation.

'Yes, that's correct. We did find some bloodstains and spatter in the kitchen but this was probably because the victim's body was found there. Most of the kitchen blood was soaked into the carpet and exhibited swipe patterns with a feathered edge, indicating a dragging motion through the kitchen.'

Becky Haversham went on to explain other parts of her findings but I was rapidly losing interest. She was so young standing there in the witness box, it made me think about her parents and whether they were proud of the career she had chosen. I thought about my father. He would be sitting at home no doubt drinking himself into a late afternoon haze. I wondered whether he was lonely all on his own. He would certainly be worried about me but as far as he was concerned all was going well and I was enjoying London. How wrong could he be? I missed him and should never have left. I suddenly felt claustrophobic. The court was stuffy this afternoon; they had got the heating all wrong. I was drifting fast, feeling a warm glow of the past filling my veins.

'I am concerned about you my child; I worry that you are going to be alright. You are leaving here tomorrow and your father is longing to see you. I shall miss you so much, my darling, but it's time you went home.'

Maria put her arm around her grandmother and hugged tightly.

'I am so sad you never met your mother Maria. She was a special woman, really special. You would have got on wonderfully.'

Maria looked into her eyes as the last few words were overflowing with emotion.

'*What was she like? Tell me about her?*'

'*Oh, she was pretty, like you. She loved your father with all her heart. She was funny but also sensitive. She was kind.*'

'*I killed her. I killed her when I was born. It was all my fault, I wish I had died, not her.*

'*Stop it child, it is time to go to bed. Come on.*'

Maria was picked up and carried back to the house as duty overtook emotion. Tarkan zigzagged behind them only a few yards behind.

Maria was asleep in her grandmother's arms by the time they got to the top of the stairs.

'Let's stop there. I think a few people are starting to falter,' said the judge as he scanned the court.

'Shall we say ten o'clock tomorrow morning?'

The usher showed the jury out and I was led back to the cells. I must have missed the end of Becky's speech because she was no longer in the court as I departed.

R. v. Maria Kayakova

Day Four

The squishing sound of a working man's stout shoes grew louder from the back of the court. I looked around and saw a proud, tall man with no hair walk towards the witness box. I recognised him straight away. This was the detective in charge of the investigation. I had met him several times during the interview process. He had been there when I gave my statements and he had asked many questions over a number of days.

When he reached the witness box the usher helped him get sworn in. He looked like a man who had done this many times before. His height made him ungainly so he had to stoop slightly to fit into the rather comedic wooden frame around the box. It was probably built a few hundred years ago and at the time not many fully grown men, I suspect, were six foot six.

'Good morning to you. Perhaps you could explain to the court who you are and your role in this case?'

'Yes, good morning to you too. Good morning My Lord!'

This guy was good. He was assured and very relaxed. I suspect Bob had saved the best until last.

'D.C.I. Blindman. I work in the serious crime unit in the Metropolitan Police,' said the witness in a rich, low tone.

'Is it correct that you are the senior investigating officer in this case?'

'Yes, that is correct.'

'I want to discuss what you found at the flat on the day in question and also some of the events which led up to Maria Kayakova and Kumara Darsha being in the flat together. I will come on to those once I have asked you about the nature of her arrest and her attitude through this process.'

'Yes of course.'

'We managed to pick up Maria Kayakova from an analysis of mobile phone records. She had called Kumara Darsha the day before his death to explain she would be late for work. She had been of interest to us after interviews conducted with other members of Kumara's staff. They had all said he was drinking at the bar with her that evening.'

'The phone she had used to call Darsha was never recovered. However, we were able to collect information from other members and former members of his staff. Mobile phone records picked up her new number down at Exeter in Devon and we were able to track her down working in a coffee shop near the cathedral. After talking to her in the shop she came with us to the local police station.'

'Did she resist in any way?' said Bob.

Blindman held his finger to his mouth for a few seconds. Eleanor looked up at him from her bench.

'Not really. I think she had a little trouble with some of the local dialect of my colleagues from Devon & Cornwall but apart from that she was happy to assist us with our enquiries.'

'Go on, D.C.I. Blindman.'

'The defendant claims Kumara Darsha wanted to have sex with her and this is the reason he stayed out with her and got her drunk. She claims she didn't want to put her job in jeopardy by being rude to him, so she agreed to stay out with him.'

'We will cover this when the defendant stands where you are now, I'm sure. What else was discussed on the journey to London?' Bob asked, trying to keep the policeman on track.

'She admitted being with him in the flat when he was attacked but claimed she knew nothing of the incident beyond her boyfriend turning up unexpectedly,' Blindman said. He paused and shifted his weight to the other leg.

'She claims her boyfriend must have hit her as all she remembered of the evening was being in the flat with Kumara one minute, then down at the bottom of the stairs the next. The rest of the evening she does not recall.'

'Thank you, D.C.I. Blindman. Perhaps we could move on to what you and your colleagues found when your officers first entered the flat.'

'My colleagues got the call that Kumara Darsha could not be located at around ten in the morning on the 17th October. Officers helped his family try to locate him but this proved to be fruitless. His mobile was not being answered and his flat was locked with the curtains closed. They then took the decision to enter his flat by force.'

'Two officers broke the door down and were immediately alerted to a strong smell of gas. One officer ran up the stairs and tried to locate the whereabouts of the gas meter in an attempt to close off the supply. Fortunately, this proved straightforward as it was located in a cupboard in the hall.'

'Once the gas supply had been switched off the officer called his colleague up the stairs and they both proceeded into the kitchen to open some windows.'

'The gas was left on?' Bob said with dramatic surprise.

'That's correct.'

Bob looked at his notes.

'Were there any signs of disturbance on the stairs or in the hallway?' Bob asked. He must have wanted Blindman to go slower. This was the important bit and it needed a build-up.

'My officers did find a shoe and a broken pair of spectacles on the stairs and in the hall.'

'Members of the jury these items have been bagged-up and are being shown to you now. My Lord, photographs of exhibits one and two are featured at page forty-eight of My Lord's bundle.'

The shoe and glasses did their rounds and each jury member studied them closely. From where I was sitting they looked like an old trainer and trodden-on pair of specs.

'Thank you D.C.I. Blindman, please carry on.'

'The two officers went from the hall and into the kitchen and this is where they found Kumara Darsha. He was lying with his head against the fire escape door. He had his hands tied behind his back and his feet were bound together.'

'What did your officers do about the smell of gas?' Bob said

'In situations like this the police need to make sure they do not interfere with anything that could be used in the investigation, so all the kitchen windows were opened once the oven had been turned off. The front door had been smashed and left open because of the force used so the gas odour dissipated reasonably quickly.'

'My men decided to call in specialist units and a crime scene was launched.'

'Members of the jury, if you could look at section three of your packs. There are images there of the flat as it was found that morning. Image four shows Mr Darsha in the position he was found. My Lord, at page fifty in My Lord's bundle. '

The jury shuffled papers and the judge turned his pages. All were engrossed in looking at the dead body – obviously more interesting than an old shoe – as Blindman spent a few more minutes explaining what Kumara was wearing and some of the obvious injuries he had.

'D.C.I. Blindman, did your team find anything else in the kitchen that morning? Anything that could be linked with this crime?'

'Very little actually, the flat was sparsely decorated and had little furniture. There was a broken chair lying by the table with one leg missing. Some glasses on the table, that was about all.'

'Did you recover the chair leg from the flat?'

'No sir, we looked but it was not there. The other rooms were bedrooms of sorts with mattresses on the floor and one or two items of clothing in cupboards. As I say the flat had basic decoration so it didn't take long to look.'

'Thank you D.C.I. Blindman,' Bob said as he sat down. He looked over to Eleanor who stood. She straightened her notes and looked at the witness for a few seconds. Blindman shifted in the box.

Good morning Detective Chief Inspector. I would like to ask how you were able to place my client in the flat that evening?'

Blindman looked at her with a frown.

'She told us she was there.'

The jury gave a murmur of light-heartedness but this was quickly stifled.

'Yes D.C.I. Blindman we are all aware of that. Was any forensic work carried out beyond the blood spatter analysis?'

'Yes of course. The team were able to put the defendant and the victim in the flat that evening from DNA found on both glasses in the kitchen.'

'Was there any evidence of the sedative the pathologist discussed?'

'No, ma'am. Both glasses contained trace elements of whisky; that was all.'

'So I can assume you have no evidence that the victim ingested the sedative found in his bloodstream at his flat?'

'That is correct.'

Thank you D.C.I. Blindman.'

Eleanor spent the next thirty minutes asking questions about my arrest paying attention to the collection of mobile phone data. Without the papers in front of me it was very hard to follow.

When Eleanor sat down the judge said he wanted to speak with the barristers in private, so he called a halt to morning proceedings. He seemed to be permanently hungry.

'We'll start again at two fifteen.'

The court stood and he left through his favourite door, back to his chambers.

Robert McOmish and Eleanor Sechford-Jones stood by the big wooden door on the main corridor which ran the entire length of the Old Bailey. Eleanor lifted her hand to knock and noticed the gold leaf sign on the door.

His Honour Judge Oliver Barniston QC

One day she thought, one day.

'Come in.'

Both barristers entered, marvelling at the quality of the artwork on the burgundy red walls. They smelt the air as they walked in. It had the aroma of intelligence, like any library. There was a long corridor of about fifteen feet with pictures all over it. To the left was a door to another room inside the chambers itself. Perhaps it was a bathroom or even a place to sleep. Eleanor could not believe the size of the chambers, it was like a flat she used to share in Fulham.

Oliver Barniston stood up as he saw Eleanor and Robert walking towards his giant wooden desk. It was covered in papers and must have been ten feet wide.

'I'm glad you could join me for lunch,' said the judge. He looked up at a clock on the wall. It was five minutes to one o'clock.

'We'd better get going, you know what they are like if you are late.'

Eleanor looked at all the law books on three of the walls in the inner chamber.

'These chambers are much larger than you realise,' she said looking back at the judge.

'Got your eye on this one have you?' asked the judge with a smile.

Eleanor could feel herself blush as the judge swept over to her. He placed his hand on her lower back.

'Come on, let's go and have some lunch.' Barniston whispered something into Robert McOmish's ear and they both chuckled to themselves.

All the Old Bailey judges have lunch together whether they are sitting on trials or not. It is an institution and has a very strict duration. Judges and their guests arrive at five minutes past one o'clock and all of them will have been fed and watered by two o'clock sharp. During this short time three courses are served which would not look out of place in a decent restaurant. Guests are offered wine with their lunch and most accepted. Everybody is served at the table and the staff ran the service like a military operation.

Oliver, Robert and Eleanor walked into the dining room which was already full of judges in their robes together with other civilian or legal guests. Judge Barniston had a custom. He always asked the two senior barristers from both sides of a trial to come to lunch with him at some point during the case. He used the opportunity to get to know them better, to understand their ambitions and interests. The trial itself was never discussed of course. Any comments the judge had to make in that regard would be done in chambers or in court.

'Thank you for letting us see this,' Eleanor said, kicking the conversation off.

'Well it's a pleasure; it is always nice to find out a little bit more about the people I work with,' said Oliver in reply.

'Tell me Eleanor, what have you done in your career so far?'

Oliver and Robert both turned to look at her.

'I have been lead in twelve trials now and this is the second time I have defended at the Old Bailey. I have been involved in quite a number of technical cases involving kidnap and torture but this is my first murder trial,' Eleanor said feeling the intensity of two pairs of eyes.

'Well it is hard to tell it is your first murder trial – you seem well composed. So what would you like to do in the future?' Oliver said taking a glass of white wine off the tray of a passing waiter.

'I would like to think I could be a judge at some stage, I haven't really thought about it.'

'Really? I find that hard to believe, I heard you have planned every part of your career so far,' Robert jumped in with a quick swipe.

'I would much prefer to carry on doing my current job and get a few victories under my belt,' Eleanor said looking directly at Robert. They both took a sip of the water they had taken off the tray.

'Shall we sit down?' Oliver raised his hand as a gong was struck softly in the corner of the room.

Everybody stopped talking at the sound of the gong and with silent determination they all turned and headed to the long tables further down the room. These were organised like a piece of railway track, about fifty feet long with places laid all the way around them. The glass sparkled and the silver cutlery shone under the light of the big chandeliers which ran down the length of the ceiling.

Soon everybody was sitting down and the conversations started again. Eleanor found herself next to another judge in robes of different colour to those of Oliver. She noticed Robert had a barrister next to him – bad luck, she thought, no upwardly slanting networking for you.

Oliver asked more questions to Robert and Eleanor over lunch. He seemed keen to focus on Eleanor's ambitions more than anything. Eleanor was happy to answer them over a light-hearted lunch but felt slightly awkward that Robert was listening in too. It was nothing to do with him.

Coffee was served with most people accepting a cup to stimulate them for an afternoon of heavy law. Eleanor saw Robert whisper something in Oliver's ear. Oliver nodded and Robert stood, spoke to his neighbour and announced that he had to do a little more preparation for the afternoon and he would have to leave lunch a little early. Eleanor nodded courteously and Robert made his way out of the room.

Once Robert had gone Oliver turned to face Eleanor directly. He had very cleverly placed himself on the corner of the long table they sat at.

'It is very important you have sponsors through your career, you do know that don't you?' Oliver said when Robert was out of earshot. There was still plenty of chat around the table so Oliver knew nobody would be listening.

'Yes, I have been trying to network with as many people as possible but it seems to me it is very difficult to find people you can actually trust. There are too many egos and not enough people interested in the future of the profession,' Eleanor said looking in the direction of Robert. Oliver seemed to get the hint.

'Well we haven't got time now as we are due back in court in five minutes. Why don't you come down to my chambers at 5.30pm and we can talk about this some more. I think I could help you out you know,' Oliver said with all the innocence he could muster.

'Really? Thank you, I would like that.'

'That's a date then,' Oliver said as he stood up. He ran his hand under his bottom to release his gown. It billowed up like he was standing over an air vent. As he turned he put his other hand down next to Eleanor's. They did not touch but she could feel the warmth coming from it. Oliver bent down and got close to her hair.

'I'll see you later then,' Oliver said in a whisper. Eleanor felt her hair ruffle from his breath.

He flew off like a vampire late for a party. Other judges from around the room were doing the same. Lunch had lasted for exactly fifty-two minutes.

Eleanor sat there watching the bat display with plenty on her mind. The outcome from lunch felt marginally inappropriate.

I climbed back up the stairs to my place in the dock. The judge and the barristers were in position when I arrived. Eleanor had suggested I used an interpreter for the next part of the trial – Bob McOmish was going to draw the prosecution's case to a close and she wanted the jury to think I was taking this seriously.

The jury filed in and Bob stood, ready to begin. He looked keen to get on, fired up almost. He looked at me directly.

Aimlessly I looked around the court as Bob reminded the jury of the places, times and people involved in the case. I lost interest during the summary – I was keen to hear Eleanor, to get on to the pieces we have rehearsed. This was the hardest part of the day for me, post lunch I found it very hard to concentrate on what was happening.

'You have heard from the victim's daughter Meniki Darsha via video link who told you about what a loving and caring father Kumara was. She told you she was unable to contact him the morning he was found.'

'Next we had the victim's brother Amal Darsha who told us more about Kumara's business activities. Now you must decide as to whether Mr Darsha is a credible witness having listened to some of the questions my colleague put to him,' Bob said, shooting a glance at Eleanor and again a frosty competitiveness had developed between them. Eleanor looked back at him with equal keenness.

'Amal Darsha told us Kumara was a happy, successful businessman who was liked in the community. On the lookout for a bargain perhaps, but he had no enemies.'

'We heard from the next-door neighbour, Helen Smallwood, who mentioned she and a friend had listened to screams and banging which went on for about an hour. Following that there were moans and thuds and continued screaming. There were male and female voices according to Miss Smallwood.'

'PC Donaldson spoke about the arrest of Maria Kayakova down in Exeter. We looked at some of the cell site analysis to show you the pattern of mobile phone use over the period when Kumara died. There was evidence to suggest Maria Kayakova had been in contact with her boyfriend Yamin that night as well as with Kumara Darsha. What conclusion you draw from that communication is your decision.'

'We continued with two witnesses who helped us set out the medical position, first we had Dr Battersby-Sykes, the pathologist asked to perform the autopsy. He explained how Kumara had died, going into detail about the injuries he suffered. He let us know the victim had been drugged with a rare organic compound which originates from the Himalayas.'

'Mrs Becky Haversham took us through the interior of the flat and the state it was in after this crime had been committed. She explained how her work into blood patterns can be used to determine what happened to Kumara that evening.'

'Finally, we listened to D.C.I. Blindman this morning. He is the senior investigating officer in this case. He told us about the time-line from the crime to the point of discovery and also told us about the gas supply being left on. Again, the significance of this you must decide.'

'So, there we have it ladies and gentlemen. I would like to leave the case for the prosecution there.'

Robert McOmish QC closed the file in front of him and sat down. I looked around to see what was next. Eleanor stayed seated.

'Members of the jury I would like to have a conference with counsel about a point of law and this may take some time. You have had a busy couple of days so go away and have some rest; I suggest we start the defence in the morning. Let's make a prompt start at 10.00am sharp,' He waved his hand in the direction of the usher and she immediately jumped to her feet. She helped the jury leave for the day.

Eleanor stood by the door she had been at only a few hours before. She looked at her watch - Five-thirty p.m. She was on time to the second as always and felt like a seventeen-year-old girl again. Prompt but panicky. What is wrong with you, she thought. You are a professional woman going to see a colleague. Pull yourself together. She knocked on the vast oak door.

No reply from inside.

Eleanor knocked again.

This time she heard a hurried hustle of papers and a muffled come in. She pushed through the large door and went down the now familiar corridor. Oliver Barniston, sitting behind his enormous desk, looked up at her as she approached.

'I'm looking forward to hearing your defence tomorrow Miss Sechford-Jones. Can I call you Eleanor?' he said in a low voice, which to Eleanor sounded normal, not the overbearing voice he used in court. In fact, without his wig, he looked much younger. It made her think just how ridiculous the wig wearing was. Just an attempt to make the defendant feel they were in the presence of an antediluvian patriarch.

'Can I?' Oliver repeated.

'Oh, sorry, yes of course.'

'In which case you must call me Oliver.'

'Ok. Oliver.'

Would you care for a drink? I have got a little whisky.'

Eleanor looked at his glass. If that was a small whisky, she couldn't imagine the size of the glass needed to accommodate a large one.

'Yes, ok. That would be lovely,' she replied. Talking about it made her notice a faint odour of whisky in the room; she wondered how long he had been drinking small whiskies that afternoon.

Oliver stood slowly and held the corner of his desk as he straightened himself.

'Ooh, my back; sitting down all day does it no good.'

Eleanor looked at him without his robes for the first time. He was thinner and certainly much younger than she would have guessed in court. Having never met him before the trial, he had been subject to her usual research process before the trial started. He had been a highflying QC for many years before becoming a judge. Being only fifty-two demonstrated just how successful he had been as a barrister – he had been called to be a judge at a very early age.

To Eleanor it looked like the desk was being held to counteract the influence of the whisky, not a bad back. Given the trial had finished early and the meeting with counsel had only taken thirty minutes he could well have been drinking in his chambers for a couple of hours.

Oliver walked over to a small table at the side of his chambers. It was covered with books and framed photographs. There were some of grown-up children but the largest showed a beautiful young woman with her hair up around her head, blowing freely in the wind. He took a glass and poured a good slug from the crystal decanter before bringing it over to the big table in the middle of the room.

'Come and sit down here,' he said, pulling an antique wooden chair out for her when the drink was on the table. As she sat Eleanor noticed a fraction had been spilt.

The table was covered with all manner of items. Legal papers were strewn all over it with the detritus from everyday life breaking up the theme. She could make out utility bills and unopened post in amongst the neatly ordered and bound legal papers. There were photographs on the table, again of loved ones but these had not been framed, just scattered around the place.

'It's a bit of a shambles I agree,' Oliver said breaking the silence.

'I'm sorry, forgive me.'

Oliver chuckled.

'It's OK, there is nothing sensitive here. It's just the accumulated junk of an old widower.'

Eleanor stared at him. That had not been in the research she had done.

'I'm sorry, I had no idea.'

'No idea I was messy or no idea my wife died?'

'The latter of course.'

Oliver chuckled again.

'I'm only teasing you,' Oliver said. He took a sip of whisky like he was steeling himself to talk about something painful.

'My darling died two years ago after a long battle. She used to do everything at home. You know, kept it looking great, fed the children. They have all left now and have flown off to university. I sold the house and bought a small flat in London. The kids can stay when they want to but of course they don't because Dad is boring and always busy.'

'I am sorry to hear that,' Eleanor said with genuine sympathy. This guy did have a softer side after all.

'Anyway, that's enough about me. I have been looking through your CV and your case history. Your career since leaving Oxford and Bar school has been very impressive. The top guys at Six Letterstone Court must be delighted with your contribution.'

Yes. Almost as impressive as yours, Eleanor thought as Oliver spoke. They both knew Six Letterstone Court was one of the harder chambers to enter. It had been the proudest moment of her life when she was offered pupillage there.

'I found when I was going through my career as a barrister that it was very important to build networks with the right people. The industry is so competitive, people do need a little help sometimes. Looking at your history and how you have performed in my court I do believe I can help you if your ambition is to be a judge. We are always on the lookout for the next wave of candidates who can make the grade.'

'That is very kind of you. I...'

'I am not sure it is kind, as I said it is imperative we find the right people to continue the judging profession. Not everybody has what we are looking for.'

Eleanor looked at Oliver for a few seconds. What did he mean exactly? There was something slightly macabre about the precision of his words.

'Well thank you. I appreciate your comments.'

'Top up?'

'Um, well only if you do.'

'Of course.'

Oliver stood and retrieved the whisky. He filled both glasses to higher than before and this time put the decanter on the table.

'I like your style Eleanor, I have to be careful discussing the current trial but I can say I like the way you conduct yourself. Robert is so harsh, so blunt. You have energy yes but grace is the key – that is what we need in this profession, more grace. You cannot teach that at Bar school.'

'To be honest I am not sure I picked a particularly good case this time, I would hate to ruin my record. When I took it Maria seemed so innocent, so vulnerable. She was wrapped up in her boyfriend and things got out of hand. I thought it would be easy to persuade the jury she was not guilty. You're right, Robert is bloody good in my view, doesn't give you an inch.'

'I bet he would give you a few inches if he could.'

Eleanor raised her eyebrows at the innuendo which had come from nowhere.

'Sorry, that was unnecessary. I think you will be OK; you have a chance to shine tomorrow. I'll look after you,' Oliver said in a lower voice. Eleanor looked into his eyes for a fraction too long.

There was an awkward pause.

'What do you do in your spare time Eleanor? Do you like opera, the theatre perhaps?'

Eleanor felt uncomfortable discussing her private life with work colleagues. She had devoted much of her life and certainly the majority of her adult life to the law. She only had a small group of close friends and had been unlucky with boyfriends. One or two through university and Bar school but nobody with the 'take him home to mother' quality. She always felt peculiar talking about it and often liked to invent a phantom boyfriend to terminate an awkward conversation. This time she would be honest, just as Oliver had been about his wife. She would respond with a question – a classic technique.

'I don't really get the chance to socialise as much as I would want. Do you like opera?'

'I hate it; all that squawked Italian and painful overacting. People like opera because they think they should like it. Very pretentious.'

'Well I am glad I didn't say yes then!'

The unease Eleanor felt at the start of their meeting dropped another notch as they both laughed. She was starting to like this old man.

'Tell me more about your wife. She looks very pretty.' Eleanor said, looking towards the photo on the table.

'She was the love of my life. She made me laugh and made me think. Most of the important decisions in my life were made by her. We met at Oxford and spent the next thirty odd years barely apart. She did law too but chose the corporate route – she was the one who earned the big money and paid the bills. She was formidable at work apparently – her colleagues called her The Tyrant!'

'Breast cancer you know. She had a terrible time towards the end. There was a lot of pain and a great deal of sadness for all of us. Such a waste. Just a…'

Oliver stopped abruptly. Eleanor could see he was upsetting himself. He tried to carry on but found the words too difficult. Eleanor put her hand on his to comfort him.

'I'm so sorry Oliver; it must have been terrible for you.'

Oliver gave a sniff and quickly wiped his eye. He was trying to regain his masculine side.

'Oh, thank you, I am sorry to burden you with this. It is a side of me very few people have seen. Sorry.'

'You are an amazing man and thank you for what you said earlier, I would be delighted if we stayed in touch with each other. I really must now be getting back to my case, I am a little underprepared for tomorrow.'

'Can you stay for one more drink?'

'No, thank you Oliver, I have had too much already. I am sure I will make some mistakes tomorrow because of this,' Eleanor said with a chuckle.

Eleanor stood and moved away from the table. Oliver mirrored her and followed her to the door.

'Thank you again,' Eleanor said.

She turned towards the door and placed her hand on the handle.

'Oh, just one more thing,' Oliver said.

Eleanor turned back.

'I would be grateful if you could keep our conversation to yourself,' Oliver said slipping back into judge-like mode.

Eleanor stepped towards Oliver keeping her eyes on him all the way. Oliver stood rooted to the spot. She stopped right in front of him still maintaining eye contact.

'Of course,' Eleanor said, placing her hand on Oliver's arm and standing on tiptoe to kiss him on his cheek.

'I must go,' Eleanor said taking a step backwards.

She tried to straighten her hair then turned back as she passed through the doorway. Oliver had gone back to his desk.

Eleanor closed the door and with a soft click it shut. Holding the handle for a few seconds she looked down at her feet. A broad smile broke out on her face. She turned and walked along the main corridor where all the judges kept their chambers. The smile lasted all the way to the exit.

R. v. Maria Kayakova

Day Five

This was my big day; my chance to shine.

Eleanor met me in my cell ahead of the ten o'clock start to run through what was going to happen. It was the start of the defence and a crucial part of the trial.

The barristers were in position, all beavering away with their boxes and files. The clerk stood and issued her customary 'All rise'. We stood and Oliver came zooming in at full speed, gown fluttering around behind him. He had a broad smile across his face.

For a couple of minutes we waited for the jury. I wondered where they came from; what sort of room did they meet in? Where did they all live? I had been remarkably selfish in my thoughts on the trial up to now – I hadn't given any consideration to what they must be feeling, what they were telling their loved ones. How quickly we all become self-centred when we are faced with danger. It is in danger the truly selfish thrive.

The jury settled down along the two benches and we were ready to start. I looked around with keen anticipation and this drew the attention of a couple of the women on the jury. They stared at me whilst the other jury members looked expectantly at the judge. Perhaps these two women could sense that I was excited by the prospect of listening to Eleanor.

'Good morning ladies and gentlemen; I do hope you are well rested. We have heard the case for the prosecution. Now it is time to hear the case for the defence. Before I ask Miss Sechford-Jones to start, can I please remind all of you to stay alert during proceedings; it is crucial you all concentrate throughout the day. If any of you feel you are unable to continue, please pass a note to me via the usher.'

I now understood part of the reason we stopped reasonably early yesterday – he must have seen one or more jurors drifting.

'Miss Sechford-Jones.'

'Thank you, My Lord,' Eleanor stood and gave a courteous smile to the judge who smiled back. My goodness, it was the first sign of normal human interaction from the judge. Unbelievable. Well done Eleanor, that's my girl.

'Today we focus on the woman you see before you in the dock. So far, my learned colleague for the prosecution has spent time running through the events of the night in question, the timings and opinions of witnesses. Now it is time to focus on Maria Kayakova.'

'Ladies and gentlemen, I want you to look at Maria sitting here in front of you. She is a twenty-year-old woman from Belarus. Her mother died when she was born and she has been raised by her devoted father. She was studying at the famous Belarus State University in Minsk then came to London to see the world with her boyfriend. She is hard working, intelligent and kind. She worked hard in Kumara's restaurant to provide some money for their stay whilst her boyfriend secured a job with the Russian Embassy. Together they were able to take a flat in West Hampstead.'

'We have heard Kumara was a good businessman. I suggest he used this acumen when he employed Maria – he recognised a talented, hard working woman and was delighted she wanted to work for him.'

'Before I ask Maria to take the stand, I need to tell you a little bit more of what was contained in Maria's statement. As I think all of you will realise, Maria does not deny the fact she was in the flat with Kumara when Yamin arrived. She had been working late at the restaurant and once the last guests had left Kumara offered her a drink at the bar. Kumara was very drunk by the time they finished and was, in Maria's judgement, unable to get home. Maria kindly made sure he did get home and up the steps to his flat. We will of course hear much more detail about what happened during that evening but it is crucial to understand that this defence is based around whether Maria was involved in the death of Kumara Darsha, not whether she was present at the time he died.'

'I will show you that Kumara did in fact want to have sex with Maria and these advances were made through the evening. We have heard the drug found in his blood can be used to promote sex drive. Maria did nothing to suggest she was interested in Kumara. She did have a few drinks with him, but it was always her intention to go home to Yamin. She kept him abreast of where she was and what was going on.'

'Now the person we would really like to talk to is, of course, Yamin. He fled the country after the incident. The police are clearly very keen to talk to him and are working with colleagues from Interpol in an attempt to trace him. Without him we have to look beyond what we can see and what we have heard. We need to use our common sense and ask what a normal person of good character would have done in such a situation. Maria had no reason to kill this man.'

I looked at the jury. They were transfixed with what Eleanor was saying. I felt uplifted when I heard her talk; it filled me with hope. Eleanor was much more gracious than Bob; he was hard and direct; she was softer, more personable. The jury seemed to respond well.

'I would like to ask Maria to take the stand. I think it is time you heard her side of the story. She has asked for an interpreter to stand with her in case there are any questions she cannot fully understand. I believe her English is good. Nevertheless, given the pressure of the situation My Lord has agreed to this arrangement.'

'My Lord, the defence calls Miss Maria Kayakova.'

The security guard stood and opened a small door at the side of the dock. As the wooden frame and the glass swung open, the guard nodded her head as a sign I should walk with her. I didn't have handcuffs on so I followed the guard to the witness box by the side of the jury. The red-headed interpreter had walked up from the benches at the back of the court and came to stand next to me when I reached the wooden witness box. The court looked different from here – the barristers faced me with more intimidation and I was just a couple of metres from the judge's bench. I could have reached out and touched the two members of the jury nearest the witness box.

The usher gave me the bible which shook as I read the script from the plasticised card placed on top of it. I had to stop and clear my throat to complete it. All present knew who I was but for the record I was asked by Eleanor to state my full name and the address in West Hampstead where Yamin and I had stayed before all of this.

'Good morning Miss Kayakova,' Eleanor was more formal than I expected. 'I would like to take you through the events of the night you had a drink with Kumara Darsha, the night when you helped him back to his flat. I would like to hear your version of events.'

The interpreter whispered the Russian translation into my left ear. I had understood the question perfectly well in English. When we sat down to plan the defence techniques, Eleanor had suggested we use an interpreter to give the jury an image of vulnerability, of a young girl lost in a foreign country. Perhaps this plan was childishly obvious but we decided to try it. I looked at the interpreter and asked her to say I understood.

'Yes, thank you. I understand,' the interpreter said with a Russian lilt to her voice.

I wondered how long we could keep this charade up. I looked at the interpreter again and told her to tell Eleanor I was happy to try and answer in English.

'I would like to answer in English,' she said to Eleanor.

'Of course, please Maria, when you are ready.'

'I was working late at the restaurant. It had been busy evening with many customers coming. All staff were tired but elated after a long and, err, happy session. There is a wonderful buzz in the restaurant when staff happy. I was standing by the bar making sure it was tidy when Kumara came up to me and offered me drink. It was approaching midnight and I wanted getting home to Yamin but given the happiness of the evening and mood in the restaurant I decided to accept. As he poured the first drink, I sent Yamin a text to tell him I was still in restaurant and he shouldn't worry.'

'Kumara seemed like he had already a couple of drinks. It was not unusual to see him in the restaurant during the serving. He often is speaking to friends or business associates at the bar.'

'What did you both drink Maria?' Eleanor said.

The interpreter stepped nearer and whispered the Russian equivalent. After a few seconds I looked back at Eleanor.

'I drank wine from bottle opened that evening and Kumara drank his rum. He likes a particular sort from the bottles at back of the bar. It was a very unusual brand, Pelican or something. Smell very strong. He told me he only one who like.'

'Did he pour the drinks for you both?'

Again, there was a pause for translation.

'Yes, he was gentleman; he poured the drinks all evening.'

'So how many drinks did you both have that night.'

'Oh, I suppose I had three large glasses of wine. Kumara drank about half the bottle of rum.'

'So Kumara was very drunk?'

'He seemed to be able to handle it through the night. I thought he must have been drinking before because he seemed to lose it just before we left.'

'Did you touch his drink at all that night?'

'No, he stayed at the bar all evening and I only went to toilet once. I call Yamin and left him message saying I was still at work and having a drink with my boss.'

'Now we have heard Kumara ingested some drugs that evening which could well have slowed him down; made him weaker than he would have been. Do you know anything about that?'

The interpreter took a little longer to explain and I didn't wait until she'd finished. I held my hand up to stop her.

'I know nothing of this. I had few drinks with him and made sure he got home safe. That was all. If he was drugged then this must have been happening before or after our drinks. Nothing happened when we were talking! Nothing!'

'Ok, ok Maria thank you. I ask you remain calm whilst we ask questions. We have to cover a lot of ground and some questions are going to feel intrusive.'

Madam Interpreter whispered in my ear as I took a couple of deep breaths. I flicked a glance towards Bob who was staring at me with such intensity that it made me look away immediately.

Eleanor broke the silence.

'What time did you leave the restaurant Maria?'

'I suppose it was around twelve-thirty. I have to say, looking at the clock was the last thing on my mind. Kumara needed a great deal of help getting out of the place. I had to bear his weight when we went through the door.'

'I managed to hail a cab and I asked driver to go to Kumara's address. It took us only a couple of minutes but I needed help, there was no way I could have walked him home.'

'You paid the taxi driver for the short journey and helped Kumara into his flat. Is that correct?'

'Yes, it took a couple of minutes to get up the stairs but then he seemed to have a second wind; is it perked up?'

'Do you think he pretended to be unable to get home himself so you had to help him? It seems odd a man can sober up so quickly?'

'I am not sure; I didn't think about it until he started asking me personal questions. You can tell when a man's interest changes. Back in his flat I think he thought I was easy target.'

'What did he do Maria?'

'He offered me another drink but I declined saying I had to get home. He insisted we had another drink. He started coming up close to me and at one point he touched my hair. I thought he wanted to have sex with me.'

'What happened next Maria?'

'That is when there was a knock on the door.'

'Let's get this clear, Kumara noticeably recovered and then started coming on to you?'

'That's right. He was interrupted by a knock on the door.'

'What happened then?'

'I went to answer the door. I looked through the little eye-hole and saw it was Yamin. My first thought was he had come to collect me. I didn't think about where I was or whether he knew I was there, you don't when you see a friendly face. Then I thought he was cross because I was in flat of another man.'

'Did Yamin get cross with you? Was he violent?'

'Yes, he did have a very bad temper sometimes. When he had been drinking he was particularly bad. He was often violent in bed.'

Oliver looked up from his notes.

'So you let him in?'

'Yes. I opened the door a little but he pushed on the door and forced me back.'

'Did he say anything to you as he went past?'

'He tried to but at that moment no words came out. He gets like that sometimes. Anyway he had a definite purpose, a drive beyond talking to me. I could see a fixed look in his eyes which didn't disguise his rage. I asked him why he was there but he couldn't answer.'

'Go on.'

'By the time I reached the top of the stairs Yamin had pushed Kumara to the floor. He was sitting on him, pushing his finger into his chest.'

'Did you try and intervene?'

'I shouted at him. I wanted to know why he was there. He did not know Kumara Darsha. He had no reason to be angry with him.' My voice was starting to wobble. An anxious feeling was stirring in my stomach.

'Yamin hit him around the head with both fists.'

'Did you attempt to stop him?'

'I got no response from him; he just kept on going.'

I paused taking a deep breath. The emotion coming through my words were clearly the product of an exhausted mind.

'Then I screamed and ran at him begging him to stop. I hit his arm with my fists trying to get him to let go of Kumara's head which he had in an arm-lock.'

'What did he do next Maria?'

'Yamin let go of Kumara's head. He turned to me and I saw the devil in his eyes. He had a fixed glare like someone I didn't know.'

Emotion was rising causing my voice to crack so I paused to draw a tissue from my pocket. The security guard had given me a wodge of them before the start of play. I used one to dry my eyes.

A perfect prop.

The judge leant forward in my direction.

'Would you like to take a few minutes break Miss Kayakova?'

'No, no I will carry on thank you My Lord.'

Eleanor took her cue from the judge.

'Maria, I understand this is difficult for you. Could you tell us what happened next?'

'Yamin pushed me away but I kept on coming back, demanding to know what on earth was going on. Kumara was on the floor trying desperately to catch his breath and I was shouting at Yamin.'

'Go on.'

'He pushed me back as far as the top of the stairs. He was not even looking directly at me. I tried to resist him but he pushed once again and I fell. That is the last I remember of that night. The next thing I knew I was back in the flat the next morning.'

There was an intake of breath from the jury. Hopefully the drama would stick in their minds.

'Thank you, Maria,' Eleanor said after a few seconds of reflection.

Eleanor asked me a few more questions that morning about timings after the attack and when I saw Yamin last. I told the court about the last time we were together as lovers; this would surely help build the perception of aggression in him.

The judge decided it was time for the jury to have a cup of coffee, a cigarette or both if required. I was asked to step down to the dock whilst they took their fixes. I had never smoked but God I would start now if I could have twenty minutes in the car park talking to normal people as a free woman.

Eleanor went to the bathroom during the interval. As she adjusted her gown and collar at the mirror she felt the silent buzz of her mobile phone against her hip. It was from Oliver.

Lunch again perhaps? Oliver

Eleanor smiled to herself in the mirror. She thought for a second then started tapping a reply.

Sorry My Lord, I am very busy. Eleanor

Eleanor switched her mobile off and left the bathroom with a smile on her face.

The jury scuttled into court with a palpable sense of anticipation. They knew it was time for the prosecution to cross-examine me. I was nervous as my security guard led me back to the witness box where I waited like a young rabbit cornered in a field.

Robert McOmish rose to his feet. He was in no hurry to start. He shifted the red file in front of him as he looked down at the notes. After a few more seconds he raised his eyes to meet mine. They were piercing and full of lust - this was what he was paid for, this was his moment.

'It was a pretty nasty way for a man to die wasn't it Miss Kayakova!' Robert shouted in a voice many decibels louder than normal. The volume gave me a start and made one of the jury members nearest me jump in her seat.

Was I supposed to answer him? I didn't have a chance.

'You plotted the death of this man with your boyfriend. You assisted your boyfriend by drugging the victim.

Eleanor stood up with the intention of objecting.

'Miss Sechford-Jones, you have had your turn thank you,' the judge said with an unfamiliar firmness.

Eleanor sat down with an indignant look on her reddening face.

'Mr McOmish?' The judge said with his hand pointing at Robert.

'Thank you, My Lord.' Robert looked at his notes wearing an almost imperceptible smirk. He had lost his place but didn't mind one bit.

'We have heard from Mr Darsha's next door neighbour there were screams and shouts from a female through the duration of the attack. It is up to the jury to decide who they should believe. You claim your boyfriend rendered you unconscious by pushing you down the stairs. How can that be if female screams continued into the night?'

'I'm telling you the truth,' I said but he wasn't listening, he didn't want anything to get in the way of his oration. All his questions were rhetorical.

'It is clear this jury must decide if you are being truthful about your involvement before and during the attack. These people must decide what you both were doing there in the first place. You claim

Darsha wanted to have sex with you and Yamin came to collect you. You claim Yamin was a jealous man and beat Darsha up because he wanted to sleep with you. You yourself have admitted Darsha was practically unable to walk when he left the restaurant. Now I believe this is because you drugged him and were under instructions to get him home. What I don't understand is what you both were doing there? Perhaps you could tell this court Miss Kayakova. What were you actually doing there?'

The last part of Robert's question was delivered at top volume. This time he paused for my response. I felt all the eyes of the court on me.

I looked at my interpreter and whispered something in her ear.

'I'm sorry sir, could you repeat the last part of the question; she is having trouble with the final part,' the interpreter said with a thick Russian accent.

'Well I put it to you Madam Interpreter, the defendant can understand every single word I am saying. I have been looking through her academic history as well as observing her in this court. Her English, both written and conversational, seems completely fluent when it needs to be.'

'My Lord can I ask that the interpreter is removed from this court? Her use is clearly a tactic to distract and to confuse the jury,' Robert McOmish said looking at the judge.

The judge looked at Robert, the interpreter, then down at his notes to give himself time to reflect. Eventually he looked up at me.

'In this incidence I happen to agree with the prosecution. I also consider the interpreter to be superfluous to proceedings in this trial.'

I looked across to Eleanor whose fixed gaze told me all I needed to know. She was being embarrassed in front of the jury. The judge continued.

'Miss Kayakova, despite agreeing to your request, I believe your understanding of the questions put to you and your ability to answer them in English, is of sufficient comprehension to manage without an interpreter. Would you agree with that?'

I looked at my interpreter and one of the jury members sniggered. Eleanor offered no support, she didn't even look at me.

I looked back at the judge.

'Yes, I think I can manage My Lord.'

The interpreter did not wait to be told to leave. She walked from my side past the jury and out of the wooden door at the back of the court.

'Good. Now we can get on with questions without unnecessary interruption,' Robert said standing up once again.

'Miss Kayakova, you will remember my last question. What were you and Yamin doing at Kumara Darsha's flat that evening? What did you want from him?'

'I was trying to help him. I did not flirt with him and had no intention of going back to his house for sex. Yamin must have arrived because it was getting late.'

'Do you expect this jury to believe you Miss Kayakova? After all we have heard about the severity of the violence inflicted upon this man. We are all aware of the screams and banging heard by a witness in this court. People don't murder people for no reason Miss Kayakova,' Robert yelled.

'Yamin was a jealous man. He was cross with us for staying out so late.'

'Members of the jury could I ask you to turn to page seven under section six of your jury information packs.'

There was a familiar rustle from the two jury benches as the page was located.

'Members of the jury, do the injuries you can see in these images suggest to you Yamin was cross with his girlfriend for being a little late with her boss, a man with whom she worked? I will answer the question for you. No, they do not. I suggest these are the actions of a man, and indeed of a woman too, who wanted something much more, something very important to them. Now it is unfortunate we have not been afforded the privilege of what this might well be. It is up to you to decide whether you are comfortable with Miss Kayakova's explanation.'

'Let me move on to the day after the carnage. We have heard Yamin left Maria that morning. She fell asleep after making love and he had gone when she woke from her post-coital slumber.'

There was a small titter from the jury and the judge looked over to them. It soon died down.

'Yamin had taken all his belongings and, we assume, fled to the airport. Some very clever criminals are capable of leaving the country without being recognised. We can find no evidence of his departure. What we do know is that he is not here. This we can believe, after all he has committed a horrible murder, so who wouldn't try and run away? My question to you Miss Kayakova is this. Why didn't you tell the police something had happened that night? Why did you run away? You could have made this terrible situation a whole lot easier.'

'I was frightened. I had no way of contacting him so I ran away. It is difficult when you have no friends or family to turn to. I just packed up and ran.'

Robert looked at me like I was a lying schoolgirl.

'Really Miss Kayakova? It seems to me remarkable that you would go so far on a whim. Did you not think it peculiar your boyfriend had just packed up and left you without saying goodbye? Were you not suspicious?'

'I didn't know what to think. I was scared of what he might have done.'

'Why did you go to Exeter?'

'A waiter in the restaurant left with his family and settled in Exeter. He went back home some weeks before all of this. I decided to go and find him. He was the only person who I knew. I had no other choice.'

'What happened to your mobile phone? We have looked at the cell-site analysis through this trial and all calls from your phone seem to stop after the incident. This is quite convenient isn't it?'

'Yamin must have taken my phone because I couldn't find it after he left.'

'Did you try and call Yamin? The analysis of the calls made on your new phone suggests you didn't try to call him.'

'I only had his mobile number stored in my old phone. I had no way of contacting him.'

'So, you contacted your friend in Exeter Miss Kayakova? I assume you did, given the number of calls to this gentlemen's mobile phone made on your new device.'

'I did locate him, yes. He offered me a bed. I found work at local coffee shop. That is what I seem able to do best.'

'Did you have any romantic link with this gentleman in Exeter? Is this the reason you went to see him?'

'No, he was friend. Just friend I could turn to. No sex.'

'Is this where the police arrested you? At the coffee shop?'

'Yes, that's right. I was working there when they came in.'

'What did you think when they came in? Did you think they wanted to talk to someone else? It was a few weeks after the attack?'

'I had forgotten about that night. I only remember the argument Yamin was having with Kumara. Only when they asked me my name did I think I was in trouble. I was so scared I just did everything the police asked me to do.'

'Thank you, Miss Kayakova, I think I will leave it there,' Robert said picking up his file and sitting down.

Eleanor stood. She looked flustered by the force of Robert's cross examination.

'My Lord. I wish to talk with my client. Could I suggest a short break?'

The judge looked up at Eleanor.

'Miss Sechford-Jones. I will decide when and for how long we break in this court. It just happens I deem a break at this juncture an appropriate action,' the judge said sternly.

'Members of the jury if you could make your way out of court; I think thirty minutes should be enough.'

The jury crept out gingerly reflecting the increased intensity of the morning session. I was led back to my normal position in the dock. Eleanor and Robert sat down in silence, one in a huff, the other with a contented grin.

Eleanor joined me in the dock and placed her hand on my shoulder as she sat down.

'Are you OK?' Eleanor said as she raised her eyebrows to the guard who took the hint and went to stand at the steps leading to the cells.

'I suppose so. Not quite what I expected. I am worried the jury will side with Robert. He was very aggressive. He even made me doubt myself,' I said looking deeply into her eyes.

'It will be alright, he was impressive but I have one final trick up my sleeve. I am going to sum up for the defence after the break. I don't think all is lost.'

Eleanor stood and walked back out of the dock. She rushed out of the court through the wooden doors. She had tried to be upbeat but we both knew Robert had been magnificent. The jury must by now think I was a liar.

Outside the court, just behind a large marble pillar, Eleanor furtively retrieved her mobile phone. She switched it on and immediately it gave a soft buzz alerting her to a text message. She looked up to check nobody was watching her then looked back at the message.

Shame. Can I see you for dinner? Oliver

Eleanor's fingers buzzed over the keypad. She smiled as she wrote.

Not sure. Being nasty to me in court doesn't help. E.

Eleanor reread it then pressed send.

As she put the phone back in her long pocket she felt it buzz again. She felt a tinkle of anticipation and pulled it back out again.

OK. Dinner tonight at my flat? 8.00pm? Ox

Just a couple of finger movements this time.

We'll see...

Eleanor replaced the phone and hurried back into court. It was time to wrap up the defence. She had told Maria about her secret weapon. She had better think of one fast.

The court reassembled after the break and the air was crackling with anticipation. It was Eleanor's turn to redress the balance during her summing up of the defence.

She stood after a nonchalant flick of an arm from the judge.

'Maria came to this country in good faith to experience our great capital city. She came with her boyfriend and they both found work here to pay the bills and provide enough cash to enjoy life comfortably. All pretty normal stuff I'm sure you would agree.'

'I would like to take a moment to tell you a little bit more about the life Maria Kayakova left behind in Belarus. This was no ordinary life. I hope you will agree with me Maria is no ordinary woman.'

'Maria spent her days caring for her father. She also managed to find time to go into Minsk from her father's house each day to attend university. She met Yamin there and they decided to go travelling together before Maria finished her course. This was because Yamin had been offered a job in London. Maria was left in a very difficult position. She cared greatly for her father but he had become increasingly violent towards her. Frankly, she couldn't cope with his brutality anymore. She was able to organise for a neighbour to come in to help her father but the decision to leave was still not an easy one.'

'I point all this out to show you this woman is a rational, intelligent human being who has had to make difficult choices through her life. To me this is not the description of a murderer.'

'We have conceded Maria was at the flat when Kumara died. We have conceded she spent the evening with him and came back to his flat when he struggled to get home. Perhaps that was foolish - I would suggest this was a mistake any young woman trying to impress could have made. Maria acted according to her instincts, not for personal gain.'

I looked across at the women in the jury. A couple of them were nodding to Eleanor's words.

This had been a good start.

'Maria did run away the morning Yamin went missing. We admit she could have phoned the police at that point and things may have turned out differently. Once again, I remind you Maria had no idea any of this had happened. Her last memory of the night in question was of being pushed down the stairs in a brutal manner – in a manner that rendered her unconscious. That is why she knows very little about events that night.'

Eleanor was on a roll.

'You may well ask about the drug. We have heard no evidence to suggest Maria had any involvement in putting any foreign substances into Kumara's drinks. She had no opportunity to. You may well ask about the gas in the flat; why was the gas left on?' Eleanor said looking out to the jury. 'Again, we have heard no evidence Maria was in any way responsible for this.'

'There are many issues for you all to deliberate in this trial, so I ask you to do just one thing for me. Please remember who this woman is, where she has come from and just how much of what you have heard is not solid evidence. It could be a matter of one person's word against another and to me the word of a hard-working, loyal daughter with good character is a very powerful word indeed. She acted under duress.'

Eleanor sat down. She took a deep breath as she looked back at the jury then at me. Finally, she glanced at the judge and gave an almost imperceptible nod.

The case for the defence was over.

His Honour Judge Oliver Barniston QC looked up towards the jury. He paused as he got their attention.

'Ladies and gentlemen of the jury, you have heard from the prosecution and the defence in this trial. I must now tell you about the next steps and your responsibilities as members of this jury. Before I ask you to deliberate over this trial in an attempt to reach a verdict, there are some important points to note. Both sides will offer a very brief summary of their case before I summarise the trial from my perspective. I will attempt to mention all that I have observed and to set out the facts as I see them. Once this is completed, we will hear from Mr McOmish and what are known as agreed facts. This is a list of points both sides agree on. This you will find invaluable when deliberating on the trial. Once this document has been shown to you, I will have copies distributed amongst you.'

The judge shifted in his large chair.

'When we have completed the summary, I will then provide my steps to verdict document. This will disclose the legal issues in this trial and again should be useful to you when you retire to discuss the case.'

'Now let's start with the summing up from both sides.'

A sense of relief went around the court when the judge started summarising the case later that afternoon. It was fairly simple stuff; he ran through each character, witness, event and time. I'm sure it was quite useful if anybody on the jury had not been paying attention at any time.

'Members of the jury, the woman you see before you in the dock must be considered by you as a person of good character. There is no reason to doubt this. You must take steps to your verdict based only upon the evidence you have heard in this trial.'

'You will now hear the schedule of agreed facts, as I mentioned earlier. This document will be printed and available for your deliberations. Mr McOmish?' the judge said raising his left hand as a signal to the prosecution.

Robert McOmish stayed sitting down. Behind him his second stood. She was a young woman who was clearly an up-and-coming barrister. I never did find out her name. Apart from the odd conference with her principle barrister this was the first verbal contribution she had made. Her red hair was tied up neatly under her wig and the pale features of a redhead showed keenness and intelligence. She was certainly a hot-shot and this was her chance to shine.

'My Lord, with your permission, I would like to read to the court the schedule of agreed facts in this case,' she said confidently with a low almost masculine tone.

The judge nodded at the procedural enquiry and she continued.

The first few points covered the place and time of death and the fact that Yamin and I were both there when he died. She read them out like a shopping list. She covered the drug Kumara had ingested and Yamin's departure, all these facts were not in doubt.

Then came a shock to us all.

'Kumara Darsha was a restaurateur and small business entrepreneur in and around West Hampstead. He was known to police in the area and had a history of low-level Class A drug purchasing and distribution in the area. Kumara Darsha was never prosecuted for any such offences. He had low-level involvement with a Sri Lankan gang and was suspected of buying drugs for this organisation from suppliers in London.'

As she spoke a sudden intake of breath could be heard from the jury. I looked over and saw a couple of the women whispering to each other. Both were smiling. Had this been something they were expecting? I had not seen or heard about any of this during my time at the restaurant. Why were they telling us this now?

'My Lord, this concludes the statement of agreed facts,' the second said looking at the judge. She checked the bench behind her, threw up the back of her gown and sat down. She looked around the court like a schoolgirl who had just completed her first solo – she was looking at the reaction of others in court.

'Ladies and gentlemen, that is the final procedure before I ask you to enter the jury deliberation room. I have prepared a 'Steps to Verdict' document to help you reach a conclusion.'

The judge looked at both barristers and they nodded their heads simultaneously.

'Good, then we can continue. Members of the jury you will need to elect a foreman whose responsibility it will be to chair your debate and who, once agreement is reached, will deliver the verdict to this court. I also ask you to be thorough in your deliberations. Always remember your duty and responsibility to see all the evidence is considered.'

'In this case I will not accept a verdict unless it is unanimous. We will sit here through the duration of your discussions so if you have any questions then please contact your usher who will hand the question to me. I will call you back into court to furnish you with the answer.'

'Your deliberations are still bound by the same principles of this court. Please keep all parts of it private at all times and do not be drawn onto the Internet or into Social Media discussions. You will be kept as a single body and locked in your room until you have reached a decision.'

The judge nodded at the usher who stood and asked the jury to follow her. This time they went out of the wooden door the judge used at the side of the court by the witness box. Once they had all snaked out, the door slammed shut behind them.

The clock on the wall said ten to three. All I could do now was wait, four-wall surrounded by my fear.

Chapter XIX

R. v. Maria Kayakova

Jury Deliberation

The first thing that hit Sam was just how much of the Old Bailey was behind the courts and not immediately obvious to the serving juror. He walked out of the court and into a vast, invariable corridor with plump oak panels protected by seasoned pictures of judges on the walls. They disappeared off into the distance in each direction like a hall of mirrors reflecting different personalities through legal history. He was met by an aroma of seriousness and anybody walking past on soft, sound deadening carpet did so as if in a library. As he trooped along with his flock, led by Chantelle, he passed doors marked with the names of judges in residence. Some doors were open which gave the prying eyes of the jurors a passing glimpse at the pinnacle of the legal profession. Soft lighting crept from each door, bringing with it a seriousness wrapped in intelligence.

The jury was brought to a halt by yet another big oak door. The usher unlocked it with an old-fashioned key which had to be six inches long. This was their door. Sam looked at a couple of other jury members with a foreboding glance which suggested they were entering a prison of their own.

'Follow me please,' said Chantelle in a hushed tone. Submissively, the twelve new inmates filed into the room which would be their own stockade for the foreseeable future.

Looking around, Sam felt he had gone back fifty years. Oak panelled walls, a big solid oak table surrounded by heavy wooden chairs, lead-lined windows with thick curtains, all completed the mood as together they let very little light into the room.

Some of the jurors were now chatting about Maria. This was the first time they had been able to share their views about the trial and clearly some jurors couldn't wait to get started. Others were just talking generally, relieving the pressure of being trapped in court all day. Sam noticed that the old-fashioned central heating was on full and had made the room incredibly hot and stuffy. He thought he might open a window but a quick glance at the thick paint around them suggested they had ceased operational duties many years ago.

Chantelle broke the prattle with a doubtless well-practiced cough.

'Ladies and gentlemen, you need to read the steps to verdict document as well as all your notes from the trial. These will be placed on the table with the other working documents from the trial. I will bring them through in a minute.'

'The first thing to decide is who your foreman should be. Once that has been established, any questions you have for the court should be channelled through the foreman by writing questions down and sending for me. I will be sitting outside and will be responsible for taking your questions to the court. If you ask a question, the judge will ask you to return to his court to hear his answer.'

'You will be locked into the room until such time as you have reached a decision, remember that the judge has asked you for a unanimous verdict. There are toilets at either end of this room, men's on the left and ladies' on the right. If any of you feel the need to smoke, then we will all leave together. We will go down to the courtyard and the smokers can smoke whilst the non-smokers watch. Sorry non-smokers but these are the rules.'

Sam opened his mouth and raised his eyebrow.

'Do we just go on all night?'

The usher raised her eyebrows in turn.

'I'm sure you could but in here the judge will decide when you should be released. I suspect the pattern will be similar to the trial itself. I will come in to tell you when you are free to go.'

'Ok, anything else? I will be outside so just knock on the door if you need me.'

With that Chantelle turned on her heels and went through the door. All the jurors heard the key turn in the lock. The action of closing the door made the room feel hotter immediately.

One of the jurors, a middle-aged woman whose yellow complexion made her look like she had smoked all her life, looked up at Sam.

'We have been talking about who should be foreman. We think it should be you,' she said with a gruff voice which had a South London ring to it. Sam looked around and noticed others around her nodding their agreement.

'But when did you talk about that?' Sam replied.

'You know, us smokers have to talk about something when we are outside. Do you want to do it?'

'Does anybody else want to do it?' Sam said looking around the room. To him it was something he would be very keen to do but he didn't want to make it look like he was too keen.

Nobody said anything. In fact, nobody was moving; eleven mannequins were staring at Sam. Had she spoken to everyone about this already?

'So, will you do it?' asked the woman with more authority. She was clearly not to be messed with.

'Sure. I would be delighted to do it.'

Human movement started again. Everybody took a place at the table. They were interrupted by the usher coming into the room with a colleague. They carried all the notes the jurors had made during the trial. Quite remarkably they placed the notes belonging to each of them in front of the right person, ready to be studied in the milky straining light.

Once everybody was seated Sam decided to take control. A wave of concern spread over him. He was foreman and now responsible for guiding these people through deliberations. Where should he start? Like most things he ever did in life, he decided to jump straight in, hoping at some point that style would triumph over content.

'Right. Thank you for asking me to be foreman. Fundamentally, I think it is important for all of us to have our say. First things first, let us all read the steps to verdict document here. Afterwards can we please go around the table and introduce ourselves. This process will be so much easier if we know each other better. I'll start and then I'll write down our names in the order we are sitting, it's probably best if we remain in our current positions. I am Sam…'

Sam drew a big oblong on a piece of paper in front of him and wrote his name down. He looked to his left and raised his eyebrows as a prompt.

As the names were called out Sam wrote them down on the paper in front of him. He also made a quick aide-memoire of each of the other jurors' characteristics on his own pad. If only they could have seen what he was writing in his illegible handwriting…

'Thank you. That will help us all,' Sam said reviewing the diagram. He placed it on a clear part of the table so others could see it. He pulled his notes closer to him.

'We have a great deal to discuss but a worthy place to start, in my view, would be to go around the table and ask each of you whether you think the defendant is guilty or not guilty. Does everybody understand?'

Sam looked around the room. Everybody nodded. Primary school teacher Sam.

Sam started with his opinion with each juror taking it in turn to give their initial thoughts. Sam jotted the results down. After a twenty second pause to think, he announced the score, laughing as he did it…

I sat in the dock staring at the judge. It felt ridiculous to be sitting in court for the full duration of the jury deliberation. It had been an hour since they all streamed out and literally nothing had happened here since. The judge was concentrating on his notes

– no doubt trying his best to finish the cryptic crossword before the jury came back. I'm sure the barristers were looking through documents which related to another trial, otherwise this would be a chronic waste of time for them. I had no word game luxury so had to be content with letting my eyes scan the court trying to find things to think about. It's a strange thing to know that there are people close by who are talking about you and your fate. What you wouldn't give to be a fly on the wall…

It dawned on me that this was the first time in my life that I needed, rather than wanted, my mother. Many times I had wondered what she had been like, what she would have thought. With my future about to be decided by a group of strangers and what they thought of my past, I felt helpless and scared. I tried to imagine my mother's voice and how it might comfort me. All I could see was my father weeping in his wheelchair.

During my random scan, Robert McOmish shook me from my thoughts. His raptor eyes were staring straight at me but this time there was a beaming smile upon his face.

After another stilted, thirty-minute discussion, Sam conducted another round-table vote. Disappointingly, the score on Sam's sheet had not changed from the first round.

Looking skyward, Sam thought for a while then told the others that he had an idea, he would write a note to the judge to clear something up. The others seemed as desperate as he was becoming and nodded their approval of Sam's idea, so he scribbled a short note on a scrap of paper in front of him.

Sam stood up and walked to the door. A soft knock brought a scrapping at the keyhole and moments later a face came slowly round the opening door.

'Hi there,' said Sam.

Chantelle's smile exposed a mighty set of gleaming white teeth. The contrast against her ebony skin was startling. Sam knew none of the others could see her.

'We haven't been properly introduced.' Sam said with a whisper suitable for the long corridor.

'Chantelle,' the usher whispered back.

'Hi Chantelle, I'm Sam. They picked me to be foreman.'

'No shit. The rest of 'em look like they can barely read or write, let alone be bothered. I don't know where they get them from. How can I help?'

'Come in,' Sam continued and opened the door so Chantelle could enter the room.

'We have a question for the judge. I have written it down for you.'

Sam handed Chantelle the note. They touched skin very briefly. Chantelle looked up as she took the note securely in her hand.

Immediately she ghosted out of the room and locked the door behind her.

As they waited, Kev did not waste a second by offering his building services to most people around the table. Honestly priced and reliable, he was able to turn his hand to almost anything. Katie promised with gleeful delight to bake some cakes for tomorrow and poor old Joan hadn't spoken with anyone. Free enterprise and loneliness locked together in the same room.

After a matter of minutes they all stopped talking in unison with the familiar sound of the key scratching the door. Chantelle came back into the room, this time with greater feminine emphasis. Sam noticed just how long her legs were as they eased in front of her gown with every step.

'The judge has read your note and would like to speak to you back in his court. Would you please follow me?'

Sam was the first out behind Chantelle, he was the foreman after all. Just as they reached the door she turned to Sam.

'No mucking about from you in here please,' she gave another trademark, haughty smile.

Sam smiled back. Shit, could he not take anything in life seriously? The future of a young woman was at stake here and all he could do was flirt with the usher.

Through muscle memory the jurors dutifully shuffled back into the same positions they had been in during the trial. Sam found it remarkable just how quickly they had all been coached to behave like schoolchildren again. Was it the controlling authority of the judge, the seriousness of the place or perhaps they all felt engaged with what was going on? Whatever it was, it certainly worked.

'Members of the jury, thank you for your question. Let me remind you that this court sits even whilst you are deliberating so it's important I answer your questions in front of you as a collective and the full court.'

'You make reference to two aspects of English Law which do need to be explained in detail. I am not surprised and am indeed pleased that you are asking me about them - they are both extremely pertinent to this case.'

'Let me deal with the two issues you raise in order. First your reference to Joint Enterprise. You will have noticed I made a point of raising this in my steps to verdict. The contemplation of this point is critical to how you reach your decision.'

'Let me put it simply; Joint Enterprise is a rule in English Law which allows several people to be charged with a crime when they are not the primary offenders. You have heard both sides agree, Yamin Shakirov is wanted in connection with this crime and you have heard he was responsible for the injuries inflicted on the victim. This point is not in dispute by either side. What you have to decide is whether Maria Kayakova was party to this offence and knew about the attack and, critically, the intention to commit it. You must gain this understanding from the evidence you have heard. You may also wish to consider her actions after the attack had taken place. Reflect upon what a reasonable person would do in the circumstances outlined. Was she under duress or party to a beastly attack? That is for you to decide.'

'I turn to your second point which asks about Intent Escalation. This is more complicated so please do pay attention to what I am about to say. The laws are valid for a single person committing a crime but also apply where there is a suspicion of joint venture. Again, as I have mentioned in my summary, to be able to demonstrate murder you have to be confident you can prove intent to kill. You have to ask yourselves whether Yamin foresaw the consequences of his actions leading to Kumara Darsha's death. If you feel there has been Joint Enterprise then all parties are guilty of the crime.'

'The escalation of intent can happen during an encounter. It may well be the individuals in this case went to the victims dwelling to cause injuries that did not result in death. You will have to look at the evidence and use your life experiences to come to a conclusion on this. If the individuals concerned did not have the intention to kill at the beginning of the encounter it is still possible to consider murder as a verdict. Intent can escalate as an individual involved in the encounter can recognise death or serious harm would be virtually certain. It is no longer necessary to prove there was appreciable time between the formation and execution of the intent. You must consider what state of mind the defendant and Yamin were in. I must urge you to use your judgement as to whether a witness to somebody attacking another could have done anything to prevent the attack.'

The judge looked directly at Sam who was caught looking up at the empty public gallery. Sam could feel his face redden like he had been spotted chewing in class.

'Let's leave it there shall we? That concludes my answers and you all look like you could do with a good night's sleep. Can you please be ready to start again at ten tomorrow morning. Please do not forget to congregate at the rear entrance to gain access during your deliberations.'

The usher stood and showed the jury out. Sam noticed the defendant looking over to him as they left. He felt a degree of discomfort he had not felt before. With his head down he scuttled off into the carpeted corridor that led to a large staircase and the rear exit. As he came out into the cold air he placed his beanie hat right down to the tops of his eyes. With yet another disguise on, he headed for the Tube.

Sam got home in time to witness the end of the boys' supper. Spaghetti was stuck on the floor and clung to their hair but hopefully some sat inside them. Sam kissed Lucy hello and rubbed the boys' hair despite the pasta.

'Hello Daddy!' the boys cried in unison. Sam would never tire of their innocent enthusiasm.

'Have you sent the naughty lady to prison yet Daddy?' Charlie said looking up. His face had not escaped the Bolognese invasion; he looked like he wore a red beard.

A natural inquisitiveness had been with Sam since birth, so he had chosen to ignore the judge's instructions and to research the crime online with journalistic rigour. He had also discussed all aspects of the trial with Lucy. He felt sure all the other members of the jury would have done the same. Surely everybody did it these days given the temptations of Google.

'Not yet darling. We are still deciding what to do.'

'Will we go to prison if we are naughty Daddy? Can Mummy come with us?'

Sam looked at Lucy and smiles grew simultaneously on their faces, smiles which they both recognised from earlier days in their marriage but which had been in hibernation for some while. Sam felt a surge of emotion run through him. It was moments like this that drove away the concerns of adult life; putting the worries over Wolfenberg back where they belonged.

Sam walked forward putting his arms around his wife. They both relaxed in the security of the moment. Only the boys climbing out of their seats and jumping onto their parents enriched the spell, peace yet further enhanced by boyish screams and messy faces.

Later that night Lucy stared at the bedroom ceiling with a radiant glow across her face. Tiny sweat beads on her brow were lit by moonlight coming through hastily closed curtains. Sam rolled over to gently kiss her cheek and whisper something that made Lucy giggle. He slid back slowly and jumped out of bed with youthful elegance.

After tiptoeing past the boys' room, he entered the upstairs study and fired up the laptop. He desperately needed to understand the definitions of Joint Enterprise and Intent Escalation. Not in the terms set out by the judge but in his own way, hopefully littered with past examples.

Hours later he had quenched his thirst for legal knowledge. He had also found an interesting newspaper article about the crime. He drained his second whisky, switched off the computer and walked to the boys' room with the afterglow of the screen still stencilled in his eyes. He kissed his sleeping sons and headed off to bed. It was midnight and he would need all his wits about him to get the jury moving forwards towards any form of conclusion.

It was a cold, bright morning so Sam decided to take the slightly longer walk from Holborn Tube station to the Old Bailey. Along Holborn Viaduct he looked up and saw the mighty leaden tower of St Sepulchre-Without-Newgate rise up in front of him. It looked stunning set against the azure blue of the morning sky. The rising sun illuminated the dirty yellow stone and made the recesses and openings in the tower darker than normal. He walked past the church entrance and stopped to read the notice board next to the railings. He had never been to see St Sepulchre's before; quite often London churches go unnoticed unless people had a reason to visit them. As the City had grown, many had been dwarfed by new office buildings. Sam looked above the sign to size up the mighty church behind it. It was easily the largest London church he had seen. Like all churches, it made Sam wonder what secrets lay behind the big wooden doors.

Sam looked at the opening times; he had to see inside. Doing this made him look at his watch - he had only five minutes to get to the back entrance. He turned and strode at a brisk pace towards the courts. A more detailed inspection of the church would have to wait.

Sam was the last juror to arrive. He apologised as they were all led upstairs by a noticeably haughty Chantelle. A perk of his lateness was the proximity he had to Chantelle's bottom as she ascended the stairs. She wore tight black trousers and a smart dark grey shirt and, for the first time, no gown. As she walked, her perfectly round feminine form flicked gracefully from side to side. She glanced round to see if her brood of jurors were following her and noticed the direction of Sam's gaze. She smiled and carried on putting just a touch more effort into the rocking of her hips.

Back deep inside Hotel Penitentiary, Chantelle showed them into their room. Time had not affected this place, neither for decades nor overnight - everything was in the same position as it was left the day before. Other jurors took their seats whilst Sam opened the only working window to squeeze some fresh air into the room.

'Once again, I will be outside the door. If you have any more questions just knock quietly and I will come in to help you.' Chantelle said, looking directly at Sam.

Sam sat in his chair. He looked around the table and saw eleven expectant faces staring back at him. Most of his professional life was planned in minute detail, a consistently full diary and preparation were part of everyday life. Somehow, he had to lead the jury to make a decision and he had little idea how to carry on. Perhaps he should start like he did yesterday?

"Right, after the judge's comments yesterday let's go around again and see where we are with the numbers.'

Shaking his head slowly he wrote the scores down on his pad in front of him. He used the procedure to try and think of what on earth he should say next. Luckily Barbara came to his rescue with a long diatribe stating exactly what she thought. She was a large, outspoken woman who took care in her appearance. Sam had identified her as dangerous in his initial notes; her comments so far had reinforced this view.

Barbara's speech had lighted the touch paper. For the next hour the debate carried on with much more vigour than before. It seemed the jury needed help warming up because the collective body was now arguing like a family stuck in a traffic jam on a long car journey. During a momentary pause for a collective breath, Sam jumped in.

'This is hopeless.' Sam groaned, not lifting his eyes from the page.

It was a full thirty seconds before he spoke again.

'I'm going to write another note to the judge. There cannot be many trials which end with a unanimous verdict. The judge might have some suggestions and give us more to work with.'

Nobody seemed to object so Sam scribbled the note on a clean sheet.

Sam folded the note and walked to the door.

'Just an excuse to talk to that pretty usher again eh Kev!' Brian declared as Sam walked past his chair.

'Your phone number on it Sammy?' Kev added with a chuckle.

'Just doing my job lads, all for the cause.' Sam retorted turning back and smiling.

A knock on the door brought Chantelle back into the room. She beamed when she saw Sam standing there with the note.

'A note for the judge, Chantelle,' Sam pressed the folded paper into her warm hand. She took it slowly, her eyes not leaving his.

'I'll be back in a minute,' she said.

Kev broke the silence.

'As I have said already if any of you want any building or plumbing work done you should give me a call. I can do most things and the price is always reasonable.'

A laugh went up in the room at Kev's second attempt at marketing his business. Sam thought it was wonderful to see the great British entrepreneurial spirit alive and well.

'I'm just saying, I'll give you my number if you want it. I am based down in Sutton but can travel anywhere. I've got all my own tools.'

Sam looked at his fellow jury members. It was clear to him that most of them wanted to go home. They had had enough of this process; the pressure of work, the need to get back to children or just a chance to resume normality with a loved one. He too was growing tired of the seriousness of the place; no free expression or fun; it was built for process and punishment. He hoped nobody was making a decision based upon a desire to get this over with and leave. That would be a tragedy given what they had been through. It was up to him as foreman to make sure a proper conclusion was reached.

The door opened knocking Sam back from his thoughts.

'Can you follow me please; the judge would like another word. When you go in could you please make sure your foreman is sitting in the position nearest to the judge on the front row? My suggestion is you go in last Sam,' Chantelle said staring at Sam. Kev nudged Brian in the ribs and gave him a wink.

Sam hung back as they filed out making sure he was at the back of the line which snaked into court number one. Chantelle was behind him having locked the deliberation room door and like a goose-herder, rushed forward and guided her livestock into the court. Just as Sam entered he felt a warm hand on his bottom. It gave him a shock from the surprise but more because Chantelle's boldness cut through the seriousness of the situation like a red-hot poker through butter. He picked up his pace and took his new position with a smile on his face. Sam looked up and the smile evaporated – this was no time for a semi. He was that much closer to the judge now and all the court officials were staring at him.

The clerk of the court stood only a few yards from Sam. She turned to face him. Sam's eyebrows lifted a touch; his heart was beating faster.

'Would the foreman please stand.'

Sam felt a wave of fear build up in his stomach. He was suddenly keen to be somewhere else. This happened occasionally when he was under significant pressure at work. He took to his feet like the headmaster had just walked in. What was going on?

'Have you reached a verdict in this case upon which you all agree?'

Sam was perplexed. What a silly question given the note. Then he realised, this was process. He cleared his throat.

'No.'

Sam looked around to gauge whether the answer to the pointless question had come in any way as a shock to the assembled crowd.

'Thank you, Mr Foreman. You may sit down.' The usher concluded and sat down herself.

What a pointless exercise.

'Members of the jury, I have read and considered your note. In the circumstances I will allow you to reach a verdict based upon a majority of ten or more. If ten of you agree then I will take that as the collective decision and will acquit or pass sentence as appropriate,' explained the judge.

'Now please do remember to take your time. You need to reach a considered conclusion. Off you go now.' The judge concluded waving his hand like a Victorian father sending his son off to bed.

The jury filed out once again – a Conga line seasoned with a touch more optimism...

With the new instructions Sam was able to inject a fresh energy into the debate. It was clear that many were getting bored of the process with some jurors not raising previous concerns and others starting to side with others.

Sam had kept his own thoughts to himself to a large degree. He had announced what verdict he thought was appropriate but had given very short answers when pressed as to why. He wanted the others to persuade him to give him insights he had missed. He knew if he got going he would very likely influence others.

'From what I have heard I think we should go around again. Many of you seem to be losing interest in this duty we have been asked to perform. This is not a game guys, someone's liberty is at stake here. Right, to my left Sonal, what do you think?'

Sam noted the remarks down as one by one, each jury member called out their verdict.

Sam looked down at his pad and added up the scores.

'Eureka!' Sam said scanning the table. There were a few nods from the people brave enough to make eye contact. The others averted their eyes trying to hide any embarrassment in a rapid verdict change.

'Good, right Katie could you call the usher in before anybody changes their mind?'

Chantelle was as quick as ever and looked mildly cross to find Katie on the other side of her door. She looked to find Sam who was still sitting.

'Another question for the judge guys?'

'We have reached a decision, here it is,' Sam said standing, folding the note in two and handing it to Chantelle.

'Back in a minute,' Chantelle said and rushed out of the room.

As soon as she left the debate rekindled. Colin and Barbara were the main protagonists in the argument. It was clear they were never going to agree. Sam decided to step in.

'Come on guys, enough is enough. We have sent our collective thoughts through now. Our job is almost done. You can all get back to your lives very shortly,' Sam suggested with a hint of irony.

After a couple of awkward minutes Chantelle reappeared.

'Follow me; same positions as last time please. Sammy, it's your big moment.'

The jury walked with some nervousness towards the court. Sam hung back again more to be next to Chantelle than because of his position at the front of the jury box. As he waited for his colleagues to file in, he felt Chantelle press something into his hand. He could feel a rolled-up piece of paper at the centre of the warm sphere. In a reflex action he stuffed it into his pocket as quickly as he could. He turned to see Chantelle beam all her big white teeth at him.

Once everyone had settled down the clerk of the court stood. This time there was much more seriousness to the situation. The court was full, packed in the public gallery and behind the court with friends and family of Kumara Darsha together with representatives from the press. There was a buzz created by the swollen numbers. They had been told it was time for a verdict. After a few seconds the clerk cleared her throat and turned to face Sam.

'Would the foreman please stand.'

Her tone matched the mood. Much more robust, like she was being filmed this time.

Sam stood slowly and placed his hands in front of him, cupped together in what he was sure analysts would describe as a defensive gesture. He moved them to behind his back but this felt uncomfortable, so he settled with them at the side. Shifting from weight on left foot to right he looked up to meet the crow-like gaze of the clerk.

'Members of the jury you have been asked to reach a verdict in the case of The Crown versus Maria Kayakova. This was a murder trial and you have been asked to deliberate upon three possible verdicts.'

'My Lord has instructed you he will accept a verdict of ten or more in this case.'

'Mr Foreman, have you reached a conclusion based upon this criterion?'

'Yes,' said Sam with a frog in his throat. His reply was not as clear as he had wanted it to be so he cleared his throat with a polite cough. He couldn't remember when he had been so nervous.

'Under the charge of murder, do you find the defendant? Guilty or not guilty?'

Sam looked at Maria Kayakova, the public gallery and then back at the judge.

'Guilty.'

There was a split second of silence. The court was still processing the word. Then all hell broke loose. There were shouts from the public gallery and busy jostling from the press getting their equipment ready.

'Order, order,' Oliver Barniston tried to settle things down. Sam's job was not finished yet. The clerk had sat down as soon as the judge had spoken. She stood again to complete her job.

'Mr Foreman, how many found in favour of this verdict?'

'Yes,' said Sam for some reason, not comprehending the question. He had been watching the reaction of the defendant, seeing her head fall into her hands. Sam felt Colin behind him; he was prodding him in the back.

'Say ten Sam, just say ten.'

'Ten,' Sam said without understanding why.

'Thank you,' the clerk said and sat down. The noise had died down but there was still spontaneous chattering, it took a stern look from the judge up into the public gallery for silence to be restored.

Sam looked across to the dock. Maria Karakova had collapsed.

'Given the time I think it sensible if I sentence the defendant after lunch. Members of the jury, your job is now complete but I am sure many of you would like to hear what I have to say regarding this matter. I would be very happy if you came back at two fifteen. I will allow you to sit in the jury benches so please leave via the rear entrance.'

'Before that Mr McOmish would like to read a statement. Mr McOmish.'

Robert McOmish stood and read a statement prepared by the prosecution. It was compiled by Kumara Darsha's children. Sam and the rest of the jury heard how much they loved and missed their father. Sam looked down the line at Kev and Barbara. They both looked like they needed a stiff drink as they listened to Robert McOmish rubbing the defendant's nose in it.

Sam collected his coat from the now redundant deliberation room. He wanted to use the next hour and ten minutes to full effect. He wanted to see inside the church of St Sepulchre's.

It was still a crystal-clear day and bright sunlight lit the pavement as Sam walked up Old Bailey towards the church. The wind had picked up during the morning and leaves, together with general city detritus, were blowing around in straight chutes and curling eddies. Smokers stood in huddles watching people walk past going through their normal routines; not many of them could know what kind of activities were conducted in the big dirty-grey building Sam had just walked out of. Sam looked up at the older portion of the building.

'Defend the children of the poor and punish the wrongdoer.'

Sam stopped and reread the inscription above the now unused main entrance. He was unsure what the first part of the quote referred to. He got the second bit but the first concerned him. Why should a criminal court single out children of the poor? Surely all children could be vulnerable.

Sam noticed a CCTV camera attached to the building on the corner of Newgate Street. He scanned around counting another ten security cameras. He decided to move on up the hill to the church. This place had an amazing ability to control you. One minute you feel calm, the next intimidation; how quickly reflection can turn to paranoia. Head down, Sam decided it was time to go.

The first big sycamore came into view. Eight of these mighty trees protected the church from all sides. What they must have seen over the past two hundred years or so. The two World Wars, the second of which resulted in the Old Bailey being rebuilt; the IRA bomb in the Seventies which struck right at the heart of English justice. Then there were the famous cases which ranged from high celebrity to the gruesome Dr Krippen, The Kray Brothers, The Yorkshire Ripper, Oscar Wilde and Ian Huntley; all infamous in their own era.

The occasional motorbike provided a metallic falsetto to the constant register of the early afternoon London traffic. Sam was relieved to see the front gates across the porch had been opened. He pushed on the oak door, which was a few steps in from the heavy front gate. A soft creaking from the reluctant door made him hesitate and look up to see if he had disturbed anyone. From what he could see the church seemed empty, so he gave it another push. Reluctantly, it gave way with a huffy shudder.

Sam's eye was naturally drawn upwards as he entered the nave. The church was enormous. The high ceilings were beautifully ornate which thrilled Sam as he looked skyward. The stunning gold leaf surrounding the lights shone brightly, trying desperately to illuminate the massive interior. Sam looked back down to see the gold theme reflected all around the organ. This was to the left on the far side of the main aisle, standing like a grand Victorian music box. Gold pipes and a skirt of dark oak.

The stained-glass windows beyond the chancel threw dappled multi-coloured light onto the altar, right at the far end of the church. Candles burned either side in preparation for a lunchtime Communion; this only added to the kaleidoscope of colours bursting through from the window. It was the most magnificent church Sam had ever seen.

Sam noticed a collection of visitors in the stalls to the right of the altar. He walked across the chessboard stone floor then turned left by the final stone pillar. There was a wooden box attached to the pillar which interested him. It was filled with two pieces of rubble. He read the script next to it. As he read Sam realised the significance of this fairly unexciting masonry lying there. They were pieces from the original Holy Sepulchre in Jerusalem, the church said to be built on the site of Christ's grave and the site of the resurrection. Sam could hardly believe such an important artefact was only protected from damage or theft in a frail wooden box. Pieces of perhaps the most symbolic shrine in the Christian world were on display with no security. How trusting was the Church believing no angel was bound to stray.

Sam turned back towards the transept and walked to the other side of the church. He had spotted some empty pews where he could sit down and contemplate.

Sam sat down in the Fusilier's chapel. This was vaulted in oak, very much like the non-public parts of the Old Bailey. Faded Union Jacks hung from the ceiling next to brighter regimental colours. Sam looked down the long wall of oak to see hundreds of names of members of the regiment who had fallen for their country during the two World Wars.

Looking around at nothing in particular, Sam considered the past week or so. It had been a fascinating adventure for him, a world away from the pressures of his normal existence. Soon he would be back at Wolfenberg to face a different set of problems, impossible short-term targets; a team which had been without its leader for two weeks, Qin and a worsening client relationship.

Sam detected an old stone archway set into the wall just where he sat. The peak of the arch was no more than three feet from the floor and bricks had been used to block any passage through it. Sam thought it looked rather like a blocked-up fireplace but the arch was wide and far too low.

Footsteps made him turn to see a woman approaching him. She had a broad, kind smile on her face as she drew close. Sam stood up to face an elegant lady in her fifties.

'Quite incredible isn't it,' she said to Sam. 'I saw you looking at the archway.'

'Yes, I was wondering what it was. It's very low to the ground.'

'Ah, you are not the first to ask that. You are looking at one of St Sepulchre's secrets. That archway used to go straight from here right into the cells at Newgate prison. Back in the seventeenth century there was a strong link between this place and what was to become the Old Bailey.'

'But it's so low,' said Sam. As the words came out he realised he sounded like a schoolboy. The compliant juror mode would take a few days to lose.

'If you can imagine the floor being excavated away, steps used to go down here and you could go through the arch into the cells. You have seen our bell haven't you?'

'Your bell?

'Yes, just here.' She pointed at the pillar just behind where Sam was sitting. Just like the masonry he had seen on the opposite side, there was a small wooden box with a glass front attached to the pillar at head height. Inside was a dark coloured bell. It was no more than nine inches tall and had lost any metallic sheen.

'What is it?' Sam asked.

'It's the Newgate Execution Bell. It has been here since 1605. The clergy would walk through the passageway and use it to wake up condemned prisoners at midnight on the day of their execution. It is a pretty gruesome story. You should have a read.'

'Thank you I will,' said Sam. He turned away from the woman and took a step towards the pillar.

'I hope you enjoy it. Are you going to be here long? We have a communion starting in ten minutes. Are you here for that? Are you joining us?'

Sam turned back, his thoughts had turned to the bell and he only heard the bit about communion.

'Sorry, emmm, no, I have to get back to court at two fifteen. I am doing jury service. Thank you though.'

The woman gave a weak, slightly deflated smile. She turned and headed back towards the church office on the far side of the organ.

Sam read the script next to the wooden casket. The bellman would pace up and down, giving twelve double rings on the hand bell. He would then recite a macabre, solemn poem. Sam read the words out loud.

All you that in the condemned hole do lie,
Prepare you for tomorrow you shall die;
Watch all and pray: the hour is drawing near
That you before the Almighty must appear;
Examine well yourselves in time repent,
That you may not to eternal flames be sent.

And when St. Sepulchre's Bell in the morning tolls
The Lord above have mercy on your souls.

Sam took a step back. The words were so powerful he couldn't quite believe what he had read. The prisoners were asked to repent their sins despite being condemned to death.

Sam looked at his watch; he still had forty minutes to kill before the judge passed sentence on Maria. Sam took a seat by the blocked-up archway and looked towards the ceiling. What would the judge do now Maria had been found guilty? Would he be lenient, could he find it in himself to show mercy at her first offence? Perhaps he would throw the book at her for lying in court. If she hadn't drugged Kumara Darsha then who did?

Sam sat back down to have a proper look at the arch. He stared at the bricks which obstructed the redundant passage. What was behind them? What was the passageway actually like? Brick by brick his mind demolished the wall. His focus was just the archway, all around him darkened as the burning focus intensified.

Through a mixture of mist and candlelight a short, plump man in heavy overcoat came walking down the steps. He had a hand bell inverted in his right hand and a bunched nose-gay in his left. His gait was slow for two reasons, the poor light as midnight approached, and the solemn nature of his purpose.

He welcomed each burning candle as they came. The stench was overwhelming, this place was never cleaned; the reek of a location notorious for malice and corruption. For the incumbents the smell of rotting matter was the last thing to worry about. For some, it was about to be the start of their last day on Earth. Leaving this degenerated place would be a blessing.

The stocky man entered the diabolical courtyard at the end of the passage. The sounds of feral men and women had joined the foul fumes at the party of the senses. Random noises of despair emanated from prison cells which lined the walls of the courtyard. Screams and hysterical cackles came from the darkened interiors of the cells. Although each had a solitary candle, this barely illuminated the cross-hatched door, let alone the occupant's six-foot square accommodation.

The man shuffled through the muddy sludge to the far corner of the courtyard. There he saw two cells, which adjoined each other at ninety degrees. A wooden cross hung below each of the candles. These were the two he was looking for; these were the Condemned Cells.

His walk always took three minutes, so he knew it was about thirty seconds to midnight. He chuckled to himself as he got to his mark. He was fastidious in his timings but he doubted many of the occupants of these cells would respect this. Squalor, imprisonment and, for some, imminent death, made them forget the subtle politeness of good timekeeping.

He pulled his hood away from his head and touched his nose against the lattice metal door of the first cell. He screwed up his eyes in an attempt to see inside the dark cell. He looked left and right but couldn't see anything.

'Argghrrhhrhhh!'

The bellman jumped back, slipping on a particularly large clump of indeterminate waste. He fell flat on his back with a wet thud. Laughter peeled on from inside the cell.

'Oh, you think this is funny do you?' The short fat man said, getting up and trying his best to wipe the thick black slop from his coat.

With aggression, he walked towards the bars of the cell. He pressed his face up to meet the head of the condemned man. He could smell his foul breath, which permeated through the iron grid.

'Your time for laughing is almost at an end, you die today.'

The commotion had stirred the occupant of the cell next door who came to the bars on that door. It was a woman.

The bellman took a step back when he saw the other prisoner. He could do both together.

'Do you two believe in God? Do you understand he can offer you salvation, even now?'

There was silence from both cells.

'All you that in the condemned hole do lie. Prepare you for tomorrow you shall die.'

The bellman rung on his bell in double strokes. He looked at both cells as he spoke.

His eyes had adjusted to the light after his unexpected fall. He could see the two prisoners standing behind their cell doors. Both held onto the metal as he spoke. They were both in hessian clothes, all-in-one garments tied around the middle with coarse rope. Both were filthy with faces covered in dirt.

'Watch all and pray: the hour is drawing near. That you before the Almighty must appear.'

'If I ever get out of here, I am going to shove that bell up your arsehole,' said the occupant of the first cell. The bellman continued regardless.

'Examine well yourselves in time repent. That you may not to eternal flames be sent.'

The bell echoed around the courtyard. Other prisoners had stepped up to their cell doors to see what was going on.

'And when St. Sepulchre's Bell in the morning tolls. The Lord above have mercy on your souls.'

'Oh, shut up you old sod. Look at you all covered in shit. You should be ashamed of yourself.'

The man in the first cell stepped right up to his door, next to the candlelight. His face was fully illuminated by the glow. Piercing eyes and tanned skin. He had a scar down past his left ear. A knife wound. He was tall and strong, military muscular, not fat. He was frightening. The woman in the other cell started to cry when the bellman commenced his monologue. Yamin the tyrant had complained but she just wept, wept for her life, for her father.

'You seem pretty comfortable with death, young man,' said the Bellman once his last toll finished echoing around the courtyard. He held on to the bell's clapper and the waist with both hands and took a step towards Yamin. He was the one who needed help.

'Are you sure you want to die? Tell me what you did? Why are you here?'

'I will tell you everything I know you fat old queer. I stitched this bitch up. Even she had no idea what was going on. I used to beat her for pleasure. We were big into drugs, East meets West via Istanbul – you know what I am talking about.'

Sam was looking back at Yamin. It had got much brighter. There was nothing else apart from Sam and Yamin now. White everywhere apart from two faces. Sam saw a tattoo on the prisoner's neck. There was a set of cat's heads intertwined with a spider's web. A Russian Military tattoo. Cat's for a gang, spider's web indicating drug addiction. It was no more than two inches long, but the image painted a thousand words. This man had spent time in prison.

'We ran drugs from Central Asia into Western Europe. Heroin, pills, you name it. We got help from the Chinese authorities to set up relations with legitimate companies in the UK. Banks and that, places which have very high standards. We set up accounts and transfer money in. We wash it through their systems and then take it out, all nice and clean. The fun part is convincing people you are businessmen when in fact all we do is distribute drugs and collect our money. This is how we ended up here. This silly cow got caught. One bloke didn't pay so I lost it with him. I fled but she got caught. I should have killed her too, the useless bitch. I had drugged his rum bottle in the bar he used to run. He was the only one who touched the stuff. I got her to work there so it looked like her. I even told her I worked for the Russian Embassy. Stupid woman – I'm far too clever for that place.'

'In a few hours you will both be dead. May God have mercy on your souls.'

'They can't stop me. I will be alright.'

'You don't have time young man; you've run out of time'

Sam was jolted from his chair. The woman he had spoken to earlier was standing next to him.

'You've run out of time, you said you had until two fifteen, you will be late,' she said looking at her watch.

Sam shook his head, trying to bring himself back into the room. He noticed cold sweat on his forehead.

'What? But?'

'It's ten past two, the judge will be furious with you if you are late. What have you been doing?'

Sam looked at her for a few seconds. He was regaining his senses.

What he had just been thinking about was so strange, like a psychedelic dream.

'Sorry.'

Sam turned and ran out of the church, his shoes clipping on the chessboard floor. People leaving Communion looked up to see what the commotion was about.

Having got through security Sam dared to look at his watch again. The woman's watch must have been fast – it was still only ten past two by his reckoning. He still had a couple of minutes to check something.

'Hi there Sam,' said Kev as Sam entered the jury deliberation room for the last time.

'Been in the pub? We thought you were going to be late.'

'Sorry, I was just...'

Chantelle entered the room as Sam spoke. Everybody stopped.

'Are we ready? You do not need to be in any order now. Just follow me please.'

Sam hung back. He had to look at his trial notes. As the others filed out, he walked to the table, found his notes and turned to the photograph they had been shown of Yamin.

There it was. Yamin had the sinister tattoo on the left side of his neck. The cats swirling around in a spider's web.

'Come on Sam. I want to get home,' Brian said as he stood by the door.

'Yes, sorry.'

Sam left his notes and jogged to the back of the line entering the Court Number One. His legs were unstable, his mind was racing. He filed in with only Maria's innocence on his mind.

> *Five little kittens sitting in a web*
> *A spider came along and now they're dead.*

The court was full of people waiting to hear the sentence. The public gallery and press benches were groaning under the weight of family, friends of the deceased and news-hungry hacks. All Sam could think about was the fact that Yamin could be Qin. He had come to see Lucy and the boys, to drop off the whisky. He had been to Sam's house; he had seen his family. Qin had gone back to Central Asia at the same time as Yamin ran away.

Maria Kayakova was sitting in the same position all trial. She had no discernible emotion on her face except the continuously sad look she had in her eyes. Sam felt he knew her better now than he did two hours ago. He had no proof of course but it did all seem to fit. The timings, the descriptions and of course the characteristics explained to him in the trial, what he heard on the telephone and from what Lucy had said.

The other jurors were looking forward to the sentencing like a group of Romans at the Coliseum, conclusion and closure burning in their eyes. Kev and Brian were rubbing their hands.

'All rise,' said the clerk of the court, much louder than normal, playing to the swollen crowd.

The judge came swooping in through the door at the back of the court. The court fell silent as he took centre stage at the front. Hamlet was about to perform.

'The defendant will remain seated until I ask her to stand.'

'Maria Kayakova. No divine purpose brings freedom from sin. You have been found guilty of murder and therefore there are guidelines and precedence I must follow in sentencing you. I am obliged to look at the detail of your trial and make allowances for what has happened. It has been established that you entered into an operation involving joint enterprise. You wilfully assisted Yamin Shakirov to assault Kumara Darsha and inflict injuries which led to his death. You drugged him in an attempt to slow him down and you befriended him to gain access to his house.'

'The gravity of the offence indicates a life sentence. Guidance suggests I must send you to prison for a minimum of fifteen years. I also need to take into account other factors like whether you pose a significant threat to the public.'

'I must turn to the issues arising from this trial. You have already spent two hundred and fifty-seven days in custody in relation to this case and I have taken this into account. You have lied to this court under oath when questioned about many aspects of this charge, most notably in regard to the drugging of the victim. You were also, in my opinion, trying to deceive the jury by asking for an interpreter who was in fact not necessary. You ran down to the South-West of England instead of reporting this crime to the authorities.'

Sam sat listening to the precision of the judge's delivery. He was shocked by the increased volume and depth of the words he used. This was the business end of the trial and each word from the judge was uttered as if chiselled from marble. Sam noticed that all eyes were on the judge as he spoke. Sam's were fixed on Maria. The more Sam thought about the truth the more she looked like a victim. This was why she looked disinterested in the judge's words. Frankly it looked like she had given up hope long ago. Her freedom had been skilfully burglarised away from her, she had been stitched up by a professional.

'Would the defendant please stand.'

Maria looked at the guard next to her to be sure. She stood and held on to the Perspex rim of the dock. Her eyes showed a slight dampness, her increasingly puffy face tilted up in a show of respect for the court.

'Maria Kayakova, I have considered all the aspects of this trial in conjunction with the guidance given to me for a crime such as this. You will go to prison for eighteen years. You may go down.'

With this there was an eruption of noise. Just as Sam's verdict had caused commotion, the sentence sparked off celebrations from the family and friends of Kumara Darsha. The representatives of the press ran from the court, eager no doubt to report the sentence.

'All rise.'

The judge left as Maria was helped out of the dock, back down the concrete steps to the cells. She was too weak to walk unassisted. Sam looked up at the public gallery. He caught the eye of a woman in the front row. She waved and lifted her thumb up to him. Her smile beamed from ear to ear. Sam just wanted to get away from this episode of his life.

'Thank you, members of the jury, you are free to go.' said the clerk of the court.

They all stood, turned to the left and walked out of the court. They were never to see each other again. As they approached the exit some of the men turned and gave a cursory nod whilst the women all embraced. Outside the court the jury melted back into normal life, like none of this had happened. The performance was over so Sam pulled up his collar, placed his beanie hat on his head and drifted to the tube station.

Sam stopped just before the entrance to Mansion House. He had walked the long way around via St Paul's just in case any family or friends wanted to talk to him. He pulled out his mobile phone, switched it on and called the network operator. He asked for the number for the Russian Embassy in London. They put him straight through.

'Can I speak to Yamin Shakirov, please?'

'One minute, Sir.'

After two minutes the lady came back onto the line. They had nobody on the directory under that name.

Part III

Shepherd the flock with justice

As a shepherd looks after his scattered flock when he is with them, so will I look after my sheep. I will rescue them from all the places where they were scattered on a day of clouds and darkness.

Ezekiel 34:12

Chapter XX

Chelsea, London

Sam sat at his desk in front of the laptop in his spare-room office. It was after ten at night; supper and children's bedtime were long gone. Lucy had gone to bed to read and all was quiet in the house. Sam poured a glass of red from the second bottle of the night.

The light from the computer screen reflected off Sam's face as he stared at the latest web page he had called up. He had spent hours looking at sites which detailed drug trafficking across the Middle East. He had to find something to neutralise his growing sense of guilt about Maria.

He had returned to Wolfenberg to suffer the same pressures that had faced him every day before the trial. Peter Heathcliff had allowed Sam only a few hours back in his chair before calling him in and lecturing him on the need to refocus on revenues and growth. His clients were just as demanding, still asking Sam to perform miracles in a stagnant equity market. He kept them at bay with the same old synthesis of bullshit and optimism.

Qin Property had been very quiet since his return. There had been the odd payment and an occasional call from Martin Zhao but nothing like before. Sam had seen this type of behaviour previously, the clients who slip into the shadowlands before making a change of manager. The silence was a waiting room which usually prompted greater effort from Sam but this time he was not bothered. He knew more than he ever should about Xanchu Qin. If they ever found out he would surely hurt Sam and his family. Sam had to look beyond this. He had to press on with his research.

The thing which concerned Sam the most about work was the change in attitude of his immediate team. Joanna and Will had become distant and seemed to have their own private understanding which didn't include Sam. He felt guilty only because he knew he had taken advantage of the people around him for far too long. Politics at any large institution required constant attention, take your eye off the ball and the walls would come tumbling down. Sam knew he was losing his grip, the truth was he didn't care as much as he used to. He was getting in later and leaving earlier. The presence of young children masked the truth in Sam's case. The storm had been rumbling on in the distance for some time but now Sam had to face the pointlessness of his career head on – he needed to clear the air. The truth was that his time at the Old Bailey had uncovered elements of the real world; barristers and judges performing important, morally sound roles which made his job of striving to make the wealthy wealthier seem trite, greedy and unsatisfying.

Sam clicked on another link. A bright blue page appeared in front of him, text on the left and a map of the Golden Crescent. This area included Iran, Afghanistan and the countries to the north including Uzbekistan and Turkmenistan. With renewed keenness Sam read the text down the side of the page.

Afghanistan contains the most sophisticated and productive opium processing plants in the region. The Northern provinces provide drugs which easily flow across the Turkmen, Tajik and Uzbek boarders. All of these areas fall under the influence of the Northern Alliance. An estimated ninety per cent of all heroin consumed in Russia is sourced from Northern Afghanistan. In turn the vast majority of heroin consumed in Europe first passes through Russia.

Sam had researched China's involvement in drug trafficking. Most searches had thrown up discussions focussing on the South-East region known as the Golden Triangle. This time he wanted to explore the connection between the Middle East and China. Sam tapped away and found another site.

Up to twenty per cent of Chinese opium enters the country from Afghanistan.

Sam felt like he was getting closer to the link between Shakirov and Qin, to the real reason he came to London in the first place. There had to be more on the links between the Russian states and the Chinese.

Sam turned as he saw Lucy enter the room.

'What is wrong with you?' she said as she stopped beside him.

'What?'

'All you do is look through those ridiculous websites,' her finger jabbed at the screen. 'When are you going to drop your silly theory so we can all get back to normal? We need your income Sam; please don't lose your job chasing whimsical fantasies.'

'I need to know the truth, darling. You have no idea how I feel. If I am right, we sent an innocent woman to prison for eighteen years. I just can't think about anything else.'

'Listen Sam, I understand how exciting the trial was for you. Heaven knows, you have talked about it enough. You have...'

'I enjoyed the whole thing, yes, but that doesn't make what

happened right...'

'Let me finish will you,' Lucy raised her voice to re-establish control.

Sam stared back waiting for her to continue. There was a mildly helpless look on his face.

'I know how you feel Sam, however you have to be practical here. You told me the judge agreed with you when he summed up. You have to let go. You were caught up in a murder trial and twelve of you sent a woman to prison. It happens every day Sam.'

'But I know she has been terrorised by this Qin man. It all makes sense Lucy. The timings fit. The descriptions match, even the way the prosecution explained his temper. They are the same person I am sure of it.'

'Fine, so what are you going to do about it? He has fled back to the Middle East and your only lifeline is spending eighteen years in prison.'

'I want to talk to her barrister. I want to let her know.'

'She will be debarred from talking to you, you'd be mad to see her. Don't ruin her career as well Sam.'

'But she could help me...'

'Sam, she will laugh at you. Laugh and then have you arrested for being a fucking idiot.'

Lucy stared at her husband with her finger against her head.

'Think about what your priorities are Sam. It's time to grow up.'

Sam stared at his wife as she turned and left the room.

'Come to bed!' he heard Lucy shout as she walked across the landing.

Sam shook his head slightly and rolled the computer mouse to the hibernate button. Just then the computer gave a soft beep and an indicator appeared next to his message icon. He rolled the mouse back over it and clicked. He could not recognise the sender for the title only contained a series of numbers and letters. It must be spam he thought. Sam clicked again to open the new message.

Please be careful.

Sam stared at the screen. Who could have sent this? Was it Qin or Martin? How could they see what he was up to?

The computer beeped again; another message from the same sender. Sam opened it immediately.

You focus on your priorities Waghorne. Concentrate at work and look after your family.

Sam stood up and took a step back from the computer. He was frightened now. Any mention of his family took his concern to a new level. It must be Martin and the boys from Qin. As quickly as he could he switched off his computer and left the study. He was determined not to give up. He had come too far and seen too much. He knew things had gone too quiet with the account. His sixth sense had been right. They knew where he lived and that made Charlie and George vulnerable. He couldn't let them near his family. If Sam's theory was right, these guys were killers.

He had to see Eleanor as soon as possible.

Chapter XXI

6 Letterstone Court, London

Sam had told Joanna he had a private appointment and he would be away from the office for a couple of hours. She had barely raised her head when she grunted a half-hearted acknowledgement. Sam thought she couldn't care less and frankly preferred it when he was not around.

A few minutes later Sam slipped through a small alleyway off Chancery Lane and entered Letterstone Court where grand stone buildings rose on both sides of the street. Each address was furnished with a wide-open entrance at the top of an imposing set of steps. Sam looked for number six. As he drew near, he could see a painted list to the side of each entrance. All of the barristers in residence at the chambers were listed on the wall. At the top of the list stood the QC's and the most experienced practitioners of the chambers. He found Eleanor's name halfway down.

Sam looked around him and mounted the stairs. Another stairwell ran up the left-hand side of the hall. He looked on the wall by a big solid oak door that felt like it had been in place for centuries. The sign was in bold italic ink indicating the clerk's office.

Sam knew a little bit about how these places worked. The clerks and particularly the Chief Clerk were in charge of booking jobs to the chamber's barristers. They were very important people who had the capacity to make or break careers. Sam had not made an appointment and it was very likely Eleanor was not in chambers. She could be with clients or even at a trial at any criminal court around the country. Sam was a gambler and had taken a chance. He would come back if she was not here, come back as many times as were necessary. He had to speak to her.

Once in the office he gave two crisp knocks on the glass hatch. He saw a short middle-aged man approach the other side. He wore a grey waistcoat and had slicked back dark hair. He was probably in his fifties and was wearing half-moon glasses. He looked extremely busy.

'Good morning sir, how can I help you?' said the man with a polite South London accent.

'Err, yes. Good morning. I, um, was wondering if I could see Miss Sechford-Jones this morning.'

'Do you have an appointment with her sir?'

'No, um, I'm sorry I don't.'

The small man stared over his glasses at Sam for a few seconds.

'My barristers are all very busy people. If you want to speak to any of them, you need to speak to us first. Miss Sechford Jones' diary is booked up for weeks in advance.'

'I just need to speak to her for ten minutes, is she in her chambers?' Sam added the second point with a good helping of hopeful inflection.

'Give me a minute sir. Can I take your name please?'

'Sam Waghorne, with an e.'

'Will she know what it is about, sir?'

'If you mention that I would like to talk about Maria that would be very kind.'

The hatch slammed shut in front of Sam's nose. He took a step back with the shock.

A minute later the hatch door swung open.

'Mr Waghorne?' The clerk's voice carried down the corridor

'Yes, sorry. Is she there?'

'Miss Sechford-Jones has a full diary today but if you hurry she can see you now for five minutes only. Second floor.'

The hatch slammed again but Sam didn't notice. He was already halfway through the door heading for the stairs.

The building grew warmer as Sam climbed the stairs to the second floor. Carpet appeared on the steps and there were pictures on the walls. He turned from the stairs and looked at each of the white doors he passed. Around the first corner he stopped. There was the name he wanted, beautifully inscribed on a brass plate in the middle of the vast door. Eleanor's room.

It was time to get his story straight. He only had a few minutes to get it across. He had prepared for this moment but still felt nervous. There was sweat on his palms and his heart was racing like an express train. This was it. He stepped up and knocked on the door.

'Yes!' A booming voice shouted from inside the room.

Sam twisted the big brass handle and pushed on the door.

Sam was not prepared for what he saw in front of him as he entered. The room was vast but a complete mess. All the walls except the one with windows were covered from ceiling to floor in bookshelves, full of legal books. There must have been a thousand leather bound books in the room. There were two sofas completely covered with bound legal papers, old newspapers, items of clothing and unopened crisp packets. The floor was littered with shoes of various descriptions and fought for space with full shopping bags and yet more piles of legal notes. There was a table in the far corner or at least Sam thought it must be a table or else even more unordered matter was levitating of its own accord – there was not an inch of the table-top visible.

In the corner by the window was Eleanor's wooden desk. This contained very much less paperwork and was illuminated by a strong light coming from a desktop lamp. Eleanor sat behind the desk and stood as Sam entered.

'Good morning, please do come in. How can I help...' Eleanor Sechford-Jones cut herself off as she looked at Sam standing in front of the closing door.

'I recognise you, have we met before?'

'My name is Sam Waghorne, Miss Sechford-Jones. Thank you for agreeing to see me at such short...'

'Your face is familiar. I...'

'I was on the jury for the trial of Maria Kayakova. You know the trial that finished a...'

'What are you doing? I cannot speak with you Mr Waghorne. Do you know anything about ethics? I would be debarred if they found out you had come to see me.'

'Yes, but I need to talk to...'

'I must ask you to leave immediately. Who did you speak to downstairs?'

'One of your clerks I assume.'

'I'm sorry but you must go.' Eleanor came towards Sam with her right arm outstretched, trying to shoo him out of her chambers.

'You have no idea how seriously they take this kind of thing. Please leave,' Eleanor placed her hand on the brass doorknob and pulled.

'I need to talk to you about Maria and Yamin. I think there has been a terrible mistake. I think she is innocent.'

'Mr Waghorne, you were the foreman of a jury at the Old Bailey in a trial of a woman I was defending. I have nothing to say to you.' Eleanor shifted her head to indicate he must leave.

'I think I know who Yamin is and where he has gone. Maria was telling the truth, she had nothing to do with the murder.'

Eleanor let the door shut and glared at Sam for a few seconds. Sam could see many calculations going on in her head. Sam had seen how ambitious she was during the trial. She must be slightly curious as to what he had to say.

After she had scrutinised his face for thirty seconds she spoke again.

'I am cross you came to see me here, Mr Waghorne. Please do not do that again. It is embarrassing to me and my chambers that you have done this. However, I am interested to listen to what you have to say. Do you have a card? I will call you.'

Sam took a business card from his breast pocket and took a pen from the opposite side. He wrote a number on the back of the card.

'Use this one. Best to keep some things away from one's employer.'

Eleanor took the card and reopened the door. Neither she nor Sam said a word as he left.

Sam bounded down the stairs and walked briskly through the hallway. As he walked towards the passage back to Chancery Lane, he didn't notice the short, spectacled man looking out of the window of the clerk's office.

Back at work Sam switched on his computer and brought up his emails. Most of them were garbage from brokers touting their latest weak ideas. Two drew his attention. The first he opened was from Martin Zhao. He was asking Sam to organise a meeting next week. They wished to run through recent portfolio performance and discuss the future with Sam. Martin mentioned they were starting to lose confidence in Wolfenberg to manage their affairs in the manner they wanted. Sam had to convince them the bank wanted them as clients. Frankly this was the last thing Sam wanted but he flicked through his diary and replied with a couple of suitable dates which were early enough in the morning to make lunch a non-starter. From the tone of the email, lunch was the last thing on Zhao's mind.

The other email that caught Sam's attention was from Aaron Snee. He read it and decided to call rather than reply.

'Hello?' said Aaron after a couple of rings.

'Hi Aaron, it's Sam. I've just read your message. I have had an email from the client – they want to meet me next week.'

'Ok Sam. I just wanted to update you on our investigations. We may have to ask them to leave the bank.'

'I want Compliance to do that if you don't mind, these guys are quite aggressive, I'm not sure it would go down too well coming from me.'

'Well we will see. I would prefer it to come from the client adviser Sam but nothing has been decided yet. I will let you know how we intend to proceed.'

'Ok, thanks Aaron.' Sam put the phone down,

'Fucking typical.' He said under his breath. They do all the easy stuff and leave the difficult bits to the front office. Martin Zhao would cut Sam's balls off if he said he had to close the account.

Sam decided on a long walk.

Sam chose a bench in the graveyard of St Sepulchre's. He sat down in front of the church and looked down Old Bailey at a dispersing crowd. Another show was over for today. The wind gently blew the leafless branches of the massive sycamores to his left. What was Maria doing now? Holed up in her cell at Holloway, trying to make the most of the situation. No doubt she was already into a sterile and tedious routine. How did people cope with prison? Did they find things to do during the day? Learn new skills that would serve them well when they got out or did they drown themselves in a sea of self-pity and regret?

Sam wanted to speak with her, to get his message across. He had to go and see her but he knew he would never get into the prison as a visitor. She didn't know who he was. His name would mean nothing to her. He didn't even know whether she was allowed visitors.

Sam's mobile rang in his pocket. It must be Joanna finding out where the hell he was. He took it out but didn't recognise the number. A sudden fear gripped him. Another Chinese threat perhaps.

'Hello?'

'Mr Waghorne?'

'Yes,' Sam said in a meek voice. Six months ago, he would have demanded who was speaking.

'This is Eleanor Sechford-Jones. Listen, I need to meet with you. Where are you?'

Sam's heart quickened with a sudden shot of adrenalin.

'Hello, yes, err, I am just taking a walk. I am just by St Paul's. Where do you want to meet?'

'Somewhere quiet, away from here. Do you know *Le Gros Boucher* in Smithfield's Market? It's on Hosier Lane. I'll be there in twenty minutes, in the basement bar.'

The phone went dead. Sam looked at the screen as he thought. Perhaps things were looking up. Eleanor's ambition might be stronger than her ethics after all. He needed to get his story straight. He also had no idea where the wine bar was. He stood and looked around. He had to get there as soon as he could. With a glass of red in his hand he could get his story straight before she arrived.

Having asked an exhausted meat market worker, Sam found the bar on Hosier Lane. It had seen better days, the black paint around the door was peeling and the odd poster in the window detailed events which had long since passed. It was dark inside and only a few customers could be seen through the dirty glass.

Sam pushed on the door and went inside the bar. A faint smell of garlic and stale alcohol greeted him as he came in. Sam wrinkled his nose and the barman saw.

'Apologies monsieur,' the barman said in a terrible French accent. 'We 'ad snails on ze menu and zey proved to be very popular.'

'Do you have a spare table downstairs?'

'Well, I sink zey are all spare, cannot I tempt you wiz a table at ze window?' said the barman.

'No, downstairs will be fine,' Sam said walking towards the small staircase at the back.

'Could you bring me a bottle of house red and two glasses?'

'Of course Sir, we 'ave a nice claret. Very good.'

Sam walked past several black and white framed photos as he climbed down into the basement bar. The lighting was even worse than upstairs. He walked past two men in chef's clothes sitting at a small table. They stopped talking as he went by, looking up at Sam like he had just ruined their day. Sam found a table at the back and sat down to wait for Eleanor.

Sam checked his watch. He had five minutes or so to get his story together. Eleanor would be brisk and pushy. He had to get as much across as quickly as possible. He would mention the Chinese clients at work and the shocking similarities between Yamin Shakirov and Xanchu Qin.

He checked his watch again then straightened in his chair. There was a creaking on the wooden stairs. Somebody was coming down.

In fact, it was two people. A woman wearing a woollen hat and high collared coat was followed by a waiter carrying Sam's order. The woman walked up to Sam unbuttoning her coat whilst the waiter brushed past to place the open bottle and glasses on the table. He scuttled off without a sound. He looked like he was used to such mid-afternoon liaisons. He was back at the top of the stairs before Eleanor spoke.

'Mr Waghorne...'

'Please call me Sam?'

Eleanor stared for a few seconds.

'Ok Sam. Tell me what you wanted to say earlier.'

Sam poured two glasses of red, pushing one of them towards Eleanor. She took it and took a healthy gulp. Sam did the same.

'I think Maria Kayakova has been the victim of a crime far more serious than any of us realised. I think she was telling the truth that she was not responsible for the murder of Kumara Darsha. I think she has been terrorised and controlled by a man working in a gang which has come to London, not to deal in low level drug trafficking but something far more sophisticated, something which covers much, much more.'

'Sam stop, what on earth are you talking about?'

'I have been caught up in something at work; something that I had no idea about before the trial. It sounds like a preposterous coincidence but I think there is a connection between Yamin and a man in charge of a company who is a client of my bank. Christ, it sounds absurd when I say it.'

Eleanor took another outsized swig of wine. Her glass was almost empty after two hits.

'Go on,' she said wiping her mouth with a lack of grace.

'Well these Chinese guys came to the bank looking for somewhere to keep their money, somewhere safe but with the possibility of making it grow. Typical client really, they wanted security and to take risks all at the same time.'

'Annoying but hardly unique.' said Eleanor. Sam realised he was dealing with a bright girl.

'Yes precisely. Anyway, I met with a group of about ten of them, a board of directors if you like. We got on well and with the help of my boss we signed them up.'

It was Sam's turn to have a drink.

'All went well for the first few months. Markets were good so the client transferred more money to us. They told us they were going to buy properties in London. Cash was coming over from their parent company. The client seemed pleased and everything was great at first. We get paid for growing the business you see so my bosses were very pleased.'

'Sorry, where is it you work Sam?'

'Wolfenberg AG, in the City. Just off...'

'Oh yes, I've dealt with them before. German.'

'I started to get requests to transfer money away; far more than normal for an account like this. First just small amounts but then much bigger flows, in and out. Our Compliance department monitor these things and they have started to become suspicious.'

'Money laundering?'

'Yes, washing criminal money through us to make it legitimate. It is what criminals try and do.'

'So, what is the link to Maria?'

'Wait, I will come to that. The Chinese client's main man started to call me directly and he sent presents to my house. He met my wife and children one afternoon. I have never met him; he was always busy when the others came to see us.'

'What was his name?'

'His name is Xanchu Qin, the same name as the company. He is a member of the family who set the business up. As I say I have never met him, just spoken to him on the phone. We deal with his number two, Martin Zhao. He and his other directors sat with us at the first meeting.'

'In recent months Martin has become aggressive on the phone - impatient. He has been telling me they are not happy with the service they are receiving.'

'Things went quiet during the trial but I have received strange emails at home. Messages warning me not to dig around, telling me to look after my family. It is almost like they are watching me or have a way to track what I am doing on my computer at home.'

'You think these are from Qin?'

'I have no idea. It is all very strange. Anyway, after a few months we were told Qin had gone back home. We were told to wire money to Uzbekistan; to a bank in Tashkent. This sent Compliance into a flat spin. Martin Zhao kept on calling me to make sure I understood what they wanted.'

'So what position are you in today?'

'I suspect they will fire us next week given recent performance. Also, Compliance want to sack them, they have had enough of all the money flows. The only person who wants to keep them is my boss. He has connections into Government and apparently there are pressures to make sure they get all they require.'

'A show-down next week, eh?'

'Yup, a right proper fuck up and I'm in the middle of it.'

'So, what is the link with Maria then?'

'It's crazy but I think Yamin and Qin are the same guy. They both went abroad at the same time. They both have bad tempers. Our Compliance team are convinced Qin is involved with drug money coming in from China and going back to drug related countries.'

'Is that it? Sam, I think you need a holiday.'

'There's one more thing. The tattoo on Yamin's neck, you know the cats in the spider's web.'

'Yes.'

'I looked into it. That represents a gang involved with drugs in Russian prisons. I can see why Yamin would have a tattoo like this but I think Qin had the same. My sons saw it on his neck when he came to my house to drop off a bottle of whisky. They were singing about it when I got home. I only realised just before the judge sentenced Maria.'

'What else Sam? Is there anything else?'

'I called the Russian Embassy. They have never heard of a Yamin Shakirov.'

Eleanor finished her glass without taking her eyes off Sam. Sam refilled it.

'It sounds like nonsense when I say it all together. I think Maria has got involved in something much bigger than we realised, than she realised.'

'What do you think you can do Sam? Maria has gone to prison for a very long time.'

'I want to talk to her. I need to tell her my thoughts. I want to know more about her; I want to know who Yamin really was, why they came to London.'

'Sam, that's impossible. She doesn't know who you are. She'll never see you.'

It was Sam's turn to stare. Sam felt like this had been a waste of time. He filled his glass to the brim.

'Sam, to be honest, I was only curious to hear your story because, between you and me, I too do not think Maria Kayakova received a fair trial. I believe the judge was far too sympathetic towards the prosecution and drew up his steps to verdict document in such a way as to make a guilty verdict very accessible. I don't think you made the wrong choice necessarily; I just feel the judge made it too easy for you to reach a guilty verdict.'

Sam was already lost.

'I'm sorry, what do you mean?'

'These things are very subtle Sam. I think he had it in for me. He wanted to derail my career.'

'What?'

'Ok, Sam I'll tell you the truth. He tried it on with me. During the trial he tried it on with me.'

'Where?'

'What do you mean where? Why does that matter?'

'At the Old Bailey?'

'Yes, as a matter of fact, in his chambers.'

'The dirty old stoat! Fuck! I'll drink to that. Weren't you tempted by all that authority, the long white wig?'

'Stop it Sam, I'm being serious. He asked me out but I cancelled at the last minute. After that he had it in for me – in truth he probably started before then. You didn't see it but after that night, rulings went Robert's way. He was short with me in court and, as I said, the way he steered the jury was pathetic.'

'Are you telling me judges can move a trial in a particular direction?'

'Of course. It's so subtle you hardly realise. They can be like magicians when they want to be.'

'It's called the Pygmalion Effect. Outcomes can be influenced by the attitude of leaders. It has been proved jurors are persuaded by a judge who believes a defendant is guilty. Whether the jury like it or not it does happen. I think Barniston made it abundantly clear what his thoughts were to you lot. Do you not agree?'

'Well, I haven't really thought about it.'

'Crap. You have thought of nothing else since you left the trial. That's obvious.'

'OK, OK. I must get back to work in a minute. I am pretty sure you need to as well. What are we going to do about this?'

'Let me have a think. I might go and see Maria to run a couple of points past her,' said Eleanor with finality.

'Do you need a Visitors Order? How do you get in to see her?'

Eleanor looked at Sam with interest.

'You have done your research haven't you? Well, don't worry; one of my clerks will talk to the Head of Operations at Holloway. Legal visitors are given access all the time; we are always coming and going from there seeing clients on remand.'

'Will you call me when you decide what we can do?'

'Yes, but Sam, don't get too excited. Your theory may have some truth but there is very little you can do about it I'm sure.'

'It might even help you Eleanor,' Sam said draining his glass. He knew this would raise the stakes.

'Perhaps Sam, perhaps.'

Eleanor reached for the bottle and poured the remaining contents into both glasses. They both picked them up simultaneously.

'Maria.' they announced together.

Chapter XXII

Chelsea, London

A few days later Sam sat at the kitchen table. It was eight fifteen and all was peaceful in the house following Lucy's and the boy's whirlwind school run departure.

Eleanor had called the day before to explain that she had organised a meeting with Maria. The clerk had contacted HMP Holloway and received a slot during visiting time. She was due to see her at eleven thirty today. Sam had other ideas.

Sam folded his paper and went to take a shower. He would call work at eight thirty to explain the mystery illness which would be keeping him from the office that day. Masculine twenty-four hour 'flu could be very sudden and equally as nasty. Once this call was out of the way there was just one more to make, then Sam would be in the clear.

Sam had a quick practice before making the call to Joanna. A few months back this would have been a light-hearted exchange. Joanna was perfectly capable of running the desk without Sam there and they both knew it. She used to relish the days he was not there; it was an opportunity to prove herself. The relationship with Joanna had deteriorated and they no longer shared the same confidence. Sam was convinced Joanna wanted to take a couple of the team and go it alone, find some other company and make a fresh start with Sam's clients. This was a consequence of Sam neglecting her, spending less and less time caring about the team. Suddenly Sam was reluctant to make the call. If he lost Joanna and others his career would be over.

Sam made the call and, predictably, Joanna seemed to be distant. They had a brief, hollow conversation on the recent features in the market; going through the motions. Joanna said things would be fine when Sam said he felt unwell and would not be coming in. His diary was free and not much was going on. She said he should take as long as he needed.

Sam rang off with mixed emotions. He was relieved to have got this hurdle out of the way; he could now get on with the main work of the day. He felt bad about Joanna though, her nonchalance made him nervous. So much had changed in recent months. Sam no longer provided support for her career development. A Pygmalion Effect in reverse perhaps – she wanted to break free now Sam had become distracted. Others in the bank had recognised her talent and were constantly telling her. Given Sam's absence, it was not surprising to see the change in attitude. She wanted to get on and Sam was not helping anymore.

That was for tomorrow.

Sam checked his watch as he stood from the breakfast table. Just before nine. He cleared his plate to the sink and practiced a London accent, one any Cockney would have been proud of. He turned back to the table and picked up the phone and the piece of paper next to it, the latter had written on it the fruits of yesterday evening's internet session. Just two telephone numbers.

Having stared at the phone for thirty seconds he started dialling the first number on the paper. After three rings the line connected.

'Oliver Barniston's chambers. How can I help you?' said a soft female voice on the line.

'Oh yes, good morning Miss. This is Miss Sechford-Jones' chambers. She has asked me to call you to fix up an urgent meeting with her this morning. Would His Honour be available around midday?'

'His Honour is not here at the moment but he has a space at lunch time. Perhaps I could call you back when I have confirmed with him.'

'Yes of course. If you could confirm that would be great,' said Sam. He read out the second number.

'Can I take a name?'

'One of us will be here,' said Sam thinking on his feet.

'OK, thanks. I'll call you back later.'

Sam hung up. He was still a terrific liar.

A glance at the kitchen clock. He would leave at ten for his appointment.

At eleven fifteen Sam asked his taxi driver to stop fifty yards from the entrance to Holloway prison. He wanted to walk the final steps with nobody watching him. He was about to take an enormous gamble. He knew he was taking a big risk but several sessions online had provided him with the knowledge to give him a chance. Eleanor would have asked her team of clerks to book up the meeting with Maria. One of them would have called the prison office. Old-fashioned approach, surname and initial. This was the risk Sam took. Meetings with barristers or lawyers were very common; with a bit of luck Sam would be shown through security if he looked the part.

There were two short beeps from his mobile. It was an SMS from Eleanor telling him something important had come up so she would not be able to make it to see Maria.

At the entrance Sam looked both ways, pulled down the brim of his felt hat and walked with purpose towards the prison office at the front of the building. Tucked under his left arm was a random selection of papers he had bundled together and tied with pink ribbon. He was proud of his home-made legal papers, this and the hat made him look the part.

In front of him the mighty walls of the main prison rose up to a height of over thirty feet. The prison had an eighties feel with most of it made of red brick - it looked new and functional; more modern university than prison. Sam saw the vast wooden doors which stood in front of him. The visitors centre was just to the right but he couldn't help thinking how intimidating the doors were, like a medieval castle only to keep dangerous people in rather than out.

After a few deep lungfuls Sam strode into the Visitor's Centre with the necessary professional purpose. He bustled up to the desk and dropped his fake legal bundle on top of it.

'Edward Sechford-Jones to see Maria Kayakova at eleven-thirty,' he declared in his best Oxford English. The words were well enunciated, clipped just like a barristers would be. Sam also tried to include as much exasperation as possible.

The security officer looked at Sam for a few seconds like he had announced he had burnt down an orphanage. Sam looked down and saw he had in fact interrupted the guard's tabloid crossword.

The guard reached across for the list of legal visitors. This was it. What had the clerk at Eleanor's chambers told them? Sam felt a bead of sweat forming on his brow just under his hat. It ran down the side of his face. Sam caught it just before it fell onto the reception desk.

Sam tried to see the name as the guard fingered the list. There it was, just the surname. Sam was so relieved he made an involuntary laugh. The guard looked up and Sam smiled back.

'In through the scanner then across the courtyard to the Visitor's Hall in the main prison. They will let you in over there.'

'Yes, thank you. I have been here before you know.' Sam spat. He was starting to enjoy the make believe.

As Sam turned to walk towards the airport-like scanner he caught a glimpse of the guard's face reflected in the glass of the window. He looked at Sam and shook his head before returning to his gentle word game.

Sam was relieved to walk through the scanner with no drama. He collected his document bundle and scuttled across the courtyard to a small door with a sign saying Visitor's Hall marked in faded letters. Despite getting through the first test of the name, his heart had quickened across the courtyard. He pushed on the door and went in.

He was immediately met by a booming voice.

'Follow me Sir!'

Sam turned to face the direction of the order. A brute of a man stood in front of him in prison officers' uniform.

'Come on Sir, you only have twenty minutes.'

'Yes, yes. Sorry,' said Sam as the guard started to walk towards a big metal door in the far corner of the room.

Sam was led into a cold, grey coloured room. He could see his breath rise up in condensed plumes in front of him as he walked just behind the guard. He was shown to a small plastic and metal table in the middle of the room. There were two simple chairs set out either side of the table.

'Have a seat Sir, the prisoner knows their guest has arrived.'

Sam felt nerves rise up again as the guard spoke. Imagine what they would think if they found out he was an imposter, a pseudo barrister here only to satisfy his own curiosity.

The guard left Sam alone in the room. The battleship grey walls looked like they may freeze a hand if touched. Service pipes ran up and down the walls like the veins of an old man's leg. There were no windows. A couple of strip lights only just threw a milky glow onto the table. The corners of the room were dark. Another door grew out of the dark on the other side of the room - the inmates entrance given the additional locks.

Sam put his stunt legal papers on the table. He thought about taking his coat off but, after quick reflection around the room, sat down with it on. He placed his hat on the papers providing some cover for the bogus document. Sam waited. Looking around there weren't any security cameras or perhaps they were hidden.

Sam looked at his watch. Five minutes had passed since he sat down. What was wrong? He looked around nervously. Had they checked the schedules? Were they calling the police? He shifted his papers on the table. This was madness, what was he thinking?

A clunking sound from the darkened door brought his focus back. Sam sat up in his chair, his eyes narrowed to see what was going on. After a couple more metallic sounds, the door opened to bring another guard in. He said nothing as he stood to one side, eyes fixed on the wall opposite.

Soft, squidgy steps made Sam get to his feet. Maria Kayakova appeared at the doorway. Sam was shocked to see her in what looked like her own clothes. No denim dungarees or orange boiler suit. Maria walked a couple of steps into the room. Sam got a better look at her. She looked good in her casual clothes with her long blonde hair tied back in a ponytail.

'Twenty minutes.' said the guard. He walked behind Maria and closed the door.

It was just Maria and Sam in the room. Maria's eyes had adjusted to the poor light and she was staring at Sam.

Sam stood staring back. He didn't seem to know what to say. Perhaps it wasn't his call.

Finally, she spoke.

'Who are you?' Maria said in a voice Sam immediately recognised. 'I was told Eleanor was coming to see me.'

Sam paused. He wanted her to recognise him. He didn't want her to call the guard.

Maria's face was fixed on Sam. There was a flicker, a brief sign. Maria's eyes narrowed as she stared. Something was happening.

'Why are you...'

Maria stopped mid-sentence. Her head gave a slight tilt to one side, an animal instinct Sam had seen in dogs.

'You were from the trial. In the jury.'

Sam felt himself nod. No words, he wanted her to carry on.

'What are you here for? I don't understand,' Maria demanded. 'What do you want from me?'

Maria flicked a look back at the door she had come from. Sam still said nothing. After another agonising pause Maria turned to the door and took a step towards it.

'Wait!' Sam said with passion. 'I need to talk with you.'

Maria stopped and turned around. It was her turn to be silent.

Sam took a step forward.

'I have been talking to Eleanor. She was supposed to come but I had to see you.'

'You were on the jury, yes?' Maria said. 'What the hell do you want from me? Haven't you done enough damage already? I came here to see Eleanor. Please leave.'

Maria turned once again and knocked on the metal door she had come from.

'I think I can help you. I think we made a terrible mistake. Yamin was not what he seemed. I believe he deceived all of us not just you!' Sam pleaded at full volume.

Maria turned her head back when she heard Yamin's name.

The door opened in front of her. The same guard appeared with a concerned look on his face.

'I heard a knock. Is everything...'

'Err, yes. Thank you,' Maria said. 'Could we get two glasses of water?'

Quick thinking thought Sam. The guard looked at Sam in a curious way then back at Maria.

'Sure.'

He left as quickly as he'd arrived, leaving the door ajar for his return trip with refreshment.

'Sit down,' Maria said in a loud but unemotional voice.

Plastic cups on the table and the door shut again; it was Maria who spoke first.

'I don't know what the hell is going on here. You have taken a big gamble getting in to see me if you have done what I think you...'

'I have.'

'Well then I am happy to listen to what you have to say.'

Maria sat back in her chair with her arms folded across her chest. The movement cast her into shadow.

'I needed to talk to you. I needed to discuss something with you. Something important. Since the trial I have been incapable of focussing on anything else. It has taken over my life.'

'It's kinda taken over mine too. Well here I am. We don't have all day so spit it out. Come on.'

'I think I have been involved with a gang of individuals at work, one of my clients I was happy to take on, people who I thought were good clients. Christ, it all started well, but things turned nasty, really bad once they got their claws into me. I...'

'What's your name?'

'Sam. Sam Waghorne.'

'Well Sam, what the fuck are you talking about?'

'Sorry, I am not making myself clear.'

'Not really no.'

'OK, sorry. I'll try again.'

'I think I have been involved with Yamin's gang in London. I think he and others have been posing as Chinese businessmen. My jury service came along when things started getting nasty. I think Yamin was running a gang pretending to be Chinese investors. We have been investing money for them. Money came into the bank from overseas sources. They claimed to be building up property investments here and needed a bank to help them. My boss gave me the client; he needed one of his more experienced directors to help him. I jumped at the chance.'

'What sort of company do you work for?'

'It's an investment bank; I work for the wealth management side. We take rich clients and manage their money. Most of the time it is fine but these guys paid lots of deposits then started paying it out again. Our Compliance department started to get nervous, worried they are laundering the money, taking bad money and washing it through us, making it clean.'

'What has this got to do with Yamin? He was working for the Russian Embassy.'

'Look,' Sam said. 'I wouldn't be here unless I had something to say to you. It all fits. I never met the main guy. Things were controlled by his number two. Martin Zhao controlled...'

'Who?'

'Martin Zhao. I met him a few times. He is the man in charge of the portfolio I run. He seemed to report to Xanchu Qin. As I said, I never met him.'

'Xanchu Qin. Sam what are you talking about? Who are these people?'

'Sorry. This is why I am here. I think Qin is Yamin. It all fits perfectly.'

'You said you never met Qin and you haven't met Yamin so what the hell do you know? Why are you doing this Sam?'

Sam stared back at Maria trying to read her face. She was getting frustrated with him.

'I think we got it wrong Maria. I think we came to the wrong conclusion about you. Qin came to see my wife and children. He went to my house Maria. My children saw him. He had the same tattoo, the same stammer as you described in court. They said he looked Chinese Maria, just like Yamin's photo.'

'Chinese? He was from Russia Sam.'

'My children are five and eight Maria; they say what they see. I suppose he had Tibetan or Mongol blood?'

'Whatever. Tell me more about what you just said, you got it wrong. What do you mean, wrong?'

'Would you agree to see me again? If I came again would you...'

'Yes. Of course. Why can't you tell me now? Why did you think I was badly treated?'

'Not now Maria, I want to ask you another question, it's much more important than the trial.'

'Go on.'

Sam took another sip.

'Did Yamin hurt you?'

'What do you mean? I...'

'Did he hurt you, physically? Was he a bully?'

'No, I mean he was violent sometimes, with me and others. That was him. He was a strong guy, liked getting his own way.'

'Did he threaten you? Hit you?'

'Sometimes.'

Sam didn't speak.

'He was kind you know, kind most of the time. He had a terrible temper. He could snap easily. I thought it was the line of work he did, security, always having to be aggressive, protecting people.'

'Did he ever talk about his work Maria, did he ever mention colleagues? Did you meet any of them?'

'No, that was always private. He never spoke about it. He was a soldier Sam, that's how we met. In Minsk. Soldiers keep things to themselves.'

'I called the Russian Embassy after the trial Maria, nobody there had heard of Yamin Shakirov.'

'Maybe they didn't want you to know. It is a very secretive place.'

'Or he never worked there. Maria I wouldn't be here if I thought all this was normal. I tell you, he was controlling you, controlling everybody. Did you know why he killed Kumara Darsha. Weren't you a little surprised when he beat him to death?'

'Yamin used a bit of stuff, you know, drugs. He was never involved with selling it. Not that I saw. I promise you I didn't see him kill the guy. Yamin pushed me down the stairs. All I remember was waking up with a sore head and not just from the wine I drank the night before.'

'So why did you look so miserable through the trial Maria. Why didn't you fight harder if you were innocent? Did you drug him?'

'I had no idea about that. It must have been from the restaurant, all I do know is it wasn't me.'

'Did Yamin know where you worked?'

'Yes, he was the one who saw the advert in the window. I went to meet Kumara the day after.'

'It was Yamin then, he planned the whole thing.'

'You need to go Sam; your time is nearly up. What about Eleanor? What if she calls the prison office?'

'She has plenty to think about I'm sure. I will talk to her. When can I come again?'

'As a civilian? Once every two weeks but as I have only had legal visitors,' Maria lifted her eyebrows and forced a half smile, 'you could come back whenever you like.'

'In a couple of days?'

'You book it up, I'll be here. Funny that…'

Both guards came in from the opposite doors after exactly twenty minutes. It had felt like five. Sam stood, shook Maria's hand and walked towards his guard with his untouched belongings. He would have to hope for different guards when he came back. Either that or another disguise beckoned.

The second meeting was much more relaxed. The prison staff had changed and there was no problem getting a time. Sam ditched the hat, choosing shabby casual clothes so nobody had any suspicions about the hour-long meeting. It seemed more compassion was afforded to private visits. He had to fill out more forms containing details of his identity but he didn't mind this now his legal mask had been thrown away along with the headgear. He felt much more comfortable talking to her about his feelings, his views on Yamin and the double life he had been living.

Maria opened up about life back in Belarus with her father, the time she had spent with him before she met Yamin. She seemed keen to talk to Sam about it. She told Sam about her father's accident in Kuznetsovsk and how this affected him. Sam listened intently as Maria spoke of her care, her father's moods swings and how they both daydreamed, a habit developed to numb the pain of their gloomy existence.

Sam asked questions about Maria's mother, learning how she had died giving birth to Maria. Soft, slow tears ran down Maria's cheeks as she told Sam she blamed herself for her mother's death and her father had never forgiven her. She blamed his anger on this. She also thought this was the reason he was so protective, so demanding of her as well. Maria was all he had in life.

Then there was Turkey, how she was sent away because her father needed to work and could not afford to care for Maria as well. Maria had stayed there until she was old enough to go to school at eight. When Maria spoke of her grandmother, calmness gathered in her voice. She seemed to take pleasure in recounting the sensual memories she clearly cherished.

It was the near-fatal accident that changed everything. Dymtrus Kayakova had been working his shift as normal when he had slipped and fallen onto a frozen path. It left him in a wheelchair, so Maria had to look after him. She had no time for friends, struggling to balance school and home life. Dymtrus became cantankerous and frustrated; he drank to help with the pain but this made him violent. Maria grew frightened of him and started to think of life beyond Belarus.

Sam learnt so much in such a short time. Now Maria understood his purpose she was willing to open up. The more she talked the more he was convinced he was right. Maria had been the victim of a monumental deception.

This time the prison guards gave Sam an extra twenty minutes. They must have been observing Maria's tears.

Back at home, Sam sat on the sofa to reflect. He had accomplished what he set out to do; he had made contact with Maria and got his side of the story across. He had also managed to find out a great deal about her. This made the next step clearer in his mind. He had to take action. Lucy was still sceptical; she didn't see any value in this pursuit. Sam had not told her of the trips to Holloway but it was obvious Lucy thought the discussions pointless. At least it was taking his mind off the pressures of work, most notably the worry about what the Chinese would do next.

Sam went to see Eleanor the week after his two meetings with Maria. He knew he had been taking too much time off work recently, so he called her in the morning and arranged to see her at lunchtime. Walking through the stone passage he felt relaxed. With Eleanor back on side he could suggest the next part of his plan.

Eleanor was waiting at the entrance to her chambers. She said hello just as Sam rounded the corner at the top of the stairs. Having shaken her hand warmly, Sam entered her room and sat down on the overloaded sofa after gently persuading some files to make a small gap for his bottom.

'I'm terribly sorry I had to cancel my trip to see Maria. Something important came up,' Eleanor started the conversation with an apology. Sam had momentarily forgotten he was responsible for the meeting she would have had with Oliver Barniston. When he remembered he turned his face away towards the window.

'Oh, yes. I hope everything was OK, you sounded somewhat flustered on the phone.'

'You would never believe what happened. I got a message from the judge'

'Which judge?' Sam said, trying to muster surprise. He kicked himself for not having practiced at home.

'The judge, Oliver Barniston. I went to see him at short notice. I told you what happened during the trial. All very embarrassing you see; I was invited to his chambers during the trial.'

'You told me.'

'He is a very clever man Sam, the only problem is he is also incredibly lonely. He had had a few drinks and got the wrong idea. I wanted to forget it. I thought he called me to apologise.'

'Did he?'

'Did he what? Apologise? No. In fact his clerk was not there when I went to see him. I caught the judge on a break.'

'So he invited you in?'

'Yes, of course. Why wouldn't he? He had asked to see me.'

Sam felt his face turn another shade redder.

'So what happened? What did he want? If he didn't apologise what did he say?'

'He was very interested in my next case. He wants me to stay in touch with him. He was a very ambitious barrister too Sam, when he was younger, he was just like me. He recognises certain qualities in me I think.'

'I bet he does the dirty old weasel. What would his wife think if she found out?'

'She is dead Sam and anyway it is not like that. Not now.'

'But you said he changed the course of the trial to spite you, he hardly said a word to you after that day. If you rejected him why would he want to see you again?' Sam said. The situation was becoming ridiculous with Sam asking why Barniston had asked her to a meeting he hadn't arranged. He must have thought very quickly when he saw her. Perhaps he was as intelligent as Eleanor suggested.

'He is still keen to watch my progress. The senior lawmakers like to watch the less experienced echelons; they like to see who is making the waves, who could be useful to them in the future.'

'I went to see Maria.'

Eleanor stared back, a frown growing across her forehead.

'I went to see her at Holloway after you told me you couldn't go.'

'But, no way, how did you get in there? My clerks would have left my name. How did you get through security? What did she say? What did…'

'They just checked your surname. The prison guards are very relaxed it seems when it comes to legal representatives. I just said your surname and they scanned me in.'

'How long were you there? What did you talk about?' Eleanor said, her voice increasing in volume. Her laser-like eyes were now burning into Sam's face.

'We were together for half an hour the first time.'

'The first time! Shit Sam, have you been more than once?'

'I have seen her twice. The second time I went as me. She was happy to see me again.'

'You went as yourself? What do you mean?'

Sam realised he had made a mistake. He was talking to a barrister after all.

'Sam, did you dress up as a barrister the first time? Tell me you didn't dress as a woman!'

'I did try to, well, put it this way, I tried to look as legal as possible from my banker's wardrobe.'

'Have you any idea the trouble you, and I, could be in? They will have you on camera. They will have records of your deception.

You could be prosecuted, I could be debarred.'

'I'm sorry, Eleanor. I had to see her. I had to get my story across to her.'

Eleanor was now furious. She stood up from the chair behind her desk.

'Did you get me to go and see Barniston? Did you send me over there so I couldn't make the meeting with Maria?'

'Yes, but please, don't be cross. It was necessary'

A paperweight flew past Sam. He ducked as it shot past his right ear and smashed into the wall at the back of the room.

'You fucking bastard! What the hell do you think you are playing at?'

Eleanor's face was purple with rage. Sam said nothing, it was punishment time. Let her get it all out. He was an expert at this bit.

'Don't you start treating me or this profession like we are part of your sordid little industry. How dare you play me like a fool!'

Eleanor reached down and picked up her coffee mug, ready to throw it. Sam stepped towards her with his arm out. He touched part mug, part hand. The mug was negotiated safely back to the desk.

'Look, I'm sorry. OK? I am sorry to have thrown you off the scent. Surely a quick visit to the old man Barniston wasn't that bad.'

'It's not that Sam. I can handle him. I am cross with you because you have put us both in serious trouble.'

'But we are both protected surely. Nothing will happen if you don't mention anything.'

'And if I do we both get clobbered. Oh, I see, Sam. Very clever. You get away with the prison break-in because I don't want to report it and risk repercussions. Good one.'

'That wasn't my plan, but now you mention it...'

'Fuck off Sam. You are an absolute shit.' Eleanor said with a growing smile. The thaw was starting.

Sam smiled back as Eleanor picked up the mug and threatened to throw it.

'You should have been a lawyer Sam; you are wasted in banking.'

'Perhaps you should have been a cricketer.' Sam said looking around at the paperweight lying on the floor.'

Sam and Eleanor sat down in unison.

'So what are you going to do next Sam? Are you seeing her again now you are best mates?'

'Probably. We still have a great deal to cover I think. The more she tells me the more I am convinced Yamin held her under duress. He constrained her life with the threat of violence.'

'I'll keep your fancy dress session a secret I promise. Just tell me you won't call Barniston again, I don't want him getting any more ideas.'

'What are you going to do about him? He must wonder why you came to see him if he didn't ask you to. He must suspect something?'

'These guys don't think like us Sam, he will be worrying about some point of law or sentencing precedence. He tried it on with me because I was there and he was lonely, that's all.'

'So does he take an interest in your development then?'

'Probably not. The only things he took an interest in last time were my tits.'

'Too old for you or do you not mix professional and social?'

'Get out before I throw this mug at you!'

Sam took his instruction and jumped out of his chair. He turned the brass knob on the door.

'Keep me in touch Sam. Perhaps you could buy me dinner when you have more to report? I would like to tell you more about what happened during the trial, what Barniston did.'

Sam left the room without another word. Eleanor was ambitious and very intelligent. Perhaps Oliver Barniston wasn't entirely to blame for what had happened in his chambers during the trial.

Chapter XXIII

The offices of Wolfenberg Bank, City of London

Sam was in the office bright and early on the day of the client meeting with Qin Property Limited. There was much to organise despite most of the work having been delegated to Joanna and the others in the team. Sam sat at his desk quietly reflecting on a busy few days.

'Are we nearly ready?' Sam enquired, turning to Joanna.

Joanna had been reluctant to help Sam but had finally agreed, knowing how important this client was.

'Yup, all the documents are done. Reception confirmed the meeting room, so you are all set.'

'Thanks Jo. I don't know what I'd do without you. Has performance been any good?'

'Terrible. Too many expensive equities and not enough gilts, given what the bond markets have done recently. All a bit of a dog's breakfast to be fair. Four per cent behind the benchmark. Martin Zhao is going to kill us.'

Sam didn't smile at Joanna's attempt at gallows humour. He

turned back to his Bloomberg screens and looked at his personal investments. He didn't receive any comfort.

'Why don't you take a holiday Sam? You look exhausted.'

Sam continued to survey his screens. He flicked a quick look at Joanna but she was not looking back. Her comment had been more of an instruction rather than a sympathetic observation.

Ten o'clock came with Sam's phone bursting into life. It was reception announcing the arrival of the delegation from Qin Property. Sam and Joanna put on their suit jackets, checked the documents one final time and went to collect Peter Heathcliff. He was wheeled out occasionally for the larger client meetings or if there was a danger of being sacked. Sam was comforted when Peter agreed to come. It was his introduction and Government contact after all.

Entering the meeting room in the client service suite, Sam shook hands with all the Qin representatives. There were polite bows from their side. Then it dawned on Sam, Martin Zhao was not in the room.

'Is Mr Zhao not joining us?' Sam said, looking around the guests.

'He sends his apologies; he has been caught up in some important company business back at our headquarters.'

Sam was surprised. Given how cross Martin had sounded on the phone it was remarkable he wasn't here.

'Please do sit down gentlemen,' Sam said with a serious tone. Client acting mode was switched on. 'Let's make a start.'

All four Qin Property representatives were on one side of the table, with Sam and Peter on the other. Joanna remained standing to offer coffee or water to the guests.

'Thank you for seeing us this morning. Mr Zhao regrets to inform you he is unable to join us this morning. He asked me to start the meeting by handing this letter to you. It has been written by Mr Qin himself.'

The letter was passed over to Peter Heathcliff who opened it without delay. He read it and handed it to Sam. The only noise in the room was Joanna taking her seat.

It was a termination letter. Mr Qin said the investment performance and client service had fallen well below what they had been expecting, indeed below the levels they expected for a bank with a reputation like Wolfenberg's. Mr Qin wished to sell all the investments, pay the proceeds away and close the account with immediate effect.

Sam knew about the consequences of this. There would be an investigation by head office and Sam would come off badly. In a company obsessed with growth the loss of such an account would go down like a shit sandwich. The thing was, Sam knew this was coming, the client had been quiet for a while and this was always a portentous sign.

Peter had a face like thunder. He knew the game, so blaming Sam was the only alternative for him. Otherwise his bosses would pick on him. The abused always kicked downwards.

'Well thank you for letting us know,' Peter said after an embarrassing pause. 'We will, of course, act on your instruction immediately and with efficiency.'

There was a knock on the door. Peter turned to Sam who turned to Joanna. She shrugged her shoulders; they were not expecting anybody.

The silence was broken as six people burst in through the door. Aaron Snee was with another man in a gabardine coat, two Wolfenberg security guards and two uniformed police officers.

'What the fuck is going on?' Peter cried as he stood up. The four Qin representatives did the same as the two policemen went to their side of the room. There was a general bustle as people grew to realise what had just happened.

The man in the raincoat was the first to speak.

'Gentlemen, you are all under arrest for crimes under the Financial Services Act 2003, in particular relation to money laundering and distributing the proceeds of crime.'

He read the usual rights as the policemen moved up to them and handcuffed each with their arms behind them. There was no fuss, no shouting. The four guests seemed to be resigned to their fate.

Sam stood watching with his mouth wide open. Aaron had come to stand on the Wolfenberg side of the table. He looked as frightened as anybody.

'Take them away boys,' said the man in the coat. 'I want to talk to you lot alone,' he added, pointing at Peter first, then Sam and Joanna.

The Qin men filed out accompanied by the policemen and security guards. The detective pushed the door shut when the party had left.

'My name is D.C.I. Boswell, financial crime unit at Scotland Yard. Apologies for the crude interruption, these things have to be done like that.'

'Perhaps you could start by explaining what the fucking hell that was all about. What is going on? These guys are, or should I say were, our best client,' Peter spurted out, still angered by the shock.

'They may have been your best client sir but we believe they have been involved in money laundering and deception. We have been working with your compliance department for a number of weeks now. We have all the evidence we need to prosecute.'

'But how come we knew nothing of this?'

'You need to brush up on your regulation sir; we cannot tell you or anybody else who has access to the client. Can't run the risk of a tip-off you see.'

'You're enjoying this aren't you Snee?'

'What about Qin, and Martin Zhao?' Sam said weakly with a dry throat.

'Don't you worry Sir. My men are looking for Mr Zhao as we speak. We are confident he will be arrested shortly. As for Qin, as I'm sure you are aware, he has left the country. We are talking to our colleagues overseas but that, frankly, is proving difficult.'

'Where is he?' Sam said with more than a hint of speculation.

'I need to get going. My colleagues will be in touch for statements from each of you shortly.'

D.C.I. Boswell turned and left. Aaron Snee didn't look sure as to what to do but after looking at Sam, Peter and Joanna, he turned and left as well.

It was all over in three minutes.

Later on, Sam took Joanna for a coffee in the shop opposite the office. Despite the usual chattering bustle, they ordered without speaking and took their drinks to a free table in the corner of the shop.

'Will the police want to talk to us again?' Joanna said, warming her hands on her oversized coffee cup.

'Undoubtedly. You know what Aaron and his crew are like; this will go on forever now. All of our actions, all our conversations will be analysed to see if we have broken the law.'

After a long pause Joanna spoke.

'Things have changed Sammy. It's not the same,' Joanna mumbled with her eyes firmly fixed on the table.

'What do you mean? Compliance has always been unbelievable in our industry. The day you take it personally is the day you need to quit.'

Joanna looked up at Sam, holding his gaze. Sam smiled to share his joke but there was no symmetry, just a serious face on the girl he had seen grow-up in front of him over the past few years. He knew his words no longer influenced her; she was able to work things out on her own now.

'I want to resign Sam.'

Although it was what Sam had been expecting for weeks, he felt regret when it came to hearing the words. In his world, the risk of raising professional progeny was the inevitability of their departure. The training of anyone involves a degree of ownership. The pupil is driven to learn of course but the tutor is driven to create something like them in part, just without the rough edges. How much of the tutor you see in the final version is a function of the success of the operation. The whole idea was to create a better version of yourself. Joanna was now better than him and he knew it.

The surprised face with the indignant look could have been sold as a fake. What couldn't be forged was the sense of defeat. He felt like he had been found out, like a chapter of his life was ending.

'What, err, what do you want to do next?' Sam said in a weak voice.

'There are a couple of things I am...'

'Come on Jo, you owe me the truth.'

'Sammy, I want to work for a much smaller company. I am fed up with big banks, all the red tape and bureaucracy. I want some freedom.'

'Will you try and take our clients?'

Joanna had learnt a lot from Sam but her blushing was of her own making, he couldn't teach her not to do that.

'I see. Well, ok. Good luck. When do you want to leave? You are on three months.'

'Straight away if possible.'

Sam's mobile rang in his pocket.
Sam took out his phone and looked at the screen. A slight frown suggested it wasn't Peter Heathcliff calling him back to the office.

'Hi, how are you?' Sam said in a familiar way. It was Lucy.

Sam listened to his wife, his eyes growing wider as she spoke.

'What? Lucy slow down, what has happened?'

'When?'

'Have you called the police?'

'Ok, ok. I will come back. Are you at home now?'

Sam took the phone from his ear. The line had gone dead before he had finished his question.

'What is it Sam, what has happened?' Joanna said, reaching out her hand to grab Sam's arm.

Sam stood up, knocking his coffee over as his knee caught the table.

'I've got to go Jo, George has been taken from the playground in Bishop's Park. He was playing with his friends and has gone missing.'

'Oh God, Sammy! Do you want help?'

Sam turned from the table.

'Sam?'

The coffee shop door slammed shut after Sam left. Joanna watched him jog past the office and raise his hand at an approaching taxi. Her resignation speech was only half finished.

Sam arrived home to find Lucy sitting at the kitchen table. It was just before midday. She looked like she had aged ten years, her face was pale, hair all over the place. Sitting next to her was another school mother who Sam had met at one of the inevitable children's parties along the way. She made an excuse and left Sam alone with his wife.

Lucy ran through what had happened. Charlie and George were playing with their friends one minute, next George had disappeared. He had been missing for two hours now. The half-term playground had been busy, Lucy and her friends had searched for George for a full hour. Organised searching soon turned into panic with mothers and nannies running all over the park in search of Sam's son.

Lucy called the police after fifteen minutes of searching. Two young women constables restored a degree of calm to proceedings, with an orderly search and questions asked to people they could see around the park. Concern turned to tears and hysterical screams as time slipped by. The police called for back-up and the search was widened beyond the park.

Ninety minutes after George went missing Lucy was told to go home. The police response team took control of the situation; there was nothing more for Lucy and her friends to do.

'Where's Charlie?' Sam said with a sudden rush.

'He's upstairs, playing in his room. He's not sure what is going on.'

'So what do we do next? Do you want me to go and look for him? Surely we can help?'

'The police say they can do more good on their own. We searched everywhere Sam, everywhere.' Lucy's voice was cracking with emotion. 'It's just not like him to wander off.'

'Do you think he could have been taken by...'

'By who? Your fucking work people, your nasty clients? Well I just don't fucking know Sam; all I know is that my darling son is missing.'

'Our son.'

Lucy burst into tears.

'Come on Lucy, we have to remain strong. I'm sure the police are conducting house-to-house searches, they will have put out a missing person's report.'

Sam and Lucy sat in the house all afternoon. Charlie came down only once to say he was hungry, the rest of the time he was firmly ensconced in the security of his bedroom, plastic dinosaurs protecting him.

At three there was a call from the police. The search had widened, other officers involved. They were speaking to other police units around London. Still no child.

When life is thrown out of equilibrium, nagging, underlying arguments are never far away. Winning the lottery or losing a child, it just didn't matter. The arguments would return whether it was good or bad news. To temper this Sam spent much of the afternoon justifying his career. Lucy often took her frustrations out on her husband and this was no different. Sam was accused of a vivid spectrum of deficiencies, from bad parenting to alcoholism. He took most of it on the chin, only getting riled when the spectrum turned into a circle. His mercantile and unworthy career caused the heavy drinking which caused the bad parenting. Dealing with criticism is easy if it is singular and mixed with balanced praise. When it becomes a rant against your base characteristics it becomes very hard to tolerate.

Sam's mobile rang.

'There you are you see, one of the office tarts no doubt. You are such a wanker.' Lucy said with venom.

Sam walked out as he answered. It was Peter Heathcliff. He wanted to see Sam immediately. Sam explained what had happened with George. Sam could sense Peter's feelings. He knew Qin had been to see Lucy and the boys; he knew there could be a connection.

'Come and see me as soon as you are back Sam. Good luck old boy.'

When Sam returned, Lucy was asleep on the sofa, all the tears had taken their toll. Gently he put a cushion behind her head and went upstairs to his study. He had some thinking to do.

It was some time later when Charlie came into the study. Sam had been looking at a map of Uzbekistan, viewing the major cities, the geography.

'Where's Mummy?'

Sam turned from his screen to look at Charlie. His elder son's hair was ruffled, he looked like he had just woken from an afternoon sleep. Sam held his arms wide open and a devilish smile came across Charlie's face as he raced across the room to jump into Sam's arms. Both hugged each other, Charlie just like normal but Sam added much more pressure and duration.

'Daddy!' Charlie said after Sam released his grip, 'what are you doing, Daddy?'

'I love you Charlie, you do know that don't you?'

'I love you too, Daddy,'

'Can I go downstairs and watch some TV?' Charlie was not stupid, realising after a hug like that any request would be met with approval.

'Mummy is sleeping in the sitting room so let's go to the playroom.'

Charlie trotted off to turn the TV on before Daddy changed his mind. At the door of the study he stopped. He turned back to Sam.

'When is George coming home? He has been ages.'

Sam stared back not knowing quite what to say. He smiled, always a good start.

'He'll be back soon, darling. Very soon.'

'Is that a lie Daddy?'

Sam sat back down in his chair. Charlie came back from the doorway and climbed up Sam's leg to settle into his lap. After a couple of minutes Charlie's ruffled hair was damp from Sam's tears.

A little later Sam awoke with Charlie asleep in his arms. He placed him on the sofa in the playroom and looked around for the permanently lost remote control.

'Can we watch the dinosaurs Daddy?' he had woken up and immediately hopped off the sofa to walk towards the DVD cupboard in anticipation of the response.

Charlie shuffled himself into position, only twelve inches from the screen and sat with eager anticipation. Sam knew he was too close but couldn't be bothered to tell him today. The playroom was now a temple to Late Jurassic worship, immediately Charlie was lost in a world one hundred and fifty million years older than him.

Happy that Charlie was settled in, Sam went to check on Lucy, she would feel better for having slept. As Sam entered the sitting room there was a knock on the front door.

Lucy came bounding through the doorway from the other side, crashing into Sam who had no chance of getting out of the way. They both looked at each other for a brief second before heading to the hall as one. Lucy opened the door.

'Good afternoon', the policeman said. 'Mr and Mrs Waghorne?'

Lucy and Sam just stared back, not saying anything. This kind of thing happened to other people.

Sam felt a tear start down his nose. He wiped it away and gave a masculine sniff. He put his arm around Lucy. Her long hair, messed up from sleeping, hid the full extent of her crying.

'Would you like to come in?' Sam said with a thin, watery voice.

The policeman didn't answer; he took a step forward, following Sam and Lucy back into the warmth of the house. Sam closed the front door and led their guest into the sitting room.

'It's about your son, George.'

Lucy put her arm back around Sam. Sam pulled her close. Her face holding years of memories together with the expectation of the worst news.

'We found him in the grounds of Fulham Palace, just down by the river.'

'Oh my God! No!' Lucy screamed.

'What? No, no, you misunderstand me. He's fine. He was with this dog which had gone missing you see. He must have followed the poor mutt into the gardens and not been able to find his way out. They were found by one of the security guards sweeping for tramps just before lock up.'

'Is he OK?'

'Bit tearful and cold but, apart from needing a spot of supper and a hot bath, he's right as rain.'

Sam and Lucy hugged for longer than Sam could remember.

'Very brave little boy you've got there. The guard said he found him curled up with the dog.'

There was another knock on the front door.

'That will be him now, we keep them in the car until we know you are here and OK, you know.'

Lucy ran to the door, threw it open and ran out. A female policewoman was standing next to George, holding his hand.

'Sorry Mummy.'

A half smile ran across the policewoman's face. She let go of George's hand when the resistance became too strong. George raced to his mother, burying his face in her knees. Lucy squatted down to hug him. George began to cry. Not the normal sort of tears, there was no emotional capital to control here. He had been frightened; seeing his mummy again provided fundamental relief.

On hearing the disturbance Charlie came into the hall. Sam and Charlie joined Lucy and George in a group hug. Eventually the sobs turned to laughter when Charlie said George had kept him from his supper.

Charlie took George by the hand and led him back to the dinosaurs. How quickly things returned to normal.

As Sam sat down to listen to the police debrief, his thoughts turned back to Qin and what his worst fears allowed him to think. He felt like he had dodged a bullet.

He must take action. Things could not go on like this. His mind was made up.

Tomorrow he would see Peter then go and see his friend Eleanor. For now, he pulled his mobile from his pocket to send a quick update to Joanna.

All good. He followed a dog.

Chapter XXIV

The offices of Wolfenberg Bank, City of London

Sam only had one thing on his mind. He wanted to talk to his boss, Peter Heathcliff.

Peter tended to be in later than the average banker on the floor. Some directors considered it perfectly reasonable to drift in at nine in the morning. To Sam it demonstrated laziness - he had been at his desk for ninety minutes before Peter could be seen marching into his office with the air of a Major General.

Sam knocked on the glass door of Peter's office five minutes later. He saw Peter look up, nod and mouth something like come in. A wave of Peter's hand confirmed his approval. Sam pushed on the glass.

'Morning Waggers, what's up?' Peter said in a jovial manner as he stood up.

'I need some time off Peter. I can't go on like this. This Qin thing has almost killed me. George went missing yesterday; he followed a dog and got lost. I thought Martin Zhao had taken him. I was pulling my hair out before the police found him. I need a holid...'

'Woh Woh, slow down Waggers! We need to talk about the

Qin business. You did everything you could there. Don't blame yourself.'

'But you don't understand Peter, I know much more than…' Sam said, stopping himself in mid-sentence. For an inexplicable reason he just stopped.

'Go on Sam.'

'Err, I know much more Peter,' Sam paused. 'Joanna wants to resign. She wants to work for a smaller organisation.'

'When did she tell you this?'

'Yesterday.'

'She has been upset by all this Qin thing. Give her a couple of days and talk to her. She's a strong girl.'

'It's more than that Peter, she doesn't want to work for me anymore. She wants to be independent.'

'She's worked out you are a lazy fucker Sam, that's all.'

'Peter, I am serious here. I need three weeks off. I need to get my life back in perspective.'

'Take two weeks and then come and speak to Joanna. She will listen. You make a great team.'

Sam paused.

'Did they catch Martin Zhao?'

'Not sure Sam. I haven't heard anything. We have a big meeting with Compliance and senior management this morning. There may well be an update then. Have a good break.'

'There was one more thing actually.'

Peter looked up; having thought the conversation was over.

'What is it?'

'Do you know anybody I could call, you know, in your old line of work? Security, ex-military, that kind of thing?'

'What on earth for Sam? Are you worried about Martin Zhao? My view would be he is on the first plane back to China. He should be if he has any sense.'

'I want to make sure Lucy and the family are OK, yesterday really shocked me. I don't feel safe Peter.'

Peter stared at Sam for a few seconds, he was contemplating something.

'There is someone who might help. Andre Otto. South African special forces. Hard bastard but also clever. Retired some years ago and now works for a private security company, you know, protection, kidnaps, negotiating with terrorists, that kind of thing. He could help you if he's in the UK, but he might be abroad rescuing somebody.'

Peter took a pen and his mobile. He found Otto's contact number and wrote it down with his name on a scrap of paper. He flicked it across to Sam.

'Give him a call.'

A sad smile crept across Peter's face.

'Come on Sam, pull yourself together. You're a strong man. Have a good break.'

Sam folded Peter's note in half, stood and walked out of Peter's office for what would be the last time.

Outside on the street Sam retrieved the piece of paper Peter had given him. He felt his heart quicken in his chest as he found his phone and called the number. After two rings there was a click, a man with an impossibly low voice answered like he was busy with other things.

'Yes? Who is that?'

'Err, am I speaking to Andre Otto?' Sam said feeling like a teenager calling a girl for the first time.

'Yes, who is this? Who gave you my number?'

Sam regretted calling without preparation.

'This is a friend of Peter, Peter Heathcliff. He gave me your number; said you could help me.'

'Where are you?'

'In the City, just by St Paul's. Could we meet?'

'I'm busy now. Meet me at 6.00pm in Brixton. There is a pub on Brixton Road, Crown & Anchor. Can't miss it.'

'Thank you.'

'Peter is a good man.'

Another click signalled the end of the conversation. Sam saved the number in his phone and screwed up the note. He sent a quick text message to Eleanor. The reply came back almost immediately. Sam smiled as he set off with renewed vigour towards Chancery Lane.

Three at a time, Sam raced up the stone steps to Eleanor's chambers. A knock on the door yielded a response so Sam twisted the old knob and pushed on the solid oak door. A fresh whiff of scent greeted his nose as he looked up. Eleanor was seated at her desk pretending to be busy. It was obvious to Sam she had spent the last ten minutes tidying both herself and her chambers.

'Short notice Sam, I can only give you ten minutes. I'm due in court,' Eleanor said ruffling the white tabs of her collar.

'Sorry, yes, err, just thought I would give you an update. Peter has given me two weeks off. George went missing you see and I...'

'Whoa, whoa. Slowdown. What are you talking about?'

'I'm going to find him. Maria has given me all she can. I have asked for some help and I'm going to bring him back.'

'Are you out of your fucking head? This guy is a trained killer; do you not remember what he did to Kumara Darsha?'

'I have to Ellie.'

Eleanor shifted her head to one side upon hearing Sam say her nickname without permission.

'I have to prove Maria is innocent. I have to show the system has failed her.'

'Sam, I really have to advise you not...'

'No point in trying Ellie, I am off to see someone now - someone to help me.'

Eleanor stared at Sam.

'I just wanted to let you know. When I return with him, I'll bring him to you.'

'Fuck off Sam, I think you are crazy, now get out of my chambers, I need to go to court.'

Sam was turning the doorknob as she spoke. He had to prepare for Otto. He had no idea what was going on, just that it felt right.

The route to Brixton was easy. Ahead of the rush hour it took Sam fifteen minutes to get the tube down to, for him, an unknown part of London. The street was all a-buzz as he emerged from the station. There was music blaring from a first-floor window and a heavy chatter of shoppers and vendors conversing in front of him, all mixed with the heady aroma of grilling chicken.

Sam had looked at the pub website before he left so had a good idea where the chosen venue was. Getting out of the way of a bustling woman with a pram who was talking to herself, he made his way south towards the Crown & Anchor.

The pub was quiet when Sam entered. There were a few locals

sitting at the bar who stopped their conversation to give Sam the once over. By the tables there was nobody who looked like Sam imaged Otto to be; just a couple clearly having an affair. They looked at Sam like he was disturbing them, so Sam quickly spun around to check out the other side of the pub. In the far corner was a man sitting by himself. He was dressed in jeans and a thick jacket and had a large neat whisky sitting in front of him. He had his back to the door so did not see Sam approach. Sam could make out longish blond hair and a strong profile – a solid chin and tanned complexion.

'Otto?'

The man turned to reveal all of his face. A large forehead and thick nose dominated his features. A scar ran from under his left eye to the corner of his mouth.

'Yup. You Sam?'

Sam nodded and pointed at Otto's drink.

'Double Glenmorangie, no ice or water.' It was a thick Boer accent. Very abrupt.

A few minutes later Sam returned with two of what Otto had ordered. He sat down opposite and took a large slug of the whisky to settle him down.

'What do you want?' Otto said after doing the same to finish his first drink. He wiped his mouth on the sleeve of his jacket.

'Peter tells me you know certain people, people who can get things done overseas. I need help to get to Uzbekistan. I know nothing about the place.

'You got any money? Any help I give you needs to be paid for. Despite giving years of my life for my country, they still kicked me out with fuck all; Special Forces to broke in three months. Queen and Country. Bollocks to that.'

'I have enough. I just need help to get to somebody – somebody who has run away.'

'Are you sure this person is in Uzbekistan? What makes you certain they have stayed there?'

'I'm not. All I know is that is where he went. It's a long story.'

Otto looked around him before taking a large slug of his fresh drink.

'I'm all ears. Start from the beginning.'

Sam sat with Otto for three hours. He told him about Maria and the trial; what Yamin looked like and how he committed murder. Otto started off with little interest but as Sam went on he became more animated, more interested in helping. Hearing about Yamin's Special Forces training was a turning point – a reason for a fight perhaps.

A plan was hatched and they settled on a fee. Otto asked for half the payment immediately with half if they completed the task. Several whiskies later Sam gave Otto his details and left. It was over to the experts now. All Sam could do was wait to hear.

Sam walked out into the cold night air. The street was buzzing with provocative music and cocky teenagers – all out for the evening. Sam found a cab and headed back to his part of London. Chelsea was safer for City bankers.

It was past nine when Sam came through the door. He was not used to drinking spirits so aggressively and was feeling very drunk. A high octane, low volume kind of drunk - but drunk all the same. Lucy was in the kitchen pretending to be busy.

'Where the fucking hell have you been? I thought the episode with your son might have changed you.' she screamed as she started towards Sam in the hall.

'Bushiness, plenty going on at wor...'

'Sam you are shitfaced again. What is wrong with you? George has been crying all evening and you have been pissing it up with those useless tarts from the office.'

'I haven't actuall...'

'Fuck off Sam. Just fuck off. I am sick of you.'

Lucy pushed past Sam and ran up the stairs.

'FUCK OFF!' came a distant cry just before the bedroom door slammed shut.

Sam sat in the sitting room with a single lamp on behind him. Pointlessly, he nursed another whisky in his hand. What would Otto come up with? Would it be possible to go and find Yamin, to bring him back to face justice? Sam's deliberations were disturbed by the sound of his mobile ringing in the kitchen. He rushed to answer it.

'Hello?'

'Sam, it's Otto. I have made some calls. We have visas and letters in place. Meet me with your kitbag and passport at Heathrow tomorrow at 7.30am. Terminal three. We are all set.'

'Shit that was quick. What are we going to do?'

The line went dead. Sam placed the phone down gently. His mind was whirring. He had to talk to Lucy.

Sam crept into the bedroom. Lucy's light was still on. She was sitting up reading. She had a face like thunder.

'Spare room!'

'Listen Lucy I need to talk to you. There is something I need to explain.'

'Which one have you fucked Sam, is it Joanna?'

Sam sat on the bed. Lucy pulled herself up nervously, looking concerned about Sam's reluctance to answer her question.

'What the hell is going on Sam? Tell me.'

'I need to go away. I need to get out of Wolfenberg for a while. It is killing me.'

'What do you mean go away?'

'There is something I need to do, someone I need to find. I will be OK.'

'Sam what the fuck are you talking about, go away? What the hell is...'

'Trust me. I am not cheating on you, I love you Lucy but there is something I have to sort out.'

'Tell me you fucker. Tell me what the hell is going on.'

Sam stood and turned to the door. Peeking around the door was George. Sam smiled but got no such response from his son. George ran past Sam on his way to his mother's side of the bed. He jumped up and gave Lucy a massive hug. She ran her hand through his hair and kissed the top of his head.

'Get out Sam. Just get out. I don't care where you go, just get out of our lives.' She had tears forming in her eyes.

Sam went to the spare room. En route he stopped at the landing cupboard and pulled out the brown leather hold-all. He placed it on the spare bed and started to think what he might need. Money and a passport was all he could come up with before he flopped onto the bed and fell asleep.

Chapter XXV

Turkish Airline flight TA012

The engines gave a reassuring hum as Sam looked out of the window of the plane. They were cruising above the clouds having left London two hours earlier. Otto was sitting next to him, his clothes mirroring Sam's. They looked just the same as all the other British passengers on-board, who were interspersed with many Uzbek nationals travelling home. The occasional baby scream mixed with the noises of the stewards starting the lunchtime service.

Sam had met Otto at Heathrow at 7.30am precisely. He had left Lucy and the boys well before they woke up. A quiet hunt for all he needed was followed by a quick taxi ride to the airport. They found a coffee shop to discuss the first part of the trip and to confirm he had made a payment to Otto's account before he left. The British Consulate had provided papers. Sam had asked questions but Otto ignored them all - he had assumed a different attitude – he was working now.

After a coagulated, unsalted lunch Sam ran through some of the things Maria had been through during his visits. Yamin had told her about various trips to Tashkent and where he liked to go in the city. She had assumed it was just a part of his training. Otto listened carefully as Sam went through as much as he could remember.

The engine tone dropped and there was a slight slowing of the plane. They started their descent into Istanbul.

Once up again after the Turkish stopover, Otto gave Sam a folder he had retrieved from his bag. It contained information on Uzbekistan and further detail on Tashkent itself. A map of the city had been colour-coded showing different areas of the capital. Important buildings and landmarks had been highlighted. The British Consulate had been ringed in red.

After filling in his landing papers, Sam reclined his seat by as much as the cheap airline would let him. With a few hours to go he needed sleep. Last night's excess and the thoughts of things to come sent him off quickly.

Sam was woken by the screech of tyres on the runway. It was black outside with glowing orange blobs illuminating only a few buildings. Sam looked at his watch. It was eight in the evening local time. They had arrived in Tashkent.

It was warmer than Sam thought it would be when they stepped out of the airport building and into the humid evening air. There were unfamiliar smells all around; burning odours mixed with the aromas of exotic foods.

At the airport entrance Sam could see a black Mercedes parked about twenty yards away. It was very dirty and not particularly new. Otto tilted his head to indicate they should approach it. Sam made sure he had the two bags he had packed and scuttled off after the South African who was already halfway there. A yard before he got there the passenger door opened. A tall man wearing jeans and a plain polo shirt got out of the car. Otto shook his hand and said something Sam couldn't hear.

'Sam?' said the man after greeting Otto.

'Hello, yes.' Sam wiped the hair across his forehead and shook the man by the hand.

'Nick Penfold. I run the British Consulate.' He spoke with a clipped accent, very confident.

'Let's go.'

After the brief introduction they all jumped into the car which sped off as the last door slammed. Sam didn't ask where they were going. On the plane he had made a promise to himself to let events wash over him. Otto was in charge here. Sam noticed the driver had a gun in a holster on his hip. He quickly looked away and turned his attention to the scenes flashing past.

'Today is the Day of Memory, the streets will be very quiet,' said Nick, breaking the silence from the front seat.

'The locals will be back out in force tomorrow but tonight it will be quiet.'

There were a few people on the streets going about their business. The men Sam could make out in the gloom of dust and orange had coloured robes with wide trousers. They looked very smart – not what Sam had been expecting. Nick turned around from the passenger seat to see Sam looking out of the window.

'They all make a special effort on a public holiday; you will see the normal scruffs tomorrow.'

The rest of the journey was made in silence, pregnant with anticipation.

After ten minutes the car slowed abruptly and ducked down into an underground parking area. From there Sam and Otto were led up into a finely but sparsely decorated building. English furniture could be seen in small quantities – like a poor aristocrat trying to kit out a large country house.

'You guys must be starving,' Nick said as they entered a small sitting room on the first floor.

'Let's have some dinner once you have had a chance to see your rooms. Shall we say back here in fifteen minutes?'

Sam was led off up the stairs by the driver. He had not said a word since Sam had arrived. He walked two paces in front of Sam eventually pointing to a door at the end of the corridor. Sam pushed the door and entered. Having put his bags on the bed he turned to thank his escort. There was no one there.

'Friendly place this,' Sam said to himself as he closed the door and went to unpack. He had brought only essential clothes, so it took him only a couple of minutes to place his things in a small wardrobe next to the bed.

Sam felt his phone vibrate in his pocket. He had had no contact from Lucy since the night before. He checked the screen.

Welcome to Uzbekistan. UzMobi hopes you have a pleasant stay.

Sam read about the charges his mobile company would make for calls and texts during his trip. He flopped down onto the bed. Should he phone Lucy? Tell her he was OK. No, she would only worry more. He decided on a text which was meant to reassure her.

The message was sent straight away. There is a better signal than some parts of London Sam thought as he went into the bathroom. He ran the cold tap as he looked into the mirror for at least a minute. What a crap message he had sent. He looked drawn, tired and dirty. What a fucking mess. He splashed water on his face and found a towel.

After changing his shirt and putting on some other shoes he grabbed his phone. No messages. He headed back downstairs to meet the others.

Sam pushed on the door and all fell quiet in the room. Otto was with Nick and a woman who Sam did not recognise.

'Come in Sam, I want you to meet someone.' Nick said as they saw Sam arrive.

The woman stepped towards Sam and offered her hand.

'Claudia.'

She was tall with dark, tanned skin. Her hair was aggressively pulled back in a tight ponytail. She was wearing fitted khaki coloured clothes, smart enough for dinner in this part of the world. Sam shook her steely hand and looked into her eyes, her attractiveness was masked by a cold professional air. Sam's inspection was broken by Nick.

'Listen, Claudia is here to help you Sam. Shall we sit down and discuss things over dinner?'

There was a table set at the end of the sitting room. Nick, Otto, Claudia and Sam sat down as if about to play cards. There was a limited amount of glassware and china on the table, in keeping with the decoration of the entire embassy. It was like they had

had an explosion at some point and they had lost half of their belongings.

A clock chimed nine-thirty as two servants came in with the food. A chorus of cutlery broke the silence. Sam and Otto were hungry from the flight so started at a ferocious pace.

'Claudia knows this part of the world very well Sam,' Otto said after a couple of mouthfuls.

'She can help us find the man you are looking for.'

'How can you be sure he is in Tashkent Sam?' Nick gave Sam a quizzical look.

'This is where his business is run from. This is his home. I will recognise him when I see him.'

'From somebody else's description of him?'

'Yes. Also how he acts. We will find him.'

'You must leave it to us Sam,' Otto added with another mouthful of food.

Sam gave a half smile as the others laughed. Sam flicked a look towards Claudia which wiped the smile off his face. She made him feel nervous.

'Have you been working in the area long Claudia?' he chanced.

'Sam, let's finish here and head next door. We have plenty to discuss and also some clothes which may help you in your quest,' Nick changed the subject with a diplomat's charm.

'Sure, sure,' Sam looked around at Otto but his face was deep in goat stew.

Once ensconced in a ruby-red sitting room from a forgotten era, Sam told them what he knew about Yamin from the trial and the meetings with Maria. Cigar smoke filled the air as ghostly servants served brandy into large balloon glasses as if in the final tragic act of a play about the British Empire. Through all of the histrionics Claudia watched Sam like a hawk, taking notes at certain points.

After half an hour Nick stood and walked towards the window, small cigar in hand.

'That's quite enough plotting for tonight,' said Nick, stubbing his cigar into an ashtray on the windowsill, 'I want you to try these on.'

Sam watched Nick cross the room and pull some robes out of a wardrobe next to the window.

Having tried on a smock, beard and sand shoes Sam looked the part. According to Nick a touch of make-up would bring his skin up to speed to complete the disguise. Otto and Claudia looked at Sam then back to each other.

'You look like a drag act Sam,' said Otto. 'I would wear metal pants if I were you, there are some serious Moffies out there, eh?'

Otto and Claudia got up and left the room, still laughing.

'Remember Sam; leave the talking to the others. Claudia speaks Russian so you will be able to get about.'

'What's the plan Nick; tell me what we are going to do.'

'Let's talk tomorrow. The holiday will be over then, things will be back to normal. Otto and Claudia are working things out now.'

'I bet.'

'Sorry?'

'Nothing, I will see you in the morning. I am exhausted.'

Sam took himself to his room. He passed a full-length mirror as he rounded the bed. He stopped and stared for a good minute.

He threw his new clothes off quickly and got into bed. He checked his phone.

Nothing.

Chapter XXVI

The British Consulate, Tashkent, Uzbekistan

When a successful game of silent British breakfast had finished, Sam, Otto and Nick sat looking at each other waiting for each other to talk. Otto lit a cigarette. For a while Sam wanted to say something, to ask about the plan but he chose to wait. He felt both an apprehension and an urge to take charge. A craving created from the difference between the two worlds he knew, one engrained and one recently witnessed.

'Listen', said Otto after indulgently blowing a long blue plume of smoke. 'We did some surveillance last night and Claudia has gone out this morning to narrow the bars down.'

'We'll wait for her to get back then check some places out at lunchtime. If we have no luck we can go back to others in the evening. She knows what she is looking for.'

'I anticipate Claudia will be back at ten so let's plan to get out by midday.'

Sam decided to try on his new outfit and go for a walk. He wanted to get a feel for the place. He located his disguise, applied his make-up and dressed. He recoiled when he saw himself in the mirror. He looked like an extra from a Bollywood film.

'These guys know what they are doing,' he said to himself as he made for the door.

Once in the street Sam was engulfed in bright radiance. It was only nine in the morning but the heat was already oppressive. The city shimmered in a hazy glow and dust was being kicked up by a jumpy zephyr, blowing across the square that the car had sped through the night before. Sam shielded his eyes from the sun as he walked towards what looked like a market, fifty yards from the embassy. Car horns and the smells of a primitive gathering completed the sensory gamut as Sam drifted up the street. There were market traders yelling at customers and customers yelling back. Live goats and ducks were being exchanged alongside vegetables and fruit.

Out of respect to the locals, Sam maintained a brisk pace past the stalls. Occasionally a bright glint of the sun's reflection made him squint and turn his head. People started to look at him with a questioning gaze. Words he did not understand came screaming from the traders. Eventually he realised they were keen for him to buy their goods. There was no doubt he looked like a local so that none of the beggars bothered him. They saved that for the occasional suited man or obvious visitor.

Children were playing football on a dirt covered pitch. The screams and shouts were more familiar to Sam. They reminded him of London. It was the universal sound of sport; only the parched pitch looked different.

Sam saw what looked like a bar through a dusty haze. Local men were drinking wine and beer at this time of the day which surprised him. Some had black tea but most alcohol. He followed his curiosity to the door.

A man waved his hand to Sam indicating him to take a seat outside the bar. Sam was not intending to have a drink but felt he had to. He had to keep in character.

'Hayirli tong?' said the waiter not even looking at Sam.

Sam had looked at some Uzbek phrases on the plane.

'Sarbast.'

'Sarbast.'

Sam didn't want a beer but this was the only brand he had seen on the plane. He sat motionless just looking at the locals. They ignored him as they chatted away, some playing dominos.

Sam noticed Claudia first. She was sitting at the bar inside drinking a black tea. Her hair was covered but when she turned her head the sun caught her face. She was talking to a local woman next to her. Claudia's hands were moving around, pulling her sleeve up and pointing at her bare arm.

Sam's beer arrived and Claudia turned to look in Sam's direction. She gave the woman she was talking to something from her fist and clearly thanked her. She came bounding over as Sam took a long draw on his drink.

'Are you a fucking simpleton?' Claudia said pressing her face into his ear as she sat down.

'What?'

'What the hell are you doing here?' 'It is pretty fucking obvious you are in disguise. Have these guys been staring at you?'

Claudia nodded in the direction of the domino set.

'No, not at all. Just having a look around. Killing time.'

'We've got to go. I have some information. Come on.'

The men nearest them looked over to Sam. Claudia's voice had broken their concentration. They muttered something to each other.

'Come on Sam, we need to go now,' cried Claudia getting up from her chair. She put two coins down on the table.

A man with a full beard and red cheeks stood at the nearest table. He stared at Sam. Sam took another long slug of beer and got up. He pushed past a chair which made a scraping noise on the stone floor as he rushed to catch Claudia.

'What, what is it?' 'Why the rush?'

'Come on. They were talking about you. They were asking who you were. Hurry.'

They walked as quickly as they could past the stalls, back to the security of the embassy.

'You English are such cock suckers, do you know that?'

'Come on Claudia, calm down,' said Otto. 'Tell us what you found.'

Sam was standing by the window, looking out at the scene he had just left.

'I was having a look arou...'

'Sam, shut it. Claudia?'

After a long pause, pregnant with anger, Claudia turned to Otto.

'I know where he drinks. I met a woman who has seen him. Three or four blocks away there is a bar. A drinking club. A group of men drink there. I think he might be one of them. Fits the alpha male description.'

'Good. We can leave in twenty minutes. Sam you do nothing. Let us control it. Nick will drop us off.'

Sam looked around the room. His stupidity from earlier had been forgotten. This was it. This was the time. His heart was beating like a jungle drum being played by an over keen teenager.

The car they arrived in shot out of the embassy into the square, throwing a hundred lazy birds perched in the trees into the scorching air. They were all in their costumes, ready for the first act.

'Stop here please,' Claudia said from the passenger seat of the Mercedes. The car came to a sudden halt.

The three got out of the car and watched it drive away. Otto pulled Sam and Claudia into a side street.

'Right, listen to me. We all walk in, sit and order. Claudia will do her thing. Sam, you just relax. All you need to do is identify him.'

Otto went first then the others followed. They caught up with him just before they reached the bar.

Smoke and the sweaty smell of men greeted them as they walked in. Most of the tables were taken but one remained, close to the back. It was just by the door to what looked like the kitchen. Claudia chatted as they sat; nobody batted an eyelid at these guests, these locals coming for an early lunchtime drink. Dominos clicked and bar life carried on as normal.

Claudia ordered three black teas and two beers, for Sam and Otto.

'So, what do we do now?' Sam said under his breath.

'Just shut the fuck up and look normal you English prick,' said Claudia with a scalding whisper. 'We are in the right place; we just have to be patient.'

'Keep your voice down Sam. Tell me a little bit about yourself,' Otto said trying to defuse the situation.

Sam looked around. Nobody was remotely interested in them. He relaxed and started chatting.

A few minutes later Claudia put her hand flat on the table. Very subtle, no noise. Just a sign. A sign to Otto that something had happened. Sam stopped talking.

'Carry on Sam, for fuck's sake,' said Otto. 'Keep talking.'

Sam turned as he spoke. Three men by the door had cleared their table and a hush had fallen on that part of the bar. Sam stopped talking.

'What is going on?' Sam said in a naive childish manner.

'Just watch. There is an order around here. Those men know what is good for them,' said Claudia, turning towards the action.

Five men walked into the bar. Two other patrons immediately stood and offered their chairs to the party. They were snatched without a word and all five sat down with arrogant swagger. The bartender came rushing over in an efficient panic. One word was said and he raised his hand and scuttled off as quickly as he came.

'Just talk, Sam. Just like everything is normal. Don't stare either.'

Otto tried to keep Sam engaged as Claudia stood up and went to the bar. Sam could see her talk to the barman. He gave Otto a worried look.

'Just calm down Sam, she is in charge here.'

Claudia came back to the table.

'I've got to go guys, sorry.'

'But, what? What?' Sam spluttered.

Claudia turned and left the bar. The five men did not notice her as she walked past in her drab clothes.

'Otto, I may be stupid but what the fu...'

'Just calm down and tell me more about your family.'

Sam stared at Otto, shaking his head.

'Lucy probably thinks I have run off with a work colleague, my sons hate me and I have gangsters trying to kill me at work.'

Twenty minutes later Sam noticed someone pushing against the front door. The bar was much busier now with many locals refreshing themselves after a hard morning in the market. Nobody seemed to notice this woman dressed in a tight skirt and faded leather jacket. She looked dirty, like she had been working the streets. Her hair was down and messy, partially covering her face.

Sam looked back to Otto when he realised it was Claudia. He hoped nobody had seen him stare at her.

'Good job eh?' said Otto, 'She is a great actress you know.'

'She looks like a hooker, do they get them in this country?'

Otto raised his eyebrows. Sam felt like he was five years old.

'Just drink your beer will you, let her get on with her job. If you want to look then go for a piss and come and sit down here.'

Otto thumped the chair next to him and two of the men next to them turned around. Sam got up and went off to do as he was told.

As he settled back down, he saw Claudia standing alone at the bar. She had ordered a beer and was drinking it straight from the bottle. Sam had a better chance to look at the group of five men. The man in the middle of the group was clearly in charge. He held the conversation as the others looked at him. He was strongly built with cropped black hair. His eyes were dark and fixed; they didn't yield even when he laughed at one of his own jokes. Despite the quality of the photos from the tube station, this was without doubt Yamin Shakirov.

A group walked in front of them obscuring Sam's view. Otto nudged Sam.

'Don't make it too obvious, they look like a rough lot. Babelaas babelaas.'

'Sure, sorry?' said Sam looking at Otto with a frown, not understanding his last comment.

'Hangovers Sammy, they all have hangovers. They're picking up from last night.'

'Here we go,' Otto said. 'Watch this. Go Loskind!'

Sam looked back. The main guy in the middle was nudging the man next to him. He had spotted Claudia at the bar. They let out a few raucous shouts aimed randomly at first and then more specifically at her. The four others were playing along to their leader's tune. They had seen he was interested and were happy to get involved.

One of them shouted out something Sam did not understand. Claudia gave a half turn towards the group, looked at the five men and then turned back to stare at the array of bottles behind the bar. This made the four men burst into raucous laughter. The main man did nothing. His dead eyes focussed on her, like she had insulted him by turning away.

Something in Sam's head clicked. The comments Maria had made to him; the evidence during the trial. Something was familiar. Sam pushed himself to the edge of his seat – this was unfolding quickly.

Sam caught his breath and gave a quick glance across the table. Otto widened his eyes and glared at Sam as if to say 'calm down you silly fucker'. Turning back Sam saw the main man stand up and push past the two men to his left. A hush fell at his table but elsewhere in the bar the chat and low hum of the music continued.

Sam felt his pulse quicken as a kaleidoscope of emotions tumbled in his head. The man walked up to Claudia who was still facing away from the table where the group sat. Sam wanted to stand, to go and help. The man's black T-shirt was tight against his muscular chest, his arms looking strong and purposeful. His flat stomach drew a line from his chest to his waist. He looked in good shape. He had a slow confident gait, one which suggested he knew what he wanted. He stopped just behind Claudia. He was close. Sam thought he was going to touch her. One man at the bar noticed what was going on and stood back not wanting to get in the way. It provided a space next to Claudia at the bar.

The other men were staring at Sam and Otto. They had noticed Sam's interest in the situation. One of them stood and came over to Sam. Otto stood to greet him.

'Is there a problem?' Otto said in Russian, stepping towards the man with aggression. This stopped the man in his tracks. After a few seconds and a quick flick to Sam he smiled at Otto and walked past to the washroom.

'He was going to fight you Sammy,' said Otto once he was out of sight. 'You have to hit back quickly with these guys.'

Sam was not listening. He was watching the bar. Yamin had whispered something into Claudia's ear and place his hand on her bottom. It was then Sam saw it. Just below his ear as he craned towards Claudia. The spider's web tattoo. He could just make out the heads of cats around the web. The whole thing was no wider than a golf ball. Sam felt a surge of adrenalin run through his veins. This was him. Shit, this was the man.

Claudia laughed and turned towards the door. Sam flicked a look to Otto. They were leaving together. The boys at the table screamed with juvenile delight as the couple walked out of the door. Otto stood and went to the bar. He came back with two more beers.

'Got to blend in Sammy, got to blend in,' he said as he put the bottles down, collected one and clicked it against the other.

'What's next?'

'Blow job I expect. Or a quick Ficken, eh?'

Sam got that one.

Five minutes later Otto touched Sam's arm.

'Let's go.'

'What?' said Sam turning to Otto. 'I haven't finished my...'

'Come on. I've had a message.'

Otto ran out of the bar and Sam followed, knocking a chair over as he went. By the time Sam was outside he saw Otto had run twenty metres up the road and was stopping next to a car - Nick's car from the embassy, parked in the middle of the road. Dust was still hanging in the air.

Sam ran to the car. Otto had already got in the back. Nick's window was down. He had dark glasses and looked altogether less diplomatic than he had three hours earlier.

'Get in Sam. Get in now.'

Sam saw Claudia sitting in the passager seat then heard Nick revving the engine.

'What's going on?'

'Get in Sam, we need to go.'

Sam jumped in the back and Nick sped away as soon as he saw Sam sit down. The door slammed shut ten yards down the road.

'What the fuck is going....'

'Claudia stuck a needle in his neck Sammy. Right into the web tattoo. He is in the boot. We need to get out of here and back to the Embassy before his friends realise.'

'You what?'

'You better be damn sure this is your man,' Claudia screamed from the passenger seat. 'There will be serious shit if he's not.'

Sam looked out of the window at the closing market as they sped past. The locals ignored the car despite it almost running two people over. This must be how they drive around here.

Sam was back in his room at the Embassy. He had changed back into his casual clothes when there was a knock on the door. It opened before Sam had a chance to say anything. Otto appeared also wearing normal clothes.

'Hi Sam,' he said in a functional manner. 'We are leaving in ten minutes. Get packing.'

'But, what is going...'

The door closed before Sam finished. He turned back to the bed and threw his bag on it.

'You OK Sam?' Otto said as the car turned into the airport. It took a different route away from the main terminal coming to rest on the tarmac next to a private jet - dark in colour and with no markings save the registration number.

'Sure, perhaps somebody could explain what the hell is going on?'

'You wanted your man, you've got him. Nick and his colleagues have organised a plane back to London. They have been doing some checks themselves. They seem happy to help. The police will be waiting for us at Biggin Hill. They are aware of what we have done.'

Sam sat staring at Otto. He could not believe this had happened so quickly.

'Where is he?' Sam said. 'Don't tell me he's in the boot.'

There was no answer from Nick or Otto. Their attention was distracted by an official walking towards the car. He checked a few details and didn't seem to be at all concerned about the three passports and papers handed to him. After a quick look at the three men inside the car he walked back into the terminal.

'We are good to go Sam. You get in the plane first, we will follow you.'

Sam did as he was told. He opened the door and went across the tarmac as quickly as he could. The noise of the airport was roaring in his ears as he went up the steps and into the jet. A stewardess was standing inside the aircraft.

'Good afternoon Sir,' she said in a low, chesty voice. 'This way please.'

Sam was shown to a seat facing away from the door. He sat down and picked up an English newspaper.

A couple of minutes later he heard Otto coming up the stairs. Sam turned and saw Otto with Yamin, dressed in a suit, next to him. Otto had walked up the stairs with his arm supporting Yamin as it was clear Yamin was still out cold. He walked past Sam, carrying Yamin's weight like a child. He put him in a seat opposite Sam and strapped him in. Yamin's head flopped to one side. Otto took a syringe out of his pocket and stuck it into Yamin's neck.

'That should keep him going,' he said turning to Sam.

'Nick says good-bye. You had to go first, you do understand?'

Sam looked out of the window to see Nick's car drive away from the plane. The stewardess had closed the door and the pilot announced their departure.

Within three minutes they were in the air heading west on their way back to London. Sam settled into his seat and stared at the prize. Amazing what money can do he thought as the stewardess handed him the largest whisky and soda of his life.

Chapter XXVII

Chelsea, London

The house was empty when Sam got home. There was no food in the fridge and no sign of Lucy or the boys. They had probably gone to Lucy's parents in Hampshire, Sam couldn't be sure. It was one less thing to worry about. He had called Lucy's mobile but it had gone straight to voicemail. He didn't leave a message.

Sam called Eleanor a few days later. She told him she had contacted the police and organised them to be at Biggin Hill. Sam had started a chain reaction which had quickly gone way beyond just him. Yamin was now in custody in the UK and the police had reopened the case against Maria. Eleanor had seen her too. She had appealed against her conviction in light of the capture of Yamin. Sam was waiting to hear what was next. He didn't understand the procedure but Eleanor seemed to think Maria had a chance of appeal if Yamin was convicted.

Sam spent the whole of the next morning writing his letter to Peter Heathcliff. Several drafts were in the rubbish bin before he was happy with the contents. Sam wrote to resign from Wolfenberg with immediate effect. He had lost interest in his job many months before and it seemed like the correct time to move on. He wanted to get his life back on track, to admit everything to Lucy, to spend time with Charlie and George. He had no idea what he would do. Retirement was out of the question but he needed to get his mind straight.

Sam walked to the end of the road to the post box. Nobody would care or be surprised he wanted to leave. They all knew his heart had been elsewhere for months despite not knowing about Qin. He paused just before dropping it in the slot. Then he let go.

As Sam heard the letter hit the other post his mobile rang. It was Eleanor.

'Sam?'

'Yes, hi Eleanor. What's up?'

'They are going to press charges Sam. Yamin is to appear before magistrates tomorrow. He is being charged with murder. The CPS wants a retrial. It is extremely rare Sam. She is going to claim duress.'

'Have you spoken to her?'

'I have been to see her Sam. I have just as much to gain from this as you, you do realise that don't you?'

'How long will it take?'

'The CPS just needs to dust off the old case. They will be ready in a matter of days. You get some rest Sam. Sort yourself out.'

'Sure. Keep me in the picture will you.'

Eleanor's phoned clicked.

Sam was thrilled things were moving quickly. He had a sudden urge, a need to speak with his wife so he rushed home and called his parents-in-law's home number. His mother-in-law answered and she put Lucy on after no chat at all.

'Darling, it's me, how are you and the boys?'

The line was silent.

'Lucy, it's Sam. Are you OK?'

'Where the fuck have you been Sam? What in fuck's name is going on? Are you banging someone from work? Tell me the truth for once in your life.'

'Lucy, please come home. I need to talk to you. I need to explain what is going on. Please.'

'It might have escaped you Sam - the boys are on half term. They go back tomorrow so we are coming to London tonight. You are such a shithead Sam.'

For the second time in ten minutes the line went dead.

Sam was happier. He detected the hint of mirth in Lucy's last remark. He would come clean and tell her the whole story. A wave of relief was beginning to flow but this was clouded by the need to get some serious thinking done. He had to get his story straight.

Using his computer, he scanned his letter to Peter and sent the email. Peter was on the phone ten minutes later.

'Waggers?' Peter said when Sam answered.

'Hello Peter. Listen, I have been doing a great deal of thinkin...'

'Save your breath Waggers. I fully understand. You have been rubbish for several months now. Mind clearly not on the job. I can redistribute your clients very easily. There is no problem. Quite a relief actually, I was getting pressure from Frankfurt about your performance with Qin.'

'Fuck Qin Peter, they are all a bunch of dirty crooks.'

The phone was silent for a few seconds.

'Be careful what you say Sam. Your opinions might get you into trouble one day. They are very influential people.'

'They are all going to prison Peter, anyway I don't care anymore. Just send me my paperwork.'

'Let's have lunch soon Sam. Be good to catch up properly.'

'Sure. That would be nice.' Sam put the phone down. Peter had been good to him over the years. He liked Peter. He would have lunch with him. One day.

Lucy came home with the boys that evening. Sam had a big speech written but only got through half of it before she melted and gave him an enormous hug. His heart was back in equilibrium. They sat talking over supper once the boys were in bed. Sam couldn't believe Lucy was being so understanding, so happy to let his story wash over her.

'Why didn't you tell me earlier? Why didn't you let me help you?'

'You know how work is. How things build up, how you dedicate your life to a company which ultimately doesn't give a shit about you.'

'What are we going to do Sam? Do you have any idea what you are going to do for money?'

'I'm not sure, I just know I don't want to work for a bank anymore, there are plenty of other things you know. I just need time to think, to evaluate. I think we should move out; to get out of London. I've had enough of this place. The boys need more space.'

'Really? I am happy to but are you sure? Sam, are you serious?'

'I think so. I want to make a break for it. It's time for a real change.'

'Let's talk about it when you know more about Maria. Let's see what happens to her first. Do you think Martin Zhao will come after you? He will be pissed off about Yaris.'

'Yamin.'

'Whatever he is called, you must be worried about what he will do? These Chinese businessmen are notorious.'

'All I know is I have tried to do the right thing. Justice doesn't work when a jury is too self-interested to care, when it doesn't look at all the facts. We were too quick to judge. Some guys wanted to go home to see their wives or watch the football. I used too much of my work life to come to a decision. It just isn't right. Maria went to prison knowing she had been abused and threatened by Yamin. There was nothing she could do about it. That needs to be stopped Lucy. Idiots should not be allowed to serve on a jury.'

'Come on Sammy, time for bed.'

Lucy cleared the supper things with a coy smile and they went upstairs. Explanation turned into harmony. Sam was back where he wanted to be, with the woman he loved, in a house where his darling children slept. He could sort out his problems tomorrow.

Sam started taking the boys to school as the first part of a more involved role at home. Packing sports kit and the right books each day, he started to understand the routine. Summer was coming and he was really starting to relax. Lucy fully understood what he had been through and had forgiven his unreliable behaviour.

Eleanor called later that week. She was clearly excited on the phone.

'Sam?'

'Sure, Eleanor, what's up?'

'There's definitely going to be a retrial. The courts have allowed it, given Yamin's return. Sam, this is incredible. If they can show Yamin was the murderer and he forced Maria to help she may get off.'

'When is it going to start?'

'Next Monday. Yamin must have said certain things to the police. They seem very confident.'

'Are you involved? Has Maria asked you to represent her again? Are you allowed to?'

'I am defending her again. Different judge and prosecution. I have lots of work to be getting on with but I will keep you in the picture. Once the trial starts, I won't be contacting you.'

'Shit, yes of course. Wow. If I can help you with anything?'

'Bye Sam, keep your fingers crossed.'

Chapter XXVIII

The Old Bailey, London

Sam went to the trial on most days. The public gallery of a minor court was always quiet as there was little interest in a drugs related murder trial at the Old Bailey, these were two-a-penny. The only faces Sam recognised were Maria's, Yamin's and Eleanor's.

Yamin was passive through the trial. His face gave nothing away. No looks to Maria, no emotion or mannerisms. Sam wanted to shout on a couple of occasions. Bits of the trial he thought were important, things he thought the jury might have missed. On one occasion his irritated shifting drew a raised eyebrow from the judge. Sam managed to control himself after that.

Sam went back to St Sepulchre's during the lunch breaks. He sat in his favourite pew by the bell. He felt happy there, he had time to think in a quiet environment. He drifted in and out of reality, allowing his daydreams to take him off, to cleanse his conscience of what had happened over the past few months. Once, as he sat, he saw the Bellman again. This time smiling. It was light and hot, summertime. The stench of burning meat and excrement had been replaced with the scent of Mediterranean flowers on a warm breeze.

'Mr Waghorne?'

Sam jumped out of his vision and spun around to see a tall man standing in front of him.

'Yes,' said Sam with surprise. 'Can I help you?'

'Sorry to disturb you sir, I hope I didn't give you a fright.'

'No, no. Sorry,' Sam said standing up to meet the only other person in the church. 'How can I help you?'

'My name is Blindman, sir. Detective Chief Inspector Blindman. You might remember me from the original trial. I recognised you from the public gallery sir.'

Sam didn't know what to do. Was he here to criticise Sam or perhaps to thank him?

'We just wanted to thank you sir, to thank you for what you have done. I know we wanted a conviction for this but getting the main man, well the Governor is very happy sir.'

'But the trial hasn't finished yet, you don't know what the outcome will be?'

'Trust me sir, we are very pleased. We wanted you to have this sir.'

D.C.I. Blindman handed Sam an envelope. Sam looked up at the policeman's eyes as he stood there with a thick envelope thrust towards him. Sam looked around despite knowing nobody was there; then he gave Blindman a squint-eyed frown.

'What the fuck are you doing?' Sam hissed, raising his voice.

'Just a thank you from the Met sir, that's all. You did a very brave thing sir. It's the least we can do. It should just about cover your costs sir.'

Blindman thrust the envelope into Sam's chest. There seemed to be a definitive 'take it' in the final prod.

Sam took the envelope still staring at Blindman. As soon as it was in his hand Blindman turned and walked out. His job was done.

Sam waited until he saw Blindman leave before he looked in the envelope. He opened it and saw two inches of fifty-pound notes trying to burst themselves out of the packet. There was something else caught Sam's eye. A photograph. Sam pulled it from the front of the wad.

Sam sat back down on his pew making a thud which echoed around the church. The photograph was of Peter Heathcliff sitting in a bar with Martin Zhao, surrounded by several beautiful young women. They were drinking champagne and laughing, completely oblivious to the picture being taken. What was this? Why had the police given it to Sam? His mind was racing again, all the pleasant thoughts evaporated in a whirl of panic.

On the sixth day of the trial the jury went out. Sam sat watching as they shuffled out through the door next to the judge. He knew where they were going, what faced them in the next few hours. Sam studied the clearing court before a tap on the shoulder told him it was time to vacate the public gallery. He knew he could not get back in so decided to go home. He would have to follow the case online now. His hope was that Eleanor would call once the jury had reached a decision. She owed him that much.

On the way to the tube Sam went past a bookmaker. He walked in and studied the form of the next race. Any connection he would back. He found a horse called Honest Jim running at Newbury and decided at 16-1 to win, this was his best shot. He walked to the counter with his ticket and placed Blindman's money on the counter.

'Can you count it please?'

The woman looked at Sam like he was mad. She started counting the fifty-pound notes with a face which suggested Sam didn't quite have legal ownership of the money he had given her. Ten thousand pounds later Sam had the receipt in his hand. He walked out of the shop and to the tube. Now all he could do was wait, wait for Honest Jim and for Maria.

The jury took only two sessions to decide on the verdict. Sam got a call from Eleanor at noon the following day.

'Sam?' Eleanor said with calm in her voice. 'Maria is free. She has been acquitted. Yamin has been found guilty. The judge is going to sentence after lunch.'

'Where is Maria now?' Sam said with excitement.

'She is with me now. Why don't you come up and see us?'

'I'll be right there.'

Sam put his phone back in his pocket and grabbed a jacket. It would take him thirty minutes to get to the Old Bailey. He would be there before the judge had finished his lunch.

Maria sat on the sofa and looked at Sam as he entered Eleanor's chambers. Sam walked over to her and she stood. They embraced each other with no words. Eleanor, in casual clothes once again, looked on as their heads blended together in emotion. Finally, they parted.

'It's great to see you Maria,' Sam said. 'You must be delighted.'

'I need to see that pig driven off to prison. I want to know he has gone.'

'I suggest we go down to the Old Bailey and watch him leave then,' Eleanor said. 'They will be taking him away shortly. Let's go.'

The three of them left Eleanor's chambers together. Maria tucked her arm under Sam's as they walked. There was a spring in her step which was accompanied by a beaming smile all the way along the short walk to the Central Criminal Court.

'Let's wait in the pub opposite,' Eleanor said as they approached. 'It's called the Viaduct Tavern and we can see everything from there.'

It was a warm day so all three ordered a refreshing long drink and sat down by the window which looked out onto the North side of the courts. This was where one of the public entrances was and also the giant doors which saw the defendants arrive and the convicted leave. Most mornings and afternoons the traffic was stopped by the police as security vans came and went. They would be alerted to any activity by the arrival of police escorts.

After twenty minutes Eleanor stopped talking. There had been a police whistle outside which was followed by the sight of two police motorbike riders flying past the window. Sam jumped up and ran out of the pub with Eleanor and Maria on his heels. They saw the traffic had been stopped in both directions. The bike riders got off their machines and had their hands up preventing drivers from passing. Sam put his arm out to stop Maria and Eleanor from getting any closer. They were twenty yards from the great doors that had slowly started to open.

'Let's wait here,' he said. 'These things have windows, there is no point showing our faces.'

Maria and Eleanor pulled back so the three of them collected under the awning of a shoe shop.

As the doors opened a white security van emerged into daylight and poked its nose out into the street. This had to be the van carrying Yamin. It was the wrong time for normal defendants to come or go. The two policemen jumped back on their bikes and turned in front of the van. The blue flashing lights reignited to stop all passers-by.

Sirens announced the start of Yamin's procession to prison. The bikes then the van sped off turning left on Newgate Street. It was then Sam noticed two further bikes holding traffic at the lights by the pub. The outriders went through the lights and approached St Sepulchre's Church.

There was a sound Sam had never heard before, a sound which stopped time. An explosion which pierced the air with a terrifying scream. The security van was stopped in its tracks and literally jumped in the air. Fire engulfed the driver's compartment and then the back door, the secure door prisoners entered, was blown off by another fireball ripping through the van. People near the church fell. Both policemen were blown off their bikes, one high into the air. The windows of the shops opposite imploded and alarms started ringing.

Maria started running, running to get a closer look at what had just happened. Sam grabbed her arm.

'No!' Sam said as loud as he could. He couldn't hear himself. 'Come with me.'

Sam pulled Maria towards him and instinctively turned towards Eleanor. She was lying against the shoe shop window, staring at Sam with a frightened look. Sam decided to leave her, he needed to do something.

On the other side of the road Sam assessed the carnage. The scene was motionless except the fire that raged from inside the van. Through the smoke Sam looked up at the bell tower of the church. This was open on all four sides and one hundred feet up.

There looking out of the tower with a grenade launcher on his shoulder was Martin Zhao. His unmistakable face was as clear as anything Sam had ever seen. Next to him was one of the gang, one of the directors Sam had been introduced to at the Qin Properties office. He held a sniper's rifle and was scanning the area like a man possessed. He was looking for someone through the smoke.

Sam grabbed Maria, pulling her away from the pavement and back across to Eleanor. She had not moved. Her eyes had closed so Sam bent down to feel her face and neck, she was cold and her pulse was weak. The window behind her shoulder was dripping red.

'We need to go,' Sam said standing up. 'I'm sure they were after you.'

As the alarms of shops screamed, Sam and Maria carried Eleanor down Newgate Street away from the courts. As they approached St Paul's Sam stopped a cab. The traffic only one hundred yards away was unaware of what had just happened.

'St Thomas's Hospital, quick as you can,' Sam said as he bundled Maria and Eleanor in. 'Please, as quick as you can.'

The cab driver gave Sam a quizzical look through his rear-view mirror as he pulled out and headed for the river. As he drove, several police cars screamed past on their way to the Old Bailey.

'Something must have happened guv,' said the driver. 'Fucking police drive like wankers.'

'Someone must have escaped,' said Sam laughing. Sam turned back to see a small plume of smoke rising above the office blocks around St Paul's.

Chapter XXIX

Kojdanava, Belarus

Maria Kayakova had stayed with Sam for three weeks. She played with Charlie and George and spent hours talking to Sam and Lucy about her life. She explained what had happened that night. The way Yamin had treated her and the sadness about her father.

Sam agreed to travel with her to Belarus. He wanted to close the issue out, to see Maria truly happy again.

Flying together Sam could see the excitement build in Maria the closer she got to home. From the airport the rain lashed down as they shot through villages and towns. Maria said very little as she watched her homeland wash back over her. Sam could see she was absorbing it again; the place she loved, the country she should never have left.

They arrived at Dymtrus' house just after two in the afternoon. The rain had stopped, being replaced by a soft mist which rose from the ground as the car pulled up.

'You wait here Sam,' Maria said. 'I'll come and get you in a minute.'

Sam nodded and got out of the car. He walked down a grassy slope to a bench under some trees. Despite a touch of damp, he sat down. A wet sensation rose up through his jeans but he didn't mind. He watched Maria take the bags from the car and head towards the house.

Maria pushed on the front door. It was open so she entered her father's house with apprehension. This was the place she had spent many months but it felt unfamiliar, like there was no warmth there anymore.

Her father was fast asleep in the same old chair facing a weak fire. He had a blanket over his knees and an overcoat covered his body. His shaggy grey hair rolled over his shoulders. He had lost weight. It was dark in the bare sitting room but light from an odd flame from the fire occasionally flickered across his gaunt face. He looked much older despite the calm only sleep can bring. Maria sat on the arm of the chair opposite him watching his chest gently rise and fall. She looked around the room. There were dirty plates and dust on the surfaces. A musty smell gave away the lack of support he must have received when there was nobody to check. Oleg must be coming in to feed him but very little else.

Maria went to the front door and beckoned to Sam. He came up to the house and entered slowly.

'Wait by the door Sam.'

Maria left Sam by the door and crossed the room. She knelt down in front of her father staring at his old face and placing her hand gently upon his. He stirred, moving his head to face her, still asleep. Maria stroked the top of his hand. Slowly Dymtrus woke, his eyes opening just a little at first. Then, like he was still dreaming, he smiled and rolled his head away. Maria squeezed his hand.

'Papa,' Maria said with a soft low voice. 'Papa, it is me.'

She said it again and this time Dymtrus' head came back to her. His eyes were half open now; the smile had gone.

'Maria?' he said in a whisper. 'Is that you my darling?'

'Yes Papa, I've come home.'

Maria could see the gradual realisation grow across his face. Tears appeared in the corners of his weary eyes. Maria tracked them as they took the rugged route south down his face. She stopped them on his cheeks with her fingers. Dymtrus raised his arms and cupped them around Maria's head. He pulled her towards him and hugged her tightly. She could still feel some strength in her father's embrace and this brought the past flooding back.

Maria could feel her father weeping uncontrollably. This gave way to chuckles and then full laughter. As they separated, they both turned to look at Sam.

'Papa,' Maria said in an emotional, croaky voice. 'There is someone I want you to meet. This is Sam Waghorne. He is a friend from London.

Sam took a pace forward but then stopped. Dymtrus looked at her then swung his head towards the door. He put his hands on the wheels of his chair, pushing the left back so he could see the person Maria had introduced.

'Where is Yamin?' Dymtrus said. 'Why is this other man with you?'

'Papa, I have a lot of talking to do,' Maria said with a smile. 'Sam is my friend; he has been very helpful to me. You will like him.'

'Well come and sit down Sam but first throw another log on the fire. It is freezing in here,' Dymtrus said in broken English.

Maria made some lunch with the few provisions Oleg had left in the house. There were vegetables and a fairly old rabbit but what she produced was warm and delicious. Maria opened up a bottle of Oleg's home-made wine which was rough and gutsy but was an excellent accompaniment to the story of what had happened in London. As they spoke Maria couldn't help going around the rooms making the place tidy again. She opened the curtains and windows to make the house light and airy once again, just as she had kept it. Dymtrus spent most of the time listening with his mouth open wide. Occasionally he would ask a question but Maria's story ran all afternoon and into the early evening.

Oleg came to see Dymtrus at six. He was embarrassed to see that Maria and Sam had now made the house warm and clean. He made excuses about his wife being ill but Maria knew this was how he had been looking after her father. This was no time to be cross so she just smiled and helped Oleg get Dymtrus ready for the evening – she would not be leaving in a hurry.

'I bring more food,' Oleg said in a humble tone. 'We have chicken. I bring chicken.'

Maria wondered what her father would have eaten if they were not there. She nodded as Oleg ran from the house to collect his guilty offering.

'Don't worry Papa, I will help you now.'

'He is a good man Maria, he helps me.'

'I know, I know,' Maria said. She went to the kitchen to see what could be used with the chicken. Sam sat opposite Dymtrus. Maria's father stared at Sam for a few seconds.

'You seem to be a brave man, Mr Waghorne,' Dymtrus said keeping the stare into Sam's eyes. 'I owe you a debt of gratitude Sam. I'm not sure I will ever be able to repay you.'

Sam smiled. Now was not the time for him to talk.

'Come closer.'

Sam got up and approached Dymtrus' chair. Dymtrus grabbed Sam's arm and pulled him down to his level. He embraced Sam with both arms.

'Thank you, Sam.' Dymtrus whispered in his ear. 'Will you stay for a while?'

Sam pulled back and sat back down.

'Yes of course, my family know I am here. I can stay for a while,' Sam said slowly.

'No joy is perfect Sam,' Dymtrus said in a lower voice. 'I need you to see something.'

Maria came back into the room. The light was fading outside so she drew the curtains and turned on the lamp in the corner of the room. Dymtrus shifted himself in his chair getting ready for another instalment of Maria's story.

As she spoke, Oleg drifted in with the chicken he had promised. He took it into the kitchen before superficially checking Dymtrus was fine for the night. He realised he was now redundant. As he turned to the door Dymtrus spoke.

'Oleg, I need you to drive for me tomorrow. Is that OK?'

'Yes of course. What time?'

'First thing; we have far to go.'

Oleg nodded, looked at Sam and Maria then left for the night. Sam looked at Maria who shrugged her shoulders silently.

Oleg arrived before the sun came up in his twenty-year-old car. Sam was woken by Maria after she dressed her father and they were all travelling south before any of them knew quite what was going on. Sam sat next to Maria in the back with Dymtrus next to Oleg in the front. Little was said in the gloom of dawn; all they knew was Dymtrus alone knew their destination.

Dymtrus broke the silence.

'Maria my darling,' he said with a willowy morning voice. 'There are some things I must tell you. I should have told you long ago.'

Maria looked forward at her father.

'What is it Papa? Where are we going? What is the matter?'

'I didn't tell you the truth about my accident. Why I was left in...'

'Papa? What is this? I have only just come...'

'Maria,' Dymtrus said, letting his voice rise just a little. 'I need to explain. Please let me.' Maria stopped. She let her father continue.

'The people who hurt me have been arrested. They are in prison.'

'Did what to you?'

Dymtrus looked out of the window as Maria stared.

'They killed my parents.'

Maria continued to stare.

'They blew them up Maria. They have hated us for a long, long time.'

'Blew up. Blew up who? You are an orphan. You didn't know your parents.'

Maria turned to Sam. She was shaking her head and laughing.

'Is this all too much for him?' she said looking for comfort from Sam.

Dymtrus was silent. Sam wanted to get out of the car. Oleg kept on driving.

'They died in Kiev. We were in a cafe having lunch, on holiday.'

'Who is they Papa? You keep on saying they?'

'My parents.'

'But...'

'The same people who hurt me. The same people who have gone to prison...'

'What are you talking about Papa? I don't understand. You haven't mentioned any...'

'It was because of my grandfather. He caused it all. He was Red.'

Sam turned to look at the back of Dymtrus' head. Oleg took his eyes off the road.

'He was a Red. He was a boyhood friend of Iron Felix. Felix Dzerzhinsky. He idolised him, they played with each other as children.'

'But why did these guys want to kill you?'

'These guys don't forget; these guys are Imperialists. They want to drive out all Bolshevik threats, before and after.'

Maria stopped. She hung her head and started crying. Sam shuffled across the seat with a reflex action.

'I'm sorry my darling,' Dymtrus said looking beyond the windscreen.

Oleg drove on in silence. Everybody was alone with their thoughts. The rain bashed down onto the car as they drove along a soaking road. Finally, Dymtrus spoke.

'Dzerzhinsky went to school with my grandfather in Vilnius. They were best friends. He saved Felix's life one day. They were playing in a river. Felix got into trouble and Grandpapa pulled him out. Felix never forgot it.'

'They stayed in touch after Felix joined the Red Army. Vladyslav had no idea of the extent of Felix's activities. No idea about the

Cheka. He was a loyal man.'

Maria watched her father talk. His voice was full of emotion as the story unravelled.

'I wanted to protect you Maria. I wanted these people to keep away from you. It was time for this all to stop.'

'Did they hurt you at Kuznetsovsk, Papa?'

'They got me twice, at Kuznetsovsk and once before.'

'Where?'

'At Chernobyl. That is where I was stationed before Kuznetsovsk. I was moved there to protect me after the first attack.'

'Chernobyl?' Maria said with surprise.

Dymtrus turned towards his daughter in the back. You could see the pain on his face from the movement. He stared at her for a few moments.

'I was there when the disaster happened – part of the team responsible at the time. They beat me that afternoon, beat me so badly I couldn't complete my shift. The reactor overheated during testing and my team failed to shut it down.'

Tears were running down Dymtrus' face.

'They left me for dead away from the explosion. I was lucky. I was found and taken to hospital away from the site. It saved my life. Most of my team were lost that day. Many people died after the accident.'

'Papa, I...'

'Wait Maria,' Dymtrus said interrupting. 'You were born two months after the accident. Your grandmother looked after you in Turkey for eight years and I was moved to Kuznetsovsk when I got better.'

'Why have you never told me any of this?' Maria said with her voice cracking. 'Why have you kept the truth from me?'

Dymtrus turned back to look at the road. Sam noticed the tears. He could not have spoken if he had wanted to.

Oleg crossed over the border into Ukraine four hours after leaving Kojdanava. They had made several stops to relieve Dymtrus' pain and bladder. Another hour passed before Sam saw the first road sign for Rivne and then to Kuznetsovsk. Sam could see Dymtrus shift uneasily in his seat as Oleg drove them to his unknown destination. The rain had got much harder, torrents were pouring down through the mass of dark grey cloud.

As they entered the town Dymtrus pointed something out to his driver. Oleg stopped the car outside a blue and white church which looked miserable in the wet. Sam wiped his window to get a better look as Oleg turned the engine off and got out. He opened the boot to retrieved a large umbrella and Dymtrus' wheelchair.

'Wait here Sam please,' said Dymtrus. 'Maria?'

Oleg helped Dymtrus out of the car whilst Maria stood next to them getting soaked to the skin. She wiped hair and rain off her face and finally took the umbrella from Oleg who got back in the car.

Maria held the umbrella to cover her father. She could not cover herself, so she resigned herself to the rain which had already made its way down inside her shirt and onto her back.

Sam wiped his fogged-up window and watched as Maria pushed her father past the church and through to the graveyard at the back.

As Maria rounded the back of the church, her father spoke.

'Down there. See?' He was pointing his arm towards a large tree.

Maria pushed on down a sloping path towards the tree. The rain was bouncing off the umbrella into her face. She didn't care now; she was soaked through.

Dymtrus held his hand up and Maria stopped. They were under the bows of the large Yew tree at the bottom of the slope. Maria stood waiting for her next instruction. Dymtrus just sat not making any signs, saying nothing. A large raindrop collected on his nose. It hung for a few seconds before cascading down into his lap. He didn't notice it.

'Over there,' he said nodding his head to the left. 'Just past the tree.'

Dymtrus looked in the opposite direction with his head hanging down.

Maria started walking in the direction her father had indicated. He had given her no clue as to what she might find. Her eyes scanned around trying to find something of interest.

Then she saw it. A small marble headstone in the grass ten feet in front of her. As she approached she felt a stirring in her chest. She knelt down in front of it.

In Loving Memory
1983-1987
Tatyana Anna Kayakova

Maria touched the headstone with her hand as thoughts galloped through her head. The feelings of what a younger sister would have been like. She gripped the stone to prevent herself from falling, then let her head fall to her chest. She cried out loud into the rain as she looked up into the sky knowing one more person was up there than she had ever realised.

Maria turned back to look at her father. He was still facing away.

'Papa!' Maria screamed out but Dymtrus didn't turn around. 'Papa!'

Maria stood to see there was another gravestone directly behind her sister's. It was smaller and made of a much cheaper stone. She moved around to read it.

God Bless my Darling
Ela Yonca Kayakova
1959 – 1987

Maria's hand flew to her mouth as reality dawned. She looked back at Dymtrus who was now staring right at her. She started jerking uncontrollably; her mouth was open as she fell to the ground engulfing her mother's headstone. She hugged it tightly letting the rain merge with her tears and the saliva from her mouth.

'It wasn't me who killed you Mama. It wasn't me.'

Afterword

They talked quietly as Oleg drove them home. Dymtrus explained what had happened all those years ago. The fallout from Chernobyl killed many people over a number of years. Radiation sickness and cancer tore many families apart. Maria had always thought her own birth had killed her mother. She had in fact died three years later together with her second born daughter. Her father had always used Maria's birth to mask the biggest tradegy of his life. It would take time for her to understand why he had done it, why love so often shields the truth.

Sam stayed with Maria and Dymtrus for another week. He sat down to listen to Dymtrus tell Maria as much as he could remember about his grandfather. When Dymtrus mentioned the funding of the Bolshevik machine it made Sam wonder. The higher echelons had relied on a primitive but growing narcotics racket organised by a few Chinese contacts. They were responsible for supplying drugs from Afghanistan and the most westerly outposts of the Russian Empire, including a small but growing production facility in the old Uzbekistan.

Sam was about to say something but stopped himself. Any connections could wait.

Dymtrus moved on to talk about that fateful night at Chernobyl and the beating at Kuznetsovsk. He spent hours explaining why

Maria had been sent away to her mother's mother in Turkey for her own protection— how this had upset Dymtrus beyond words – but he had to care for his heavily pregnant wife. Now he spoke with a weight off his mind; it was something he had wanted to share for years. The full expression of his love came through as he talked with Maria. Through the discussions, Sam gave them plenty of space, allowing father and daughter time alone to come to terms with a rapidly revealing truth – to replace restlessness and disturbance with calm and stability.

Eventually it was time to say goodbye and, predictably, Dymtrus was distraught. Sam had been the catalyst; he had provided an old man with an opportunity to get things straight. He wept with joy as Sam bent down to shake his hand. Dymtrus pulled him close, hugging him with all his strength.

'You and I are very similar Sam. Go well.'

Maria stepped forward to give Sam a protracted embrace before he got in Oleg's car for the final time. They squeezed each other without any word – something was merging between them as both of their shoulders were soaked with each others' tears. Eventually, as Sam touched the door handle, she spoke.

'Глаза боятся, а руки делают.'

Sam gave her a quizzical look with a half-smile.

'Be strong Sam,' she said. Tears streamed down her beaming face like a drenched sponge. 'You are an honourable man, keep your promise. You remind me of the best of my father.'

Sam arrived at Heathrow and immediately called Joanna. She had changed her mind after Sam's resignation. She had been given all his clients and seemed much happier now that Sam had left. Martin Zhao had been found and arrested. Peter Heathcliff had been cautioned and was helping the police with their investigations. Wolfenberg was served a huge fine from the Regulator and the UK Chief Executive had been fired. Most notably Yamin had been killed in the rocket attack and it had been confirmed in a shocking story in the press that he and Qin had been the very same. Yamin had trained as a soldier as a prelude to returning to run the Qin business. Sam had been right.

Eleanor had made a full recovery from a sniper shot to the chest that had managed to miss all vital organs. She was back at work reflecting on a bullet which had been meant for somebody else. Sam would see her again in time he was sure.

Sam's life had moved on; he was back with Lucy and his boys and wanted more time to think about the whys and less about the whats and the hows. The boys had made welcome home cards which Sam looked at with unbridled joy before placing them delicately on the mantelpiece where they would stay for a very long time. This made him emotional whereas before it wouldn't have, a reflection of the scale of the change that had taken place within him. It was over and he was home, a place he now realised was the best place on earth.

Sam went upstairs and sat in front of his laptop. He had no job but felt free. He did have two things to do, however. He checked Honest Jim. It had come last. He took the betting slip out of his wallet. As he pulled it out, another piece of paper fell onto the desk in front of him.

It was Chantelle's telephone number from the trial. He played with a few images in his mind as the devil on his shoulder grew. Perhaps he could send a quick text. He reached for his phone.

After ten seconds of tapping he stopped, deleted the message and threw Chantelle's number in the bin, watching as it fluttered all the way to the bottom.

'Those long legs...' he said, chuckling as he switched on his computer.

Sam started typing. Whilst in Belarus he had promised Maria he would tell her story.

He hopes you enjoyed it.

Printed by Amazon Italia Logistica S.r.l.
Torrazza Piemonte (TO), Italy

16095302R00253